S0-BMT-848

BESTSELLING AUTHOR COLLECTION

In our Bestselling Author Collection,
Harlequin Books is proud to offer
classic novels from today's superstars
of women's fiction. These authors have
captured the hearts of millions of readers
around the world, and earned their place on
the *New York Times, USA TODAY* and other
bestseller lists with every release.

As a bonus, each volume also includes a
full-length novel from a rising star of series
romance. Bestselling authors in their own
right, these talented writers have captured the
qualities Harlequin is famous for—heart-racing
passion, edge-of-your-seat entertainment
and a satisfying happily-ever-after.

Don't miss any of the books in the collection!

**Praise for *New York Times* and *USA TODAY*
bestselling author Susan Mallery**

"Susan Mallery is one of my favorites."
—#1 *New York Times* bestselling author
Debbie Macomber

"Mallery has once again proven to be
a superb writer; romance novels
just don't get much better than this."
—*Booklist*

"If you're looking for heart-tugging emotions
elaborately laced with humor,
then Mallery is the author for you."
—*RT Book Reviews*

Praise for bestselling author Teresa Southwick

"*Winning Back His Bride* has it all—
rich characterization, a powerful conflict
and sizzling sexual tension."
—*RT Book Reviews*

"[Teresa] Southwick, a true wordsmith,
cuts to the core. She has the ability to
make every word count, even as her story
achieves magical harmony."
—*RT Book Reviews*

BESTSELLING AUTHOR COLLECTION

New York Times and *USA TODAY* Bestselling Author

SUSAN MALLERY

Lone Star Millionaire

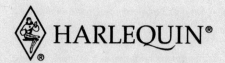

HARLEQUIN®

TORONTO • NEW YORK • LONDON
AMSTERDAM • PARIS • SYDNEY • HAMBURG
STOCKHOLM • ATHENS • TOKYO • MILAN • MADRID
PRAGUE • WARSAW • BUDAPEST • AUCKLAND

If you purchased this book without a cover you should be aware that this book is stolen property. It was reported as "unsold and destroyed" to the publisher, and neither the author nor the publisher has received any payment for this "stripped book."

Recycling programs
for this product may
not exist in your area.

ISBN-13: 978-0-373-38997-1

LONE STAR MILLIONAIRE

Copyright © 2010 by Harlequin Books S.A.

The publisher acknowledges the copyright holders
of the individual works as follows:

LONE STAR MILLIONAIRE
Copyright © 1998 by Susan W. Macias

IT TAKES THREE
Copyright © 2004 by Teresa Ann Southwick

All rights reserved. Except for use in any review, the reproduction or
utilization of this work in whole or in part in any form by any electronic,
mechanical or other means, now known or hereafter invented, including
xerography, photocopying and recording, or in any information storage
or retrieval system, is forbidden without the written permission of the
publisher, Harlequin Enterprises Limited, 225 Duncan Mill Road,
Don Mills, Ontario, Canada, M3B 3K9.

This is a work of fiction. Names, characters, places and incidents are
either the product of the author's imagination or are used fictitiously,
and any resemblance to actual persons, living or dead, business
establishments, events or locales is entirely coincidental.

This edition published by arrangement with Harlequin Books S.A.

For questions and comments about the quality of this book
please contact us at Customer_eCare@Harlequin.ca.

® and TM are trademarks of the publisher. Trademarks indicated with
® are registered in the United States Patent and Trademark Office, the
Canadian Trade Marks Office and in other countries.

www.eHarlequin.com

Printed in U.S.A.

CONTENTS

LONE STAR MILLIONAIRE

New York Times and *USA TODAY* Bestselling Author
Susan Mallery

SUSAN MALLERY

is a *New York Times* bestselling author of more
than ninety romances. Her combination of
humor, emotion and just-plain-sexy has made
her a reader favorite. Susan makes her home
in the Pacific Northwest with her handsome
husband and possibly the world's cutest dog.
Visit her Web site at www.SusanMallery.com.

Chapter 1

"Madam must agree that it's very beautiful," the store clerk said.

Sabrina Innis stared down at the diamond tennis bracelet glinting on her wrist. "Madam agrees," she told the well-dressed young man, then glanced at her boss. "Stunning. And ten carats, too. Are you sure you wouldn't rather buy her a little car? It would be cheaper."

Calhoun Jefferson Langtry, all six feet three inches of him, raised his eyebrows. "I'm not interested in cheap. You should know that by now. I want to send something meaningful, but elegant." He motioned to the diamond pin the clerk had first shown them. "Nothing froufrou, though. I hate froufrou."

The "froufrou" in question was an amazing diamond-and-gold pin that cost what the average family of four earned in three or four months. It had clean lines, a zigzag ribbon of gold dividing a stylized circle, with a large four-carat diamond slightly off center. Sabrina loved it and would have chosen it in a hot minute. But the gift wasn't for her.

She unclasped the tennis bracelet and placed it next to the other finalists—a gold bangle inlaid with diamonds and emeralds, and a Rolex watch. "I sense a theme here," she said. "Things that go around the wrist. Shackles, in a manner of speaking. Is this your way of telling Tiffany that she shouldn't have tried to tie you down?"

Her impertinence earned her a scowl. She smiled back. Cal's temper existed mostly in his mind. Compared to the screaming in her house when she was growing up—four siblings all with extreme opinions on everything—his mild bouts of ill humor were easy to tolerate. Not that the man couldn't be stone cold when it suited him. She made sure never to cross him in important issues and counted these tiny victories as perks of the job. If nothing else, they kept her wit sharp—a definite advantage when dealing with the wealthy and privileged.

"This one," she said, pointing to the emerald-and-diamond bracelet.

The clerk paused, waiting for Cal's approval.

"You heard the little lady. Wrap it up."

"Yes, sir."

Sabrina rose to her feet. After six years of being in Texas, she'd grown used to being called "little lady." She often accused Cal of being trapped in a John Wayne western. Not that he couldn't be urbane when he chose. When it suited his purposes, he could talk about world events, pick out the perfect wine and discuss the changing financial market with the best of them. But with her, he was himself—Cal Langtry, rich, Texas oil tycoon and playboy. She looked at the piece of jewelry the clerk tucked into a velvet box. A soon-to-be unattached playboy.

"Does Tiffany know?" Sabrina asked as Cal signed the credit card receipt. The clerk held out the bag, not sure to whom to hand it. Sabrina took it. Even though the gift wasn't for her, she was responsible for mailing it to the recipient, after she'd composed a suitable note.

Cal led the way to the front of the store, then held open the door for her. "Not exactly."

Sunlight and the spring heat hit her full in the face. Despite having lived here six years, she still wasn't used to the humidity. She felt her hair start to crinkle. So much for the smooth, sophisticated style she'd tamed it into that morning. The hair-care industry had yet to invent a hair spray that could outlast the Houston weather.

They crossed the sidewalk to the waiting limo. As always, Cal politely waited until Sabrina had settled into the seat. She liked to think it was because he enjoyed watching her skirt climb up her thighs. The truth was, he never bothered to look.

It was better that way, she told herself, wondering when she was going to start believing it. After all, if she was as good-looking as her boss, they would cause a stir wherever they went and all the attention would grow annoying. As it was, she was able to slip into the background and live her life in peace and quiet.

She chuckled softly and glanced out the window.

"What's so funny?" Cal asked.

"I was wondering if we were going to have a storm this afternoon," she said. It was almost the truth. She'd really been wondering if her outrageous lies, told only to herself, would cause her to be struck by lightning.

She set the carefully wrapped gift between them. "Tiffany's for Tiffany," she said, pointing to the name on the bag. "I wonder if your soon-to-be ex-girlfriend will appreciate the irony."

"Don't start with that, Sabrina," Cal warned. "Tiffany was a splendid girl."

"I couldn't agree more."

He eyed her, as if he didn't believe what she was saying.

"Okay, so she wasn't the brightest person on the planet," he admitted.

"Now, there's an understatement."

He narrowed his gaze.

Sabrina feigned fear by sinking back into the corner of the limo. "Oh, Mr. Langtry, please don't punish me for my impertinence. I'm just the hired help. I desperately need this job to support my orphaned brothers and sisters. I'll do anything to get into your good graces."

She fluttered her eyelashes for effect.

Cal faced front. "Dammit, Sabrina, I hate that I can't stay angry with you. Why is that?"

"Why do you hate it or why can't you stay angry?"

"Both."

"You can't stay angry because I'm nearly always right, and you can't hate it because deep in your heart you know I'm incredibly bright. Smarter than you, even. So you spend your days intimidated by me but determined not to let me know."

"In your dreams." He pointed at the bag. "Why'd you pick that bracelet over the other one or the watch?"

She stared at him. "Do you want the truth?"

"Oh, so I'm not going to like your reasoning. Sure. Tell me the truth."

She shrugged. "Tiffany is a sweet girl, but young. Her taste is a little, shall we say, undeveloped. While the diamond bracelet was beautiful, I thought it would be too plain. The emeralds give the bangle flash and she'll like that."

"Agreed. Why not the watch?"

"We're talking about Tiffany here, Cal. The watch wasn't digital, and I'm not completely convinced she can tell time the old-fashioned way."

"Remind me to fire you when we get back to the office."

"You asked me for the truth."

"So you're telling me it's my fault?"

"You're the one who chose Tiffany, and now you're the one who doesn't want to deal with the hassle of ending it. What do you want the card to say?"

He shifted on the seat. "Something nice. That we had a great time together, but we don't want the same things. You know. The usual. And stop looking at me that way."

"What way?"

"Like you disapprove. Your face gets all scrunchy. It's not attractive."

Sabrina resisted the urge to whip out her compact and peer at herself. She doubted that she was the least bit scrunchy, but she hated not knowing.

"I don't have an opinion on your personal life."

"Liar," he countered. "Why are you always telling me what to do and always disapproving of the women I pick?"

"Tiffany was all of twenty. You're using the term *woman* very loosely. I'd be willing to accept *mature girl,* or even *postadolescent.* If you actually picked a woman, I might not disapprove."

"Colette was nearly twenty-eight. That counts."

He had a point. Before Tiffany had been Shanna, and before her, Colette. "Okay, she counts as a woman."

"Colette was also bright. She'd been to college and everything." He sounded smug, as if pleased he was going to win the argument.

Sabrina shifted until she was staring at him. "For all we know, Colette was a rocket scientist, but that's hardly the point. The woman, and I'll concede that she was a woman, was French. She barely spoke English, and I know for a fact you weren't the least bit interested in her brain. She was a lingerie model. Did you actually ever hold a conversation with her?"

"Sure."

Sabrina raised her eyebrows and waited. Cal had many flaws, but dishonesty wasn't one of them.

He sighed heavily. "Okay, it was a short conversation. What's your point?"

"I'm not sure I have one, aside from the usual. You're reasonably intelligent—"

He glared at her and she ignored him.

"Reasonably attractive—"

The glare became a scowl. She was also lying through her teeth. Calling Cal attractive was in the same league as describing New York City as a "large village."

"Somewhat articulate, very successful man who in the six years I've known you has yet to have anything resembling a normal long-term relationship. You're thirty-four. When are you going to settle down?"

"I've had long-term relationships."

"Taking your suits to the same dry cleaner for six or seven years doesn't count. Face it, boss, you're not actually interested in anything but the chase. You want them until you catch them, then you lose interest. Don't you ever think about something more than that?"

His brown eyes darkened. "My personal life is none of your business."

She picked up the bag containing Tiffany's parting gift. "You make it my business," she said, no longer teasing.

He grunted. She'd heard enough of the sound to recognize it as a dismissal. He didn't want to talk about this anymore. There were times when she ignored the dismissive grunt, mostly because whatever they were talking about was important, but in this case, she let it go. Except when ending one of his relationships became her duty of the day, she really tried to stay out of his personal life. She admired Cal in many areas, but that wasn't one of them.

The limo pulled up to the west side high-rise in the Galleria district of Houston. Sabrina braced herself for the heat, slid across the seat and stepped out onto the sidewalk.

She smiled at Martin, Cal's private driver, then followed her boss into the building that housed the corporate offices of Langtry Oil and Gas.

The business occupied the top three floors. While Cal headed directly for his suite in the southwest corner, Sabrina stopped to collect mail and chat with her secretary, Ada.

"What did you pick?" Ada asked, leaning forward and smiling. The older woman had worked for Langtry Oil and Gas for years. When Sabrina had been hired, she'd taken her time choosing an assistant of her own. Ada had a reputation for being a little grumpy and stubborn about doing things her own way, but she knew everyone in the business and had probably heard every whisper uttered in the company since the 1970s.

Sabrina handed her the Tiffany's bag. Ada raised her eyebrows. "Tiffany's for Tiffany? You know the subtlety is going to be lost on the girl."

"My thoughts exactly, but it was still fun."

As Ada opened the box and gazed at the bangle, Sabrina flipped through the mail. "What's the word on the street?" Sabrina asked.

"Number ten should be hitting oil tonight, tomorrow at the latest, even though the engineers say another three to four days of drilling. The only other piece of news is that the clerical supervisor is still having trouble keeping his hands to himself. He cornered another two employees by the copier. They're filing official complaints right now."

Sabrina looked up from the mail and frowned. "He's been warned. Cal doesn't tolerate that kind of behavior."

Ada slipped on the bracelet and shrugged. "Apparently he's bought into Cal's good ol' boy act and thinks the fact that the boss invited him to lunch once means they're best friends. I'm not sure. I'm just telling you what's happening."

"I appreciate it, Ada, and I'll tell Cal. He'll take care of it immediately."

Ada set the jewelry back in the box and sighed. "You did very well. She'll love it."

"That's the idea. To ease the pain of losing the man. Personally, I'd rather have the cash."

"Me, too. Tell Cal I'm ready to start our affair anytime he likes. Or we can skip the affair completely and just get right to the parting gift. I want something that can be easily returned. Remember that, Sabrina, when you're picking it out."

Sabrina laughed and rose to her feet. "I'll be sure and tell him, although I don't think he'll appreciate the fact that you're only interested in the gift and not the man himself. Cal considers himself something of a prize where women are concerned."

"Oh, he is. But we all know I'm old enough to be his mother. You, on the other hand—"

"Stop it, Ada. You know I'm not interested, either." She headed down the hall. "Talk to you later."

"You can't stay immune forever," Ada called after her.

"Oh, yes I can."

Sabrina ignored the elevator and climbed the elegant spiral staircase that led to the executive level. She'd offered Ada an office of her own up there, but her assistant claimed she had to stay down with the "little" people in order to hear all the good gossip.

As she climbed, Sabrina finished sorting through the mail. Nothing pressing, nothing she couldn't handle on her own. She reached her office, collected the messages Ada had left for her, then continued through to Cal's suite.

Floor-to-ceiling windows filled two walls of his huge office. Aside from the requisite desk big enough to land a Harrier jet on, a conference table and two leather sofa groups to encourage chatty conversations, he also had a big-screen television, every computer game known to man and a temperature-controlled wine "closet" that stored a few dozen of his favorites.

There was a full kitchen and dining room beyond, an oversize bathroom complete with shower and Jacuzzi tub and a private elevator that led directly down to the parking garage.

As Sabrina approached the desk, she tried to ignore the view out the windows. Houston was about the flattest place on earth, and if she bothered to look, she could see forever. She'd watched thunderstorms roll in, perfect sunsets and, once, even a tornado dance across the land. In her opinion, Texas had too much weather. She missed Southern California, where the only way to tell the changing of the seasons was by the clothes being sold in the department stores.

Cal finished his call and motioned for her to take a seat across from his desk. She sank down into the leather chair and set Tiffany's parting gift on the chair next to hers.

Her boss met her gaze then looked away…almost as if he was embarrassed. How odd.

"Anything the matter?" she asked.

"No," he answered. "Just following up on something. It's… personal."

"Oh." Although she didn't know everything about Cal's life, she knew *almost* everything. And it had been a long time since he'd kept anything "personal" from her. At least she thought it had been.

"It's nothing important. Any of that for me?" he said, referring to the stack of mail in her hand and deliberately changing the subject. He wasn't the least bit subtle, she thought, and decided to let it go.

"Nothing I can't handle," she told him. "A few invitations."

He grimaced. "Charity functions."

"Of course."

"Just send a check."

She kept her smile hidden. If Cal wasn't "involved" with

a woman, he got fairly reclusive. Society matrons loathed his dry spells, as he was often the life of their parties. It would take him a couple of months to find someone to replace Tiffany, then his social life would be off and running.

"I've heard from the number ten rig," he said. "The engineers figure another three to four days, but I think they're going to hit in the next twenty-four hours."

He never ceased to amaze her. Ada's contacts had said the same thing. The difference was Cal made his assessment from his downtown office with nothing more than daily reports to guide him. Ada's source was an old oil man from way back who phoned her when they were getting close.

"What does Ada say?" he asked.

Cal watched as Sabrina tried to hide her annoyance at his question. She didn't like that he knew about her "source" in the office and would have preferred him to think she figured everything out on her own.

"The same," she admitted. "Within the day."

"Anything else I should know about?"

"The clerical supervisor is still having trouble keeping his hands to himself. A couple of staff members are filing official complaints."

Cal leaned back in his chair and rested his hands on the padded leather arms. "I can't say that I blame them. I hate it when this happens."

The coolly spoken words were enough to make Sabrina straighten. She reached for a pad of paper on the edge of his desk and grabbed a pen. "Go ahead."

"He's already been warned. Have Human Resources investigate the allegations and prepare the case, then fire him. Oh, I want them to promote from within this time—all the better if it's a woman so we can regain a little trust in that department—but tell them to be sure it's the best candidate, someone with a good record of employee interaction."

"That's it?"

He gazed at his personal assistant. Her wide blue eyes met his unblinkingly. "What did you expect? That I would call him out at dawn? Pistols at twenty paces?"

"I thought you'd at least threaten to beat him up."

Cal thought about the self-important young man who had been with the company less than a year. He'd been hired out of college, all cocky and convinced he was the next industry leader. Cal had put him in a supervisory position to season him. Obviously it hadn't worked.

"I would like nothing more than to show him what it was like to be physically intimidated by someone with the authority to hire and fire, not to mention someone physically stronger. However, letting him go under these circumstances is going to be plenty of punishment. He'll be left with a black mark on his employment record. So much for a rapid rise to success."

"Do you want to give him an exit interview?"

Cal grinned. "Let Ada do it."

Sabrina shook her head. "You are too cruel. That's perfect. He'll hate it."

"And Ada will adore it. I call that a win-win. Oh, and set up a department meeting with the clerical staff in the next few days. I want to talk to them myself. I don't approve of that kind of behavior. It's illegal and immoral. I want to reassure everyone that the situation is being corrected. Immediately."

Sabrina nodded as she took notes. She bent her head slightly, and the afternoon sunlight slipped through the window and caught in her short red hair—a layered cut falling just to the bottom of her collar. Her features were even, pleasant, if unremarkable. She had a nice smile, intelligent blue eyes and a figure that, after six years, was still something of a mystery to him. Despite the fact that she'd accompanied him on several working vacations, she always wore tailored clothing. Even her shorts-and-shirt sets had been proper and slightly loose. The only time he'd seen her in a bathing suit, it had been dark, and the shadows had prevented him from catching more than a glimpse of the occasional curve.

Not that he was overly interested in Sabrina's body. It was more male pride than desire. She was the perfect assistant—smart, attentive and not afraid to say what she thought. She had a gut instinct he'd come to rely upon, about people and situations. She didn't call attention to herself, and when he asked, she was willing to take care of his dirty work. The fact that she didn't turn him on was a plus. He didn't want the distraction and he couldn't afford to lose her.

He wondered what her reaction would be if he told her that the phone call she'd interrupted had been with an editor from *Prominence Magazine*. A letter had come to his house yesterday, telling him that he'd been named one of the world's most eligible bachelors by the magazine…and he'd been trying nicely to withdraw himself from such an "award." Unfortunately, he'd hung up agreeing to do an interview instead. He could just imagine the way Sabrina's eyes would sparkle with amusement once she heard about his most recent "honor." He would definitely wait to tell her.

They spent the next hour going through business. "Don't forget the trip to Singapore at the end of September," he said. "We're discussing the joint drilling venture."

She continued to make notes. "I remember. Maybe we can stop by Hong Kong on our way back and have some Chinese food. There's a lovely little restaurant there." She glanced at him, and her expression was innocence itself.

"I remember," he growled.

"Oh, Cal, you're not still sore that I beat you, are you?"

"I was never *sore* about anything. You got lucky in the fourth quarter."

"I was ahead the entire year. You've just conveniently forgotten that part." She grinned. "I'm also ahead this year."

He ignored her comment. For the past five years they'd had a bet on the stock market. On January first, he fronted them both ten thousand dollars to play the market. Whoever had the most money at the end of the year was the winner. The loser had to treat the winner to lunch anywhere the winner said. Last year, Sabrina had won and had claimed a taste for Chinese food...from Hong Kong.

"Actually, this year I've been thinking of Italian," she murmured.

"Rome?" he asked.

"Maybe Venice. I've never been to Venice."

"You've never been to Rome, either."

"I know, but Venice sounds so fun. All that water, those boats. Venetian glass."

She was already up twenty percent. It was his own fault. When they'd started their game, she'd insisted on a handicap. He wasn't allowed to invest in oil or gas stocks, the one area he was guaranteed a win. She, on the other hand, invested heavily in his own company. Last year that had been enough to push her over the top.

"I know a great Italian restaurant in New York."

The phone rang. She reached for it and grinned. "Don't even think about weaseling out of it," she said before picking up the receiver. "Mr. Langtry's office. This is Sabrina."

Cal didn't pay attention to the call. It hadn't come in on his private line, and Sabrina took care of most of his other business.

After a couple of minutes, she put the line on hold. "You'd better take this one," she said.

"Next year the rules are changing. Either I can invest in my industry or you can't, either." He put down the paper he'd been reading and glanced at her. "Otherwise— Sabrina, what's wrong?"

She'd gone pale. She didn't have much color in her face, anyway, but the little that was there had drained away, leaving her ashen.

"Is it Tracey?" he asked, knowing his older sister was usually responsible for any trauma in his life.

"No. It's your lawyer." She motioned to the phone. "You'd better talk to him."

Before he could ask her anything else, she rose and crossed the room, then let herself out. Cal frowned. He couldn't think of a single thing he and his lawyer had to discuss that would require privacy. Sabrina knew almost all of his secrets. It was part of her job.

"Jack," he said, when he'd picked up the receiver and released the hold button. "What's going on?"

"Are you sitting down, Cal?"

He didn't like the sound of that. "Get to the point, Jack. Whatever you said chased Sabrina from the room, and she's pretty unflappable."

"Okay. Do you remember a woman named Janice Thomas? You had a relationship with her back in college."

Cal frowned as the memory fell into place. "That was about twelve or thirteen years ago. Between college and grad school. We went out for a summer. What does that have to do with anything?"

"It seems she had a baby. A daughter. From what I've found out, when she discovered she was pregnant, she approached your parents. She wasn't interested in marriage as much as money. They agreed on a very tidy sum with the understanding that you would never know about the child. Unfortunately, Janice died in childbirth. The baby was given up for adoption. Her adoptive parents were killed in a car accident nearly a year ago. She's been living with an aunt in Ohio, an older lady who no longer wants responsibility for the girl. That's why I'm calling. I thought you'd want to know. If you don't take the girl, the aunt is going to make her a ward of the court."

Cal knew intellectually there weren't any fault lines in Houston, so the sudden tilting he felt couldn't be an earthquake. But that's how it seemed. As if his whole world had just been jolted from its axis.

"Cal, are you still there?" his attorney asked. "Did you hear me? You've got a twelve-year-old daughter."

A daughter? From Janice? The enormity of the information stunned him. Nothing made sense. A child? Him? No wonder Sabrina had left the room.

"I heard you, Jack." He'd heard, although he didn't have a damn clue as to what he was going to do now.

Chapter 2

"I don't know what to say," Cal told his attorney. He turned in his chair so he was facing the window, but he didn't even see the view. Instead, images of Janice filled his mind. He remembered her as being of average height and pretty. They'd met while interning for the same oil-and-gas firm one summer. "Are you sure about this? Why didn't she tell me she was pregnant?"

"Like I said, she was after money, not matrimony. I guess she knew about the trouble your parents had with Tracey and figured they would be willing to pay her off. One of the retired partners here at the firm prepared the paperwork, Cal. I've seen it. In fact, telling you this raises some issues regarding attorney-client privileges within the firm. But this is important enough that I'm willing to deal with any backlash. Janice was offered a sizable amount to keep quiet and stay away from you. If she hadn't died unexpectedly, she wouldn't have had to work again for life."

Nothing made sense. Cal tried to pick a rooftop outside and focus on it, but the task was too difficult. Janice had gotten pregnant? She'd gone to his parents instead of him? She hadn't wanted to get married, she'd just wanted the money?

"I don't want to believe any of this," he said, too stunned to be angry. "I tried to get in touch with her when I went back to college. She just disappeared. I thought she'd run off with someone else."

A child. He couldn't imagine that being real. That one of those long summer nights had resulted in a new life.

Jack cleared his throat. "Look, Cal, I'm your lawyer, not your conscience. You say the word and I'll pretend this conversation never happened. You don't know this kid from a rock and that doesn't have to change. Let the aunt turn her over to the state. It's probably better that way. The reports I have say she's been having problems. Poor adjustment in her new school, falling grades, antisocial behavior. Do you really want that kind of mess right now? Face it, your life is pretty damned good. Why change that?"

Cal knew Jack was just trying to do his job—which was to make his most wealthy client's life easier, however possible. Cal supposed there were many men who would simply walk away from this kind of information—he had a feeling he was going to wish he had. But he couldn't.

"If she lost her parents less than a year ago, I'm not surprised she's having trouble adjusting," Cal said. "Everything's been taken away from her. She's living with an aunt who doesn't want her. She probably knows she's going to get thrown out any minute. These circumstances wouldn't make anyone look like a poster child for mental health."

"You're right, of course," Jack said. "I'm not the enemy here, I'm simply pointing out different options."

"I know. I'm sorry," Cal said. "This is impossible for me to believe. I can't help thinking I would have known if Janice was pregnant, but that, as Sabrina would gladly tell me, is male arrogance at its worst."

"I understand. You're going to need some time to think about this. The aunt will keep her about two more weeks, so no decisions have to made today. There are a lot of different ways to play this one. I suspect with a little financial encouragement, the aunt might be willing to keep her longer. If you want, I can look into boarding schools. Or, as I already mentioned, she can go into foster care. You don't have to do anything if you don't want to."

Cal felt as if he'd been blindsided by a tanker. He heard his attorney's words and knew he had plenty to think about, but one thing was certain. "I'm not going to let her go to the state. If there's proof she's my daughter, then she's my responsibility."

"Oh, there's proof. Your parents had her checked when she was born. She's yours."

That was all Cal had to know. He'd done a lot of things in his life that he wasn't especially proud of, but he'd never walked away from his responsibilities. "I have a few things to take care of. Sabrina or I will be in touch in the next day or so with the particulars. In the meantime, call the aunt back and tell her I'll be out to pick up my daughter before the end of the week."

"Are you sure you want to do this?"

No, he wasn't sure he wanted to. He only knew he *had* to. "If she's mine, Jack, I don't have a choice."

His lawyer sighed. "I figured as much. I'll let her know."

"I'm going to New York to talk to my mother. If you have to get in touch with me, the office will know where I am."

"Will do."

Cal was about to hang up the phone when he heard Jack call his name. "What?" he asked.

"Don't you want to know her name?"

The question shocked him. Giving the child a name made her more real—an actual person with an identity. "Yes."

"Anastasia Overton."

"Anastasia? What the hell kind of name is that for a twelve-year-old kid?" He shrugged. "I know you can't answer that one, either. Okay, Jack, I'll talk to you later." He hung up the phone.

Silence filled the room. Cal leaned back in his chair and swore. He pushed to his feet and stalked to the window. "What the hell is going on? How did this happen?"

He didn't even know what he was asking. Did he mean how had Janice gotten pregnant? That would be pretty easy to answer. Maybe he meant how had the pregnancy been kept from him? Or maybe how had his parents thought they could get away with keeping news of his own child from him?

But they had, a small voice whispered inside his head. For twelve years his mother had sat in silence. She'd sacrificed her own grandchild for the greater good. At least that's what she would tell him. He could already hear her voice.

The quiet got to him, and without thinking he turned back to his desk and hit a button beside his telephone. Less than thirty seconds later Sabrina stepped into the room.

Her usually animated face was strangely solemn. He half expected a crack, then realized that was never her style. She liked to banter and fight with him, but only on even terms. She would never attack him when he was vulnerable.

"How much did Jack tell you?" he asked.

Sabrina walked to one of the leather sofas and gracefully sank onto a cushion. He walked toward her and took a seat at the far end of the same sofa. He wanted to be close, but he found he couldn't face her. Odd, because Sabrina knew the worst there was to know about him. Knew it and didn't judge him. That was one of the reasons he kept her around.

"He said that you'd been involved with a young woman about thirteen years ago and she'd gotten pregnant, apparently on purpose. When you went off to grad school, she approached your parents, promising to stay out of your life if they paid her enough. They agreed. When the woman died in childbirth, the child was put up for adoption. She's now living in Ohio with an elderly aunt."

He faced front and braced his elbows on his knees, then clasped his hands together. "That about sums it up. Her name was Janice—the woman, not the kid." He glanced at her. "This is one of the bigger messes you've had to help me clean up. I guess you're going to be expecting a substantial raise this year."

She gave him a slight smile. "This isn't a mess. I would never think that. You didn't know about this. Jack told me he'd only found out about it a couple of days ago."

"You believe him?" He asked the question casually but suddenly found that her opinion mattered.

"Of course." She angled toward him. "Cal, you're nothing like your sister. Tracey is spoiled and willful. If this were her problem, she would have let the child go without giving him or her a second thought. You're not like that. If you'd known about your daughter from the beginning, you would have done the right thing, whether that meant marrying Janice or just providing for your child."

Her expression was earnest, her words sincere. He appreciated that. Jack had claimed not to be Cal's conscience, and Cal agreed. But there were times he wondered if that was actually part of Sabrina's job. Knowing that he was going to have to look her in the eye often influenced his behavior, and for the better.

"You're right. So thirteen years after the fact, I'm going to do the right thing. But first I'm going to New York to talk to my mother."

Sabrina raised her eyebrows. "I'm surprised."

"That I'm going to take my daughter or that I'm going to visit my mother."

"Both, although I'm more surprised about your mother. I don't remember you ever going to see her."

Cal grimaced. "We're not what you would call a close family. I think I've seen her twice since my father died, and that was nearly ten years ago. She wasn't the maternal type. Mother is very big on how things look rather than how they are. This situation proves that."

"Have you thought this through?" Sabrina asked.

He knew she wasn't asking about the visit. There was no reason to consider that. He needed information and his mother was the best source. After all, she and his father had been the ones to make the decision for him.

The shock was starting to fade, and he felt the first flicker of emotion since receiving Jack's phone call. It wasn't paternal pride at finding out he had offspring, or even curiosity at what his daughter would be like. Instead, what he felt was rage. Cold, dark rage. He told himself his parents had never considered his opinions or feelings before and he shouldn't be surprised they hadn't where Janice was concerned. Based on his thirty-four years as their son, nothing about their actions should shock him. Yet he was appalled at their complete disregard for his rights as a father and their callous disposal of their grandchild. As he had often thought in the past, he would have been better off being raised by wolves than Mr. and Mrs. Jefferson Langtry.

Sabrina leaned toward him. "We're talking about a growing child. She's nearly a teenager. Have you thought about what this is going to do to you and your life? If you really mean to take care of her, everything will have to change."

He stood up and paced in front of the sofa. "No, I haven't thought it through. I haven't had time. Right now I can barely grasp the concept of having a child. I haven't had a chance to internalize the information. But that doesn't matter. The girl exists and she's my responsibility. I'm not going to let her become a ward of the state. She didn't ask for her circumstances. She's a kid, and as far as she knows, no one in the world wants her. I might not be anyone's idea of a perfect father, but I'm not going to turn my back on her."

Sabrina smiled at him. "Every now and then you do something that reminds me why I like working for you."

"So it's not just about the money?"

"Not today."

He shoved his hands in his trouser pockets. "The good news is, once Tiffany finds out about my daughter, I won't have to worry about breaking up with her. She'll run so hard and fast, she'll leave skid marks."

"You don't know that. Maybe she would revel in the chance to show what she's made of."

Cal stopped pacing and stared down at Sabrina. Her blue gaze was steady. "I do know that," he told her. "I went out with her for nearly two months. While I don't know everything about her, I'm quite aware of her character. Besides, she's too young to be responsible for a twelve-year-old."

"But not too young to be dating that twelve-year-old's father?"

She asked the question with a straight face, but he saw the hint of a smile teasing at the corner of her mouth.

"You never give me a break," he complained.

"It's not in my job description. Besides, there are enough people thrilled to do that every chance they get."

"So you want to spend your time taking me down a notch or two?"

"No. It's not that personal. However, my job description *does* include telling you the truth, even when you don't want to hear it."

"It's your favorite part of the job," he grumbled.

"Sometimes." This time she did smile. "And I think there's a chance you could be wrong about Tiffany. She's not bright, but that doesn't mean she's heartless. She might surprise you."

Cal didn't want to be surprised. Even if Sabrina was right, it didn't matter. He wouldn't want someone like Tiffany near his daughter. Which was a pretty sad state of affairs, he told himself. He was willing to date and sleep with Tiffany, but he wouldn't want her hanging around his kid. So what had he seen in her in the first place?

He thought about her perfect twenty-year-old body and got a little of the answer, although he didn't like it. When had he gotten so damn shallow? Was this what he wanted *Prominence Magazine* to tell the world? Thank God he had Sabrina. He knew he could count on her. He also trusted her.

Sabrina glanced at her watch. "You could still catch a flight to New York this evening. You'll get in late, but that would allow you to see your mother tomorrow. I'm assuming you want this over as quickly as possible."

He nodded. "I want to get Anastasia in the next couple of days. She's living with an aunt, and the woman has made it clear to everyone that she's not interested in keeping the girl. That's a hell of a thing for a twelve-year-old to know."

Sabrina stood up and started toward his desk. "Let me see what I can do about getting you a seat. One night in New York, or two?"

"Make it two. I don't know how long I'll be with my mother, but I doubt we'll have a big family reunion. I already know our conversation is going to make me angry, and I'll need some time to get over it before going to Ohio. Oh, and book two seats, Sabrina. I want you to come with me."

His personal assistant looked at him. Wide blue eyes darkened slightly. "You want me to come with you while you talk to your mother?"

"Let's just say I haven't lost my temper with her yet, but I've come close. If anything was going to push me over the edge, this would be it."

"I'm not big enough to wrestle you into submission."

"I know, but one of your icy stares is usually enough to remind me to behave."

"Okay. I'll come, too. After all, I'm yours to command."

"Cheap talk. I command you to stop winning on the stock market."

She blinked slowly. "I'm sorry. Did you say something? I heard a faint buzzing, but no real words."

"Just as I thought. Selective hearing."

"I listen when you say something worth paying attention to."

He pointed at the phone. "Get us seats. If you promise to behave, I'll let you have the window."

"What a guy."

She picked up the phone on his desk and dialed from memory. While she talked with the airline, Cal crossed to the window and stared out. It was nearly dusk and lights were coming on all around him. He stared into the twilight and wondered about the little girl living somewhere north of here. What did she look like? He could barely remember Janice's face, although other images were clear to him. The sound of her laughter, the feel of her hands on his body.

There had been, he was willing to admit, an instant attraction between them. A fire that had burned hot and bright. He didn't remember asking her out, though. At the time, it had sort of seemed to happen on its own. Now, with the hindsight of age, experience and knowledge, he wondered if it had really been that casual. Had she set him up from the beginning, then engineered the entire relationship?

He remembered that the sex between them had been intense. With her claim of being on the pill, they hadn't worried about precautions. She'd always been eager and willing. At times, she'd been the one pulling him into bed. He remembered being flattered by her attentions and what he'd thought at the time was her insatiable desire for him. Now he realized she had just been making sure she got pregnant. He'd been a fool.

He remembered her tears when he'd left for graduate school, her promises to stay in touch. He remembered how he'd tried to call her, but her phone had been disconnected with no forwarding number. His letters had been returned without a forwarding address. It was as if she'd disappeared from the face of the earth. He supposed she had—after all, seven or eight months after they'd spent their summer together, she'd died.

He tried to feel regret for her loss, but he couldn't. He'd never known her. Whatever parts of herself she'd shown him had been designed to get him into her bed. Obviously he, too, had been born with the Langtry ability to completely screw up personal relationships.

How much had they offered her? What was a child worth these days? He pressed his hand against the cool glass and wondered how it was possible that his parents had performed this hideous deception. Then he reminded himself nothing they did should surprise him. With his family, he should know to expect anything…and nothing.

Chapter 3

Sabrina leaned back into the comfortable leather seat of the sleek limousine and told herself to relax. This wasn't her problem; she was simply an interested bystander. Cal wanted her along to provide moral support, nothing more. But the sensible words didn't stop her from clasping her hands together over and over.

She tried to distract herself from her nerves by staring out the window. As always, the city enchanted her. She'd never lived in Manhattan but had enjoyed her visits. She liked the contrasts of the city—the huge buildings, the large impersonal crowds, the street vendors who sold food and drinks on the corners and, after two days, recognized her and grinned as they asked if she would like her usual. She liked all the city had to offer culturally, she loved the theater and the restaurants. When she traveled with Cal, they stayed at beautiful hotels—as they had last night—but they didn't limit their culinary experiences to upscale, pretentious eateries. Instead, they found strange little places with unusual cuisine and often fabulous food. She liked the potential for adventure and the fact that no two visits were ever alike.

Under normal circumstances, she was usually thrilled to be in the city. Today, however, she would gladly give it all up to be back in the heat and humidity of Houston.

She didn't want to think about the upcoming visit, so she rolled down her window. It was a perfect New York spring day. Clear, warm but not muggy. The scent of blooming flowers occasionally overpowered the smell of exhaust. A burst of laughter caught her attention. She looked across to the sidewalk and saw a young father carrying his toddler son on his shoulders.

She swallowed. A child. She hadn't really allowed herself to think about children. She was still young and there was plenty of time. But children had always been a part of her future. She'd just assumed that one day she would have them. Cal was different. As far as she knew, he'd never even thought he would marry, let alone have a family. Here he was being presented with a half-grown kid. How on earth was he going to handle it?

She glanced at her boss. He stared straight ahead, and for once, his handsome face was unreadable. He didn't show his feelings easily, but over the years, she'd learned to read him. Until today. She knew he was in shock and he was angry. She couldn't blame him for either emotion. Bad enough to find out a former girlfriend had betrayed him in such a calculated way, but that information was made more horrible by the realization his own parents had joined the conspiracy.

Cal's father had died before she'd been hired and she'd never met his mother. She'd heard rumors and stories, mostly from Ada, about a cold society woman who put up with her husband's chronic philandering in order to keep her lifestyle intact. The marriage had been a business arrangement. One half had brought in land rich with oil; the other, technology, engineering know-how and a small infusion of cash. Separately the families had been struggling, together they formed an empire. An empire that, according to Ada, hadn't left any time for raising children. Cal and Tracey had been put into the custody of an ever-changing staff.

"What are you thinking?" Cal asked.

"That a twelve-year-old is going to change your life."

"I know."

"I don't think you realize how much. Children are a big responsibility. I remember helping Gram with my younger brother and sisters after our parents died. They were a handful."

He shrugged. "I don't have a choice. I'll learn what I have to. At least I want the girl. That's more than her aunt can say. That should count."

"It will." But would it be enough? Sabrina wasn't sure. After all, Cal wasn't into long-term commitments. His idea of a serious relationship was one that lasted two months. His record to date was ninety-three days. Still, a daughter was different from a girlfriend.

The limo pulled up in front of an East Side high-rise co-op. One of the uniformed doormen stepped to the curb and opened the door. Sabrina accepted his assistance from the vehicle, then waited for Cal to lead the way inside. She'd worked for him for several years and thought she'd grown used to their difference in background and wealth, but occasionally obvious signs of his family's impressive fortune intimidated her.

"I didn't call to say we were coming," she murmured as they stepped into the elegant foyer and walked to the elevators.

"I did. She's in this morning. She has a lunch appointment, but I told her this wouldn't take long."

Sabrina smoothed her hair, then tugged on the skirt of her hunter green silk suit. It was the most expensive work outfit she owned and she'd brought it deliberately. No doubt Mrs. Langtry would consider her beneath notice—after all, she was just the hired help. But she also figured she would need all the confidence-boosting she could get.

Instead of opening into a hallway, the elevator doors pulled back to reveal a huge living room. Marble floors and glass tables reflected the light from outside…light that flowed in through floor-to-ceiling windows. Unlike Cal's office view, this one didn't show a flat world, but instead stretched across Central Park, to the equally impressive buildings on the other side. The windows on her left looked south, and Sabrina realized Mrs. Langtry not only had a penthouse, but one on the corner.

Must be nice to be the other half, she thought, before the click of approaching heels caught her attention.

A very elegant, very beautiful older woman swept into the room. She had to be in her late fifties, but she looked substantially younger. Sleekly styled brown hair hung to her shoulders. She was thin, well-dressed and had the air of one born to society and money. Sabrina instantly felt dowdy. Her instinct was to take a step back in the presence of someone so different. Instead, she forced herself to square her shoulders and stand her ground.

"Good morning, Calhoun," his mother said. "You're looking well. Taller than I remember. You get that from your father, of course. The Langtrys are always tall. We'll talk in the morning room. It's this way." She motioned to a doorway on their right. "Your secretary can wait in the kitchen." Mrs. Langtry offered Sabrina a slight smile. "It's through there, dear. Just past the dining room. Cook will get you some coffee and maybe a pastry."

Before she could move, Sabrina felt Cal's hand on the small of her back. "That won't be necessary, Mother. Sabrina isn't my secretary, she's my personal assistant. I don't have any secrets from her. She'll be joining us this morning."

His mother's expression didn't change, but her nose twitched slightly as if she'd accidently inhaled an unpleasant odor. Sabrina resisted the urge to tell Cal she was more than happy to wait in the kitchen with Cook. For one thing, she would like to find out if Cook actually had a first name, and maybe even discover the gender of that person.

Nerves, she told herself. Okay, so she wasn't a Langtry, but she was an Innis, and while they weren't exactly top drawer, she'd graduated at the head of her class at UCLA. She was bright, funny and good at her job. So what if no one in her family was listed in the social registry?

"As you wish," Mrs. Langtry said, and led the way.

Sabrina stared at the woman's beige silk blouse. The fabric looked as if it was made from starlight, it was so smooth and flowing. Did the rich get fabric from a better class of silkworms? Did silk still come from worms? She would have to look that up when they got back to Texas.

The morning room was spacious and bright, with overstuffed sofas and a low table set with coffee service. Sabrina saw there were only two cups. Mrs. Langtry pushed a button on the wall. When a young woman in a black dress with a starched white apron appeared, she ordered a third cup and some pastries.

Cal motioned for Sabrina to sit on one sofa. She was grateful when he settled next to her. She leaned close and whispered, "So do the afternoon and evening rooms get progressively bigger? I have no experience with this, you know. Back in California, we had one little old living room. It was good enough for the likes of us."

Cal grinned. "I'll fill you in on architecture of the rich on the way back to the hotel. It's pretty interesting."

"I'll bet."

She glanced up and saw Mrs. Langtry frowning. Sabrina doubted the older woman had heard any part of their conversation, so she must be unhappy with their obvious familiarity. She thought about telling Cal's mother that there was nothing going on between them, nor was that ever going to change, but she figured the woman wouldn't believe her, and even if she did, she would pretend not to care.

The maid returned with a third cup, then quietly left the room, closing the door behind her.

Mrs. Langtry poured coffee. She handed Cal his black, then looked expectantly at Sabrina. "Sugar? Cream?"

"Cream, please."

Mrs. Langtry complied, then held out the cup. When Sabrina took it, the older woman's attention turned back to her son. "I still think whatever you want to discuss would be better done in private."

"Sabrina knows it all, Mother. Well, not all. Obviously there are secrets even I'm not aware of, but those are the exception. After all, who do you think worked out the details of paying off Tracey's last husband?"

Mrs. Langtry's mouth pursed. "I see."

Sabrina resisted the urge to hunch down on the seat. But she *had* been the one to take care of Tracey's problem. Cal's older sister had a bad habit of falling for men who were only interested in her money. She'd been married six times and had had an assortment of lovers, all of whom used her, taking what they could and leaving as soon as the funds dried up.

It was sad, she thought to herself. All this money and no one was happy. She remembered Ada's comments about Cal's mother being a cold witch. What no one could figure out was, had her husband fooled around because life was icy at home, or had his philandering caused the chill in the first place? Considering how they'd been raised, maybe it wasn't surprising the Langtry children hadn't found marital bliss, or even a decent relationship.

Cal set his cup on the coffee table. "Does the name Janice Thomas mean anything to you, Mother?"

"No." She took a sip. "Should it?"

"Yes, actually it should. Unless Tracey has a couple of kids that I don't know about, Janice was the mother of your only grandchild."

Mrs. Langtry drew in a deep breath. Her dark eyes, so like her son's, didn't waver. She took another sip, then nodded. "So you found out about the child. I suppose it was foolish to hope that unfortunate incident wouldn't come to light. Oh, well, you know about it now. No harm done."

Sabrina felt Cal start to burn. The heat of his anger singed her skin. She placed a hand on his forearm and gave a quick squeeze. His glance of thanks told her that he had been about to lose control.

"I don't know which comment to address first," he said, his voice low and controlled. "Your calling it an 'incident' or the statement of 'no harm done.' You played with lives, Mother. You kept information about a woman's pregnancy from me. You kept my child from me."

She dismissed him with a wave. "You don't know what you're talking about. You were what, twenty-two? Did you actually want to marry the little gold-digger? I don't think so. Your father and I knew exactly what had to be done. Janice Thomas didn't want to marry you, she wanted money. Under the circumstances, it was simpler to pay her off. I don't regret it for a moment, and you shouldn't, either. We were prepared to set her up for life. It's hardly our fault that she died."

Sabrina knew that Cal's mother was cold, but she hadn't expected to feel the frost seeping into her body. She was stunned by the woman's callous words and had to consciously keep her mouth from hanging open.

"We are talking about my daughter and your grandchild. You had no right—"

The older woman set her coffee cup on the table and glared at him. "We had every right," she said, cutting him off in mid-sentence. "Your future was set, or it would have been if you'd ever bothered to settle down. You were going to run Langtry Oil and Gas. You barely knew the girl, so don't try to tell me you lost the love of your life. The truth is, you haven't thought of her once in the past thirteen years. All this righteous indignation over what? She was money-hungry trash. She got what she deserved."

Cal set his teeth. "I'll admit I didn't fall in love with Janice. I take issue with your comment that she got what she deserved, but that is not the point. I had a child and you kept that information from me. You let your own grandchild be adopted. I'll bet you didn't bother to keep track of her."

"No. Why should we? All this fuss. What's the point? The past is over. You wouldn't be interested in a child with a mother like Janice. I don't know how you found out about her, and I don't really care. If you want a child so much, marry someone suitable and have one. Stop chasing around with those young girls. You and your sister. Whatever did your father and I do to deserve such children?"

Cal rose to his feet. "Nothing, Mother. You two did nothing."

"Where are you going?"

"Why does it matter?"

"You're going to do something stupid, aren't you. Something with the child. This is why we didn't tell you about Janice all those years ago. You would have married the mother, or at least taken responsibility for the child. We saved you that, but you're not grateful. You don't understand. You've never understood."

"You're right, Mother. I don't understand. And yes, I'm going to go get *my* daughter, and I'm going to do my damnedest to be a good parent to her. But that's something *you* wouldn't understand."

Sabrina didn't remember standing, but suddenly she was at Cal's side and they were leaving the room, closing the door behind them. Mrs. Langtry continued talking, her words fading as they moved away. Sabrina was grateful. She didn't want to hear anything else. She was too shocked. Knowing that Cal's mother was a cold woman was very different from experiencing it firsthand.

They crossed the living room and waited in front of the elevator. Cal pushed the Down button.

"Cal?"

Both he and Sabrina turned toward the soft voice. Tracey Langtry stood in the shadows. She was a beautiful female version of her brother, or she had been at one time. The morning light was not kind, highlighting the lines on her face. Her lifestyle had not allowed her to age well, and she looked far older than her thirty-eight years.

Worn jeans hung on too-narrow hips.

"Cal, I need some money. I've used up my allowance."

Cal didn't look at her. Instead, he stared impatiently at the closed elevator doors as if willing them to open. "Who is he this time?"

"Oh, he's lovely. A race car driver. Very good, very young." She giggled. "Very nice in bed. I—" She hiccupped, then covered her mouth. "I like him a lot."

Sabrina realized the other woman was drunk, and it was barely ten in the morning. She considered herself fairly so- phisticated, but this was too much. She took a step away from Tracey and toward Cal.

"There's a race and he needs the entry fee. Plus, traveling around gets so expensive. Please, Cal, just ten or twenty thousand. You won't even miss it."

He didn't answer. The elevator doors opened and he guided Sabrina inside, followed her and pushed the Down button. As the door closed, he didn't bother saying goodbye.

They reached street level and walked toward the limousine. Sabrina didn't think the silence between them was especially awkward, but she felt obligated to think of something to say. Something to tell Cal that she didn't judge him by his family. But she couldn't find any words. Not without making a difficult situation worse.

After they were settled in the car and he'd given the driver instructions to return them to their hotel, he finally looked at her. Something dark and painful lurked in his eyes.

"When I was a kid, I used to pretend that I'd been left on the doorstep by Gypsies and that one day they would come back to get me. At this point I would be grateful just to have been adopted. I'm not happy to have that gene pool floating around in my body. I could turn into one of them at any moment."

"If it was going to happen, it would have happened already. You're safe."

"You think so?" He turned toward the window. "I'm not so sure."

"Cal, you're a good man. If you were like them, you wouldn't care about your daughter. You would have let her go into foster homes or arranged boarding school. You're making an effort. That counts."

She wanted to tell him that she admired him. When she thought about all he'd been through as a child, of the horrible life he'd had, she was amazed that he'd turned out as well as he had. It was a testament to his character. Sometimes she forgot there was a real person behind the handsome playboy facade, then something like this came along and reminded her.

"I'm sorry you had to see that," he continued. "But I'm not sorry you were there. Lord only knows what I would have done to that woman if I'd been alone."

She wasn't sure if he was talking about his mother or Tracey, and realized he probably meant both of them. She didn't doubt that in a couple of days he would tell her to send his sister a check. Maybe not for the amount she'd requested, but for enough to tide her over until her next trust fund payment.

"Every family has dirty laundry. You'd be shocked if you knew some of my secrets."

He looked at her and smiled. "Yeah, right. You have secrets? What? That you went to bed without flossing twice all of last year?"

She glared at him. "They're more interesting than that."

"I doubt it. You are not the kind of woman who has deep, dark secrets. Don't worry, Sabrina, I'm not complaining. Far from it."

Before she could protest that she could be bad, too, if she wanted, he did the most extraordinary thing. He reached out and took her hand in his.

Sabrina blinked twice, then stared at their linked fingers. She and Cal often touched. A light brush of his arm against hers when they walked together. A teasing poke in her side if he thought she was being too stuffy. He'd hugged her a half dozen times or so over the course of their working relationship. But those had all been impersonal buddy-type contacts. This was personal.

She felt his heat and strength. His long fingers and broad palm dwarfed her hand, leaving her feeling incredibly feminine. A strange lethargy stole over her, and it was only when her chest started to get tight that she realized she'd stopped breathing.

She forced herself to draw in a deep breath, then release it. This wasn't happening. She glanced down and saw that it was. He was actually holding her hand. Then, as if he'd read her mind and realized what he was doing, he squeezed once and released her.

Sabrina sat next to him, feeling as if she'd just survived a force three tornado. Her entire body felt buffeted. Every cell was on alert, her skin tingled where it had been in contact with his, and if she allowed herself to notice, she would have to confess to a definite hint of dampness on her panties.

Danger! a voice in her head screamed. Danger! Danger! Do not do this to yourself!

She straightened and gave the voice her full attention. Every word was true. Cal Langtry was deadly to women everywhere. He was only ever interested in the chase. Once he'd caught his chosen prey, he lost interest and ended the relationship. She'd seen it happen countless times. Besides, they had a perfectly wonderful working relationship. She adored her job, she was well paid, and she wasn't a fool. Not only would she jeopardize everything if she started thinking of Cal as a man instead of her employer, she would be wishing after the moon. After all, she wasn't his type.

As painful as it was, she forced herself to remember a phone call she'd overheard nearly six years before. She'd been working for Cal all of two or three months and had been fighting a serious crush. It had been late and she'd entered his office unannounced.

He had his back to the door and didn't notice her in the shadows. She still didn't know who he'd been talking to and she didn't want to know. What she recalled most was that he'd been talking about her.

"Yes, my new assistant is working out great. I'm impressed with her." He'd paused to listen. "I did say 'her.' Sabrina is very much a woman."

She thought about how her heart had leapt in her chest and her knees had grown weak. Was it possible he'd been attracted to her, too?

"No, you've got it all wrong. She's perfect for me. She's bright and too good for me to ever want to let her go. She's attractive enough so that no one is going to think she's a dog, but not pretty enough to interest me. It's great. No matter how closely we work together, Sabrina Innis will never be more than office equipment to me."

The words had laid her soul bare. She'd crept out silently

and spent the rest of the night crying away her foolish dreams. In the cold light of dawn, she'd made a decision. She could continue to want what she could never have, or she could make the best of what was a wonderful job. With Cal she would make enough money to put her three siblings through college and provide for Gram. She would also be able to build a nest egg for herself. The position of Cal's assistant meant travel, all of which would be first class, a chance to meet interesting people and gain experiences she would never have otherwise. Did it matter that she didn't turn the man on?

In the end, common sense had won out over ego. She'd ruthlessly suppressed every hint of her crush until her wayward emotions fell into line. Now she could look at Cal and see him for the handsome bachelor he was without feeling anything but friendship. She'd bought gifts for his women and had made arrangements for romantic weekends away all without a twinge of jealousy or regret. So what had just happened?

Sabrina thought about all that had occurred in the past twenty-four hours. It must be the tension, she told herself. She hadn't slept much the previous night. Dealing with Cal's family was difficult for both of them. He'd reached out for comfort and she'd happened to be the closest person. She'd reacted because he was a good-looking man and she'd been living like a nun. Wayward hormones and close proximity. Nothing else. She didn't have any romantic feelings for the man. How could she? She knew the worst about him. She still liked him, but she sure wasn't fooled by his charming personality. Cal Langtry might be an incredible catch, but he had flaws, just like everyone else.

The limo pulled up in front of the hotel. She looked over at her boss. "What do you want to do?"

"There's no point in staying here. Let's change the flights and go to Ohio this afternoon. I'll call Jack and have him notify the aunt. If I can, I want to get my daughter as soon as possible."

Chapter 4

The town was a three-hour drive from the airport. Cal slowed at the intersection. There were only two other cars in sight and both of them were at least ten years old. Although he'd traveled to many unusual places, he'd always lived in large cities—Houston, Dallas, New York for a short time. In the back of his mind, he'd wondered what it would be like to live in a place where everyone knew everyone else.

"Follow this street about a mile," Sabrina said, consulting the handwritten directions Jack, his attorney, had provided them. "Then turn right. Oster Street. There should be a stop sign."

There were small business on both sides of what was obviously the main road. A diner, a barber shop, a closed five-and-dime. He was about to say it didn't look as bad as Jack had made it out to be when he noticed the peeling paint on most of the buildings. Some of the windows were boarded up. The farther he drove into town and away from the highway, the more run-down everything seemed.

He turned right where Sabrina indicated. Commercial and retail areas gave way to houses. He saw a lot of broken or missing fences, cars up on blocks. Side yards contained clotheslines with drying garments flapping in the brisk breeze. Porches sagged, yards were overgrown with weeds. They passed a block with five houses for sale, four of which had signs proclaiming the price had been reduced.

"This place is dying," he said.

"I know. It's sad. Jack said the main factory closed and there's no employment. A lot of people have already gone, and those who stayed are having trouble earning an income. In a couple of years, there won't be anything left."

Their rental car was a plain General Motors four-door sedan, nothing fancy. But it was relatively new and seemed out of place on the narrow street. "I'm glad we didn't take a limo."

"I agree. Turn right at the stop sign." Sabrina rolled down her window and took a breath. "I feel badly for these people. You can smell the poverty." She shivered. "What's that saying? 'Been there, done that, bought the T-shirt.' I don't want to go back."

Cal frowned. "You told me that you grew up without a lot of money, but things were never this desperate, were they?"

"Not really. We didn't have extra spending money, but we got by. After my folks died and we moved in with my grandmother, we had a few months that were pretty difficult, before the social security kicked in. Then it wasn't so bad. Besides, Gram was a hoot to live with. I remember her standing at the stove fixing macaroni and cheese. We had it about three times a week because it was cheap and all us kids liked it. Anyway, she would stir in that orange powder stuff, look at me and say, 'Sabrina Innis, being poor sucks. You make sure you do better.'" Sabrina laughed. "She was wonderful."

"Yeah." He thought about his half dozen meetings with Sabrina's grandmother. The feisty old lady was opinionated, but charming as hell. "Why don't we have her out to visit soon?"

"I'd like that. Thanks. But we're going to have to wait. She's planning a summer trip to Alaska. I know she's going on a ten-day cruise, and after that, she and her friends are taking the train through the state."

Cal knew exactly who was paying for Gram's vacation. "You're generous with her."

"She was good to me and I love her. I want her to be happy."

"You also listened to her statement that being poor sucked. Is that why you took the job with me?"

When Sabrina had graduated from UCLA, she'd had four serious job offers with Fortune 500 companies. Cal had been recruiting for his firm as well, and when he'd first interviewed Sabrina, he'd realized she could be a great assistant for him. As the job didn't come with room for advancement or a lot of corporate exposure, he'd sweetened the pot with promises of travel and a generous starting salary.

Sabrina chuckled. "Are you asking if I only want you for your money? Cal, it's not like you to be insecure."

"I'm being serious."

"Oh, serious. That's different." Her blue eyes twinkled. "Okay, the money was a large part of it. I wanted to help Gram out and I had three younger siblings heading for college. But that wasn't the only reason I took the job. I knew I would be giving up some things, but working for you offered the opportunity to travel, to learn about a major corporation from the top down. There was also the issue of moving to Houston. I was ready to be on my own, and getting out of Los Angeles made that possible."

He had the oddest urge to ask her if she had any regrets. Regrets about not taking the other jobs. He told himself he was reading too much into her words. At times the job was difficult, but he knew Sabrina enjoyed her work. If she didn't, she would have moved on a long time ago.

"Were you heartbroken when you realized I wasn't a Texas cowboy?" he asked, his voice teasing.

"Oddly enough, no. I already have to put up with you calling me 'little lady' every couple of days. I don't need to add the smell of cow manure to the equation. You're a good ol' boy, Cal. That's plenty. Oh, this should be the street. The address is 2123. There it is, on the left."

He parked their rental car and turned off the engine, but made no effort to get out. For a moment he could only stare at the small house.

The walkway was cracked and overgrown with weeds. Any grass had long since died. There were missing panes in the windows, and those remaining were too filthy to see through. The screen door hung on the top hinge only.

"This can't be right," he muttered. "Jack said Anastasia's adoptive parents were middle class. Not rich, but nothing like this."

"These aren't her parents," Sabrina reminded him. "The woman she lives with is an aunt, maybe not even that closely related. Jack wasn't sure."

"My daughter can't live here," he said, then swore. "How could my parents have let this happen?"

"You're going to fix it. That's what matters, Cal. You came as soon as you found out about her."

Her. My daughter. The words were spoken, but they had no meaning. On the other side of that door was a child he'd never known about. A flesh-and-blood person with hopes, dreams and feelings. What was she going to say when she saw him?

He pushed away the question because he didn't have an answer, then got out of the car. Sabrina did the same and came around to his side.

He gave her a brief smile. "Thanks for coming with me. I would have hated to do this alone."

"No problem. I'm happy to help." For once she didn't tease and he was glad.

He studied her, the short, layered red hair, the familiar face, the concerned expression. She wore tailored khaki slacks and a cream blouse. As always she was sensible and in control. He admired those qualities in Sabrina, and right now, he was depending on them.

He nodded toward the house. "Let's go."

He led the way to the front door and knocked. There was nearly a minute of silence that left Cal wondering if they had the wrong place or if no one was home. Then the door opened. A woman in her late fifties or early sixties stared up at him.

"What do you want?" she asked, her voice throaty and her tone annoyed. "I ain't gonna buy anything, so don't bother trying to sell me whatever you've got."

"Mrs. Sellis?" Cal inquired politely. "I'm Cal Langtry. I believe my attorney spoke to you on the phone. I'm here about my daughter."

The woman was small, not much over five feet, and very thin. Her clothes were worn and stained. Gray streaks highlighted her short, dark hair. She looked Cal up and down, then grinned, exposing yellowed teeth and three empty spaces.

"So you decided you wanted the brat, did you? I can't figure out why, but you'll save me the trouble of filling out paperwork, so that's something. You'd best come in."

She held open the screen door. Cal led the way inside. The living room was small and dark, with tattered drapes hanging over the dirty windows. Pizza cartons and empty potato chip bags littered the floor. The center of the sofa looked as if it had been hit by a bomb, with springs poking up through a large hole in the dark brown tweed fabric and bits of stuffing burping out onto the other cushions.

The woman shuffled to a rocking chair in front of a new television and sat down. The tray table next to her contained a pack of cigarettes and an overflowing ashtray. She took a cigarette and lit it, then inhaled.

"You're early," she said. "We wasn't expecting you until the end of the week."

Cal glanced at Sabrina. Mrs. Sellis hadn't invited them to sit down, and neither of them made a move to settle on their own. For one thing, the couch looked filthy and uncomfortable. For another, he wanted to bolt.

"I finished my business more quickly than I expected," he said. "Is Anastasia here?"

"Of course she's here. Where else would the girl be? She's twelve. I don't let her run around on her own. She might not be blood kin, but I've done good by her. She's had a place to stay and food to eat. There are some who wouldn't have been so kind."

Sabrina touched his arm. He knew what she was trying to tell him—that this woman had probably done the best she could. Maybe it wasn't her fault she lived in such a poor house. Of course, she could have bothered with picking up the trash at least.

Mrs. Sellis took a deep puff on her cigarette and coughed. When she'd caught her breath, she yelled, "Anastasia, get your stuff and get on out here, girl." She turned her attention back to Cal. "She'll be right along. Did you bring the check?"

Cal stared at her. "What check?"

"Figures." She stubbed out the cigarette. "I'm not handing the girl over to the likes of you for free, you know. Her fool parents up and died without a penny to their names. Her daddy had just changed jobs, so there weren't any life insurance yet. I took the girl in because I'm family—" She frowned. "After a fact. They did adopt her. Well, I did the right thing and it's been nearly a year. I get a little something from social security, but it's not enough."

Mrs. Sellis pushed herself to her feet. "She's nothing but

a trial, I don't mind telling you that. Sassy mouth on her, always talking back. She won't do her schoolwork. Grades falling, getting in trouble at school. She ran away a couple of times." The woman glanced around her living room. "From here, if you can believe it."

"Mrs. Sellis, the social security check would have adequately provided for Anastasia's needs," Sabrina said quietly. "Mr. Langtry's attorney didn't mention that any reimbursement sum had been discussed."

Cal recognized Sabrina's tactic instantly. They were going to play good cop, bad cop. He wanted to protest that he usually got to be the bad cop, but in this case, it was probably better that he come off as the good guy. After all, his daughter might be eavesdropping on the conversation.

Suddenly reminded of the girl's presence in the house, he glanced around the small room. To the left was a tiny kitchen with an even smaller eating area. To the right was a single door. It would lead to a hallway, he thought, or maybe just to the only bedroom in the house. Again he was stunned that his child had been living under these circumstances. If only he'd known sooner.

"You his wife?" the woman asked.

"No, Mr. Langtry's personal assistant."

Mrs. Sellis cackled. "Is that what they call it these days. Oh, my. An assistant."

Cal's temper flared. "Name your amount. I will be happy to write you a check. In return you'll sign a paper saying you never want to have anything to do with the girl again."

"Well, that's the truth, I'll tell you. If I never see her again, it'll be too soon. That one's nothing but trouble." Her dark eyes glittered. "Of course, she's your own flesh and blood and that should make a difference."

The anger increased. He didn't like this woman. At first, he had felt some compassion for her circumstances, but now he didn't give a damn. "I would like to see my daughter."

"I know, I know. Anastasia, get out here, girl. I mean now!" She turned from the door. "What kind of a name is that, I ask you. Anastasia. Like she's someone important, instead of a skinny brat with a nose for trouble."

The door opened. Cal stared, his heart pounding as he waited to catch his first glimpse of his daughter. Someone stepped into the room. A young preteen, caught in that awkward stage between childhood and physical maturity.

She was about five foot five or six, just a little shorter than Sabrina, with large dark eyes hidden behind glasses. Her hair hung to the middle of her back. He registered those facts before getting caught up in horror at how painfully thin she was. Her too-small, worn T-shirt clung to her, exposing her bony shoulders and rib cage. Her cheeks were sunken and her mouth pinched. Jeans hung off her hips.

There was dirt on her face and hands, and her hair was greasy. He couldn't tell if she was pretty or not. He couldn't do anything but stare in shock.

"What the hell have you been doing to her?" Cal demanded in a roar. "There are laws against this kind of neglect."

The girl's eyes widened. "I'm not going to the state home," she shrieked. "I'll run away and you'll never find me! I swear, I'll die first."

She made a quick move as if to run out the door. Cal stepped forward to block her. "You're not going to the state home," he said quickly. "I'm not from the government. I'm your father."

He said the words without thinking, then the meaning sank in. Her father. This was his child. Not at all what he'd pictured, but no less his.

Sabrina felt as if she were caught up in a movie. Everyone was reacting to a script, but she didn't have a copy of today's dialogue. She stared at the girl standing—shaking—in front of them and her heart went out to the child. What terrible pain had she endured in the past year? No wonder she'd been a discipline problem. From the looks of things, Mrs. Sellis wasn't overflowing with compassion and concern.

The girl watched Cal warily, as if deciding whether or not to trust him. He took another step toward her. Sabrina wanted to warn him to take things slowly. After all, if she was having this much trouble absorbing what was happening, Anastasia would be suffering with the same problem.

But she couldn't get it together enough to speak. She was too stunned by Anastasia's appearance and this tiny house that smelled of neglect and poverty.

Cal reached out to touch his daughter's cheek. She spun away and glared at him. "You're not my father," she spat. "You're just the bastard who knocked up my mother. Go to hell."

With that, she raced for the bedroom and slammed the door behind her. Sabrina flinched at the sound. Cal looked as if he'd been sucker punched. Only Mrs. Sellis didn't react.

"I told you she was difficult. So, about the check. I think eight thousand ought to cover it."

"If you think—" Cal began, then visibly took control of himself.

"Excuse us," Sabrina said, then moved close to him, took his arm and pulled him into the kitchen. "Cal, look at me."

"That woman," he growled. "She's been starving her. That kid hasn't eaten in days. Longer. Don't try to tell me she's got an eating disorder. This isn't about trying to be thin enough. We're talking about neglect and possibly emotional abuse. I can't believe—"

He stopped talking and ran his hand through his hair. "Dammit, Sabrina, did you hear what my own kid said to me?"

"I know, but you can't take it personally. She's scared. She doesn't know you from a rock, and here you are, ready to take her away."

"Anything would be better than this place."

"She doesn't know that. This is all she knows right now. Okay, it's horrible and she hates it, but at least it's familiar." She gazed at her boss. "What do you want to do?"

"I want to get my kid out of here."

She thought for a moment. "Why don't you talk with Mrs. Sellis and I'll collect Anastasia. I think I'm less of an emotional button for her right now. As far as how she was treated, you can call Jack when we're in Houston and let him take care of it."

Cal swore, then pulled Sabrina close and rested his chin on her head. "Thanks. I wouldn't be able to get through this without you. I'd want to tear that old lady apart, limb by limb."

Sabrina ignored the fluttering in her chest and the heat from Cal's body. "You wouldn't like prison, Cal. I don't think you'd do well there."

"Probably not." He took a step back, then shrugged. "She's going to come around, isn't she?"

She knew he meant his daughter. "She's been through a lot and it's going to take some time, but sure, she'll come around. You're going to be a great dad."

She spoke with more confidence than she felt. While she didn't doubt Cal's abilities, she was concerned about Anastasia. She'd suffered tremendously, and she'd had to do it alone. That kind of experience could leave a person scarred for life.

She and Cal went back into the living room. Mrs. Sellis watched them, her dark eyes glowing with greed. Sabrina ignored her and crossed to the closed door. She hesitated, almost afraid of what she would find on the other side, then drew a breath and turned the handle.

The bedroom was tiny, dark and even more dirty than the living room. Sabrina didn't want to think about what might be living under the bed. Clothes were scattered all over. There were dirty plates, glasses, torn magazines and dirt everywhere. Anastasia lay curled up on the bed, with her back to the door. Her shoulders shook, but she didn't make a sound.

Sabrina stared at her and tried to decide the best way to handle the situation. Her instinct was to offer the girl comfort, but her gut told her that was wrong. Right now Anastasia was scared and angry. Compassion would be viewed as weakness. She decided to go for logic.

"Boy, were you stupid," she said, her tone conversational.

That got the hoped-for response. The girl stopped crying.

"Talk about blowing a perfect setup. Look at this place. It's disgusting. I know you hate it here."

"No, I don't" came the defiant response.

"Oh, so that's why you ran away a couple of times. And now this basically nice guy shows up, a guy who is, by the way, your father. He just found out about you and he wants to take care of you. Instead of saying thanks or even hi, you call him a bastard and run out of the room. Like I said, not really bright. I guess you want to go to that state home, huh?"

Anastasia rolled over and glared at her. "No, I don't. I won't go there. I swear, I'll die first."

Sabrina shrugged. "You want to stay with Mrs. Sellis?"

Anastasia wiped the tears from her face. The moisture smeared the dirt there. "She hates me. She only wants the money the government sends." Full lips trembled. "I want to go home."

Sabrina's chest tightened. She knew exactly what the girl meant. She wanted her old life back—the one where her adoptive parents were still alive and she was allowed to live in blissful ignorance about the tragedies of life.

"I know," Sabrina told her. "Unfortunately, no one can

make that happen. But living with your dad might not be so bad. You could at least try it."

Anastasia glared at her. "Who are you? His wife?"

It was the second time that day she'd been asked the question. "No, I work for him."

"Oh, the secretary." The dismissal was clear.

"No, the personal assistant. I'm the one who makes his life run smoothly. If you're smart, you'll realize I'll have the same power over your life. I'm not so bad, kid. I have two sisters and a brother, all three younger than me, so I'm on to you. You can't scam me. I know this isn't going to mean anything now, but I'm more than willing to be your friend." She held up her hand. "Don't say something you're going to regret later."

Anastasia just glared.

Sabrina smiled brightly. "So what's it going to be? You want to throw a tantrum or two and stay here? I think Mrs. Sellis is serious about sending you away. Or you can take a chance on your dad and come along. Houston is kinda hot in the summer, but it's nice." She looked around the room. "Nicer than here. With a little luck you might be happy there."

"If I was lucky, I would still have my parents." Anastasia sat up. "Why does he care about what happens to me?"

Sabrina assumed the "he" in question was Cal. "Because he's your father. He wants to take responsibility for you. Foolishly, I'll bet he even wants to care about you."

The girl's mouth twisted as if there was no way she was going to believe that.

"It's up to you. You coming or not?"

Anastasia drew in a deep breath, then rose to her feet. "I guess."

They were standing pretty close. Sabrina noted the dull cast of her skin and the unwashed smell of her body. This kid needed someone to care about her, and she was willing to bet

Cal was the man for the job. It wasn't going to be easy, but it would be worth it in the end.

She motioned to the room. "Do you have a suitcase?"

Anastasia stared at her as if she'd grown another head. "I'm not going to bring anything from here. I want to forget I ever saw this place." She headed for the door, then changed her mind. "Wait." She bent down, drew a tattered shoe box out from under the bed, then clutched it to her chest. "I'm ready."

Sabrina stared at her dirty face and thought her heart was going to break. She knew better than to ask about a doll or other toy. Anastasia wouldn't have any. Obviously taking clothes would be a waste of time. They would all have to be thrown out, anyway. She swallowed the lump forming at the back of her throat and led the way to the door.

They entered the living room. Mrs. Sellis stood holding a check and looking stunned.

"Let's go," Cal said, and motioned for them to leave.

Sabrina touched Anastasia's thin arm. "Do you want a minute to say goodbye?"

Anastasia didn't even glance at the woman who had taken care of her for the past year. Instead she marched outside without once looking back. "Is that it?" she asked, pointing to the rental car.

"Yes."

She walked toward it, then climbed into the back seat and slammed the door shut. She sat still, staring straight ahead.

"My lawyer will be in touch," Cal told Mrs. Sellis.

"You tell him to call me and I'll sign whatever you say." The woman smiled. "She's a fine girl. You're going to be happy you took her."

Cal let the screen door slam into place. He put his hand on the small of Sabrina's back and ushered her toward the car.

"A fine girl?" she questioned. "So how big was the check?"

"Ten."

"Thousand?" She went on without waiting for a response. "She doesn't deserve anything but a trip from social services. No wonder she suddenly thinks Anastasia is a prize."

"Anastasia is my daughter, and the old woman *has* custody of her. It would have taken time to get custody if she didn't hand it over. And I wasn't going to leave Anastasia there another minute."

They paused by the car door. Cal glanced at her. "She called me a bastard."

"She was upset."

"She's only twelve. How does she know language like that?"

"Cal, they say words like that on television."

"I guess. It's just…"

"She's not what you were expecting."

"There's an understatement," he muttered.

"You're the one who said she'd been through a lot," Sabrina said, reminding him of his words.

He grunted in response, indicating he wanted to change the subject. She wasn't going to let him get away with that.

"Either you understand or you don't," she said. "You had to know this was going to be difficult. If you're not up to taking responsibility for her, decide now. She's not a puppy you can return to the breeder if it doesn't work out. She's a human being, with feelings and hopes and dreams. Right now she's an ill-tempered bratty girl who has not only lost her parents but lived with that woman for the past year. It's going to take a lot of time and love to help her heal. It may never happen. Are you prepared to take that chance?"

Cal stared back at the small house, at the weed-filled lawn and the crooked screen door. "You don't think much of me, do you?"

"Actually I think a lot of you. However, I'm not sure you're prepared to deal with this reality."

He wanted to tell her she was wrong, but he knew better. Everything Sabrina said was the truth. He had thought Anastasia would be different. At least cleaner. But that wasn't her fault. Was he willing to be responsible?

"She's my child," he said. "If I'd known about her, I would have taken care of her when she was born. I'm still willing to make sure she's all right. I don't expect it to be perfect."

"Or even easy."

He glanced at the sullen child in the car. "It's not going to be easy. I've already figured that part out."

He walked around to open Sabrina's door, then returned to the driver's side and stepped into the car.

"Did Sabrina tell you I live in Houston?" he asked as he fastened his seat belt.

Anastasia didn't acknowledge he'd spoken. He checked in the rearview mirror. Her gaze remained fixed straight ahead.

"We'll be flying there. Have you ever been on a plane?"

She shrugged faintly. "No, but it's no big deal. Even dorks can fly."

He swallowed the flash of irritation and the sharp retort that followed. "I know this is hard," he said, gentling his voice. "I just found out about you yesterday, so we're both kind of in shock. I want—" He paused, not sure what he did want. "I want you to be happy with me. It will take some time for us to get to know each other, but that won't be so bad."

She didn't respond.

He glanced at Sabrina, who gave him an encouraging smile. "I'm sorry about your adoptive parents," he told his daughter.

She raised her head and glared at him. Even in the reflection of the rearview mirror, he felt the intensity in her gaze.

"They're not my adoptive parents," she said loudly. "They're my real parents. Get it? Real. As in the only parents I've ever had and the only ones I want. I don't want you.

You're not my father, you're some, some sperm donor. I don't want to be here. I don't want to go to Houston. I don't want to talk to you or anyone, so just leave me alone."

Cal turned in his seat in time to see her fold in on herself. She wrapped her arms around her chest and rocked back and forth. Sobs caught in her throat like hiccups.

He was furious at what she'd said, surprisingly hurt by her assessment of his value in her life, uncomfortable and confused by her tears. So far, parenting was a bitch.

Sabrina reached out and touched Anastasia's head. The girl jerked back. "Leave me alone," she muttered.

His assistant shrugged. "You're not going to take her back to that woman, so let's just drive to the airport. We can figure this all out later."

Cal started the engine. They drove in silence. Eventually Anastasia's tears slowed. She curled up on the seat, and by the time they'd traveled about ten miles down the interstate, she was asleep.

He looked at Sabrina. "Thank you," he said.

"For what?"

"For just being with me. I couldn't have done this without you."

She smiled. "That's why you pay me the big bucks, boss."

He knew she was more than an employee. Their relationship had always been largely undefined. Sometimes strictly business, sometimes more like friends. He didn't care what people called it as long as she stayed right where she was.

Chapter 5

The flight to Houston was going to take about three hours, and they'd already been in the air for nearly two. Cal leaned back in his seat and tried to relax, but he couldn't. Again and again his attention strayed to the seat across the aisle where Anastasia lay curled up, asleep.

"You can't solve all the world's problems today," Sabrina said, repeating a phrase he often used on her.

"I hate it when you throw my words back in my face," he muttered. "And I know it's true. I can't. But what about her?"

The first-class section of the aircraft had two seats on either side of the aisle. Sabrina had taken the single seat across from the two together, but Anastasia had wanted to switch. Obviously she wasn't interested in sitting next to her father.

Cal tried not to take her actions personally. The kid had known about him only a few days, and they'd been in each other's company for less than five hours. She was alone and scared, and the past year of her life had been hell. It made sense that she would do her best to protect herself against what she saw as threats to her safety. But telling himself was one thing, while believing it was another.

He looked at the child he'd fathered, at her dirty hair and thin face. He wondered what Anastasia thought of her first plane trip, of the amenities of first class. Then he reminded himself she had nothing to compare any of it to. At least he knew she'd enjoyed the food. She'd gobbled her dinner with a haste that had made him wince.

"What are you thinking?" Sabrina asked.

He forced himself to relax a little. "I was wondering how long it had been since the kid had eaten."

"She was enthusiastic about her meal," Sabrina agreed.

She glanced down at her list and crossed off another item. Since the meal service had ended, Sabrina had been making arrangements and ordering things for his daughter. He was, Cal realized, pitifully unprepared for the arrival of a child into his life. Just thinking about the professional but impersonal decorations in the guest room made him wince.

"No," Sabrina said quietly. "You're not allowed to think that you made a mistake."

"I wasn't thinking that."

"Something close." She laid her hand on top of his forearm. "You're not to blame for Anastasia being so unhappy, nor are the circumstances of her life your responsibility. You never knew about her. If you had, you would have done something. As soon as you found out, you took measures to get her."

Her touch comforted him. He looked at his daughter. "She's not exactly what I imagined."

"Remember what you told Jack. That she's been through a terrible year. No one would thrive living with Mrs. Sellis. Add the loss of her parents and you have a recipe for disaster."

"Are you saying there's nothing to be done? That she'll never come around?"

Sabrina shook her head. "Of course not. But she's going to need a lot of time and love. If there isn't some progress in the first couple of months, counseling might not be a bad idea."

Cal grunted. Counseling he could handle, but the love part... What was that? To the best of his knowledge, his parents had never loved him or Tracey. He knew he'd never really loved anyone, and none of the women in his life had ever felt that emotion for him. Love. Maybe it was all a fantasy.

It was his fault. He'd pictured the meeting between him and his daughter as something of a cross between a television sitcom and the musical *Annie*. The thought of his daughter being someone like Anastasia had never occurred to him. Of course he probably wasn't what she wanted, either.

He looked at his daughter. Curled up in the wide seat, she seemed so small and painfully thin. "I don't know what to do with her. I don't know what to say."

"Say that. Tell her you're just as confused as she is. When a child loses his or her parents, everything in the world changes. One minute you're secure and innocent in your belief that life as you know it will go on forever. The next minute, that innocence is ripped away. It's a painful process. Kids aren't sure they can ever risk trusting anyone again. What if they do and that person goes away?" She tapped her pen against the paper resting on her tray and shrugged. "You can get over the pain, but I doubt anyone who has been through that ever forgets."

"How old were you when you lost your parents?"

"Fourteen. So a couple of years older than Anastasia. I also had the advantage of my brother and sisters around me. Gram stepped right in to take care of us, so we never had to move.

That was something, but it wasn't enough. That was the hardest thing I've ever been through. Your daughter had it much harder than I did. Try to remember that."

"The next time she calls me a bastard?"

"Maybe it will help."

A faint smile tugged at the corners of her mouth. Cal studied Sabrina's face. So familiar, so comforting. He'd grown used to asking her advice and listening to her words. She was his sounding board, his trusted adviser, his friend and sometimes his conscience.

"All right, little lady," he drawled, knowing she hated to be called that. "I'll take what you said into consideration."

"Toad." She removed her hand from his arm.

"It occurs to me," he began, "that you're the one with the expertise in this area."

She turned toward him and shook her head. "Don't even think about it," she warned. "I mean it, Cal. For one thing, Anastasia isn't a mess to be tidied. For another, she's your daughter and you have to take the time to get to know her, not to mention letting her get to know you. That's important. I know it will be hard, but you have to struggle through this on your own."

He resisted the urge to whine that he didn't want to. Mostly because he knew she was right. "I don't know how to do this."

"I'll help," she promised. Her eyebrows pulled together in a frown. "I know it's none of my business and you don't have to answer if you don't want to, but what was it like for you, when you were growing up?"

He shrugged. "Different from what you remember, I'm sure. We had a big house in River Oaks," he said, naming the exclusive area of Houston. "My father traveled a lot. My mother had charities and luncheons all the time. There was a staff, although we never kept anyone for too long. For reasons I'll never understand, my mother always hired young, attractive women to work in the house. My father didn't believe the rules of fidelity applied to him, so he took advantage of the 'landscaping,' as he used to call them. Mother would find out and fire the women. Anyone lasting three months was considered a family retainer."

Sabrina's blue eyes darkened. "Cal, that's horrible. You knew about your father and what he was doing?"

"Sure. He bragged about it. Kept telling me that I was just like him." Cal stiffened in his seat, then had to consciously force himself to relax. "I swore I would be different. That's why I only date one woman at a time. No commitment, but complete monogamy."

She angled toward him and rested the side of her head against the seat back. "I shouldn't have asked."

"It's not a problem. You probably need to know this. In case I get weird with Anastasia or something. My parents were never much interested in us unless they needed to parade us out, or wanted to be seen at a sporting event or recital. I was the serious kid, did well in school, that kind of thing. Tracey was born wild. She's four years older, and I think I was about ten the first time she ran away. By the time she was fifteen, she'd already had an abortion. She didn't get into drugs much, but she loves her liquor."

"I'm sorry," she said.

"Nothing to be sorry for. I survived. Look at where the company is now. We're earning four times what we did when my father was still alive."

"But that doesn't make up for the past."

She saw too much. In an effort to distract her, or maybe because he needed the connection, he took her free hand in his.

Her skin was smooth, her nails short and neatly filed. She didn't resist the contact, nor did she encourage him by responding. He was, he knew, getting close to a line he'd never crossed with her. For one thing, he refused to be his father, who had been forever after the hired help. For another, he respected Sabrina too much to play games with her.

But this wasn't a game. Maybe it was Anastasia. Maybe it was that they'd been working together for so long. Whatever the reason, lately he'd been feeling that he needed Sabrina. Thank the Lord she was happy in her work. He would never get through this without her.

"Think there's a class in parenting I can take?" he asked.

She laughed. "Sure, but it's going to be about dealing with newborns. Most people learn to be a parent while their offspring learn to be kids. You're jumping in the middle. Give yourself a break, Cal, and don't expect perfection the first time."

"I don't expect anything close to that. I just don't want to screw up too badly."

"I promise to point out any gross errors."

"I bet you can't wait. You always get a kick out of telling me I'm wrong."

"I know." She sighed. "One would think I would get tired of that, what with you giving me so many opportunities."

The insult sunk in and he squeezed her fingers. Not enough to hurt, but enough to get her attention. "You, little lady, are being disrespectful."

"You, Mr. John Wayne wannabe, earned it."

Her smile was contagious. Cal felt some of his tension ease. He'd never failed at anything in his life. There was no reason to think he couldn't have a good relationship with his daughter.

Sabrina freed her hand and tucked her short hair behind her ear. In the soft overhead light, she looked younger than thirty. While she wasn't his type, she was pretty enough. Her mind was razor sharp and a constant challenge. She was funny, sensitive and easy to be with.

"So why aren't you married?" he asked.

Sabrina stared at him. "Excuse me?"

"You've been working for me for over six years and I've never once heard you mention having a man in your life. Why?"

"I don't have time."

"That's a crock. You have evenings and weekends off, not to mention four weeks of vacation a year."

"Cal! Be serious. I'm usually with you until you leave for your dinner date, which means seven or seven-thirty. A lot of times, I still have more work to do. We travel constantly. More weekends than not I'm in the office, or following you around some event. As for vacation, last year I took two long weekends to visit my family. According to Ada, I've accrued about ninety-seven vacation days."

Had he really been working her that much? "You could have said something."

"I'm not complaining, I'm stating facts. The truth is, I haven't minded. I knew what the job would be like when I took it. For the past few years, career has been more important to me. When that changes, I'll do something about it."

"Just don't take those ninety-seven days all at once. Everything would fall apart." And he would miss her. Cal pushed that thought away.

"I won't, I promise."

"So there's no one who's caught your eye? No young executive or engineer in the company?"

She covered her face with her hands, then let her arms drop back to her sides. "Do not even think about fixing me up with one of your executives. I told you, it hasn't been important to me."

He studied her for a minute, then snapped his fingers. "Someone broke your heart," he announced, pleased he'd figured out the mystery. On the heels of pleasure came concern. "Who was he?"

She glared at him. "I'm not even going to ask how you

figured that out. Okay, yes, there was this guy, but it was a long time ago and it's not really important."

He leaned toward her. "Tell Uncle Cal everything."

She took a deep breath. "I was in college and I fell for this guy. He was very popular and handsome. You know the cliché. I couldn't figure out why he would want to date me, but he did. Anyway, we were together nearly two years. I thought we were going to get married. He thought he would use me to get his grades up high enough to get into a great law school. And he did. He left for Harvard and never once got in touch with me again."

She told the story easily, as if it didn't matter. Enough time had passed that maybe it didn't. But Cal thought he saw tension in her body.

"Do you still miss him?"

She looked at him as if he were insane. "Of course not. He was a jerk."

"But he broke your heart."

"Let's just say he made it difficult for me to trust easily."

He wanted to ask her if she trusted him. Not that it mattered, he told himself. They had a relationship based on the fact that she was his employee, nothing more.

"Don't worry about me," she said. "For now, this works."

He didn't like the sound of that. "And when it doesn't work?"

She raised her eyebrows. "You didn't expect me to stick around forever, did you?"

Actually, he'd never thought about her leaving. "So you're going to leave me for a man. That's just like a woman."

"It's just like a man to say 'just like a woman' when he's trying to get his way." She gave him a quick smile. "Don't worry, Cal. I have no plans to leave anytime soon. I'll be around to help you with your daughter."

He'd nearly forgotten. Cal turned and looked at the sleeping girl. She was much quieter when she was asleep and he found he liked that. It gave him time to think and try to figure out what on earth he was supposed to do with her now that he had her.

"You can't leave," Cal said, his voice low but frantic.

Sabrina raised her eyes toward the heavens and planted her hands on her hips. "I can't stay here forever. Face it, you're going to be alone with your daughter eventually. Why not get it over with now? In time it will get easier."

He glanced over his shoulder. They stood in the living room of his penthouse condo. Anastasia was checking out the rest of the place. "Nothing about the girl is easy. I don't understand why you won't make an exception to your rule. This is important. It's not just about what's easier for me, either. Anastasia would feel better with a woman around."

She groaned. Damn the man, he was probably right about that. Because she wasn't emotionally involved in the situation, it was easier for her to deal with the preteen. So far all of Anastasia's smart-mouthed comments had been directed at her father.

But move in? Here? "I can't," she said.

"You won't. There's a difference." He glared at her. "There are four bedrooms, so don't tell me this is a privacy issue. I'm not asking for anything permanent, just for a few weeks until things are settled."

She crossed to the window and pulled open the blinds. The city stretched out below, all twinkling lights and endless night sky. Everything Cal said made sense. It wasn't forever. Why was she resisting so hard?

Sabrina folded her arms across her chest and sighed. Because, she thought. Because there was an inherent risk involved with moving in. Warning bells went off every time she thought about it. Over the past few years, Cal had mentioned that life would be easier if she were closer. But she'd resisted. She hadn't wanted to be a part of his social life, and she refused to live at his place while he was entertaining one of his women. Going to dinner was one thing, trying not to hear them doing the wild thing was another.

But Anastasia wasn't one of his women. He *had* just ended things with Tiffany, so he wouldn't get involved with anyone else for a few months. Maybe longer. So that wasn't a problem. Still, the warning bells told her too-close quarters would be a risk. If only she could figure out why.

"We need you, Sabrina."

She'd always been a sucker for being needed. Cal knew that, too, and he was using it against her. She could feel herself weakening. He made matters worse by coming up behind her and placing his hands on her shoulders.

"Please?"

His voice was low and seductive. A blend of masculine charm and Texas accent. When he was like that, he was irresistible. Thank goodness he didn't know.

"All right," she told him. "I'll move in for a few weeks. But don't think I'm going to take responsibility for your daughter. You need to get to know each other, and that's not going to happen if you thrust her on me all the time. The quicker you bond with her, the better for both of you. For me, too."

Cal swept her up in a bear hug. She felt the length of his hard body against hers and wondered at the quirk of nature that made him so incredibly attractive to her, while he barely noticed she was female.

"Thank you," he said, spinning her around once before setting her on the floor. "You won't be sorry."

"Why do I doubt that?"

"No one knows but you. So now what?"

"Now I head home to get some sleep and pack up my stuff. You get to work bonding with your daughter."

"She's not interested in bonding. She hates me."

Sabrina shook her head. "She's alone and she's scared. Think of a wild animal lashing out, only instead of using teeth and claws, she uses words. It's the only way she knows to protect herself."

Cal grunted.

Ah, the signal to change the subject. This time, because she'd said as much as she wanted to, she didn't pursue the matter. She could see that Cal understood what she was telling him, even if he didn't want to.

"The things I ordered from the plane will be here shortly," she reminded him. "Take them to her."

"A bribe?"

"Think of it as a peace offering." She crossed to the door, grabbing her purse on the way. "I'll see you in the morning. Don't worry, you'll survive."

"I doubt it." He opened the door and stared out forlornly. "Get here early, okay?"

"I promise."

She met his gaze. He looked lost and abandoned. She had the strangest urge to offer some kind of comfort. But the only thing that came to mind was a hug, and maybe a kiss. Ridiculous, she told herself. Cal didn't think of her that way, and she'd taught herself to ignore the fact that he was a good-looking man. She must be tired if she was forgetting that particularly hard-won lesson.

"I'll see you in the morning," she said, and started for the elevator.

Cal hovered outside his daughter's room. He wanted to talk to her, but he didn't know what to say. First of all, he wanted to apologize for the sterile decorating. He hadn't expected the room to be occupied by a twelve-year-old. Then he wanted to explain that he was nervous, too, but that they might be able to at least be friends.

He knocked on the closed door. "Anastasia?"

"Go away."

At least she was a straightforward communicator, he told himself as he retreated. He paced in the living room, not sure if he should try knocking again, or maybe just barge in. After all, the door didn't lock. But he hated to invade her privacy, and he wasn't sure what he should say. If Sabrina were here, she would know what to do.

He glanced at his watch and saw that she wouldn't have had time to get home yet. Damn. He would have to wait to call her. Then he would—

The doorbell rang. He sprinted toward it, incredibly grateful for the interruption. Maybe Sabrina had come back to rescue him.

But instead of his assistant, he found a young man in the hallway. He carried a half dozen shopping bags all bearing the logo of a local department store.

"Delivery for Mr. Langtry," the man said. "Here you are, sir."

Cal tipped him and collected the packages. Sabrina had ordered clothes and other things for Anastasia. Cal grinned. Now he had an excuse to talk to his daughter.

He headed down the hall and knocked on her door.

"I already said 'go away.' Do I have to spell it out on the door for you to understand?"

"Not really." Cal shifted the bags to one hand and opened her door.

Anastasia had been lying on the bed. She shrieked and jumped to her feet. "I could have been getting dressed."

That hadn't occurred to Cal, then he realized that wasn't possible. "You don't have any other clothes."

"That's not the point."

"If you'd been polite enough to let me in, opening the door wouldn't have been an issue."

"I didn't want to see you. Besides, why should I be polite?"

"Because you're in my home and I expect common courtesy from you."

She glowered but didn't answer.

Cal set the bags on the floor. She stared at them with undisguised curiosity but didn't mention them. Good. A little anticipation might soften her up.

"How are you doing?" he asked.

She shrugged.

She'd showered. Her hair was damp, her face clean, although her clothes were still filthy and hanging on her. Her glasses slid down her nose and she pushed them up.

"I didn't have enough time to get the room ready," he said. "Why don't you think about how you'd like to change it?" He motioned to the plain dresser topped only with a glass sculpture that was more blob than person, although the decorator had assured him it was stunningly representational of true love. "Maybe some different furniture and wallpaper or paint."

Anastasia shrugged again as if it was of no importance to her. "There's no TV," she complained. "Or books or magazines. Don't you read? Or does your assistant read to you?"

Irritation flared and he carefully banked the feelings. She was just a child, and as Sabrina had reminded him, she was lashing out so that he wouldn't know she was scared.

"There are a lot of books and magazines in my study," he said calmly. "Many of them are about business, so I don't think you'll find them interesting. However, we can go to a bookstore in the next couple of days so you can get some reading material." He remembered the packages. "Sabrina may have ordered some when she called about clothes."

He picked up the bags and set them on the bed. "She made sure when she was on the plane that these things would be delivered tonight. I don't know if they'll fit, but they're a start. I guess a shopping trip is in order. I'll put it on the schedule."

Anastasia stared at the bags. "Those are for me?"

"Sure."

Mistrustful brown eyes turned in his direction. "All of that, or just some of it?"

"All of it. I wouldn't have brought it in to you if it wasn't yours."

She bit her lower lip. "I don't have any money. What do you want for them?"

People talked about their hearts breaking. He'd never understood the concept or felt anything close to a snap. But at that moment, with his daughter staring longingly at the packages but not daring to step closer to them, he felt something. If not a break, then certainly a major crack.

She was only twelve. She shouldn't understand the concept of having to offer something to get something. Gifts and surprises should be a part of her life. There had been surprises, he thought grimly, but only the tragic kind.

He crossed to her and placed his hand on her shoulder. She froze. He half expected her to shrug him off, but she stood there, trembling like a cornered kitten. "Anastasia, I want you to have these things because I want to take care of you and I want you to be happy. You aren't expected to pay for them except to say thank you."

She glanced at the bags, then at him. "Thank you." The word was a whisper.

She moved to the bed and dumped the contents of the first bag on the plain navy comforter. Cal saw what looked like shorts and T-shirts, some underwear and something that might have been pajamas. Working quickly, she upended the other bags. There were sandals, bathing suits, a robe, several books and in the last bag, a large stuffed bear.

Anastasia fingered the soft-looking fur, then shoved it away. "I'm not a kid," she said defiantly. "I don't play with stuff like that."

Considering how stubborn his daughter was, he figured she must like the bear most of all, but she wouldn't dare show that for fear it would be taken away. Dammit, what had she endured in the past year?

He pushed the clothes aside and sat on the bed. She remained standing. "I know this is hard for you," he told her. "You don't know me, this is an unfamiliar place. We're talking about a lot of scary stuff."

"I'm not scared."

"Really? In your position, I would be terrified. Probably peeing on the rug like a puppy."

That earned him a slight smile, which she quickly suppressed.

"I've never been a father before."

"Duh."

He ignored her. "But I was a kid. Some would tell you I was a kid for longer than I should have been. The point is, I know you're nervous and concerned about what's going to happen. I want to try and make you happy, but you have to try, too, Anastasia. We need to work on this together."

Her chin raised slightly. "I'm not going to be happy ever again."

"I see. You know, being happy doesn't mean you won't still love your adoptive parents. They wouldn't want you to spend your whole life mourning them."

"What do you know about them?" she demanded. "You don't know anything. And they're not my *adoptive* parents, they're my real family. You're not my father, you'll never be my father. I had the best father in the world, and no one will ever be better than him."

Tears spilled out of her eyes and slid down her cheeks.

"I know that's true," he said, ignoring the jab of pain in his chest. "He will always be exactly perfect. I accept that. But that doesn't change the fact that you live with me now, and I am your biological parent. You're my daughter."

"No!" She wiped her face, but more tears fell. "No. You didn't want me before so I don't care that you want me now."

"I didn't know about you before. I just found out about you yesterday."

A sob shook her. She shuddered. "You should have known. If I was really your daughter, you should have known about me. You should have come and taken me away. But you d-didn't."

She ran into the bathroom and slammed the door shut behind her. He could hear the sound of her crying. He ached for her—no one should ever be that unhappy.

He stood up and crossed to the door, but this one he left closed. He had no right to intrude on her pain. Instead he walked out of the room and went into his study. After pouring out a stiff drink of Scotch, he took a sip and wondered what he was supposed to do now. He wasn't prepared to be responsible for his daughter. He didn't know how to be a father. He was probably doing everything wrong. He'd never loved a child or even been loved *as* a child. He was completely in the dark on this one.

He took another drink of the Scotch and decided it would be a great night to get drunk.

Chapter 6

Sabrina walked to her window and glanced out. The view wasn't nearly as nice as it was at Cal's condo, but she didn't mind. The lush garden, overgrown into a tangle of fragrant flowers and vines, reminded her of a New Orleans courtyard. She rented a two-bedroom guest house on a stunning estate in the River Oaks district of Houston. The place had its own single car garage, and the owners of the property were gone more than they were home. The location put her only a couple of miles from Cal's place and the office. Best of all, the rent was reasonable. Ada had found it for her when she, Sabrina, had first moved to Houston. Back then, every dime had been important, and she'd been thrilled with both the floor plan and the price.

Now, although she could easily afford to pay three times as much in rent, she didn't want to move. She'd grown used to the neighborhood and being close to everything. She liked the quiet of the estate…at least she had until tonight. For reasons she couldn't understand, this evening the quiet made her restless.

Or maybe it was something else, she mused as she moved from the window to the sofa and thought about sitting down. She could read. Although she wasn't someone who watched a lot of television, there was always her collection of movies. Or maybe a nice hot bath. The larger of the two bedrooms had a beautiful bathroom, complete with separate stall shower and oversize Jacuzzi tub.

None of the suggestions sounded right. She strolled into the kitchen and pulled open the refrigerator. Nothing inside called to her. There was some triple chocolate ice cream in the freezer. She grabbed a spoon, took a mouthful, then set the pint carton back on the shelf. No, she wasn't hungry. She was looking, but for what?

Maybe the past couple of days had upset her more than she'd realized. Learning that Cal had a daughter was one thing, but actually meeting the child was another. Anastasia. While Sabrina understood the girl's fears and her need to protect herself by lashing out, she didn't envy Cal the job of "taming" the angry child. It was going to take a lot of love and patience. She'd seen her boss take as much time as was necessary to close a deal, but he'd never been as willing to go the distance with people. Certainly not with the women in his life. But Anastasia was his daughter and that would make all the difference in the world. He might just surprise them.

She returned to the living room and sank onto the sofa. What was he doing right now? she wondered. It was after ten, so Anastasia was probably asleep. Did she like the clothes? Sabrina had had to guess on the sizes, but she was pretty sure she'd gotten them right. They would go shopping in the next couple of days and pick up some other things for her. After all, she'd arrived with nothing.

Sabrina thought about the tattered clothes the girl had

worn, the dirt on her face and how thin she was. No child should have to live like that, with both physical and emotional neglect. It wasn't right. She pulled her knees up to her chest and reminded herself that things were going to be different. Anastasia had family now. Cal might not be anyone's idea of a traditional parent, but he wouldn't turn his back on his responsibilities.

The restlessness grew. Sabrina frowned. She was going to be spending the next couple of weeks at Cal's condo. If she knew her boss—and she did—he would try to talk her into staying longer. So this was her last night alone for a while. She should enjoy it.

Yet, for once, the solitude didn't heal her or comfort her. Something was off, something she couldn't put her finger on.

Maybe if she called a friend, she thought as she rose to her feet and crossed to the phone. It wasn't too late. She could call one of her sisters on the West Coast, where it was two hours earlier. Or she could—

Like most revelations, when this one occurred it was both startling and unpleasant. Sabrina stopped in the middle of the floor and turned slowly in place. She took in the neatly decorated room with its pine furniture, cream sofa and contrasting Colonial blue wing chair. She'd collected the artwork herself, buying a piece at a time, some from galleries, some from estate sales. A few were framed posters. Her collection of movies and books filled a cabinet in the corner. Each of the other rooms in the house had been decorated with the same care and attention to detail.

It was a facade. A pleasant, pretty facade that hid the truth from everyone—even herself. But reality had just hit her upside the head and there was no escaping the truth.

She didn't have a life. She hadn't had one for years. At least not one of her own. There were no friends she could call in Houston. Oh, she had some acquaintances from work, women she went to lunch with occasionally. She was still close to her sisters, but college kept them busy and they had their studies and their friends. Phone calls every two weeks weren't a substitute for actual emotional intimacy.

Everything she had, everything she thought and everything she was had been linked with Cal. She had become her job with nothing left over for herself.

She returned to the sofa and sank down. When had it happened? She shook her head, already knowing the answer to that one. During her first interview, Cal had warned her that he demanded long hours and plenty of travel. She'd been thrilled with both the opportunity and the starting salary.

Cal had been an answer to her prayers. Between salary, raises, bonuses and stock options it had taken less than four years to fund everyone's college plans. Two of her siblings had opted for the more inexpensive state colleges, while the youngest had been offered a partial scholarship to Stanford. Once they were taken care of, Sabrina bought Gram a condo by the ocean, one close to her friends and the social activities she adored. Now everyone had been taken care of, even Sabrina herself. She'd been investing her money. She'd learned a lot working for Cal and now had a nice nest egg. *And no plans for a future,* she thought.

The truth was she would never have a life as long as she worked for Cal. He was like the sun. If you stared at it, the light was so bright, you couldn't see anything else. As long as she was around him, she wouldn't be able to deal with what she wanted. The job had been perfect…at the time. But times had changed. Maybe she should plan to move on.

She ignored the voice inside that cried out she didn't really want to leave. This was comfortable and familiar. There had to be a compromise. She ignored the vague feeling of apprehension. Change was never easy, but sometimes it was the right thing to do.

She walked into the guest bedroom and moved to the desk against the far wall. There, in a file, were the letters she'd received over the past few months. Letters from head-hunters telling her about jobs available to someone like her. She'd been recruited before but hadn't been interested. If it was time to move on, then these companies were her ticket out.

She stared at the file. Did she really want to leave Cal? Did she have a choice? She'd gone as far as she could go professionally. There would be more money, but that wasn't enough anymore. The other reality she tried to ignore but couldn't was that the longer she stayed, the more she was at risk emotionally. Cal was the kind of man she could fall for big time. She'd gotten over her initial crush, which was good. But now she actually knew him and liked him, despite his flaws. If she got emotionally attached to him, then what? He wouldn't be interested in her—he'd made that very clear. She wouldn't want to settle for an affair, and he didn't do anything else. Besides, Cal only wanted what he couldn't have. He was interested in the chase. She was already a part of his life, so there wouldn't be much of a hunt.

She carried the folder to the kitchen and set it on the table. It was definitely time, maybe past time, for her to do something. Before she left for Cal's in the morning, she would make a few calls and see what was available. She wasn't ready to make a decision, but it wouldn't hurt to ask around.

It was nearly midnight. Cal was well and truly on his way to being drunk. The buzz had become a roar, but it wasn't going to be enough to let him forget.

He rose from his desk and moved into the hallway. There, he stared at the closed door, behind which slept his daughter. Son of a bitch, what was he doing with a kid? He didn't know the first thing about raising a child. She was almost a teenager, which made matters worse. Plus, she hated the sight of him. How was he supposed to make this work?

Bracing himself for the tirade if she was still awake, he slowly opened her door. He paused before stepping into the darkness.

Enough light spilled in from the hallway to allow him to see the bed. Anastasia lay on her side, curled toward him. Her brown hair had dried from her shower and lay across the pillow. She'd exchanged her dirty clothes for a new nightgown. There was something dark by her midsection. He stepped closer and saw she clutched the teddy bear to her chest. One arm was tightly wrapped around the toy, as if even in sleep she was afraid someone would take it away.

In the shadows, she appeared small and defenseless. He could see the faint tracks of her tears, and his heart went out to her. He was worried about her, about what was going to happen, and he was a grown-up who was secure in his life. Imagine what this twelve-year-old must be feeling. Everything she'd known had disappeared. The people who had raised her were gone, the woman she'd been thrust upon had made it clear she was unwelcome. Now a stranger had swept her up into an unfamiliar world. No wonder she lashed out.

Unfamiliar emotions filled him. There was a tightness in his chest, along with a burning at the back of his throat. He wanted to go to her and hold her close, promising that everything would be fine. But the words held no meaning. Everything wasn't going to be fine and they both knew it.

He wished Sabrina was with him. She could explain this to both of them. She always knew the right thing to say. Thank God she was moving in tomorrow morning—otherwise they would never make it.

As he watched this child who was his daughter, he tried to figure out who she looked like. He saw traces of Janice in her—also flashes of himself. Her mouthiness and temper, for example. Pure Langtry.

Janice. He backed out of the room and returned to his study. He didn't want to think about her, but he didn't have a choice. He couldn't change the past, but he had to learn to deal with it. A woman he'd trusted had betrayed him in a significant way. She'd used him to get pregnant so she could go after the family's money.

He sank back into his chair and poured another Scotch. So he'd been a fool. He wasn't the first man to be taken in by a woman and he wouldn't be the last. So what?

But it was more than that, he thought grimly. He should have known, or at least guessed there was a problem. How could he have been so stupid? Why hadn't he seen through her?

Maybe he hadn't wanted to, he admitted. She'd been young and pretty and very willing. At that age, sex had been more important than feelings. Janice had encouraged him, making love wherever and whenever he wanted. Looking back, he realized she'd been far more experienced than he. He hadn't been looking for anything long term, but he hadn't expected betrayal, either.

He didn't understand her motives and he never would, although it was safer to think about her than to remember his parents and their part in what had happened. He wasn't ready to rage at his mother for her thoughtless interference. Damn the woman.

"Why are you surprised?" he asked aloud, before downing half his drink. "These are the Langtrys, after all."

They were all sharks. Even him. He didn't want to be like them, but sometimes he was. Blood would tell and all that. They were the reason he avoided commitment and love. He wasn't even sure love existed. He'd never seen it at home and wasn't sure it could survive in the world. So where did that leave Anastasia? With a father who didn't know the first thing about loving a child.

Maybe, he thought as the alcohol gripped his brain and

made the edges of the room start to blur, just maybe she would have been better off as a ward of the state.

He'd forgotten that sunlight could hurt so much. Cal blinked as he stepped out of his bedroom. There were skylights in the hallway. He winced and squinted, but it didn't help. The pounding in his head only increased. He had no one but himself to blame—after all, he knew the potential effects of too much alcohol. He'd been trying to bury his pain, but it was back in full force and this time with nasty physical manifestations.

Coffee, he thought desperately. He needed coffee.

He headed for the kitchen, only to stop in the doorway when he saw Anastasia sitting at the table in the corner. She'd poured herself a bowl of cereal and was in the process of opening a milk carton. She'd brushed her hair back from her face and secured it in a braid. A red T-shirt and matching shorts hung loosely on her slender body, but they were an improvement over the rags she'd had on the previous day. She was pale and skinny, but she looked a lot better. She was, he realized with some trepidation, going to be a pretty young lady.

She glanced up and saw him. "You look terrible." Her voice was loud and the tone was exactly high enough to start a series of jackhammers going in his head.

"I know," he muttered. "I feel terrible. I just need some coffee, then I'll be fine."

"Why do adults drink coffee?" she asked. "It tastes gross. It's all dark and yucky. You should try milk. It's much better."

His stomach lurched at the thought of him swallowing milk at that moment in time. "Maybe later," he said as he hurried to the cupboard and fumbled for a filter. There was a can of grounds in the refrigerator. After measuring out enough for a pot and filling the reservoir with water, he flipped the switch, then prayed it wouldn't take too long to brew. In preparation, he got down a mug and waited impatiently. At least he'd had the good sense to get a coffeemaker that would allow him to pour a cup before the pot was full.

Anastasia took a bite of her cereal and chewed. The crunching sounded overloud to him. He tried not to wince.

"There's not much food here," she said when she'd swallowed. "Just this cereal and milk. You don't eat here often, do you?"

"No." He made the mistake of shaking his head and had to swallow a groan. The pounding by his temples was rhythmic—keeping time with his heartbeat. A nice steady *thunk, thunk, thunk,* at about sixty beats per minute. He felt clammy and his skin was one size too small. He didn't want to think about the army currently camping on his tongue.

"Mrs. Sellis didn't like me to eat too much. She said food was expensive. Is it going to be like that here?"

There was a note of worry in her voice. Cal forced himself to ignore his symptoms and look at his daughter. Before he could answer, she squared her shoulders and shrugged.

"I don't give a damn," she said. "I don't need you, you know. I can run away from this place, just like I ran away from hers."

"Tell you what, kid," he said, forcing himself to remain calm, knowing giving into irritation would only make the hangover worse. "You stop swearing and I'll make sure you get enough to eat. We'll go to the grocery store as soon as Sabrina arrives."

She eyed him mistrustfully. He had the feeling he was being measured against some invisible benchmark, and he knew in his gut he was going to come up short.

He waited for her to ask the inevitable "And if I don't?" for which he had no answer. But she didn't. She shrugged again, as if to say it didn't matter to her, then shoved a spoonful of cereal into her mouth.

Cal inhaled the scent of coffee and realized the pot was full enough for him to pour a cup. He'd just taken his first healing sip when Sabrina breezed into the kitchen.

"'Morning, all," she called in a bright, cheery, migraine-inducing voice. She looked at him and came to a stop. "You look—"

He held up his hand to stop her. "Don't say it. Please. I know how I look. I feel worse, okay?"

"You earned it, Cal. You know better than that."

"I know." But even as he said it, some of the pain in his head receded. He had a feeling it had more to do with Sabrina's arrival than the miracle worked by coffee. "You brought luggage, didn't you?"

"Of course. I already put it in the other guest room." She crossed to the table and sat across from Anastasia. "'Morning," she said. "How'd you sleep?"

"Fine." The preteen didn't bother looking up from her cereal.

"I hope you checked the dump date on the milk," Sabrina said. "Your dad isn't one for keeping many groceries around. He eats out a lot, but I guess that's going to change."

Anastasia didn't respond. Cal figured the only reason he wasn't being called the bastard who wasn't her father was because of the promise of food. He supposed he should feel some small sense of victory, but he didn't. No child should understand what it was like to be hungry.

Sabrina was unaffected by the silence. She tucked her short red hair behind her ears and leaned forward. "You look much better than you did yesterday. Did you sleep well?"

"I guess."

"The clothes seem to be okay. They're a little big, but when you gain a couple of pounds, they should fit. We'll stop by the mall, too, later today to fill out your wardrobe."

"Whatever."

Sabrina glanced at Cal. "So what's the deal? You're deducting a dime from her allowance for every word she speaks?"

"No, but I did ask her to stop swearing."

Sabrina's blue eyes twinkled, although her expression

stayed serious. "Maybe she doesn't know any other words. It could have been the school system."

Anastasia rolled her eyes. "I know plenty of words. I just don't want to talk to you. Why is that a big deal?"

"Oh, it's not, I guess," Sabrina said. "I understand why you want to be sullen. After all, you've got a nice place to live, a father who wants to take care of you, a fun, witty and incredibly intelligent woman who would like to be your friend, new clothes and a chance for a new life. What a drag. I'd have a long face, too."

Twelve-year-old lips twisted. "Very funny."

"See? Witty as promised." She got up and crossed to the cupboard, where she removed a bowl. When she returned to the table, she poured herself some cereal and picked up the milk.

As Cal watched her movements, he tried to figure out what was different. There was something about Sabrina this morning, something that—

He arched his eyebrows, then regretted the movement as more pain shot through his head. The woman was dressed in jeans. He'd seen her in slacks plenty of times, those loose-fitting tailored ones that always looked so businesslike. But this time she wore butt-hugging, curve-tracing, washed-enough-times-to-be-soft-as-a-baby's-rear jeans.

Hot damn! He eyed the exposed flare of her hips, the dip of her waist, before moving to her legs. Now, if he could just get her to exchange that green T-shirt for something a little more form-fitting, he would be a happy man.

Anastasia finished her breakfast and stood up. "What do you want from me?" she demanded. "I didn't ask to be here."

"I know," Sabrina said. "But you are and it's not a bad idea to make the best of things. As for what we want, I can't speak for your dad, but I'd like you to give this place a try. I doubt it can be much worse than what you've been through. You might think about being civil. Cooperating is much nicer than fighting all the time. Try a smile."

Anastasia curled her fingers up into fists. "I don't feel like smiling."

"I know, honey. It's hard to lose your family, then come to a strange place. No one is asking you to—"

Tears filled the girl's eyes. "You don't know. You don't know anything. It's horrible. It's the most horrible thing ever."

With that, she ran from the room. A few seconds later, her bedroom door slammed shut. The sound reverberated through the condo. Cal winced.

He took another sip of coffee. This was harder than he'd thought. "How long is she going to keep doing that?" he asked. "Running away and slamming doors."

Sabrina shook her head. "For as long as it works."

Chapter 7

Sabrina pushed the grocery cart around the corner and glanced at the boxes of cereal. Why did there have to be so many choices? She looked around for Anastasia to ask the preteen what she liked best, then wondered if Cal had a preference.

She glanced at her boss who had gotten quiet in the past hour or so. "All the shopping getting to you?" she asked.

Cal shrugged. "It's not so bad." He turned, as if checking for his daughter, then lowered his voice. "She hasn't been fun, but she's been more pleasant than I expected."

Sabrina thought about Anastasia's sullen expression and lack of communication. "Gee, you weren't expecting much then, were you?"

"Not really."

Sabrina drew in a breath. "That's probably wise. I'm sure she didn't sleep that well, what with being in a strange place. This is unfamiliar for all of us and it's going to take some time to adjust."

"Yeah." Cal stared at the row of cereal and reached for a box of chocolate flavored crisps. "I haven't had these since I was a kid. I didn't know they still made them. Great." He tossed the box in the cart, then caught Sabrina's eye. "What?"

"This is your way of setting a nutritional example for your daughter?"

"They've been fortified with several essential vitamins and minerals."

"Oh, there's a defense. And when combined with milk, they're part of a wholesome breakfast."

He grinned. "Exactly. You saw the commercial, too."

"Yes. The difference is I didn't buy into it. Cal, you cannot have this kind of cereal in the house. It's disgusting."

"So is that bird feed you eat. Real people don't dine on raw grains."

"Real people can do what they want."

"Maybe but this is my house and I'm the one paying for the food."

They stared at each other. She knew she wasn't going to win this one. Cal would buy his disgusting cereal and there wasn't anything she could do about it, except maybe pick out something slightly more nutritional and hope that Anastasia had a little common sense.

"Fine." She grabbed a box of whole grain cereal and tossed it in the cart as well. "You're determined to always get your way."

"I know. It's why you like me."

She didn't reply to that. What was the point? She couldn't deny that she did like him, for an assortment of reasons. Having won the current skirmish, he strolled ahead of her. She watched him go, trying not to notice the way he moved with an easy male grace. His legs were long and muscled. His butt, well, religions had been based on less impressive shrines. He was a package worth remembering, but not for her. She might be susceptible, but she wasn't stupid.

She followed him up the aisle. "You're going to have to hire a housekeeper," she said. "Now that Anastasia is living with you, cleaning people every couple of weeks aren't going to be enough. Someone will have to cook and be there to look after her when she comes home from school. Maybe a live-in, or at least someone full-time."

"I agree."

"I'll add it to my list of things to do," she said, having known when she mentioned the subject that she would be the person calling the agencies and interviewimg candidates. It was, after all, part of her job. "Until we get someone in, I can take care of the cooking."

Cal looked surprised. "You can cook?"

"Most people can fix a few things. Don't look so surprised. I make a terrific spaghetti sauce, not to mention a meat loaf that could win awards."

"A woman of many talents. What else have you been keeping from me?"

Brown eyes focused on her. She felt her heart pick up the pace a little. Ignore this, she reminded herself. Cal was her boss and nothing else.

"You'll have to wait and find out," she told him, then deliberately turned away to study the display of coffee. Perhaps reading about different kinds of beans would be enough to distract her.

Anastasia rounded the end of the aisle and started toward them. She was still too thin, but at least she looked better in her new clothes. She was pale, but she would tan quickly, Sabrina thought, then added sunscreen to the lengthy shopping list.

"I forgot to ask," Sabrina said as the girl got closer. "Do you have any food allergies?"

The preteen shrugged. "I hate vegetables."

Sabrina shot Cal a warning glance before he chimed in that

he did, too. "Hating isn't the same as being allergic, so the short answer is no, right?"

Anastasia's mouth twisted into a frown. "Vegetables make me throw up."

"Oh, is that all? You're going to have to work harder than that if you plan to avoid eating them." She made a couple of notes on her list.

Anastasia tossed a box of cupcakes into the cart. Sabrina stared at the treat. She'd forgotten what it had been like when she'd shopped with her brother and sisters, but it was all coming back.

"I'm buying enough food for about six days," Sabrina said. "You're welcome to select a treat for yourself, but only one and it has to last all six days. So if you want that box of cupcakes, it's fine with me. But that's it. No chips, no candy. Or you take it back and pick something else. It's up to you."

Anastasia stared at her uncomprehending. "He's rich."

Sabrina assumed the "he" in question was Cal, and that the statement about him being rich meant that money wasn't an issue.

"So?" she asked.

"So I should get what I want."

"That would be a no. There aren't many 'shoulds' in this household. However, there are plenty of 'wills' as in you will follow the rules and this is one of them. You can get what we decide you can get, and for now, that means one treat for the week. I would suggest picking something with six servings so you can enjoy it every day, but that's up to you."

Sometime during the conversation Cal had come up behind her. Sabrina felt his presence. For a second she wondered if he was going to contradict her, but he didn't. When Anastasia turned her attention to him, he grinned. "She's right, kid."

The girl grabbed the box of cupcakes. "I hate you both," she said, and started down the aisle.

"That was pleasant," Sabrina said, trying to keep her voice even. She had known it was going to be tough; she'd even known she was going to be more involved with Anastasia than her job description indicated. But being right wasn't always enough to make up for the difficulties of the moment.

"I know what you're thinking," Cal said.

"Somehow I doubt that."

"You're thinking that she's scared and alone and that she needs to figure out how far she can push us."

Sabrina stared at him in surprise. "I would have guessed the 'alone and scared' part, but I hadn't thought about boundary testing. You're exactly right. This is an unfamiliar situation for her, and she needs to learn how far she's allowed to go at any given time. I'm impressed."

"Hey, I'm an impressive kind of guy."

He was, she thought with resignation. Always had been, always would be. The truth was, Cal never lacked for female companionship because most women found him completely irresistible. No doubt Anastasia would soon join the fan club.

They rounded the next aisle and saw Anastasia reading a teen magazine. When she glanced up and noticed them, she scowled and moved away.

"She wasn't kidding," he said unhappily. "She really hates us."

"Everyone needs to adjust, Cal. You can't take it too personally."

"She's my daughter. How am I supposed to take it?"

"Slowly. Carefully. There aren't going to be any easy answers."

He nodded. "I didn't think it would be like this."

"I know." He thought it would be simple. But few things in life ever were. "The good news is, you won't have to do this on your own for very long."

"I don't have to do this on my own now. I have you."

She grabbed a couple of cans of tomatoes, along with some tomato sauce. If she was going to make Gram's famous spaghetti sauce, she needed all the ingredients. "That's not what I meant," she told him. "I'm talking about something permanent."

"You're permanent. Aren't you?"

Oops! She hadn't meant to hint at anything. "Okay, bad word choice," she said, recovering quickly. "What I'm trying to say is that I just work for you. Even if you're right about Tiffany running in the opposite direction to avoid being a step-mother, she's not the only single woman out there. A lot of them would be pleased to help you with Anastasia. In fact, you're going to have to be careful, because more than a few of them will use Anastasia to get to you."

"Great." He shoved his hands into his jeans pockets. "I'm not going to worry about it now. I can't imagine going out with anyone. As far as I'm concerned, the only two females in my life are you and my daughter."

She told herself that her sudden response was triggered by the sight of him walking in front of her, which gave her far too much opportunity to stare at his rear. Or maybe it was guilt over the fact that she was really going to contact those head-hunters to find out if there was life after Calhoun Jefferson Langtry. Or maybe it was that she was tired from not having slept much the previous night. Whatever the reason, when Cal said she was one of the two females in his life, she wanted to melt. Right there…knees buckling, muscles giving way until she was just a puddle in the canned goods aisle.

"How long is that going to last?" she asked, then went on without waiting for an answer. "My point is, you're not always going to be on your own with Anastasia. You two will come to some kind of understanding, then you'll find someone and it will all work out."

"That's really likely. Thanks."

She ignored his sarcasm and continued down the aisle.

Sabrina paused in front of the magazines and picked up the current issue of one popular with girls Anastasia's age. "For later," she said, hiding it under a package of paper towels. "Surprise her when things are going well. She'll like it."

"You're assuming that will happen before the issue is outdated," he muttered.

Sabrina chuckled. "So the surly nature is inherited. Like father, like daughter?"

"I am not surly."

"I can see that. You're also not cranky when you don't get your own way."

He gave her his steely-eyed glare. It worked on most business opponents, but she'd seen it enough to be pretty immune.

"Yup," she said. "Just like I thought. Surly. I'll bet you were a sulker, too, when you didn't get your own way as a kid."

"I resent this, Sabrina. Make no mistake, you are an employee and can be replaced."

She laughed. "Uh-huh. Sure, Mr. Langtry."

Before he could reply, Anastasia approached the cart. She had a bag of chips in one hand and chocolate in the other. "This is what I want," she said. "Both of them."

Sabrina stared at her. She knew she'd been speaking English just a few minutes ago. Then she recognized the challenge in the girl's eyes. Fine, if she wanted to do a little testing, Sabrina was more than up to the task.

Cal shifted uncomfortably. "Well, the bag of chips looks small," he said. "It wouldn't last a chipmunk for a week."

Sabrina looked at him. He clamped his lips together and nodded. "Okay. One treat, Anastasia. Just one. Decide."

His daughter glared at him, then tossed the candy into the cart. "I can't believe you're doing this," she said before she flounced off.

"Me, neither," Cal said softly, watching her go. "Jeez, Sabrina, I wouldn't be able to get through this without you. I feel like I'm going to mess up every time I turn around."

"You'll get the hang of it. I have the advantage of younger siblings that I helped raise. But it's not so hard."

"That's what I tell everyone about finding oil, but no one believes me." He touched her upper arm. "Thanks."

He headed for the front of the store. Sabrina forced herself to concentrate on her list rather than watching her boss walk away. The tingling in her arm subsided after a couple of seconds and she was soon able to draw in an undisturbed breath.

This whole situation was incredibly dangerous to her. She hadn't seen that at first, but she was figuring it out, and fast. Normally they spent a lot of time together, but there was always business between them. Even when they traveled, it wasn't *personal*. But this was. Having to deal with Anastasia put them into a situation they'd never experienced before. They were talking about many things best left unsaid, seeing sides of each other that should remain hidden. Cal could probably get through this without giving any of it a moment's thought, but she wasn't that disinterested. No matter how she tried to ignore the reality, the man got to her.

Him needing her, depending on her, the sudden intimacy of family, all conspired to make her think about belonging…about this being real.

"You know better," she said aloud. She'd always known better. She wasn't Cal's type, he didn't find her attractive, and even if he did, what was the point? Cal thrilled to the chase, but once he'd caught his flavor of the month, he wasn't that eager to keep her around. She didn't want a brief affair. Actually she didn't know what she wanted, but she believed with all her heart it was much safer to stay professional, no matter how strong the temptation to make it more.

* * *

Cal watched as Sabrina stepped into his study and hit the switch by the door. He blinked in the sudden light.

"What are you doing?" she asked.

"Sitting in the dark," he said. "Pretty pathetic, huh?"

He leaned back in his desk chair and motioned for her to take a seat on the leather sofa by the bookcase. She did as he requested.

"Want to talk about it?" she asked.

"I'm not sure there's anything to say. I feel as if I'm in the middle of a war, but I can't figure out if I'm the enemy or she is."

The "she" in question was, of course, his daughter, he thought. Right now Anastasia was watching television in the other room. She'd spent the later afternoon and early evening alternating between vaguely pleasant and a complete brat.

"You want a drink?" Sabrina asked as she rose and moved to the wet bar in the corner.

"No, thanks. I tried that last night and all that happened was I woke up feeling lousy."

"I think I want to double-check your findings," she said, and poured herself a small glass of brandy. She carried the snifter back to the sofa and took a seat.

They sat in silence for a while. The lamplight made Sabrina's red hair glow like fire. He'd always been a man who preferred blondes, but there was something appealing about her bright coloring. With her face partially in shadow, her eyes looked more smoky gray than blue, but they were still large and fringed with dark lashes. She'd been in her jeans all day, but he hadn't gotten used to seeing the actual shape of her hips and thighs. To be honest, he liked it. Sabrina wasn't model thin. She had curves, like a real woman. Curves a man could cup and stroke and—

Down boy, he ordered himself. He had no business going there. Sabrina was off-limits for a lot of reasons. For one, she was an employee, and he didn't mess around where he did his business. For another, she deserved his respect. Finally, he wasn't stupid. If he made a pass at Sabrina, she would probably haul off and hit him. Worse, she might want to quit, and right now he couldn't survive without her.

"Who would have thought it would come to this," he said.

"Meaning you never thought you would be a father?"

The question surprised him. "Maybe. Kids." He shook his head. "I suppose they were part of my plan, but a vague part, somewhere in the distant future. I never expected to have one thrust upon me like this. Anastasia and I are a real pair. God knows what she needs from me, but it's unlikely I'm going to be able to provide it."

"I think you're selling yourself short," Sabrina told him. "So far, you're doing fine."

"Yeah, right. She told me I should have known about her. I should have made it my business to know, or somehow sensed it."

"You know that's not true," Sabrina said gently. "You don't have psychic powers. She's thinking in terms of fairy tales and television. This is real life."

"Maybe she's right. Maybe I should have known."

Sabrina leaned forward. "How?"

"If you're going to get logical, we can't have this discussion," he warned.

"Oh, I see. So you should have had a dream or a vision?"

She had a point. "I understand that Anastasia is reacting from the point of view of a hurt child, but she's not completely off base with her accusations. If I didn't know about her, I should have at least had a clue about Janice. I was intimate with the woman. How could I have let her deceive me that way?"

"You didn't *let* her do anything. She tricked you. She deliberately set out to get pregnant. You couldn't have predicted that."

She was right. He knew that in his head, but his gut told

him otherwise. In his gut, a voice whispered that there had been clues, but he'd missed them.

"Maybe you'd feel better if you pounded on the wall and called her a name," she suggested.

"Always practical."

"Just trying to help."

"Thanks, but I don't think breaking my hand is going to improve my mood. Besides, Janice isn't the only person I blame for this mess."

"The other two are your parents, aren't they?"

He nodded. His parents. The two people who were supposed to love him and look out for him. Instead, they'd made decisions for him, had kept the truth from him.

"They had no right," he said, trying to block the tide of anger swelling inside him. "I know they were reacting to years of dealing with Tracey. I can't remember how many times she ran away, how many times she thought she was pregnant. It was grim for everyone."

"It's going to take some time to come to terms with this," Sabrina said.

Cal wasn't sure he ever would. "They never gave me the chance to make a choice."

"Because they knew what you would do. Maybe you're looking at this all wrong. There is a bright side."

He raised his eyebrows. "Illuminate me."

"The big concern for your folks was that once you found out about Janice, you would want to marry her, or at the very least, take responsibility for the child."

"So?"

"So?" She smiled. "Cal, what does that say about the kind of person you are? They knew you would do the right thing. Even then, they knew you were a good man whom they couldn't manipulate. That speaks highly of your character. That should make you happy."

He didn't think he could use that word to describe his state of mind right now, but he understood her point. "You know the real tragedy in this?" he asked. "My mother won't want anything to do with her. Anastasia is her only grandchild. But my mother will never forget who Janice wasn't, in terms of money and social standing. So she won't bother. I can forgive a lot, but I know I'll never forgive her that."

"That's good," Sabrina said. "You seem to have all the characteristics of a great father in the making. Maybe we should get a couple of books on parenting to bring you up to speed. After all, your daughter is practically a teenager."

He groaned. "I don't want to think about that."

"It's going to happen whether you want it to or not. It won't be so bad. At least funding her college tuition isn't going to be a hardship."

As consolations went, it wasn't much of one. What Sabrina didn't understand and what he couldn't find it in himself to explain was that he was terrified. How was he supposed to father this soon-to-be young woman who had entered his life? He'd never been very good at relationships of any kind, let alone important ones. He had a few friends from his school days that he was still in touch with, but only on a casual basis. He'd been involved with women, but never for very long. Hell, if the truth be told, Sabrina was not only his most reliable friend, but his most successful relationship, and they got along because they'd never tried to make it personal. He didn't know how to love someone, and he knew instinctively that's what his daughter needed most.

"College," he said. "That's so far off. It's late May and I'm worried about getting through the summer. School doesn't start until August. What are we going to do until then?"

"We'll figure something out," she promised.

He knew she was right. Somehow they would struggle

through this. "So I should probably put some money in a mutual fund for her," he said. "For her education."

"Not a bad idea."

He looked at her. "Did you get your college loans paid off? I know you had a scholarship and a grant, but didn't you owe money?"

She laughed. "Oh, Cal, I took care of that years ago. I believe it was my bonus the second year that paid off those debts. And before you ask, I've already taken care of my siblings' college and Gram. There's plenty of money."

He nodded. He was glad she was okay. Now she could put something aside for herself. Knowing Sabrina, she already had. "So you're saying you don't have to work for a living?"

"I do have to work, but not very hard."

He'd been teasing when he'd asked his question and she'd responded in kind. But instead of chuckling with her, he was struck with an unwelcome thought. That she didn't need him anymore.

Her job was interesting, he knew that. She enjoyed the travel, the different people she met, but she didn't *have* to work for him. Not like at the beginning, when her family had depended on her.

So why did she stay?

The question startled him, and he didn't want to think of an answer. What if there wasn't one? What if he couldn't come up with a good reason for Sabrina to stay? How long would it be before she figured out she would be better off somewhere else?

As he had the night before, he wandered the halls. It was after midnight and he couldn't sleep. This time Cal couldn't blame the alcohol, mostly because he hadn't had any to drink. Worries, concerns, what if's, all conspired to keep him awake.

He walked toward the two guest rooms. Both doors were

closed. He paused outside of Sabrina's but didn't open it. He wondered if she was awake and what she wore to bed. A sensible pair of pajamas, or maybe an oversize cotton T-shirt? Or did she wear something sexy and soft, keeping that side of her nature private?

Error, he thought as his mental questions formed images that had his blood heading south. That was inappropriate and dangerous. So he left his assistant's door and moved to his daughter's.

Here he did turn the knob and peek inside. As she had the night before, Anastasia lay on her side facing him. She clutched the teddy bear close to her chest, hugging it as if she would never let go. By day the toy was tossed casually in a corner as if she didn't want anyone to know how much it mattered, but at night it was her talisman against the scary place that was her world.

He ached for her. In his heart he felt a distinct thaw of emotions, and he sent up a prayer that God would help him to figure out how on earth he was going to be anything close to a decent father.

His gaze settled on her, on her pretty features, her thin shape under the covers. She appeared more vulnerable in the dead of night, more at risk, and he wanted to protect her. The problem was, he didn't have a clue as to how.

Chapter 8

When Cal walked into the kitchen he noticed two things. One was the smell of coffee, the other was the sight of Sabrina standing with her back to him. The coffee would get his blood flowing, something he needed after a second restless night. And Sabrina, well, she was part of his world and he liked that she was there when he woke up.

She turned toward him and held out a steaming mug. "'Morning, boss," she said.

She was fresh from the shower. Her hair was still a little damp, her face scrubbed clean. She didn't wear a lot of makeup, but he rarely saw her without any. Her skin was faintly freckled, her lashes a little on the pale side. She looked wholesome, he decided. Like a young woman selling dairy products in a television commercial.

He let his gaze linger over the blue T-shirt she'd worn over white shorts. Her feet were bare, and he was surprised to see that she painted her toenails a soft peach. Interesting.

He sipped the coffee and moved to the table. His daughter was already sitting there. She looked at him, dark eyes staring, measuring. He braced himself for the opening salvo. Anastasia didn't let him down.

"What are you going to do with me?" she asked abruptly. "You can't take me shopping every day. School's out, so you won't be able to dump me there, at least not for a while. Plus you have a job, right? I mean you have to do something, you're not just rich."

Cal didn't know how to answer the question of what to do with her, nor did he feel he had to justify his existence or his employment. Still, her comments were valid. What *was* he going to do with her? Unfortunately, he hadn't had enough coffee to get his brain going.

Sabrina crossed to the table and put her hand on the girl's shoulder. "That's not a very pleasant way for anyone to start their day, is it? What about saying 'good morning,' or even just 'hi'?"

Anastasia blushed and ducked her head. "Hi," she mumbled, then shoved a big spoonful of cereal into her mouth.

"Good morning," he said, and took the seat opposite her. "Did you sleep well?"

She nodded.

A pleasant almost-conversation. It wasn't much, but it was progress. He glanced at Sabrina. She grinned. He returned the smile and something flashed between them.

Cal was so startled that, had he been drinking, his coffee would have gone down the wrong way. He couldn't define the flash, but in its aftereffect, he found himself wanting to walk around the table, pull her close and kiss her.

The thought was more unexpected than unpleasant. Kiss Sabrina? Where had that come from? It's not that she wasn't attractive, in her own way, she just wasn't his type. In his mind, she'd always been more office equipment than actual female.

Strange, he thought. Maybe it was the change in circumstances, or the shorts. He eyed her long legs. They were shapely enough. If she were a different kind of woman or he was a different kind of man, he would enjoy imagining them wrapped around his waist, pulling him closer as he—

Enough, he ordered himself. This was too dangerous. He needed Sabrina, and he wasn't about to risk messing everything up now. Not when he had a new daughter to worry about. Sabrina was his lifeline with Anastasia.

He smiled slightly as he took another drink of coffee. If the truth were told, even if he wanted to start something, he wouldn't have a chance with Sabrina. She knew him too well, knew his patterns with women. If she thought he was the least bit interested, she would run screaming in the opposite direction. She often told him he was a complete cad—even though she agreed he didn't do it on purpose.

"How about a bagel," Sabrina said, moving back to the counter.

"Sounds great."

She sliced one and popped it into the toaster, then carried over a bowl of fresh fruit.

She moved around his kitchen with a familiarity he lacked, even though it was his place, not hers. He didn't do much cooking, preferring to eat out with friends, or Sabrina, if he didn't have a date. She was, he realized with some small shock, his best friend. When had that happened?

Before he could find an answer or even decide how he felt about the revelation, Sabrina handed him a plate with his bagel and a container of cream cheese. She took the seat next to his and served herself a bowl of fruit.

"Anastasia has a point," she said. "We are going to have to find some things for her to do. I suspect it's too late for summer camp, but I can check."

Anastasia rolled her eyes. "Camp? I'm not a kid."

"You're twelve," Sabrina pointed out. "You're not an adult yet, therefore, by definition, you *are* still a kid. Some camps are fun."

"How would you know? Have you ever been to one?"

"Nope. I grew up poor." Sabrina made the statement cheerfully. "But then I had a brother and two sisters to keep me company, not to mention a warm and friendly personality that allowed me to have lots of friends."

Anastasia opened her mouth, then clamped it shut.

A second bagel popped out of the toaster. Sabrina retrieved it and continued her conversation. "But we are going to have to come up with some kind of a plan. Not just for the summer, but also for the fall. Where is she going to school?"

Cal finished with the cream cheese and passed it to her. "Isn't there one close by? She'll be in middle school, right?" He looked at his daughter. "Sixth grade."

"Yes."

"Middle school is a possibility," Sabrina said slowly. "But there's an excellent all-girls' school not too far from here. I've heard wonderful things about it. They do a great job with manners and social skills, as well as academic subjects."

Anastasia's face paled as her eyes widened with horror. "A girls' school?" She turned to him. "You wouldn't do that to me, would you?"

He caught Sabrina's wink and had to smother a smile. "I haven't made a decision yet. Let's see how the next few weeks go."

Anastasia looked as if she was going to protest, but she seemed to decide it wasn't the right time. She nodded once, then pushed back her chair. "May I please be excused?" she asked tightly.

Cal waved her off. "Of course."

She nearly ran from the room.

Sabrina took a bite of her bagel and chewed. Her expression was completely smug.

"You did that on purpose," he accused.

She shrugged. "She has good manners and can be pleasant when she wants to be. But most of the time, she's a little witch. I understand that adjusting is going to take time, but I don't want her thinking she has the upper hand. One of my sisters went through a stage like this. It was hideous. Gram kept saying all she needed was firm rules, consistent discipline and plenty of love. I'm hoping it will work with Anastasia as well as it did with Melissa."

Cal understood about firm rules and being consistent, but he wasn't sure about the love part. Growing up, he always felt his parents were only interested in him for bragging rights. As long as he did what they expected and didn't embarrass them in front of their friends, they were content to leave him and his sister in the care of the ever-changing staff. Tracey had fought against the neglect by rebelling. He'd made his own life, one that didn't include family. He'd made it a point to never care too much about anyone, and that philosophy had eventually become second nature. He wasn't sure he could go back and learn to love, even if he wanted to.

Sabrina finished her bagel and took the plate to the sink. "Let me get my notes," she said. "There are a few pressing issues." She grinned. "Some of them are even about work."

While she collected her papers and her computer, he poured them each more coffee and settled back in his chair.

"Ada says they hit oil, just like you expected," Sabrina said, handing him a lengthy fax.

Over the next half hour, they got through the faxes and notes. Cal put down the last paper. "How are the interviews going to replace old octopus hands?"

She consulted a file in her laptop. "According to the memo Ada sent me, it's down to three people, all women, all highly qualified. Someone will be in place by the middle of next week."

"Good."

Sabrina hit a couple of keys. "All right, now that the easy stuff is taken care of…"

Her voice trailed off and he groaned. "I know. Anastasia. I know she wasn't polite about it, but you and she did have a point this morning. We are going to have to do something with her. It's only late May. From what I remember, school doesn't start until mid-August. As she said, we can't spend every day at the mall."

"If I were an incredibly cruel person, I would tell you this is not part of my job description and that you're on your own with this one," Sabrina teased. "But I'm not."

He ignored her threat, mostly because he knew it was meaningless. Sabrina would never leave him in a lurch.

"What about summer camps?" he asked. "*Is* it too late?"

"It is for the one at Rice University. It's been full for months." Sabrina rested her elbow on the table and her chin on her hand. "The problem is, neither of us knows anyone with kids her age. Well, that's not completely true. Ada has a couple of nieces about her age, but we can't impose on her too much. Anastasia likes to read and there are always movies, but that's a solitary way for someone to spend the summer. I'd like to see her get out and make some friends. Then she wouldn't feel so alone."

"It might improve her disposition, too," he grumbled. He consoled himself with the fact that it was going to get better, and at least her comebacks showed that she was a fast thinker and incredibly bright.

"I could check the local parks program," Sabrina said, typing on her keyboard. "Maybe there's an art school or something."

She focused on the computer. Cal watched as her gaze narrowed. She sat cross-legged in the kitchen chair, which she

Susan Mallery

rarely did at the office. Her hair had dried and fluffed up some, with a couple of wisps brushing against her cheek.

He raised his hand toward her face, as if to tuck the curls behind her ear, then pulled back. The gesture was too personal, which was odd, because he'd hugged her before and hadn't thought twice about it.

She wrinkled her nose. "Swimming, maybe? Lessons if she doesn't know how. It's too hot for tennis. Some kind of club." She pressed more keys.

How long had she been pretty, he wondered. He remembered when she'd first hired on. He'd thought she was presentable, but nothing even close to his type. At the time, that had been a blessing. The last thing he'd wanted was to be attracted to his personal assistant. But she was pretty now. Had she changed or had he? Was it just the circumstances, their being thrown together in a way that hadn't happened before?

Pretty was all right, he told himself. She could be pretty, and he could even think about wanting her. Sex was completely safe. It was the liking that got him into trouble, and that was part of the problem. While he'd just figured out that Sabrina was pretty, he'd always liked her. So what the hell was he going to do about that now?

"I think she's darling," Ada said three days later, then took a sip of her coffee. "So sweet and well mannered. Do you know she actually came into the kitchen and asked if she could help me with dinner last night? You tell Cal he got lucky with that young lady. My nieces are great and I love them, but they have no manners at all."

They were sitting in Sabrina's office, on the sofa that faced the window. Sabrina set her cup on the glass coffee table and stared at her secretary.

"We *are* talking about the same girl, right? About five six, dark hair and eyes, glasses, Cal's new daughter?"

Ada dismissed her with a wave. "Don't you dare say anything bad about her. She's a charmer. I adore her. She can come and stay with me anytime. I don't care if my nieces are spending the night with me or not. I'd love to take her out and spoil her with shopping and movies." The older woman smiled. "You just want to hug her."

Sabrina's phone buzzed. "You around?" Cal asked.

She stood up and crossed to her desk. "Right here. Want me to come up?"

"Please."

"Be right there." She released the button. "Sorry, Ada, the boss calls."

"No problem." Her secretary started for the door. "Tell Cal what I said. I'm happy to babysit or whatever. Anastasia is a wonderful girl."

Sabrina was still shaking her head when she walked into Cal's office.

"I'm brilliant," he said, handing her a file.

She glanced at the tab and raised her eyebrows. "This is about the joint venture. Did you get a meeting finalized?"

He grinned. "For next month, in Hong Kong. If you're very good, I'll let you come and we can go back to your favorite Chinese restaurant."

"The one we ate at last year when I won our stock bet?" she asked.

He glared at her. "That would be the one, yes. Put it on the calendar."

"Okay." She made a note in the file. "I was just talking to Ada about Anastasia's visit."

Cal leaned back in his chair and loosened his tie. It was late in the afternoon, and he'd long since rolled up his shirt-sleeves to the elbows. Now he opened his collar and tossed his tie onto the desk.

"How bad was she?" he asked.

"According to Ada, your daughter is sweet, well mannered and a charmer."

Cal stared at her. "This is my daughter we're talking about? Anastasia? The same one who called me a sperm donor?"

"That would be her. Apparently she knows how to be polite, she simply chooses not to be around us."

"Great. I feel so special."

Sabrina leaned toward him. "Cal, you know she's testing you. She's still scared about being here and not sure you're going to keep her."

"I don't mind the testing," he grumbled, "but I'm ready to get a grade already. If I had to pick, I suppose it's better that she's well behaved outside the home."

Sabrina laughed. "Oh, Lord, you're turning into a parent. Have you been reading those child-rearing books I gave you?"

"I've skimmed a couple. I don't think I agree with everything they say, but it's interesting." His warm gaze settled on her. "Thanks for all your help, Sabrina. I couldn't have gotten through the last week without you."

"No problem. It's kinda fun. After all, if she gets really hideous, I can escape back to my own place." She made the statements lightly, but inside she felt the heavy weight of guilt.

While she was happy to help Cal, she knew she wasn't going to be around as long as he thought she was. So far she'd spoken to a couple of different headhunters, and both of them had felt she wouldn't have any trouble finding work with another company. Between her education and her unique work experience, she was a prize. Sabrina didn't feel very prizelike at the moment, but maybe a job offer or two would change that.

She pushed the guilt aside and reminded herself that she wasn't doing anything wrong. She'd been a good and loyal employee for Cal, but she hadn't signed a lifetime contract.

She needed to make her own way in the world, and that wasn't going to happen while she was with him.

His phone rang and he picked up the receiver. She watched him, the way the afternoon sun brought out the gold highlights in his brown hair. He was so handsome—it wasn't fair. How was she supposed to resist his good looks along with everything else? Life would be a whole lot easier if she could just hate her boss. But she didn't. She liked him…a lot. They were friends and she knew she would miss him when she left.

When he hung up, she glanced at her watch. "I've got to go pick up Anastasia. The movie gets out in twenty minutes and there's going to be traffic." She rose to her feet and crossed to the door. "Don't use this as an excuse to work late, young man. I'm not your live-in babysitter."

"Yes, ma'am. I have a couple calls to make, then I'll come straight home." His grin broadened. "What's for dinner, dear?"

"I'm thinking of a couple of words," she called over her shoulder as she headed for the door. "They're not polite words. Actually, the second one is fine. It's the first one that's gonna get me in trouble."

She was still chuckling over their conversation when she pulled up in front of the movie complex. Anastasia was waiting with two other preteens. They all saw her, and Ada's nieces waved. Anastasia said something to them, then walked to the car.

"Hi," Sabrina said when she climbed in and fastened her seat belt. "How was the movie?"

"Okay, I guess."

"Ada said you had fun last night."

Anastasia looked out the window. "Uh-huh."

"She also ratted you out, kid. So the act isn't going to fly for much longer."

Anastasia stared at her. "What do you mean she ratted me out? I didn't do anything wrong. I was polite and everything."

"I know. That's my point. She told me you were a pleasure to be around, well mannered and all the rest. So how come you give us the surly treatment at home?"

Instead of the flip comeback she'd expected, Anastasia turned back to the window and sniffed. "I d-don't know."

"Yes, you do. We all do. I understand that you're scared, but it's going to be fine. You have to trust that."

"Who are you?" Anastasia asked. "You work for my dad, but now you're living at his place. But you're not the housekeeper. It's too weird. I don't know you and I don't know him. I miss my parents. I just want things back the way they were before."

"I know, honey. It's hard."

A strangled sob caught in her throat. "You don't know."

Sabrina sighed. "Actually, I do. I was fourteen when my parents were both killed in a car accident. It was the most horrible experience of my life."

Anastasia looked at her. "Yeah?"

Sabrina nodded. "I would have given anything to have them back. I couldn't figure out what I'd done wrong to make them go away. I mean, I knew it was an accident, but I didn't believe it."

The preteen wiped at her tears. "I know," she whispered.

"I had my brother and two sisters to help me get through it. I also had a grandmother, but it was still awful. You've had a difficult year, but now you have a father who very much wants to be a part of your life. He cares about you."

"He doesn't even know me. How can he care?"

Then Sabrina got it. She wondered why she hadn't seen it before. While Anastasia was fighting the fear of an unfamiliar place and different circumstances, she was also terrified that her new father wouldn't like her. After all she'd been through, she wouldn't survive another rejection in her young life. It was safer to lash out, to create distance so nothing could hurt her ever again.

"You're not making it easy for him, are you?" she asked softly.

"Why should I?"

Good point, Sabrina thought. That was the parent's job, not the child's.

"He's just playing at being a father. He's not interested in me at all."

Sabrina heard a familiar echo in those words. "That's not you talking," she said. "That's your aunt."

Shrug. "Does it matter? It's the truth."

"No, it's not, but I guess you're going to have to wait and see who's right on that one."

They were silent for the rest of the drive. Something was going to have to be done, Sabrina thought. Cal and his daughter needed a chance to bond, and it wasn't going to happen under the present circumstances. Cal needed to spend time with the girl, but in such a way that it wasn't forced or too awkward for either of them. And she knew just how to make that happen.

"This is getting to be a habit," Cal said as Sabrina joined him in his study. It was nearly ten and Anastasia was in bed.

Sabrina smiled. "A nice one, I hope." She poured them each a brandy and sat in the chair across from his desk.

"Very nice." He took a sip of the drink. It *was* nice. He enjoyed having her in his house. He liked the close contact, finding her in the kitchen first thing in the morning, the way she insisted on taking her own car to the office because she would need it to pick up Anastasia. He liked talking with her about his concerns, listening to her opinion—she had one on everything—watching her absently touch his daughter's hair or shoulder in an unconscious gesture of affection.

Nights were the best...and the worst. He couldn't stop thinking about her at night. He looked forward to the moment she would walk into the study and take a seat. He liked looking at her in the subtle light. He enjoyed watching her relax, kick off her shoes and slump down in the chair. Sometimes, if he wasn't careful, his mind took the image further. To her slowly peeling off her blouse and letting it fall to the floor, followed by her bra. He pictured her bare breasts, the peach-colored tips pouting at him as they puckered. He thought about himself circling the desk and pulling her close, kissing her, holding her, running his hands all over her back and shoulders before finally—

"A penny for your thoughts," she said. "You're a million miles away."

He shifted uncomfortably as he realized he was rock hard. Thank God the desk was between them. "Not that far," he told her. "And definitely not worth a penny."

"If you say so." She slumped down in her chair. "I had an interesting talk with Anastasia when I picked her up from the movies. Apparently her aunt said that you were just playing at being a father and Anastasia is afraid that's true. She's not willing to give you the benefit of the doubt because she can't afford to be wrong. If she starts to care about you, then loses you, she won't be able to recover. The girl has no emotional reserves."

Cal listened to the words and shook his head. "Great. It makes sense, but how do I change that? She's barely civil to me, let alone pleasant. I don't know what to say to her or what to do with her." He ran his hand through his hair. There was nothing like a little emotional inadequacy to take care of a man's libido. The last lingering physical traces of desire faded.

Anastasia was smart to be wary of him. He didn't know the first thing about parenting and he was bound to screw it all up. "Maybe I should have made other arrangements for her," he muttered. "Sent her to people who know what they're doing."

"Don't even think that," Sabrina told him. "You're her father and you want to care about her. All the expertise in the world can't take the place of that. Give it time, Cal. It's barely been a week. You two will figure out how to be a family. I've been thinking about this, and one of the problems is location."

He glanced around the study. "You don't like my condo?"

"No. It's fine. The problem is that it's summer break, and she doesn't have any friends or ways to fill her time. You've got work, I have my own life. So no one is a hundred percent focused on the problem. I suggest a vacation. The three of us go away, maybe for a month or so, and you two spend some time getting to know each other."

As long as Sabrina was going to be there to keep him from making too big a mistake, he was in favor of the idea. "Where would you like to go?"

"Maybe the beach."

"Corpus Christi is a great idea. I know a couple—"

Sabrina covered her face with her hands and groaned. "Not there, Cal. It's still the gulf and really hot. Let's go somewhere nice and cool. I was thinking of Balboa Island in Southern California. It's a little crowded, but fun. There's lots to do and it's not like a steam bath."

He chuckled. "You still haven't adjusted to the Texas summers, have you?"

"No, and I don't want to adjust. Come on. A month on the California shore. Balboa would be fun. There's boating and the beach. We could go in-line skating. Disneyland is about thirty minutes away. Some of the restaurants in Newport are fabulous, and there is the most amazing mall."

"Oh, well, a mall. You've convinced me."

She smiled at him. "Is that a yes?"

He could deny her nothing, he realized with some amazement. At that moment, he would have given his soul to make Sabrina happy. What was happening to him?

"Cal? Say yes."

"Yes," he told her, because he didn't have a choice.

Chapter 9

The sun had set a couple of hours before, but it wasn't completely dark down by the beach. There were lights from other houses, the streets and the docks, not to mention the glow from the amusement area on the peninsula.

Sabrina settled back in her chair and sighed. "This is how the good Lord intended life to be," she said. "The water, the stars, the cool night air." She glanced at her boss. "Cool air. You remember that, Cal, don't you? I realize it's been about four months since summer started in Houston, but we did have those three days of spring. It was cool then."

"I get enough sass from my daughter," he said. "I don't need to hear it from you, too."

"Sure you do. It keeps you in touch with the little people."

His response was a grunt, a surefire signal he wanted the subject changed. Sabrina chuckled. At this point, she was so happy to be back in California and on the beach, she would have agreed to almost anything.

They sat in silence for a while. Faint music drifted to them from one of their neighbors. There was the sound of laughter and conversation.

"They must be having a party," Cal said, motioning to his left.

"Probably. Maybe next time they'll invite us."

Cal stretched out his long legs and reached for his can of soda on the plastic table beside his chair. "It's not what I thought," he admitted. "But I like it."

Property was a premium on Balboa Island, and the houses pressed up against each other. They were mostly long, narrow structures, two stories, many with apartments in back or on the second floor. Sabrina had rented a three-bedroom single family house right on the water. Their front patio opened onto the boardwalk, with the boats and the water beyond.

Anastasia was already in bed. Sabrina found herself wishing they'd left on a light in the living room so it wasn't so cozy on the patio. She wanted to inch her chair away from her boss, or maybe jump up and go for a walk. Without warning, her muscles got all twitchy and she felt as if her skin was two sizes too small.

It was the close confines of the house, it was traveling together, it was the sea air and it was the man himself. He got to her. With his good looks and his easy smile. That damn Texas drawl. Why couldn't he be a troll, or at least have a few really annoying personal habits? In the regulated world of work she found it easy to confine herself to business, but here, like this, it was too much like a real vacation, which meant her guard kept slipping. If she didn't watch her step, she was going to do something really stupid, like notice her boss was a single guy and very appealing.

She ducked her head to hide the smile. Okay, so she'd already noticed. Noticed and admired and wanted. She bit back a curse, she who rarely swore.

"Tracey didn't. She's nearly forty and she's dating boys half her age." He raised a hand. "I know, I know, it's a double standard. I suppose I shouldn't mind or be critical. If I thought they cared about her, it would be one thing, but they're all after money. We are a poor excuse for a family. I want more for Anastasia."

"You're giving her more. You're spending time with her and getting to know her. That's important."

"And I've got you. My ace in the hole." He rose to his feet, then bent over her chair. "Thanks."

He brushed a kiss across her forehead, straightened and walked into the house. Sabrina sat immobile for several seconds as she willed her heart rate to return to normal.

Cal had just kissed her. It didn't mean anything more than a friendly moment between people who'd been through a lot together. She knew that in her head. But in her heart, and other places slightly more interesting, she didn't want to believe it. She wanted to think that it meant something. She wanted him to be feeling the same heat, the same growing desire flickering through his body.

Close proximity, a charming man whom she genuinely liked and way too many years of celibacy. It was not a good combination. If she wasn't careful, she was going to end up doing something incredibly stupid and then where would she be?

Cal strolled through the kitchen into the living room. Anastasia lay stretched out on the floor, watching television. A series of tall, slender models paraded across runways while rock music blared.

He crouched down next to his daughter. "What are you watching?"

"It's a show about the fashion industry. You know, what's going to be hot for fall, that kind of stuff." She pushed her glasses up her nose. "You wouldn't like it."

He settled next to her on the floor. A large area rug covered the bleached hardwood. After grabbing a cushion from the sofa, he shoved it under his head and prepared to get comfortable.

"How do you know?" he asked. "I might enjoy fashion. So what is hot for fall?"

She rolled her eyes. "You like those detective shows, or the business reports. This is only on another half hour, then you can change it."

"That's okay. I want to watch this with you. We can bond."

On their trip to the grocery store, he'd picked up a couple of parenting magazines. He needed the information to get the jump start he needed to catch up on this parenting stuff. It was harder than he'd thought. One of the articles had mentioned parent-child bonding, using television as a neutral medium.

He pointed at the screen. "That dress is nice."

The garment in question was long and black, with very little top and, when the model turned, almost no back. "Well, not for you," he amended.

Anastasia rose to her feet. They'd spent most of the three days they'd been in California outdoors. Despite the sunscreen Sabrina had insisted they all wear, his daughter was getting a faint tan. She'd gained a little weight and her face had lost its pinched look.

"Why are you doing this?" she asked. "I don't want to bond with you. Watch your own stuff and leave me alone."

The sharp anger in her voice shocked him. In the past couple of days, they'd actually been getting along. What had happened to change that? "Anastasia," he said, his tone warning.

"What? What are you going to do to me?"

"Anastasia, I—" A thought distracted him. He sat up and looked at her. "Who named you? Was it Janice or your adoptive parents?"

"My *mother*," she said, emphasizing the last word. "My real mother. Not Janice."

"Was it a family name? It seems a little old-fashioned."

"You want to talk about *my* name?" she asked. "You're Calhoun Jefferson Langtry and you think my name is funny?"

He realized he'd hit a nerve. "It's not funny. I think it's very pretty, if a little unusual."

"I don't care what you think." Her hands curled into fists and her eyes filled with tears. "I don't care about you at all because you never cared about me. Why didn't you use birth control? Why didn't you check on Janice? Why did you just go off and leave her? She *died!*" Her voice rose. "She died and I was all alone and no one cared about me. You're supposed to be my father. You're supposed to care, and you didn't even bother to find out the truth. You should have come for me."

She seemed to fold in on herself. Her shoulders hunched forward and her face scrunched up.

"Anastasia."

But he was too late. She turned to the stairs and raced up. Seconds later he heard her bedroom door slam shut.

Cal rose to his feet and stared after her. What had happened? He'd come in to join her while she watched television. Instead of sharing some quiet time together, he'd obviously hurt her terribly and sent her from the room in tears.

"You okay?"

He turned and saw Sabrina standing in the doorway. "I'm the wrong person to ask." He pointed to the ceiling. "She's the one crying."

"I don't know. You look a little shell-shocked to me."

Cal sank onto the sofa. "What the hell happened? One minute we were discussing TV shows and the next—" He shook his head. "I'm the last person in the world to be raising a kid."

"For what it's worth, I think you did the right thing."

Then why did he have a knot in his gut and a cold, ugly

feeling that he was destined to hurt the child he only wanted to love? "About what?" he asked.

"You didn't tell her the truth about Janice. She told you she was on the pill, didn't she?"

"Yeah, but that's not something I felt I should share with a twelve-year-old. Anastasia's right. I should have checked. Somehow. I should have done a lot of things differently."

The problem was, he could be as logical as he wanted. Janice had lied. That wasn't his fault. He'd tried to get in touch with her, but she hadn't wanted him to find her. He had excuses for all of his daughter's accusations, save one—that he should have known about her. He bought into that theory, too. Even now he found it hard to believe that he'd had a child and never once sensed her presence in the world. He *should* have known. If he was any kind of father, he would have known.

"You're beating yourself up for being human," Sabrina said. "For what it's worth, I think that's a waste of time. You can't change that, and you can't erase the past. Today is what's important."

"Explain that to her," he said, jerking his head toward the ceiling.

"Oh, I intend to."

Sabrina left the room. She wished there was more she could say to Cal. His obvious concern and pain touched her. She wanted to find the right words to make it all better. Unfortunately only time would allow him and Anastasia to form a relationship. That and maybe a firm dose of reality.

She walked into Anastasia's room without knocking. The girl was curled up on the bed, her back to the door. She clutched her teddy bear against her chest.

"For one kid, you sure put out a lot of water," Sabrina said lightly as she sat next to the preteen and pulled her into her arms.

Anastasia came willingly. Sabrina stroked her hair and rocked back and forth. "I know," she murmured. "I know how it feels, and before you snap at me and say that I don't, I'm going to remind you that I lost my parents, too. Remember? I know this is painful and scary. The most scary part is that you're starting to like him and you don't want to. After all, what if he changes his mind and sends you to the state home? Or what if he dies, too?"

Anastasia raised her head. Tears streaked her face. Behind her glasses, her eyelashes were spiky and wet. She sniffed. "How'd you know?"

"It's not so hard to figure out. I worried that Gram would die, or that I'd lose one of my sisters. Most of the time I didn't really care about my brother because he was a real pain."

The joke earned her a slight smile.

Sabrina brushed away the tears. "Cal is a pretty great guy. He's never been a dad, so he's gonna make some mistakes. It wouldn't be so bad to cut him a little slack. You're the experienced one in the group. Maybe you could help him along. He's got flaws, but he's not a quitter. He's committed to you, Anastasia. He's not going to send you away."

"You don't know that."

"Of course I do. I make all his appointments and he hasn't talked to anyone about getting rid of you." Sabrina took a deep breath. "He's just as scared as you are. He has this idea that he could really mess you up. We both know that's not true, but he believes it. See, when he was growing up, his parents didn't bother with him. They were gone a lot, and they thought he and his sister were just in the way. The staff took care of them. But the staff was always changing, so there wasn't ever anyone to worry about him, or love him. He wants more for you."

"But he was rich."

"He was lonely. And you know what that feels like, right?"

Anastasia nodded. "I get scared, and then I say stuff I don't really mean."

"He knows that, but it would be nice if you could tell him yourself. Honey, he just wants to love you and take care of you. I think you two could have a wonderful relationship, but you need to meet him halfway. He'll never take the place of the father you remember, but there's still room in your life for him. It's okay to love them both. Hearts are funny that way. No matter how many people we love, there's always enough room for one more."

Anastasia hugged her bear close. "You think so?"

"I promise."

That evening Cal stared at the television, but he wasn't paying attention to the show. He was straining to hear something from upstairs. It had been a couple of hours. Sabrina had come down and said to let Anastasia work it out for herself, but he wasn't sure he could take much more of this. He felt that every time he turned around, he was doing something else wrong.

He heard footsteps and looked up. Anastasia paused in the entrance to the room.

"Hi," she said.

"Hi, yourself. You okay?"

She nodded. "I'm—" She cleared her throat. "I'm sorry about what I said before. I didn't mean it. Sometimes I just—" She shrugged. "You know. Say stuff. I don't even want to. It just comes out. I'm sorry."

He crossed to her in three strides. Once he reached her side, he didn't know what to say. "Anastasia, I—"

She stared at her feet. "I know. It's pretty dumb, huh?"

"Not at all." He reached out and took her hand in his. "It makes sense. But thank you for apologizing. That takes a lot of courage."

She raised herself up on tiptoe, pressed a kiss to his cheek, mumbled a quick "good-night" and raced up the stairs. Cal stood staring after her. He felt like Sally Field at the Academy

Awards all those years ago when she'd said, "You like me, you really like me."

His daughter liked him. Hot damn.

He knew he was grinning like a fool and he couldn't help it. Anastasia had made him very happy. He crossed the room and stepped out onto the porch. Sabrina stood at the railing, staring out over the water.

"Did you tell her to apologize to me?" he asked.

Sabrina turned toward him. In the half light spilling out from the living room, her red hair looked darker than usual. Shorts exposed long legs, although a loose T-shirt kept the top half of her charms completely covered.

"Anastasia?" she asked, then continued without waiting for an answer. "Of course not. I did talk to her and explain that you were her father and willing to meet her more than halfway. It was up to her to make the rest of the journey. I'm glad she decided to make it easy."

He shifted from foot to foot. "I know this is really dumb, but she kissed me good-night. For that second I felt like her dad."

"You are her dad."

He moved next to her and looked out at the water. Lights from boats reflected in the moving surface. "I can sniff out an oil field a hundred miles away, but I don't know the first thing about raising a daughter. And I'm obviously a lousy judge of women. I still believe I should have known what Janice was doing, but I never guessed."

"This is getting redundant, Mr. Langtry. None of that is your fault. You were willing to take responsibility as soon as you found out about your daughter. That's what matters. Let the past go, Cal. Worry about today and maybe a little about tomorrow. You and Anastasia have a chance to be a family together. Don't let go of that."

He hoped Sabrina was right. "I like her," he said. "I know she's a real brat at times, but I like her."

"If you can say that after everything she's said to you, then you're going to be a great father."

Cal bumped his shoulder against hers. Sabrina bumped him back, telling herself the action was just playful. He was thrilled that Anastasia had apologized for what she'd said. It was a big step in forming a bond. He had every reason to be happy.

She was happy for him. At least that's what she told herself. She was also on fire from standing so close to him. Had he always generated this much body heat or was she just now noticing it? And when had it gotten so warm in the evenings around here? She thought it was supposed to be cool at night.

She had to get out of here, she told herself. Before she said or did something really stupid. Her hormones were out of control, she couldn't stop thinking about Cal. If only he would dress in his suits, or even jeans. But the shorts were driving her crazy, what with the way they left his powerful legs bare. Sometimes on the beach, he wore no shirt at all and exposed his flat belly and the dark hair that taunted her. She wanted to put her hands on him and see if he was as hard as he looked.

She swallowed. Hard. Bad, bad choice of words. It made her think of other things being hard, of—

Stop it! she commanded herself.

"Thanks, Sabrina."

Before she figured out what he was going to do, he turned toward her and pulled her close. She was too stunned to resist or pull back, then suddenly she found herself pressed against him—chest to chest, thigh to thigh, his face inches from hers.

"You're the best, little lady," he said, deliberately exaggerating his drawl.

He was teasing and she was slowly melting. Well, at least he would never know how she felt, or how much she wanted him to kiss her. Pride wasn't much to keep her company, but it was going to have to be enough.

"Thank you, cowboy," she said, but her voice sounded funny. Low and husky.

Cal's expression shifted from teasing to something else. Dear God, please, he couldn't guess. That would be too humiliating for words.

"Sabrina?"

She started to pull away. Really. That was her intent. But without warning, he dropped his head slightly and pressed his mouth to hers. Then she couldn't move, she couldn't think. She could only feel… The soft, firm pressure of his lips against hers, the way his hands cradled her so gently, the heat of him, his strength, the wanting that flooded her until she thought she would drown in the sweetest way possible.

She told herself it was a "thank you" kiss, that it didn't mean anything. But the seconds ticked by and he didn't bother pulling away. If anything, he deepened the pressure, as if testing…or waiting. For her? For a reaction? For her to jerk back and slap him, or did he want something else from her? Surrender?

Involuntarily, because she sure hadn't given them permission, her hands crept up his chest to link behind his neck. She raised herself up on her toes and angled her head slightly. That was it. She didn't do a single thing about his lips pressed against hers, but apparently the other cues were enough because he began to move.

He parted his lips and brushed them back and forth against hers. The gentle caress stole the last strength from her legs and she sagged against him. Her blood raced faster as a tingle started in her toes, working its way up her body, setting tiny fires of need as it went.

She'd thought about kissing Cal. Sometimes, when it was late and her defenses were down, she allowed herself to imagine what it would be like, but all that wondering hadn't even come close to reality. The taste of him, his scent, the powerful wall of muscles supporting her—he was so much more than she could have dreamed. She wasn't even sure this was real. Maybe it was a fantasy brought on by the night.

"Sabrina."

His voice was thick with desire. A shiver of anticipation rippled through her. As if he read her mind, he opened his mouth a little more and touched the tip of his tongue to her bottom lip. If she hadn't already been leaning against him, that single stroke would have brought her to her knees.

She clung to him. Her fingers curled into his muscles as she clutched his shirt. He, too, wore shorts, and the hair on his legs tickled her skin. Her breasts swelled, her nipples grew hard, and between her thighs the ache increased as her body grew slick in anticipation of a hoped-for invasion.

His tongue swept into her mouth and she was carried away. Everywhere he touched, she melted and wanted more. So much more. It was chemistry, or maybe physics, the attraction of magnets that sealed themselves together, or maybe molecules binding into more stable compounds.

One of his hands cupped her head, as if to hold her in place. As she answered his kiss, his touches and strokes, with playful forays of her own, she knew she had no intention of pulling back. But she liked the feel of his fingers in her hair.

With his other hand, he followed the curve of her hip, then moved around to squeeze her rear. The contact brought her pelvis forward. She felt his hardness, the proof that he wanted her as much as she wanted him. As she'd always wanted him. It was—

Her heart froze in her chest, her breathing stopped and she knew she was going to die. Right there on the porch on Balboa Island. Words replayed in her head. *As she'd always wanted him.* It couldn't be true. Not that. Not Cal. She knew better. He didn't really care about her, not as a woman. He didn't care about anyone romantically. She knew that. Falling for him would be incredibly stupid. She'd protected herself…hadn't she?

Cal stepped back. "Sabrina, what's wrong?"

She realized she'd stopped kissing him and had dropped her hands to her sides. She shook her head, more to clear it than to answer his question. "Nothing. I'm fine. It's just..." She touched a hand to her lips. "I'd better go upstairs now."

"Sabrina, wait. I'm sorry if I offended you. I didn't mean—"

But she was already running up the stairs and she couldn't hear him. She hurried to her room and closed the door behind her. Her heart had resumed beating in her chest, but now it was pounding so hard she thought it might explode.

As she crossed to the window to stare out at the night, she fought against the tears burning in her eyes. It had happened. She hadn't known, or she would have tried to stop it. She knew better, but in this case, that wasn't enough. Perhaps she'd been foolish to think she could escape. Close proximity and genuine affection had conspired against her. For an assortment of reasons, some that made sense and some that didn't, she'd fallen in love with Cal.

When had it happened? These past few weeks? She leaned against the window frame and closed her eyes. No, it had been longer than that. She wasn't sure how long, but at least a year. Maybe she'd always loved him.

A single tear escaped and rolled down her cheek. She brushed it away. There was nothing to be done, she told herself. She was already making plans to leave, so she would be safe. Her only concern was to keep Cal from finding out the truth. In the best-case scenario he would be momentarily interested, but it would only be in the chase. Once he caught her, he wouldn't want her. The worst-case scenario would be that he would only pity her, and she couldn't stand that.

Best of all was for him to never find out. Once she was free of him, she would find a way to get over him. Then she would be fine. It wasn't as if she was going to love him forever.

Chapter 10

Cal rinsed the lettuce in the sink, then tossed it into a drainer. After nearly a week at their beach house, Sabrina had announced it was his turn to cook dinner. He'd tried protesting, but she'd informed him that even he could grill hamburgers on the built-in barbecue in the corner of their patio. He'd tried pouting and complaining, but she'd stood firm. They'd made a quick trip to the grocery store for supplies, including an assortment of salads from the deli. So here he stood, getting together lettuce, onions and tomatoes, along with pickles and mustard.

The kitchen opened up onto the living room. Beyond that he could see Sabrina and his daughter on the patio. They were playing a board game. Although the sliding glass door was open, their voices didn't carry to him. Still, he enjoyed watching them together.

Anastasia continued to gain weight. Her face had filled out, and her eyes didn't look so huge and lost behind her glasses.

In a couple of more weeks, she would lose the gaunt appearance of an underfed child. She continued to tan. Just yesterday, he'd caught a couple of teenage boys giving her a second glance. Fortunately Sabrina had noticed his reaction and had pulled him into the car before he could walk over and tell them to leave his daughter alone. She was only twelve.

Cal washed the tomatoes. As much as he wanted to change things, he couldn't. His daughter was practically a teenager, and the trauma of her dating was only a few years away. He could already feel his hair turning gray.

The sound of laughter caught his attention. He glanced up. Sabrina and Anastasia bent toward each other. The setting sunlight glinted in their hair. His daughter was dark like him, but Sabrina's hair glowed like fire. She tossed her head and flame-colored strands danced against the back of her neck.

Without wanting to, he remembered the feel of that skin against his hand. He'd touched her there, the night he'd kissed her. He'd stroked the softness, had experienced the warmth.

He told himself not to go there, but in the past two days, he hadn't been able to think about much else. What had started out as an impulsive, maybe even friendly kiss, had turned into something very different. Before he'd done it, he'd never really thought about kissing Sabrina. She wasn't that kind of woman, at least not to him. But when she'd been so close and he'd inhaled the scent of her body, something had happened. Something he couldn't explain but that he would very much like to repeat.

Sabrina. Who would have thought she could store all that passion inside and he would never have known? Once he'd gotten the idea to kiss her, he'd thought he might enjoy it, but he hadn't expected to be blown away.

Thoughts of kissing led to other thoughts…of things like making love with her. They'd fit so well together. That had surprised him. He'd liked how she felt in his arms and the way her body had pressed up against his. He'd enjoyed the taste of her, the need he'd felt, the explosion that had nearly flared out of control. He couldn't remember the last time a woman had made him want to lose control.

Anastasia said something and Sabrina laughed again. He smiled as he watched the familiar crinkles appear at the corners of her eyes. He'd known Sabrina for years and he'd never suspected the truth about her. In his mind, she'd been a friend, an employee, someone he could work with, respect and even like. But desire? He shook his head. She wasn't his type. No obvious beauty, no flash. Just a quietly attractive, very special woman.

He wanted her. He wanted her in his bed, naked and willing. He wanted to know if there was the same magic between them as there had been when they'd kissed. Even though he knew better. He knew what happened when he went after a woman. He wanted her until he caught her. Once he'd won the chase, he was no longer interested in the prey.

He couldn't afford that with Sabrina. She was too important to him. He didn't want to have to worry about getting rid of her or having to replace her. For one thing, she was damn good at her job. For another, he would miss her. So, for the sake of his business, their friendship and his daughter, he would keep it platonic.

Which meant no more kissing.

He sliced the tomatoes and placed them on a plate, then dried off the lettuce and tore it into hamburger-size pieces. When everything else was ready and on the table, he returned to the refrigerator and reached for the hamburger patties. Of course there were going to be regrets, he thought. He regretted that he couldn't find out if they would be as good together as he imagined.

He was halfway across the kitchen when the realization hit him. The answer was so incredibly simple he didn't know why he hadn't thought of it before. It was true that he was more interested in the "getting" than the "having" where women were concerned. But he already knew and liked Sabrina. So once he had her and lost interest, all that would change was that he wouldn't want her in his bed. He would still need and trust her as both an employee and a friend. Their relationship would return to its pre-kiss uncomplicated state and his curiosity would be satisfied. The perfect solution. All he had to do was seduce Sabrina into agreeing with his plan. Fortunately, seduction was something he was very good at.

"But I don't want to," Anastasia whined the next afternoon.

Sabrina told herself to stay patient, that the girl was just reacting to the unfamiliar, but her patience was being stretched thin. What she wanted to say was "Shut up. We're doing this so you'll have a good time and enjoy life, but if you want to go sulk in your own room, fine." Instead, she smiled brightly.

"Anastasia, in-line skating is a lot of fun. You're going to like it. The beach is a great place to learn. When we get back to Houston, you'll be able to do it there, too, because it's practically the flattest city on the planet. I've seen tons of kids your age in-line skating all over. You'll be able to meet them and hang out."

Anastasia looked around at the boardwalk. They were outside a rental shop. It was midweek, so the skate-bike-people traffic wasn't too bad. "I'm not good at this kind of stuff. I'm gonna fall."

Cal plopped down on the bench next to his daughter. "Hey, kid, there's plenty of padding. You might end up with a bruise or two, but it'll still be fun." He leaned close and wrapped his arm around her shoulders. "Look at it this way. Sabrina and I are way older than you and we can both blade. You're young and athletic. Once you've picked up the sport, you'll be skating circles around us. Isn't that worth a couple hours of looking awkward and silly?"

The girl shrugged. "I guess."

"I guess," Cal mocked. "There's enthusiasm. I don't know, Sabrina. What do you think? Should we just lock her in the car while we go have a good time without her?"

Sabrina pretended to consider the suggestion, then shook her head. "No, let's give her a chance."

Hearing Cal teasing his daughter and watching him smile was enough to blow away her ill-temper. It wasn't Anastasia's fault, she reminded herself. She, Sabrina, had been out of sorts ever since the kiss.

She followed father and daughter into the rental shop. Telling herself it had just been a kiss didn't seem to be helping. No matter how many times she thought she'd put it into perspective, it just kept coming back. At night, before she fell asleep, she relived the moment. At odd times during the day, when Cal smiled at her, or accidently touched her, she thought about it again. To make matters worse, he seemed to be touching her a lot. It was starting to drive her crazy. Because when she thought about the kiss for very long, it was too easy to think about other things, like touching him back all over— and having him kiss her on places other than her lips.

They rented skates for the three of them, then went outside. Cal helped Anastasia into her gear while Sabrina slipped on hers. She hadn't been skating in a while, and the narrow wheels felt awkward. But after a couple of minutes, she was able to glide up and down the boardwalk.

"See," Cal said, pointing. "She's kinda old and she can do it."

Anastasia giggled. Sabrina gave him a mock glare. "'Kinda old'? I don't think so. Anyway, if I'm kinda old, what does that make you? A fossil?"

"I'm a man in my prime. Everyone knows women don't age as well."

"Hit him!" Sabrina commanded. "Hit him, then hold him until I can get there."

Anastasia laughed out loud. Sabrina skated toward them. Cal easily sidestepped her, caught her hand as she came around and pulled her close. He hadn't bothered with his skates yet, so she was nearly at eye level.

"I could take you out with one punch," she told him.

"You and what army?"

Amusement glinted in his brown eyes, amusement and something that called to her. Desire? That's what she wanted it to be, but she wasn't sure.

"Should I try to stand?" Anastasia asked, breaking the mood.

"It's a good place to start," Cal said, releasing Sabrina and moving to his daughter's side.

She rose to her feet and wobbled back and forth. Cal put his arm out and let her steady herself by holding on to him.

"Why don't you show her what to do," Cal said, glancing at Sabrina and smiling.

It didn't mean anything, she reminded herself. They'd always worked well as a team. That's all this was. Teamwork to help his daughter.

"In in-line skating, the key is to keep your center of gravity as low as possible," Sabrina said. "So skate with your knees bent. When you feel yourself losing your balance, the instinct is to reach up and back. That's just going to ensure that you fall. Instead, drop into a crouch and bend forward."

She demonstrated the action.

"That's important to remember," Cal said. "You've got knee pads, elbow and wrist guards. If you fall forward, you're protected. If you fall backward, you're going to get bruised."

Anastasia looked doubtful but took a tentative step forward.

"Glide," Sabrina instructed. "Push out to the side, not forward."

"Come on, you can do it," Cal told his daughter. "I'll stay right with you."

It was a perfect summer afternoon, with the sky clear and the ocean sparkling just beyond the beach. Not that many people were out and they had a lot of room to practice. Anastasia was slow and off balance, but she managed to skate a few feet without holding on to her dad's arm.

She was tall and thin, still awkward, but Sabrina saw the hint of elegance in her carriage and facial bone structure. In just a couple of years, she was going to be a beauty. She was bright, sometimes too bright, and she was a survivor. All in all, Cal had done well with his daughter, and the young girl had gotten lucky with her father.

In the past few days, they'd started making peace with each other. They still had a lot of things to work out, and Anastasia wasn't going to be an easy teenager at times, but Sabrina knew they would form a bond that would last them forever. The love would be more precious for having been hard won.

When Anastasia could skate about a block without wobbling too badly, Cal put on his rented skates and joined them.

"Race you to the ice cream store," he said, pointing to a bright pink building up about two blocks away. "Winner has to buy."

"There's motivation not to win," Sabrina said, and laughed.

"You know I'm going to buy, anyway," he told her. "Where's your competitive spirit?"

"In my suitcase." She eyed his easy grace on the skates. While she could hold her own on a straight path, she wasn't the least bit athletic. Cal, on the other hand, could skate backward, do crossover turns and had, a few years before, spent a summer playing in a roller hockey league. His constant travel had forced him to drop out.

A warm breeze caressed them. Sabrina inhaled the scent

of salt air and ocean and knew that whatever happened she would remember this time with Cal and his daughter.

"Dad!" Anastasia called as she realized the boardwalk had taken a slight dip and she was moving faster than was comfortable. "Help me."

Cal stood frozen in place, his expression wide with shock. "Catch her," Sabrina told him, and gave him a little push in his daughter's direction. She knew exactly why he was so stunned. She felt herself tearing up slightly as Anastasia plowed into her father.

The preteen probably didn't realize what she'd said, and if she did, she might get scared and embarrassed, only to retreat into sullen silence or rudeness. But she and Cal had heard it, had heard his daughter call him "Dad" for the first time.

Cal wrapped his arms around the girl. "Good going," he said, his voice gruff. "You're doing really well."

"Think so? It's fun. A little strange, but fun. Back in Ohio, a few kids had skates, but not that many. They're kind of expensive, aren't they?" She sounded wistful.

"If you want to start skating, I think we might be able to buy you a pair," he said. "I like skating. It could be something we do together."

Brown eyes met brown eyes. They were both a little scared, both wanting to reach out but terrified of rejection. Sabrina held her breath.

"Okay," Anastasia said shyly. "Can I get pink ones?"

Cal gave her a hug. "Sure. The brightest pink they have in the store. Maybe Day-Glo so you can put them on your bookshelf in your room and read by them instead of a lamp."

His daughter giggled.

"Now, what about that ice cream?" Cal asked. He looked at Sabrina. "I'll give you a head start."

"Five minutes," she called, and started skating.

"No way. A minute." His voice carried on the wind.

"Two," she yelled back, but it was too late. She heard Cal starting out behind her. His stride was long and powerful and she knew she didn't have a chance.

"Dad, wait," Anastasia said, unable to keep up.

Sabrina glanced over her shoulder and winked. "Yeah, *Dad,* wait for your daughter."

He shrugged. "Can I help that I'm a sucker for the kid?"

"No, and I'm glad you can't."

"You're just excited about winning." With that he slowed and waited until Anastasia caught up with him.

Sabrina didn't bother racing ahead. She would rather they went together, so they moved up the boardwalk at the preteen's slightly awkward pace. On the way, they passed a couple of kids throwing a baseball back and forth.

Cal stared at them for a second. "You like baseball?" he asked. "There are two local pro teams here. One down here in Orange County, the other up in Los Angeles. I bet we could get tickets to a game."

They reached the ice cream stand. Anastasia sank onto a bench out front and sighed. "I've never been to a game. Is it fun?"

"You bet. There's hot dogs and peanuts still in the shell. This guy walks around the stand and tosses them to you."

Sabrina chuckled. "The game is fun, too."

"Oh, that," Cal said. "So you want to go?"

"Sure."

The girl smiled, and Sabrina realized for the first time that she'd inherited her smile from her father.

"Great. Okay, what flavor ice cream?" Cal asked as he fished some bills out of his shorts pocket and started for the shop. "Sabrina, I know you like rocky road. On a cone, right?"

She nodded.

"Anastasia?"

"Chocolate, on a cone, too, please."

Sabrina raised her eyebrows. Please? That was a new one. Apparently the message about trying to be pleasant to make things easier had gotten through.

Cal returned in a couple of minutes and handed each of them their cones. He perched on the bench between the two females, his long legs pressing against Sabrina's. His free hand casually rested on her thigh, as if he'd done that a thousand times. As if he had the right. The heat from his fingers burned her skin. She thought about protesting, but the truth was, she liked him touching her, even if she didn't understand why he was doing it.

She wanted him. Lord help her, she also loved him. It was a deadly combination, and she didn't see a way for her to win in this situation. The most she could hope for was to entice Cal to her bed. For years she'd known he never thought of her as more than an employee and maybe a friend. But something had changed. She wasn't overly experienced, but she knew that while he'd been kissing her, he'd wanted her. Since then she'd caught him looking at her in a way that led her to believe he'd been thinking about her and their shared kiss as much as she had.

But then what? He might come to her bed and make love with her, but that would be the end of it. She knew Cal. He was loyal and faithful while he was interested, and then it was over. She didn't delude herself into thinking she might be the one woman on the planet who could actually figure out how to keep him around. The last thing she needed was to get her heart broken by him. She also didn't want to be used as a stand-in mom for Anastasia.

She had to be strong, she told herself. But when Cal told her she had a smudge of ice cream on her cheek, then brushed her skin to supposedly wipe it off, being strong seemed incredibly overrated.

* * *

Sabrina read the page for the third time, then put down her book. She wasn't getting anywhere in the story, and this was a new release by her favorite author. But today she couldn't concentrate. The phone sat next to her on the end table and she stared at it longingly. She'd sent out feelers to the head-hunters and had initial phone interviews. Both had promised to be in touch with her soon. So why weren't they calling her back? She needed to find out if there were jobs available to her. She had to get out of here before Cal drove her crazy.

It wasn't fair, she thought as she rose to her feet and crossed to the window. Anastasia and Cal had gone sailing for the afternoon, but she'd begged off. Privately she'd told Cal it would be good for him to have some time alone with his daughter. However, that was only part of the truth. The other part was she couldn't take much more of his attention.

In the past week…the seven days since their kiss…he'd been incredibly attentive. He was always close to her, touching her, smiling at her, flirting with her and generally going out of his way to make her feel special. She hated it. She loved it. She was slowly going insane.

Every part of her body was on fire. She couldn't look at him without wanting him. She had hormones pumping out chemicals that were leaving her edgy, while the voice of reason in her head kept screaming out warnings. The situation was intolerable and unlikely to get better anytime soon. If only…

She leaned her forehead against the sliding glass door and stared at the ocean. If only things could be different. Isn't that how it always went? If only her parents hadn't died. If only she could have kept from falling in love with her boss. If only she knew what to do with the rest of her life.

"We're back!"

The words were punctuated by the slamming of the door

that led in from the garage. Sabrina quickly returned to the sofa and picked up her book. She forced herself to smile brightly. "Did you two have a good time?"

Cal flopped next to her on the sofa. "Great. The kid's a natural on the water."

Anastasia glowed. "I *love* sailing. Dad let me steer the boat and everything. We were going really fast and we tacked around this big cabin cruiser, but we're the sailboat so he had to give us the right of way and it was so cool!" She headed for the kitchen. "I'm going to get some water. Anybody else want anything?"

Sabrina tried to ignore Cal as he put his arm around her. "No, thanks," she said. His thumb brushed against her neck, the slow stroking igniting a passionate fire deep in her belly. "So you had fun?" she asked brightly.

"Uh-huh. She's really changed. I think she's starting to trust me."

"Oh, she is. It's wonderful to watch the two of you bond." The simple sentence was tough to get out because Cal had leaned close to press his lips against her throat. Her breath caught. "I don't think that's a good idea," she murmured.

"Why not? You like it. I can feel your pulse fluttering." He moved so that his mouth hovered over the hollow where her heartbeat gave away her aroused state.

"Anastasia will be back any minute." She tore herself away and pushed to her feet. "The baseball game's tomorrow," she said loudly so the girl could hear her. "Are you looking forward to it?"

Cal reached for her, but Sabrina managed to sidestep him. Anastasia walked back into the room.

"Sure," she said. "I think it will be fun." She took a sip from her glass, then moved to the sofa and plopped down next to her father. "I'm tired."

Cal ruffled her bangs. "Me, too, kid. You wore me out."

Anastasia giggled.

Sabrina watched them. Her heart ached. Not just from wanting Cal and being confused by what he was doing, but also because she was a bit player in a story that would never include her. Cal and his daughter were forming a family unit. She would always be the hired help. No matter how much she wanted it to be otherwise, she knew the truth. So it was better for everyone that she move on.

Oh, but it was going to hurt to go. She'd been in love with Cal for years and was only now admitting it. Even if it only took half that time to get over him, it was going to be a long while before she would be able to look at another man and not wish he was Cal Langtry.

Chapter 11

The phone call came early. As Cal rolled over to grab the receiver, he glanced at the clock. It was barely after five. "Yes," he said.

"Hey, boss, it's Griffin. Sorry to wake you up, but we got a problem with the Atlas rig."

Cal came instantly awake. He sat up in bed. "Explosion?"

"No, there was a fire. No one's hurt bad, but there are some injuries. We've got containment on the leak. No environmental damage. The media team is already gearing up to answer questions and there will be an investigation. I thought you'd want to know, is all."

Cal rubbed his eyes. "I'll get a plane out this morning," he said. There was a direct flight from the Orange County airport to Houston in a few hours. "I'll phone the office once I'm on board and give them my exact arrival time. The helicopter can meet me at the airport. I'll be on the rig by this afternoon."

"Sorry, boss. I know you're on vacation."

"Accidents happen. Hang tight, Griffin. I'll see you soon."

After hanging up, Cal stood and stretched. So much for the plans they'd made for the day.

A faint knock made him look up. Sabrina stood in the doorway. "I heard the phone," she said. "Is everything all right?"

Her hair was all mussed and her eyes were heavy with sleep. She wore an oversize cotton T-shirt that fell to mid-thigh. As she moved toward him, he was mesmerized by the sway of her breasts.

"There's a problem with the Atlas rig."

"An explosion?"

"Just a fire."

"Okay." She moved to the desk in his bedroom and picked up a pad of paper. After taking a pen, she walked to the bed and sat down. "What do you want me to do?"

What he wanted was for her to lie back and let him take her in his arms, holding her close as he kissed her all over, then strip her of her T-shirt and slowly make love to her.

Casually, so she wouldn't guess that the combination of her scanty attire, appealing body and his wayward thoughts were causing an obvious and predictable reaction, he slipped on his robe. For one thing, there wasn't time. He had to be at the airport in less than an hour. For another—

"Dad?"

Anastasia had only been calling him that for a couple of days, and every time she did, he felt a jolt of happiness in his heart.

"I heard the phone."

"It's all right," he said, and walked over to give her a hug. "There are a few problems with work. There was a fire on an oil rig."

She looked up at him. "That's bad, huh?"

"Very bad. It sounds like we were lucky, but I have to go make sure." He released his daughter and turned to Sabrina. "Call the airlines and get me on the seven o'clock flight to Houston. Griffin is supposed to make sure the helicopter is waiting for me, but double-check with Ada. I'll want to go directly to the rig."

"You're leaving?" Anastasia's voice was filled with outrage. "You can't leave. We've going to the baseball game tonight."

Cal had forgotten. "I'm sorry to miss that, but I don't have a choice. I have a responsibility to the rig and my men. I have to be there to oversee everything. It's my job."

Her eyes filled with tears. "You were lying about everything. I don't matter at all."

"Anastasia, that's not right and you know it. I'll only be gone a couple of days. You and Sabrina can stay here and continue with your vacation. I'll be back before you know it," he said, but it was too late. She'd already run from the room.

Cal stared after her, torn between what he wanted to do and what he had to do. He glanced helplessly at Sabrina. She shrugged. "You're between a rock and a hard place, Cal. You're right about the rig. You *do* have a responsibility to your men. Unfortunately, the timing stinks. She's just starting to trust you, and from her point of view, you've just let her down. She'll understand in time."

"How much time?"

"I don't know. This is hard for both of you. But you'll get through it. I just wish I could go with you."

He'd known from the moment he received the phone call that Sabrina would have to stay with Anastasia, but he hadn't actually pictured himself making the trip without her. Except for a couple of vacations with girlfriends, Sabrina was always with him.

"I can manage on my own," he said lightly, knowing that what he was going to miss wasn't her efficiency, but her company.

"I know." She wrote a couple of more lines on the pad. "Okay, why don't you go shower and get dressed? In the meantime, I'll start the phone calls."

Twenty minutes later he walked into the kitchen to find Sabrina hanging up the phone. She looked up at him and smiled.

"You're all set. The 7:00 a.m. flight to Houston. First class, window seat. The cab is on its way to take you to the airport." She handed him a cup of coffee. "I spoke to Ada. The helicopter will be waiting when you get off the plane." She pointed to a carry-on bag. "I packed you enough for three days. That should do it."

She still wore that damn T-shirt and virtually nothing else. He wanted her. Worse, at this moment, he felt like he needed her. He who had never needed anyone. And not just in his bed. Straight desire would have been a whole lot easier. The problem was, there wasn't anyone else he would trust to take care of Anastasia. He could deal with this crisis knowing his daughter was in good hands.

He glanced toward the stairs.

"I know what you're thinking," Sabrina said. "She'll be fine."

"I hate leaving her like this."

"I know."

"I looked in on her, but she was asleep, or at least pretending to be," he said. "Tell her goodbye for me and that I'm sorry about the game."

"I will."

Had her eyes always been that blue? he wondered as he put down the coffee and stepped toward her. Her skin looked so incredibly soft, and he had the strongest urge to touch her.

She swallowed. "Cal, the cab will be here in a couple of minutes."

"I know."

"I like working for you and I really don't want to—"

He pressed his mouth to hers. If she'd resisted, he would have stopped. Instead, she sighed and cupped his face. Her lips parted. He slipped his tongue inside, rediscovering the pleasure. Need mounted.

He rested his hands on her hips. Below the T-shirt, she wore

panties and nothing else. Her breasts pressed into his chest. His groin tightened. He wanted her. Why hadn't he seen that before? How could he have worked with her all these years and not know?

Her arms came around him and she pulled him close. He angled his head so he could deepen the kiss. A faint sound distracted him. It was repeated.

She broke away. "The cab is here."

He cupped her cheek. "Take care of yourself. I'll call when I can."

She nodded.

He wanted to say something else, something significant that would let her know that even though he was leaving without her, she would be on his mind. But it was time to go and he couldn't find the words.

She walked him to the door. As the cab drove off, his last image was of Sabrina waving goodbye from the front porch of the rented beach house. An ache started in his chest. He had a bad feeling it wasn't going to go away until he was able to return to her.

Sabrina went upstairs to check on Anastasia. As Cal had suspected, the girl wasn't asleep. She sat up when Sabrina walked into the room.

"Is he gone?" she asked, her voice sullen.

"Yes, although you didn't give him much of a send-off."

The girl shrugged. "He doesn't care. He promised to take me to the baseball game and he left, anyway."

Sabrina looked at her, at the mussed hair and pouting mouth. She didn't know whether to shake her or hug her. "This isn't about a baseball game, is it? You know the two of us are still going to go."

Anastasia flopped back on the bed. "I don't care what we do."

"Yeah, right. Like I'm going to believe that." She sat on the edge of the bed and took the girl's right hand in hers. "You know he cares about you. Having him leave is disappointing for everyone, but he doesn't have a choice. There are times in life when people have to take care of their responsibilities, even if they would rather be doing something else. You're old enough to know that."

Dark eyes met her gaze. "I know," she whispered. "It's just—" A single tear trickled down her temple.

Sabrina squeezed her fingers. "Oh, honey, why are you making this so hard? Cal wants to love you and take care of you. Just believe him. Stop looking for trouble where it doesn't exist."

The tears flowed faster. "What if he doesn't miss me while he's gone? What if he decides he doesn't want me anymore?"

Sabrina caught her breath. So they'd finally gotten to the reason behind Anastasia's actions. She hated that the preteen girl had so many doubts. She was at an age when life should be fun for her.

She opened her arms. "Come here." The girl sat up and Sabrina hugged her tight. "You know that's not going to happen. He's your father. No matter what, he'll always be your father. Trust him just a little. I promise he won't let you down."

Anastasia nodded. "I'll try."

Sabrina held on for a few minutes, then released her and brushed away her tears. "I have an idea. How about you and I try to get some sleep? Then after we get up, we'll have a girl day. We'll get our hair done, play with makeup, have dinner out, then head over to the game. What do you think?"

She smiled shyly. "I'd like that."

"Me, too." Sabrina kissed her forehead. "Go back to sleep." She rose and walked to the door. She knew that finding another job was the right thing to do, but leaving was going

to be difficult. Before she'd just been worried about missing Cal, but now she had to worry about missing his daughter, as well.

Cal stretched out on the hotel room bed. It was late—too late to call—but he picked up the phone, anyway. The crisis was resolved and he would be heading back to California in the morning. His news could wait. Yet he needed to hear Sabrina's voice.

She answered on the third ring. "'Llo."

"I woke you."

He heard covers rustling, then she cleared her throat. "It's nearly one in the morning, of course you woke me. What did you expect?"

"I'm sorry. I should have waited."

"No, I wanted you to call. I turned off the other extension upstairs so you didn't wake Anastasia. How are you? How are things?"

He pictured her in that same T-shirt, lying on her back, the sheet pulled up to her shoulders. Ruffled hair, bare face, sleepy eyes. He got hard just thinking about it.

"I'm good. Everything is solved. We had a couple of mechanical problems, but the pumping is on schedule. The injuries were minor. The men are already out of the hospital. The other rigs are being checked, although I don't anticipate this happening again. I missed having you with me."

"Of course you did."

He heard the laughter in her voice and smiled. "I had to do all the work myself."

"Instead of having me at your beck and call. It must have been tough."

"I survived. Tell me about your day."

She chuckled. "You would have hated it. We went to a salon in one of the department stores and got the works. Hair, manicure, a new look with makeup."

Cal groaned. "You're right—I would have hated it. Hey, isn't she a little too young to be wearing makeup?"

"She's about the right age to start experimenting, and I don't think she'll be wearing it every day. But it was fun."

"My daughter is wearing makeup. Now I feel old."

"That's because you *are* old."

"Is this where I remind you that I sign your paychecks?"

"Actually, you don't. Franklin, your chief financial officer, signs the checks, or should I say, approves them to go into my bank account."

"You know what I mean."

Her voice was teasing. "Yes, boss, I know exactly what you meant. I wasn't, however, very impressed with the argument. Oh, I should warn you, Anastasia cut her hair."

"What?"

"Don't panic, she looks great. Actually it was her idea. We were both going to get a trim, but while we were waiting she looked through a few different books and picked out a couple of styles. We all talked about it and agreed on what would work. Her hair is shoulder length and she's got bangs. Actually her hair has a lot of curl and the shorter length shows that. She's already a beauty, Cal. You're going to have to fight off the boys with a stick."

"I'm happy to do it," he growled. "Makeup and a haircut. I've had my baby girl for all of three weeks and she's already growing up too fast. I don't think I like that." He shoved a couple of pillows behind his head to get more comfortable. It was late and he should let Sabrina get back to sleep, but he didn't want to hang up. Not yet. "Tell me about the game."

"It was fun. We beat them five to three. The seats were fabulous. We were close enough to admire the players' butts."

"Tell me you didn't actually discuss that with my daughter."

Sabrina laughed. "Of course not. She's too young to appreciate that sort of entertainment. But I did my share of looking, and let me tell you, it was very nice."

"Hmm." He didn't like that, but he didn't feel he had the right to complain. Sabrina was his employee and friend, not his wife. She was allowed to look at all the butts she wanted, even though *he* only wanted her looking at his.

"We had hot dogs and peanuts, so we're full up with junk food. I'm sorry you had to miss it."

"Me, too. I'll make it up to you both, I promise."

"I know. Better, I think Anastasia knows it, too."

"Thanks for telling me that. You talked to her, didn't you?" he asked.

"Yes. She feels badly about what she did this morning. Sometimes she gets scared and acts without thinking. But she's better."

"I'm glad you're there with her. At least that part is familiar."

"I like her," Sabrina said. "She's a good kid. Although it was kind of strange to be left behind."

"I missed having you with me." He spoke without thinking, then realized it didn't matter. What he said was the truth. He *had* missed her.

"Oh, you did fine without me."

"That's not the point. I'm used to having you around."

He heard a faint sound, as if her breath had caught in her throat. He wanted to ask what she was thinking, but he didn't have the nerve. "I'm looking forward to being back with you both," he said, coming close to the point but still avoiding it.

"We're looking forward to having you back. Get some sleep, Cal. I'll check in the morning and get the flight information, then Anastasia and I will be there to meet your plane."

"I'd like that. Thanks, Sabrina. 'Night."

"'Night."

After they hung up, Cal got undressed, then climbed back into bed. As he lay in the darkness he found himself thinking about his daughter. He'd spent so much of his life avoiding romantic entanglements, yet here he was, taking responsibility for a child. There was no going back with Anastasia. He couldn't take a couple of months to figure out if he liked the situation, then change his mind. He'd made a commitment and he was going to keep it.

The concept should have terrified him, but it didn't. He found himself looking forward to having her be a part of his life. He wanted to watch her grow up and become an adult. His only regret was all the time he'd already missed.

From there his mind drifted to Sabrina. He missed her, too, but in a different way. He wanted her in his bed, next to him. He wanted to feel her passion, to touch her and kiss her. He wanted to see her face change as passion overtook her. He thought about what it would be like to wake up next to her. Not just once, but a couple of times. Maybe with her, once he had her, he wouldn't be so eager to let her go.

"I see you eyeing those balloons," Cal teased.

His daughter grinned. "No way. I'm too old." But her gaze followed the balloon vendor as he made his way through the crowd at the fair.

"We'll get you one on the way out," Cal promised. "Because there's no way it would survive that!" He pointed ahead, to the small roller coaster that promised a wild ride unlike any ever experienced before.

Sabrina looked at the rickety track. "You two go ahead, because I'm not sure my life insurance policy is paid up."

Cal made several clucking sounds. "You're afraid," he said. "Sabrina's nothing but a chicken."

"Call me all the names you'd like, but I'm going to sit right here." She pointed to a bench outside the entrance to the ride.

Anastasia grabbed his hand. "Come on, Dad. It'll be great."

He held back long enough to touch Sabrina's cheek. "Are you sure you'll be all right by yourself?"

She smiled. "I promise." She patted her stomach. "I know we stopped at that deli for lunch a couple of hours ago, but it hasn't been long enough for me. If I went on that, I would toss my cookies, as they say. It wouldn't be pleasant for anyone close. I don't mind waiting. Really."

"Da-ad!"

"I'm coming, I'm coming," he told his daughter. "See you soon."

Sabrina nodded as he was led away.

Twenty minutes later, he and Anastasia were soaring to the top of the track. From there he could make out the whole fairground. As it was midweek, the crowds weren't too large. They'd already been on most of the rides. Then the car slipped over the top of the track and everyone started to scream. He grinned.

"What do you think about going to the exhibit booths?" he asked as he and Anastasia caught up with Sabrina. She handed them each a paper cone topped by a football-size serving of cotton candy.

"Sounds great," she said, and swiped a handful of the sticky confection.

"Sure," his daughter agreed. "I don't care what we do. This is fun."

Cal put his arms around the two females. Both moved closer to him. This was what he wanted, he realized, recognizing contentment, probably for the first time in his life. It wasn't flashy or something a lot of his friends or even his mother would understand, but it made sense to him. Anastasia and he had talked when he'd returned from his trip yesterday. She'd apologized for acting so badly, and he'd taken the time to explain why sometimes business would get in the way of their plans.

With Sabrina there'd been less to say. She understood about business because she was usually a part of it. What he couldn't tell her, or confess, was the thoughts he'd been having. Even today, at the fair, he felt like a kid on his first date. He'd found excuses to touch her and be close to her. A couple of times he'd even taken her hand and been thrilled when she hadn't pulled back.

Sabrina swiped another bit of the candy, then turned away. "Oh, look, a booth for frozen bananas."

"You're going to make yourself sick eating all this," he warned.

"I don't care. I don't get out to places like this much anymore. When I was growing up, we always went to the county fair and I loved it."

"You should see the Texas State Fair," Cal said. "It's huge."

"Yeah, yeah, everything is bigger in Texas. I keep hearing that, but have seen little proof."

"Is everything bigger there?" Anastasia asked.

"Well, little lady," Cal drawled. "I've been fixin' to talk to you about that."

His daughter giggled. "You talk funny. It's that accent. Kinda like a hick."

"A hick?" He pretended outrage and attacked her, tickling her and making her squirm and squeal.

"Daddy, no, stop!" She thrust her candy at Sabrina, then used her free hands to push him away. "Stop tickling me. I'm not really ticklish."

Cal swooped her up and hugged her. "Yeah, brat, I can tell."

She wrapped her arms around his neck and squeezed. Cal felt an answering tightness in his chest, as if a band had just bound his heart. This young girl meant the world to him.

He turned and caught Sabrina's gaze. She smiled. "I told you so," she murmured.

She'd been right. About how wonderful it was to love a child.

Later, on the drive home, Anastasia fell asleep in the back seat. Cal checked on her in the rearview mirror, then reached over and took Sabrina's hand in his.

"I had a great time today," he said.

"Me, too. Coming to the fair was a lot of fun. I know Anastasia enjoyed it, and I'm sure it went a long way toward making up for your missing the baseball game."

"Sabrina…" His voice trailed off as he tried to figure out what to say. He wanted to invite her into his bed, or get an invitation into hers. "You've really helped me out these past few weeks and I'm grateful."

She gave him a quick smile. "No problem."

He cursed silently. *Smooth, Langtry, really smooth. You're making her sound like a housekeeper, not a lover.* "What I meant is—"

She pulled her hand free and rolled down the window.

"What's wrong?" he asked.

She shook her head. "I don't know. I don't feel that great. Are we almost back to the beach house?"

"Sure. About five more minutes."

"Good." She sucked in a deep breath.

Cal glanced at her as he drove down the dark streets. It was nearly ten and there wasn't that much traffic. As they neared the house, Sabrina moaned softly.

"I don't think I'm going to make it."

"Sabrina?"

She waved a hand at him. "Just drive. Please. Oh, God."

He pulled into the driveway and hit the button to release the garage door opener. She opened the passenger door and bolted for the house. Before he could go after her, Anastasia sat up.

"Daddy, I don't feel very good."

"Hold on, kitten, we're nearly there." He drove the car inside and turned off the engine. When he glanced back at his daughter, he was shocked to see her face was pale and coated with perspiration.

"I'm gonna be sick," she mumbled, then stepped out of the car.

She made it as far as the trash can before throwing up.

Chapter 12

Cal hovered outside the bathroom door. He listened to the sound of running water. When it stopped, he tapped lightly.

"Sabrina? Are you all right?"

He heard a muffled groan. "No. Go away. I want to die in peace."

"I don't think you're going to die, I think you have food poisoning. Anastasia has it, too. She's been throwing up and feels pretty bad. As far as I can remember, the only thing you two ate that I didn't was the potato salad we got from the deli. I guess it had been left out too long."

"I guess."

He heard a thud. "Sabrina? What's going on?"

"Nothing. I'm just sitting here on the floor waiting until the next time I have to puke my guts out. Or deal with whatever is left in my system leaving the other way. I know, I know, more information than you wanted. Go worry about your daughter. I'll die quietly. Tell my family I want a simple funeral and I don't want them wearing black."

"How about a catered lunch?"

"Oh, God, don't mention food."

"Sorry." He pressed his hand against the door. "When you feel better, let me know and I'll get you something to drink. I don't want you getting dehydrated."

"Just go check on Anastasia, Cal. I have to be sick now and I'd like to do that in private."

"I'll be back."

"I'll try to get excited about that fact."

He moved down the hall and into his daughter's room. She lay on the bed, her face pale, her eyes dark with suffering. "Daddy, I feel terrible."

"I know, honey. You've got food poisoning. It'll take a few hours, then the bad food will be gone and you'll start to perk up." He pointed to the glass of water on her nightstand. "Have you been drinking?"

She shook her head. "It's too hard."

"Anastasia." He sat next to her and pulled her into his arms. She leaned against him, her body limp and trusting. "Come on. Just a couple of sips. Okay?"

She nodded.

He held the glass and she sipped. When she was done, she pushed it away and leaned her head against his chest. He put down the drink.

"You're going to be fine," he promised as he got more comfortable on the bed and stroked her hair.

"How come you're not sick?"

"I didn't eat what you did. Which is good. Someone has to take care of you two."

"Sabrina got it, too?"

"Uh-huh. Right now she's in the bathroom threatening to die."

Anastasia raised her head and looked at him. Her expression turned stricken. Cal instantly realized his mistake. He kissed her forehead. "Sorry, honey. That was a stupid thing to say. Sabrina's fine. She's not going to die. She feels pretty bad right now, but in a couple of hours, she'll be able to get some sleep, and by morning, it will all be over. I promise."

"I don't want her to die."

"I know. I'm sorry I said that. It was supposed to be funny."

She nodded. "I don't want you to die, either."

"I'm not going to."

"Promise?"

He made an *X* on his chest. "I'll do everything I can to stay alive so I can be with you. We have a lot of time to make up for."

Anastasia rubbed her eyes and looked at him. "Am I bad for liking you?"

"No. Of course not. Why would you think that?"

"I just—" She shrugged. "My other parents. I still miss them so much, and I want them to come back, but I know they're really gone forever." Her brown eyes filled with tears.

He cupped her face and brushed away the tears. "Anastasia, you've had more than your share of heartache, haven't you? You're confused about all of this and I can't blame you. I'm the grown-up and I get confused, too. Your parents, the ones who adopted you, will always be your Mom and Dad. You love them." He touched the spot just below the hollow in her throat. "They'll live in your heart."

"Sometimes it's hard to remember them."

"Do you have a picture of them?"

"Yeah. Two."

He stuffed the second pillow behind his head. "Do you like looking at the photos?"

She nodded.

"Then keep them out on your dresser. I won't mind. I want

you to remember them. When you're feeling better, I'd like you to tell me about them. They took care of you when I didn't know about you. I'm grateful that they were good people and that they loved you. That's what I would have wanted if I couldn't have been there myself. I'm glad you love them."

She glanced at him. "Sabrina says it's okay to love lots of people."

"That's true."

"They won't be mad?" she asked in a whisper.

"If there's a little girl in heaven with no one to look after her, will you be mad if they take care of her for a while?"

Anastasia thought about that one. "They'll still love me, right?"

"Of course."

"Then I wouldn't mind. It's scary to be alone."

Cal thought about his life. He knew that demon personally. "You're not alone anymore."

Anastasia rested her head on his shoulder. "I know, Daddy. I have you and I have Sabrina."

He stroked her back. Somehow he'd gotten lucky with his daughter. He didn't know what he'd done to deserve having her in his life, but he was damn grateful she'd shown up.

She sat up suddenly. "Daddy, I'm gonna be sick again."

"All right, honey. I'll carry you to the bathroom."

But as he reached for her, he was too late. Anastasia threw up over him, the sheets, the blankets and herself. When she was finished, she burst into tears.

"It's no big deal," he said, and picked her up. After carrying her into the bathroom and leaving her with orders to get out of her dirty clothes and put on a clean nightgown, he stripped off his shirt and snagged another before returning to her bedroom. It was a mess. He glanced at the clock. Nearly nine. He had a feeling it was going to be a long night.

* * *

Cal finished filling the dishwasher. There were bowls from the soup he'd made for Anastasia and Sabrina, not to mention plates from toast and pots from his own food. It was nearly three in the afternoon. As he'd suspected, he hadn't gotten a lot of sleep the night before. Anastasia had made steady trips to the bathroom, although after that one accident, she'd managed to make it on time. Sabrina had retreated to her bedroom about midnight and, to the best of his knowledge, was feeling better. She'd spent the morning lying low.

When he'd finished in the kitchen, he went upstairs to check on his daughter. Anastasia lay curled up on her side, asleep. She'd taken a shower early that afternoon and had asked him to change the sheets. Which reminded him—they were still in the washer.

On the way to the laundry room, the phone rang. He picked up the receiver. "Hello?"

"Mr. Langtry, good afternoon. This is Ada, Sabrina's assistant. I hope I'm not interrupting."

"Not at all." Cal carried the remote into the laundry room off the garage. He moved the wet sheets from the washer to the dryer and pressed the Start button. "What can I do for you, Ada? Is there another crisis?"

He grimaced. If there was, this time he was going to have to get someone else to take care of it. He needed to be here.

"Not really."

He frowned. "Ada, something's wrong. I can hear it in your voice."

She cleared her throat. "Nothing's wrong. It's just…" What he heard sounded suspiciously like a strangled laugh. "You received a phone call a few minutes ago. From a magazine editor. She didn't want to give me the information, but when I told her you were on vacation and couldn't be reached, she agreed to tell me what she wanted. I said I would relay the information to you so you could get in touch with them."

A suspicion arose in his mind but he refused to voice it. "What is it about this time?" he asked instead, hoping it wasn't what he was afraid it was.

"It's certainly unique. Are you familiar with *Prominence Magazine?*"

"Of course." Damn, he'd forgotten all about them and their silly World's Most Eligible Bachelor story. "But I don't think I'm their style." It was true—at that very moment, he felt anything but "eligible."

"On the contrary, Mr. Langtry," Ada continued, her amusement more evident now. "You appear to be exactly their style. You see, they're doing a year-long series of articles on, well, bachelors. The world's most eligible bachelors, to be exact. And you're one of the twelve."

Cal tried not to sound annoyed...or embarrassed. "Just my luck. I was hoping they would forget all about me."

"You knew?" Ada's surprise overwhelmed her amusement for just a moment. "But I just got the information now. How did you know?"

"They contacted me a couple of weeks ago. When I called to tell them I wasn't interested, the editor somehow convinced me to do an interview."

"And a photo shoot."

"They want pictures?" Cal didn't think it could get much worse.

"Yes, sir. I understand there's going to be a large spread in each issue. I think you're Mr. June!"

He swore under his breath. Mr. June? He didn't want to think about the board's reaction to any of this. They would tease him for months.

"Anything else?" he asked.

"No, that's it."

"Go ahead and e-mail me the info, so I can access it later. I'll call them in a few days. Thanks for letting me know."

"Mr. Langtry, it was my pleasure."

He thought about how quickly word would spread in the office. "I'll just bet it was," he said, and couldn't help smiling ruefully. If this were happening to anyone but him, he would get a big kick out of it, too.

He returned the remote to its base, then climbed the stairs to check on his daughter. She was still sleeping soundly. So far she hadn't been sick that day and she was keeping down fluids, so she seemed to be on the mend. He made his way to Sabrina's room and knocked on the door.

"Come in," she called.

He stepped inside. She sat up in bed, reading a book. She, too, had showered earlier that afternoon. She wore a different oversize T-shirt and no makeup. In the afternoon light, she looked younger.

"How do you feel?" he asked.

"A lot better."

He motioned to the tray on the dresser. She'd finished off a large bowl of soup and some toast. "You're eating well. If I didn't know better, I would say you've been faking it."

She fluttered her eyelashes. "Not me. Why would I want to do something like that?"

"Oh, I don't know," he said as he settled on the edge of her bed. "Maybe to force me to take care of Anastasia so we could bond some more."

"What a clever idea," she said, still all innocence. "But you're giving me way too much credit. I wish I'd thought of that, but I didn't."

He leaned forward and touched his index finger to her nose. "Liar."

"Me? Lie? Never. I might not have been as sick as Anastasia, and I'll admit that I've stayed in bed even though I'm probably well enough to get up, but I didn't fake it." Her mouth twisted. "I spent way too much of last night barfing my guts up."

He winced. "There's an attractive visual. Thanks for sharing."

"Anytime. So how's it going?"

"Anastasia is fine. She's weak, but eating a little, and she's able to keep it down. Right now she's asleep." He cleared his throat. "Whether or not you planned it, we've bonded. We talked about her parents, the ones who adopted her. She's concerned about divided loyalties. I explained that it was okay to care about them and me." He frowned. "At least I tried to make that clear."

"Cal, I'm sure you did great. You have to trust yourself with this stuff. I'm really impressed with how well you're doing. You're a natural at being a dad."

He appreciated the confidence, even if he wasn't so sure it was deserved. There were still many things he didn't understand. "I like that she calls me that. Dad, I mean."

"I thought you might."

"It's strange how much that means to me."

She put her book aside and pulled her knees to her chest. "I don't think so. She's your daughter and you're learning to care about her. It's only natural you want her to care back. People tend to get nervous when they put their heart on the line, but the other person doesn't."

He knew what she meant. He had the same type of concerns with his relationship with her. Except he wasn't putting his heart on the line. Wanting wasn't the same as loving. But he did *care*. He'd always liked Sabrina.

As a friend, he reminded himself. Which was different from wanting her. Now he had both feelings to wrestle with. There didn't seem to be any easy answers.

"I haven't loved anyone in a long time," he admitted. "Not since Tracey and I were kids and I loved her."

"You love your parents," she told him.

"Maybe." He shrugged. "Probably. If you can love someone without forgiving them for what they've done."

"You mean keeping Janice's pregnancy from you?"

"That and letting Anastasia be adopted when Janice died. To me, that's unforgivable. I might reconsider if my mother showed any interest in her granddaughter, but I know that's never going to happen."

Sabrina looked unhappy. "I want to disagree with you, but I can't. I don't see her coming around, either. It's a difficult situation. The good news is that you have Anastasia with you now." She stretched. "Is there any news from the office?"

Cal thought about his call from Ada.

Sabrina raised her eyebrows. "Wow, what is it? I don't think I've ever seen that particular expression on your face before. An odd combination of embarrassment, resignation and—" She peered at him. "What's that last emotion? Amusement?"

"You look tired. I should let you get some rest."

He started to stand. Sabrina leaned forward and grabbed his arm, then pulled him back onto the bed. "No, you don't. Obviously this is very interesting, and I want you to start at the beginning. Tell me everything and speak slowly."

Cal hadn't minded when Ada had first mentioned that *Prominence Magazine* had called, but now, sitting next to Sabrina, he felt himself flushing. "It's nothing."

"You couldn't be more wrong." She shifted until she'd tucked her legs under her. "Come on, Cal. You can tell me anything. We don't have many secrets from each other."

He wondered what her secrets were. What did she think about that she didn't want him to know? A couple of weeks ago he would have said he didn't have any secrets from her. She knew the worst about him and still kept coming back, which was one of the reasons he liked her so much.

"Ada called," he admitted. "*Prominence Magazine* is trying to get in touch with me."

Sabrina clapped her hands together. "They want to do an article? That's great!"

He cleared his throat. "Not exactly."

"Then what?"

"Apparently they're doing a special series. The World's Most Eligible Bachelors or something like that. I've been chosen for one of the months. You know, sort of as the bachelor of the month."

Sabrina could be annoying, stubborn and argumentative, but she rarely disappointed him. This was no exception.

She stared at him blankly for two seconds, then started to laugh. "Bachelor of the month?" she asked, then continued laughing when he nodded.

The hearty chuckles filled the room. She clutched her stomach and rolled onto her side. "Oh, Cal."

He wrestled with mild annoyance. "What seems to be so funny? I'm wealthy, single, and there are those who think I'm decent-looking."

She could only gasp for air. "I can't stand it. Are they going to run a profile, complete with statistics and a post office box so you can get fan mail?"

"I don't know, but if you keep this up much longer, I'm going to make you answer all the fan mail and send back a picture with the response."

She coughed and raised herself up on one elbow. Her face was flushed, her eyes damp from tears. "Oh, my. I haven't laughed like that in far too long. I work for one of the world's most eligible bachelors, huh? So how have I managed to escape falling for your charms all these years?"

She'd been teasing him, so he teased her back. He touched her cheek. "I'm not so sure you have."

Instead of bursting out into more laughter, Sabrina froze. Her blue eyes widened as she stared at him. "I don't know what you're talking about."

But the disclaimer came too late. Her shock had been

genuine, as had the flash of guilt. She *had* kept secrets, and one of them was about him.

He didn't know what exactly she felt about him. For all he knew she'd wrestled with a crush for the first couple of days she'd worked for him but had recovered nicely. But he hoped it was more.

"Sabrina."

"No!"

She started to scramble off the bed. He caught her and pulled her against him.

"Wait. We need to talk about this," he said.

"There's nothing to say."

One of his hands rested on her hip. Her T-shirt had pulled up to her waist and he was touching the place where her silky panties ended and bare skin began. She pushed at his chest.

"Cal, I don't—"

"Yes, you do," he said, cutting her off. "We both do. We have for a while. I want to kiss you."

She shuddered as if he'd threatened her. Maybe he had.

"Sabrina, I—"

She cupped his face in her hands. "So do it."

"What?"

"Kiss me."

Chapter 13

There wasn't a doubt in her mind as to where this was heading. Sabrina wished she could find the backbone to be strong, to resist Cal and his passion, but it wasn't going to happen. At least not today. She'd wanted him—*loved him*—for far too long. She knew the pitfalls, the fact that he would quickly grow tired of her. She knew that he would break her heart without ever once having a clue as to her feelings. Maybe it was better for that to happen. At least when the time came, she would be motivated to leave. But for now…there was this moment and the magic she felt in his arms.

He kissed her gently, yet thoroughly, brushing his mouth back and forth against hers, as if he had to convince her to cooperate. She thought about pointing out the fact that kissing had been her idea to begin with, but that would mean speaking. She didn't want to do anything that would separate his mouth from hers. Not when keeping them joined felt so incredibly right.

She parted her lips in anticipation of him deepening the kiss, and he didn't disappoint her. His tongue moved inside, exploring, perhaps remembering. She met him, and they stroked each other. The sensations were more intense than she recalled. More perfect. This was Cal, this was who and what she'd always wanted. Even if she'd wanted to resist him, she no longer had that option.

In his effort to keep her from getting off the bed, he'd grabbed her and pulled her close. She straddled one of his thighs, his hands resting on her waist, hers clutching his shoulders. Her breasts hovered close to his chest without touching. She could feel her nipples getting hard, and that secret place between her legs getting wet.

"Sabrina," he murmured as he moved his hands up and down her back. "You are incredible."

The words washed over her like a caress. For today, for this moment, she would believe him, because she wanted to. She wasn't foolish, in fact she rarely did anything without weighing the consequences. So she was due for an afternoon of not thinking. While in his arms, she would only feel.

He raised his arms and used his right index finger to trace a line from her forehead, down her nose to her mouth. "Hold that thought," he said.

She stared at him. "What?"

"I need you to hold that thought. I want to go check on Anastasia to make sure she's asleep, and I want to get something from my room." His dark eyes burned with passion and intensity. "I know it's a risk leaving right now. Don't you dare change your mind."

Then he was gone. Sabrina stared after him. He'd left her? Just like that? She slid off the bed and started toward the door.

Some of the need and the desire faded. Maybe it was a good thing, she thought. Maybe she should come to her senses. This was her boss, after all. Yes, she was planning on quitting her job, but she hadn't yet. How was she supposed to face him tomorrow? As far as career planning went, this was *not* an intelligent move.

The half-closed door opened and Cal stepped back inside. He took one look at her face, crossed to her and pulled her hard against him. "Uh-oh, I knew it would be a mistake to leave you. Unfortunately, I didn't have a choice." He kissed her until she was once again weak in his arms. He slowly withdrew from the kiss and murmured, "The good news is Anastasia is fast asleep. We're also protected."

He pulled something out of his jeans pocket and tossed it on the nightstand. Sabrina looked at the small square package. He'd gone to get a condom.

She swallowed. Should she be pleased that he wanted to take care of her or horrified that she hadn't thought of that herself?

She pushed away from him and sank onto the edge of the bed. "I'm way too out of practice to be doing this with you."

Cal crouched in front of her. "What does that mean?"

He looked so handsome and so damned earnest. How was she supposed to resist him? His mouth was still damp from their kisses. She touched his lower lip and a thrill shot through her. Was it so wrong to want to make a few memories? Realistically she knew they were all she was going to be taking with her. Memories to get her through the night. Would she rather be able to look back on how it was once, knowing she could never have it again, or would she rather just wonder how it might have been?

She traced his eyebrows, then his mouth. He touched her finger with the tip of his tongue and she was lost. Better to know, she thought. Better to remember than to wonder.

She leaned forward and kissed him. Keeping his mouth firmly against hers, he rose to his feet, pulling her along with him. They pressed together from shoulders to thighs. He was strong and broad, all hard muscles and lean lines. His arousal lay against her stomach. Her throat tightened slightly as she leaned in a little more so she could feel all of that part of him. She loved knowing he wanted her. She still wasn't sure what had changed his mind or why he suddenly found her attractive, but the physical proof of his desire couldn't be ignored.

"Sweet Sabrina," he murmured against her mouth.

He cupped her head, then moved one hand down her back. On the return trip, he went under her T-shirt and stroked the bare skin at the small of her back. She shivered. Her whole body felt tingly, as if a million tiny bubbles floated through her bloodstream.

There were too many sensations. How wonderful he tasted. The warm, wet stroking of his tongue against hers. The ache of her breasts as they flattened against his chest. His strong fingers tracing an ever-smaller circle on her back, the dampness between her thighs, the hard ridge of his need. It was too much. It wasn't enough. She flexed her hips against him.

He broke the kiss, swore softly and pressed his forehead against hers. "When I was about sixteen or seventeen, I used to get into trouble when I kissed girls. About an hour of passionate making out and I would—" He shrugged. "Lose control. They didn't have to be touching me. It just happened."

Their breath mingled. His hands tugged at the hem of her shirt and she wanted him to just pull it off.

"I don't understand what that has to do with this."

He smiled. "Just that I'm in danger of that happening now. It's one thing at seventeen. It's quite another at thirty-four."

Dear Lord, she wanted to believe him. She wanted to think that she could turn him on that much. It wasn't true, of course. He was just being kind. But it was so sweet of him.

"Thank you," she whispered.

He glared at her. "Thank you? That wasn't a gift, Sabrina. It was the truth. I want you so damn much."

He clutched her upper arms and pulled her hard against him. His grip was nearly unforgiving and she grabbed him back, just as hard. Their kiss was intense, a sensual assault of lips and tongues. The passion built, as did the heat. A whimper caught in the back of her throat.

"Please," she managed to say against his mouth.

"I want you," he told her. "More than you can imagine."

He released her and jerked his shirt over his head with one strong, fluid motion.

Sabrina stared at his bare chest, at the dark hair forming an inverted triangle, at the sculpted beauty of his muscles. She'd seen his chest before, of course. But seeing it from a slight distance was very different from having it right in front of her. This time, she was allowed to touch.

She placed her hands on his shoulders and let his heat seep into her. Then she moved her hands down…slowly…very slowly. The hair was a cool and ticklish contrast to his skin. Muscles rippled under her touch. She stroked up a little, then continued the journey, pausing to let her fingertips trace tiny circles on his nipples.

Instantly the two points hardened. He caught his breath. "Is that what it feels like when you're touched there?" he asked.

She looked at him. "What do you mean?"

"It feels great. If I'd known what it was going to be like, I would have requested it sooner." At her continuing confusion he shrugged. "No one's ever touched me there…like that before."

Sabrina felt a thrill of satisfaction. She'd worried about measuring up to the other women is his life. She didn't consider herself ugly, but she wasn't an eighteen-year-old, either. Cal seemed to prefer spectacular women, and she was simply average.

But maybe it wasn't just about appearance. She had other things to offer, apparently things those women hadn't thought of.

She flicked her nail over the taut peaks. "So you like it."

"Yes, I—"

She bent forward and kissed him there, then stroked her tongue against his skin. He swore under his breath and jerked hard. "You're determined to make me embarrass myself, aren't you?"

"Of course not. Although I wouldn't mind if you did."

"No. I want this to be great for both of us."

He touched a finger to her chin and drew her upright. When she had straightened, he turned her gently until she had her back to him.

"Stay still, just like that," he murmured, then kissed the nape of her neck.

Shivers rippled down her spine, and goose bumps erupted on her arms. He moved to the curve by her ear, tracing it to the neckline of her T-shirt, then up to her jaw. His warm breath contrasted with the dampness his open-mouthed kisses left behind.

Strong hands rested on her hips. He moved them around and up, sliding from her waist to her ribs to her breasts. He hovered slightly below for a few seconds. She tensed in anticipation. Her breathing increased; she felt her nipples harden. The ache intensified. She *needed* him to touch her or she wouldn't survive.

"Cal," she breathed.

"What, lover?"

"I…"

"Tell me."

"I can't." She didn't dare say the words. What if he changed his mind?

"Tell me what you want. Or if that's too hard, show me."

He stepped closer and brushed his arousal against her derriere. "You have proof that I want you. I'd like to know the same."

At first she thought he was teasing. She spun toward him, determined to scold him for playing at a time like this. But when she saw his face, she knew he wasn't kidding. Doubt flickered in his eyes. The fire nearly hid it from view, but she knew him well enough to sense he was serious.

If he'd wanted to reassure her, he couldn't have picked a better way. Knowing that he was also a little nervous about the whole thing made her own self-doubts much easier to bear.

"Is this different?" she asked. "Am I different from the other women?"

"Of course. They were just people I dated for a while. But you and I—" He shrugged. "I *like* you." As if liking was significant. Maybe it was.

"Oh, Cal, you are the most difficult man." She cupped his face and raised herself up on tiptoes so she could press a kiss to his mouth. "Yes, I want you. Better now?"

"Some." His expression turned wicked. "I'd like proof."

She thought about the hard points of her nipples. He could see them through the thin cotton of her T-shirt. But there was other, more graphic proof. Her panties had been wet from their first kiss. Did she dare?

This was, she reminded herself, Cal. She doubted there was anything she could do to shock him. They would have only this one time together. Maybe it was time to let go, to just experience the moment.

She took his hand in hers and drew it to her belly. She slid his fingers lower beneath her panties until he tangled in the red curls. She was wet and swollen. There was no way he could miss the signs of her arousal.

He didn't. When he touched her there, he sucked in his breath. "You feel great," he murmured, then lowered his mouth to hers.

While they kissed and his tongue brushed against hers, his fingers provided a sensual counterpoint below. He explored her, discovering secret places, the tiny bud of pleasure, the waiting heat that would soon welcome him. He dipped inside, going deep, then rubbed against the slick walls. He circled the swollen knot so gently and so perfectly she made a half cry, half moan in the back of her throat. Her thighs trembled, her knees buckled and she had to lean against him to keep standing.

He tore his mouth away. "I can't believe how much I want you," he said, then picked her up and set her on the bed.

Before she could lie back, he tugged her T-shirt over her head and pulled off her panties. She didn't have time to be embarrassed. Even as the first self-conscious thoughts formed, Cal was reaching for his belt. To be completely honest, she admitted she was far more interested in seeing him naked than she was concerned about him seeing her.

He kicked off his shoes, then pushed down his jeans and briefs in one quick movement. As he bent to pull them off completely, he also removed his socks.

And then he was naked. Tall, lean, powerful and very male. She reached for him. He grabbed her wrist. "You can't," he said. "I swear I'll explode if you touch me there."

She tilted her head and pretended genuine concern. "You know, Cal, I've read some articles and I understand there are some techniques that can be used to help with that problem."

He drew his dark eyebrows together. "I don't have a problem."

"I know it's difficult for a man to admit that everything isn't perfect in the bedroom, but sometimes—"

He lunged for her. She tried to scramble away, but he was quicker. Before she reached the far side of the bed, he had a hold of her ankle and was steadily pulling her back.

"Cal! No! Stop!" she said between giggles.

She tried to kick him, then realized they were both naked and she was exposing herself in ways she normally tried to avoid.

He knelt on the bed, flipped her over, then straddled her thighs. "So I have a problem, do I?"

The promise of retribution in his eyes made her squirm. "No. I don't know what I was thinking. You're perfect. Really."

"Uh-huh. Sure. You say that now."

He tickled her ribs. She wiggled and twisted, all the while laughing and trying to catch hold of his hands to make him stop.

"Cal—"

She had to gasp for breath. He grinned down at her. "You are so beautiful," he said.

The unexpected compliment took away the last of her air. She couldn't do anything when he encircled her wrists, raised her arms and pinned her hands above her head. Then she didn't care because he leaned over and kissed her.

"I have ultimate power," he said, moving his chest gently over her nipples and making her gasp with pleasure. "Say it, Sabrina."

He was laughing, but at that moment it was completely true. "You have ultimate power."

"I know." He released her hands and cupped her face. "But you have a lot of power, too."

"Just not ultimate?"

"Sorry, no."

She hadn't known it would be like this. That the teasing in their regular relationship would spill over into bed. That she would enjoy not just the lovemaking, but the connection.

"So, you *are* a natural redhead. I'd wondered."

She blinked while his comment sank in. Then she felt herself blushing hotly. "Cal!"

He flashed her another wicked grin, then lowered his head to her left breast. As his mouth closed over her nipple, she sighed. If him thinking he had ultimate power meant she got to feel this good, she didn't mind at all.

His mouth was wet and warm as he caressed her. He moved his hand to touch her other breast, his fingers mimicking the movement of his tongue. He flicked over the taut bud and she felt the fire shoot down to her thighs. She arched into him. In response, he began to move his hips. As he still straddled her thighs, that most male part of him rubbed against her nest of curls. Close, but not touching that most sacred place, the contact aroused and frustrated in equal measures.

She rolled her head from side to side, not sure how much of this she could stand. She ran her hands up and down his back, then wove her fingers through the silky strands of his hair. She could feel herself getting more and more wet as her body prepared itself for the ultimate release.

He raised his head and looked at her. Passion darkened his eyes. "I want you," he said. "All of you."

"Yes, Cal. I want that, too."

He shifted off of her, urged her to part her legs, then knelt between them. He put his hands on her ankles and slowly slid his fingers up, taking his time, making her wait. The slow, sensual stroking made her quiver inside. She clutched at the blankets and held back a whimper.

When he'd completed the journey, he brushed his thumbs against her curls. As he had just a few minutes before, he touched close, but not *there*. She thought she might die from needing him so much.

"Sabrina," he murmured, then lowered his head. He pressed a kiss to her belly. His thumbs parted the delicate folds of her femininity, exposing her to him, then he gave her the most intimate kiss of all.

The first touch of his tongue nearly drove her off the mattress. She drew her heels toward her rear and bent her knees.

Every muscle tensed. He circled the special spot, getting close, but not pressing directly on it. Tension increased, as did her breathing.

A part of her disconnected enough to look at the situation. She'd always wondered what Cal would be like in bed. After all, he was single, good-looking and rich. For most women, he would just have to show up and they would be happy. But he wasn't like that. He took his time pleasing her. She could tell he was experimenting with different touches, trying to see which she enjoyed the most.

She felt herself building toward release and she wanted to hold back. Not just because she was enjoying what he was doing, but also because she wasn't sure she was ready to let him witness her loss of control. There was something frightening about being that exposed to a man. No, she thought. There was something frightening about being that exposed to Cal. It was specifically about him. If she gave in—he would see her soul. After that, when he walked away, she would be in that much more pain. So maybe she wouldn't let herself go all the way. Maybe she would hold back.

As plans went, it was a good one…in theory. Then Cal turned his attention to the tiny button. He rubbed it lightly but quickly and she began to spiral out of control. When he gently inserted a finger and pressed up from the inside, as if to caress her from both sides, she lost the ability to reason, or remember why she was trying to hold back. There was only the magic she felt and the onward pressing for release.

When it flashed through her, she wasn't prepared. The exquisite pleasure captured her and flung her around, filling her, buffeting her, tossing her into the air, before letting her float gently back into reality. As her body stopped trembling and the soft cries died in her throat, she found herself in Cal's arms.

A thousand thoughts crowded in. She was embarrassed by

her vigorous reaction to what he'd done. If she'd had to come, couldn't she have done so quietly and with dignity? She wanted to know what he was thinking, and if he was turned on by what had happened, and she was really dying to know if he was still hard, but she didn't dare look.

He touched her mouth. "You are so amazing," he said quietly. "I felt so connected to you that I almost lost it."

As he spoke, she felt the nudging against her thigh that told her he was still aroused, and if the light in his eyes was anything to go by, more than ready to have his way with her.

"Thank you," she whispered.

He smiled. "No, Sabrina. Thank *you*."

He slipped on his protection, then moved back between her legs. She was slick, but he still stretched her as he entered her body. When he braced his hands on either side of her shoulders, she looked at him. He met her gaze and began to move.

It was something she'd never done before. She'd never made love while looking into the eyes of her partner. The intimacy terrified her, but she couldn't look away and she wasn't going to be the first one to close her eyes.

The pressure built, as did the promise of another release. Cal moved slowly at first, then faster, building a rhythm that matched their need. His expression tightened. She felt him getting closer. That knowledge drew her along with him and she clutched at him.

"I can't hold back," he breathed.

"I'm right with you."

He stiffened and moaned. "Sabrina!"

"Yes."

Her body convulsed around him, pulling him in. She drew her knees back and arched her hips, taking all of him.

And still they looked at each other. She saw the fire in his eyes, the moment of perfect pleasure, the easing of tension, the half smile of a satisfied male.

He rolled onto his side and pulled her against him. As he held her close, he stroked her back and her hair. She sighed in contentment.

"Who knew?" he asked, his voice low and lazy.

Who indeed, she thought.

Cal woke as the first hint of light appeared at the edge of the blinds. He glanced at the clock, but it was barely six, so there was no need to get up and return to his own bed just yet. He had a little time.

He shifted so that he could turn and watch Sabrina as she slept next to him. Her short red hair was mussed. The sheet and light blanket had slipped enough to expose one bare shoulder and her arm. She looked sexy and adorable and he found himself wanting her again.

Cal grinned. He had to admit, he'd impressed himself. A couple of times the first night wasn't that unusual. After all, it had been a while and he was with someone new. But sometime after midnight, when they'd been doing nothing more erotic than talking about business, he'd found himself hard and desperate for her. Fortunately, Sabrina hadn't taken much convincing.

In the privacy of his mind, he was willing to admit he'd been terrified. After they'd made love for the first time yesterday afternoon, he'd left her room. Anastasia joined them for dinner, although she and Sabrina hadn't had much to eat. But when his daughter retired for an early evening, Cal hadn't known what to do. He'd wanted to spend the night with Sabrina. Not just to make love with her, but to enjoy time with her, too.

He'd hovered in the hallway, not sure of his reception. He'd been thrilled when she'd opened her door to come looking for him.

They were good together, he thought, as he resisted the urge to stroke her face. He wanted to touch her, but she needed her sleep. He hadn't given her much chance for rest last night. And there would be plenty more time for them later.

He quietly got out of bed and reached for his clothes. After pulling on jeans, he made his way to his room where he showered and dressed. As he shaved, he thought about Sabrina and wondered when the familiar restlessness would strike. It usually happened right after he'd been with a woman. By the second or third time they were together, he was already fighting the need to get away.

But he didn't feel anything like that this morning. He only wanted to be with Sabrina more. He could imagine waking up next to her for a while. He put down the razor and rubbed his face. What did that mean? Was it different because he'd known her for so long? Because he already liked and respected her? Or was it something specifically about being with Sabrina? Chemistry? Or fate?

Three hours later he still didn't have any answers, but as Anastasia demanded something substantial for breakfast and Sabrina teased him about his coffee, he decided it didn't matter.

"I'm glad my two girls are feeling better," he said.

Anastasia had dressed in shorts and a T-shirt. Her shorter, wavy hair fluttered around her shoulders. It had only been a few weeks, but already she looked completely different from the malnourished waif they'd rescued.

"I feel great. Can we go in-line skating later? I think I'm getting better on the skates."

"You couldn't be getting worse," he teased.

Anastasia rolled her eyes. "Da-ad. I'm pretty good. Sabrina said so. And there are these two cute guys who always—"

Cal held up his hand. "You are twelve years old and you're not allowed to notice cute guys. Not until you're thirty. Understand?"

Sabrina chuckled. "Ignore him, kid. All fathers are like this. You're just gonna have to learn to deal with it."

Anastasia apparently chose to take her advice. "So can we, Dad?"

"Skating, yes. Guy noticing, no. How many pancakes?"

"Three for starters."

He turned his attention to Sabrina. She'd also showered and changed. Her shorts and T-shirt were similar to his daughter's, but his reaction to them was very different. While he thought Anastasia looked cute and stylish for a young girl, he thought Sabrina was about the sexiest creature he'd ever seen. Despite the mundane activity of preparing breakfast, he wanted her as much as he had before they'd made love.

"And you, young lady?"

"I'll start with a couple," she said, and touched her hand to her stomach. "I want to make sure I'm completely healed before I go showing off."

He wanted to be with her. On the beach, under the stars. He wanted—

"Let's go to Hawaii," he said without thinking.

Both females turned to look at him.

Cal shrugged. "Why not? It would be a real vacation. We'll get a bungalow on one of the islands." He looked at Anastasia. "You could learn to surf, we can go sailing. The weather is perfect. What do you say?"

"Oh, Dad, can we?"

"Sure." He turned to Sabrina. "You're quiet."

Her expression was unreadable and that made him nervous. "Cal, if you and Anastasia want to go, I think it's a great idea, but I'm afraid I can't join you."

He stared at her. What the hell was she talking about? "What do you mean? Of course you can join us." Didn't she want to be with him the way he wanted to be with her?

"I can't. I'm leaving." She looked away, but not before he caught the flash of guilt in her eyes. "It's just for a couple of days, but—"

"Leaving? You mean you want time off?" He knew he sounded stupid, but he couldn't help it. She'd never left before. If she wanted to visit her family, she did it while he was out of town. Did she want to get away from him?

"I have plenty of vacation time available," she snapped. "I'm taking a few days off. It's no big deal. I work for you, Cal, but you don't own me."

With that she stalked out of the room. Cal stared after her. He felt as if he'd been broadsided by a train. What had gone wrong?

"Daddy?" His daughter sounded shaken.

He gave her a quick hug. "I know, sweetie, but don't worry. I'll find out what's going on."

"You can fix it, can't you? You won't let Sabrina go away."

"I'll do the best I can." He kissed her head and wondered if he was about to let his daughter down.

Chapter 14

Sabrina crossed to the window in her room and figured she had about thirty seconds of privacy before Cal came barging in to demand an explanation. She supposed she could have handled the situation worse, although right now it was hard to imagine that. Why had she reacted so badly? Why hadn't she said, in a calm voice, that she was thinking of visiting her family, or any other of a dozen acceptable excuses. Instead, she'd gotten angry and reminded him that he didn't own her. Dear Lord, had she really said that?

The answer to that and several other difficult questions was about three feet behind her. She'd gone to the trouble to make the bed, but the act of smoothing the covers and making sure the bedspread was centered didn't do much to erase the memories of the night they'd spent together. She wasn't stupid, so it didn't take her long to figure out that she'd reacted so badly because she was still reeling from the impact of their lovemaking. For Cal it had been…she shook her head.

She didn't know what it had been to him. But for her, it had been a life-changing event. She knew that whatever happened, she would never love another man, or make love with another man, the way she'd loved and made love with him.

Talk about a sobering experience. Her life had been completely turned around, and for all she knew, he'd simply scratched an itch.

It had been more wonderful than she'd thought it could ever be. She hugged her arms to her chest and rested her forehead against the cool glass of the window. Even now, when her body was pleasantly sore from all that they'd done together, she still wanted him. In her heart, she knew that she would always want him. That same organ informed her that he would never feel the same way about her. Sometimes the truth was ugly, but that didn't make it any less valid.

"Sabrina?"

She hadn't heard him enter the room, and it took a conscious effort not to flinch when he spoke. His voice rippled over her like warm water.

"I shouldn't have blurted it out like that," she said. "I don't mean to be difficult, but the truth is, I do have a lot of vacation time and I would like to take off for a few days."

"This isn't about you needing time away, is it? It's about last night."

She sucked in a breath. Dear Lord, give her the courage... The half-formed prayer trailed off. No, she wasn't about to pray that she lied well. She was going to have to figure out how to do that all on her own.

She opened her eyes and turned to face him. It was worse and more difficult than she'd imagined. He looked so perfect this morning, all freshly showered and so damn masculine. She wanted to weep. Now that she knew the truth, it was going to be harder than ever to walk away. Now that she'd felt his strength, and his gentleness, now that she'd tasted him, had him taste her, now that she'd experienced the passion and the need and the magic. She didn't think she had the strength to leave. But she knew she didn't have the strength to stay and watch him grow tired of her, then turn his attention on someone else. She could suffer deeply and quickly, then get over it, or she could die a little each day.

It wasn't much of a choice.

"I was going to tell you later," she said. "Last night has nothing to do with it. I do need some time off. But not to visit my family."

He frowned. "You need to get away from me?"

She smiled. "Amazingly enough, Cal, this isn't about you at all. I got a phone call yesterday morning. Do you remember?"

He nodded.

"It was from someone in New York. A headhunter. He's set up a few interviews for me. That's where I'm going. To New York. I'm leaving the company."

Until she said the words, she hadn't been sure she was really going to go through with it. But as soon as she spoke, she knew she'd made the right decision. It would be so easy to stay and love Cal forever, to make the decision to die day by day until there was nothing left but an empty shell where a heart and soul had once lived. This was harder, but ultimately better.

Which didn't explain why she felt as if she were bleeding to death.

She'd thought about this moment a hundred times. She figured Anastasia would express sorrow, but Cal would just take it in stride. She'd pictured the moment, the quiet raising of one eyebrow, the faint smile. "I hate to see you go, but you have to do what's right. Are you sure there's nothing I can do to make you stay?" He would be disappointed, maybe even a bit uneasy about breaking in a new assistant—but he wouldn't be devastated. She'd schooled herself to accept *his* acceptance with equal, casual grace.

She hadn't expected the color to drain from his face or his expression to freeze. She hadn't expected him to glare at her accusingly. "You're leaving?"

His question put her on the defensive. "It was bound to happen. You can't have expected me to work for you forever."

He shoved his hands into his pockets and stared at her. His silence made her uneasy.

"It's not that I don't like my job," she said. "I do. I love the travel and the challenge. You're great to work for. But I need more. I need—"

"What? What do you need? Explain it to me."

She shrugged. "I don't know how to put it into words." Actually she did, but what made sense in her head had the chance of sounding stupid in real life. "The work is demanding." She held up a hand to keep him from interrupting. "I don't mind that. In fact I like it a lot. But I don't have any time left over for a personal life."

"You have days off. Evenings, too."

"When you travel, I go with you. When you want to work late, I'm there at the office. The only time I get to be on my own is when you're out on a date. If you're between women, we're together constantly. That has made it impossible for me to make friends and see them."

"You mean a man."

"I mean friends. My whole life revolves around you, Cal. I haven't minded. In fact, I still don't mind, but I need more."

"I see." But his tone told her he didn't see at all.

Sabrina was confused. If she didn't know better, she would say that Cal was hurt by what she was telling him. That didn't make sense. She'd hoped he would miss her, but this silent accusing reaction was unexpected.

"I've really enjoyed working for you. I've learned a lot, but it's time to move on."

"So you're leaving." It wasn't a question.

"Yes."

"And last night? That wasn't an attempt at a relationship, was it? You were interested in stud service."

She winced. "Cal, it wasn't like that."

He took a step toward her, then stopped. Fire flared in his eyes, but this time it came from anger and hurt, not passion. "It sure the hell wasn't for me. I don't know what you were thinking, though. 'Hey, I'm outta here so let's screw the boss once, just so I can say I did.' Is that it?"

"No, never. I wanted—" She pressed her lips together. She didn't know what to say. In an odd twist of events she didn't completely understand, *she* was the one on the defensive. She was pretty sure the nagging feeling at the back of her mind was guilt.

"I haven't done anything wrong," she said hotly. "I refuse to feel bad about what happened. You wanted it, too."

"Yes, I did." He stared at her. "Why, Sabrina? Why did you want to make love with me?"

She couldn't answer that one. The truth would only make things worse. He wouldn't want to hear it and she couldn't stand the humiliation. "What was last night to you?" she asked, hoping to shift the focus of the conversation.

His mouth twisted at the corner. "Very special. Something I'll treasure always."

That hit her where she lived. She felt her eyes burn and had to fight tears. "I refuse to feel guilty about leaving," she whispered. "I have every right to go."

"Yes, you do."

"I worked hard for you. I gave you everything I had. I was worth every penny."

"That was never in question."

The tears came, anyway. She felt them roll down her cheeks and had to brush them away. What had gone wrong? When had she lost control of the conversation?

"I'll be gone only a few days," she said. "When I get back,

I'll start looking for a replacement." She sucked in a breath. "As of now, I'm giving you thirty days' notice that I'm quitting."

Cal flinched slightly and headed for the door. She wanted him to yell at her and refuse to let her go. She wanted him to throw her on the bed and make love with her until she changed her mind. She wanted him to tell her that she would never be happy with anyone but him. She wanted him to say that he loved her.

He said nothing.

When he reached the doorway, he turned back to face her. This time she was sure she saw pain in his eyes and in the lines bracketing his mouth. But she was confused and didn't know what it meant.

"I don't want a replacement, Sabrina. I've only ever wanted you," he said, then left.

She stared after him, knowing that he was talking about work and desperately wishing he meant something else.

As Cal headed downstairs, he tried to think. Sabrina couldn't be leaving. It wasn't right. She'd been a part of his life for so long, he wasn't sure he could survive without her. This wasn't just about business, either, although he would miss her presence in that area, too. But mostly this was personal. He'd come to depend upon her. He cared about her and had believed she cared about him. How could she walk away from all that?

He crossed to the patio and stared out at the ocean. She was leaving to have a life. What was wrong with the one she had here...with him? Why did she need someone else? He knew that's what she was talking about. Dating, falling in love, maybe even getting married.

He frowned, trying to remember if Sabrina ever dated. He recalled her mentioning a couple of guys, but that had been a while ago. There hadn't been anyone special in the past couple of years. He'd had a series of women, but she'd been alone.

He didn't like it, but in a way he could understand it. Sabrina was a lovely, vital, giving woman. She needed more. If only—

"Daddy?"

He turned as Anastasia rushed at him. There were tears in her eyes. He held out his arms and she ran into his embrace.

"Daddy, don't let Sabrina leave. I don't want her to go."

He hugged his daughter close. "I don't want her to go, either, sweetie, but we don't get a choice in this one."

"No!" A sob shook her.

"I know it's hard to understand, but Sabrina has her own life. She only works for me, and that means she's free to leave whenever she wants."

Anastasia clung to him. "She's going forever?"

"Right now she's leaving for a few days. Then she'll be back."

He figured there was no point in dumping the rest of it on his daughter. The time would come when he would have to explain that Sabrina had given notice. But he wanted Anastasia to get used to this smaller hurt, first.

He rocked her in his arms. When the crying slowed, he suggested a board game to distract them both. They'd been playing for about an hour when Sabrina walked out onto the patio. She'd showered and changed. Instead of casual shorts and a T-shirt, she wore tailored slacks and a silk blouse. She had a jacket slung over one arm.

"I have a flight to New York later this morning. The shuttle will be here in a few minutes."

It hurt to look at her. Cal didn't want to think about how bad it was going to be when she was gone. "You don't even want me to drive you to the airport?"

She flinched. "It wasn't that." She motioned to the game. "I didn't want to disrupt your game."

"I see." But he knew the truth. She didn't want to spend any more time with him than she had to. "How long will you be gone?"

"A few days. Maybe a week. I'll be in touch."

He shrugged, as if it didn't matter. Inside, though, he could feel a sharp pain building. He had a feeling it would never go away. "Don't worry about us. We'll be fine."

Sabrina nodded. She bit her lower lip. "I'll miss you, Anastasia."

The girl turned toward the view. Cal saw her wipe away a tear, but her voice was strong and uncaring as she said, "I won't miss you, Sabrina. You're just the hired help. I'm sure my father will find someone to replace you."

Sabrina winced. "I'm sure he will." She turned to Cal. "I'm really sorry about all of this."

Anastasia's chair scraped against the cement patio as she pushed it back and lunged for Sabrina. Tears streamed down her face.

"Don't go," the girl sobbed. "Don't go away. I'll miss you so much. I didn't mean that. I will miss you."

Sabrina pulled her close. "I know, honey. I'll miss you, too."

"Then why are you leaving?"

"Good question," Cal told her.

Sabrina stared at him. "I have to."

Anastasia stepped back and wiped her face with the back of her hand. "Is my dad leaving next? Are you all leaving me?"

Fresh tears rolled down her cheeks. Cal rose and moved next to her. "I'm not leaving you, Anastasia. You're my daughter and you're going to be with me forever."

The preteen shook her head. "No. Everybody leaves me."

Sabrina touched her hair. "It's not like that."

"Yes, it is."

Cal hugged her. "No, it's not. I have a lot of flaws, kid, but I always keep my word. You can ask Sabrina. I promise I won't leave you, Anastasia. No matter what, I'll be here for you."

"Sabrina?"

Sabrina gave her a shaky smile. "He's right. He does keep his word. You can trust him."

Cal felt his daughter's thin arms wrap around him. She shook as she cried. Over her head, he met Sabrina's gaze. He wanted to ask why she was doing this to them. Where else was she needed as much? But he couldn't speak. The words got stuck in his throat, and by the time they were loose, the shuttle driver had knocked on the front door.

"Cal, I—"

"No, Sabrina. It's what you want. Just go."

She left without saying goodbye. He told himself they would all be fine. That time was a great healer. But as he held his devastated daughter and felt his own heart slowly crumbling, he wasn't sure he believed it was ever going to be true.

That night, Cal lay stretched out on top of his daughter's bed. Anastasia was next to him, curled close under the covers. He turned the page in the book and kept reading. When he reached the end of the chapter, she glanced up at him.

"I'm way too old for this," she pointed out.

"I'm reading to you because we both like it, not because of your age. It's fun."

"I know, but it makes me feel like a kid."

"I hate to point this out, but you are a kid."

"Na-uh."

"Uh-huh." He touched the tip of her nose. "You're my kid."

She leaned her head against his arm. "She's not going to call tonight, is she?"

He knew the "she" in question was Sabrina. He glanced at the clock. It was nearly ten. Her flight had taken off around eleven that morning, which put her into New York about eight, East Coast time. She would have reached the hotel by ten, which was only seven, their time.

"No," he said quietly. "She's not going to call."

He wanted to protest the unfairness of it all. When he'd gone away, *he'd* called. She should have the common courtesy to do the same. But there was no one to complain to.

"I miss her," Anastasia said.

"Me, too."

"But we're gonna be okay without her, aren't we? I mean, we're fine on our own."

Her need for reassurance was painfully obvious. He kissed the top of her head. "We're better than fine. We're perfect in every way."

His daughter giggled. "Da-ad."

"It's true. You and I are doing great. We had a rocky start, but we've recovered. We're getting to know each other. The whole parent-child relationship can be difficult for both sides, and we're going to have things to work through, but I'm not worried. You're a good kid."

She smiled. "You're a good dad."

Her brown eyes were similar to his. He'd often searched her features, trying to figure out what came from him and what she'd inherited from Janice. In many ways, Anastasia was her own person. Perhaps he recognized that more easily than most parents because he'd only recently met her. He hadn't had a part of her early years.

"I'm sorry I didn't know about you before," he said. "I would have liked to have been there from the beginning."

"Really?"

He nodded. "You're very special."

He felt that tightening in his chest again and recognized it for what it was. Love. He, who had grown up in a cold, unwelcoming home, had finally learned how to love someone.

"I love you, Anastasia. No matter what, I'll always love you." As he spoke the words, he felt a great warmth inside.

She buried her head against his chest. "I love you, too, Daddy," she whispered.

He closed his eyes to savor the moment, to try to make it enough, but it wasn't. No matter how much he loved his daughter, he still missed Sabrina. How had he let her go? How was he going to survive without her around? What choice did he have but to figure it out? As much as he wanted to, he couldn't *make* her stay.

Anastasia read his mind. "What about Sabrina, Daddy? She needs to be with us."

"I know it feels that way now, but we'll get used to having her gone."

"I don't think so."

"We don't have a choice. We can't force her to stay. She wants her own life. She likes her job, but it's just that. A job. She's not family, like you and me."

His daughter drew her knees up to her chest and smoothed the covers. "If you married her, she'd be a part of the family and she'd stay. Married people live together."

She imparted the last tidbit in the tone of someone sharing a seldom-discussed fact.

Cal opened his mouth, then closed it. Marry Sabrina? *Marry* Sabrina? "I can't," he said without thinking.

"Why not? You like her, I know you do. If you get married, she'll have to stay. We'll be her life."

Cal felt as if he were tumbling through space. It wasn't that the thought of marrying Sabrina was so horrible. The idea stunned him, but he had a feeling he could get used to it. The difficulty lay in the asking.

"It's not that simple."

Anastasia rolled her eyes. "Adults make everything so complicated."

"That's true."

Later, when she was finally asleep, he walked out onto the beach and stared at the waves. In the darkness they were vague shapes topped by white foam. He inhaled the scent of salt, sand and sea. For the rest of his life, when he thought of Sabrina, this is the smell he would remember. This and the sweetness that was her body.

Marry her, Anastasia had said. It would solve all their problems. Cal was willing to admit that, in theory, that was true. It sounded so simple. Just ask her. Be with her. Love her.

He closed his eyes. Loving Anastasia was safe. She was his child and that bonded them together. But Sabrina was different. She was a woman, at times a difficult and challenging woman. He admired her and respected her and wanted her. But love her? Did he dare?

It would be too easy to let himself fall for her. Maybe he already had. And then what? She could never love him back. That was what he couldn't explain to his daughter. Sabrina knew the worst about him. She'd seen into the darkness of his soul. She liked him. Apparently she even wanted him in her bed. But love? She was too good. She would choose a very different kind of man.

The truth was, Anastasia was the first person to ever love him. His parents hadn't, his sister had been too self-absorbed. The women who came and went in his life saw him as a means to an end. He didn't try to fool himself about that. Even Janice hadn't wanted to be with him longer than she had to. She'd gotten herself pregnant but had been careful to ensure they didn't have to marry.

Sabrina was worth ten of Janice. She was an amazing woman. And she'd seen him with Tiffany and Colette and all the others. She knew how he operated. She would never trust him. She would never love him back.

The kindest act would be to let her go.

Sabrina had indulged herself with a first-class airline ticket. Traveling with Cal had spoiled her, probably for good. The flight attendant offered her wine, but she refused. She had too much thinking to do and she needed a clear head.

The time in New York had gone by quickly. She'd had two job offers in the past five days. One with a firm in New York, the other with a company based out of Chicago. The jobs were equally fabulous with great pay and benefits and lots of room for advancement. It was as if each company had read her wish list and decided to make her dreams come true. All she had to do was decide.

So in this moment, when she should be celebrating and planning her future, why was she so sad? Why did she keep thinking about Cal and Anastasia and wondering what they were doing? Why was she still hurt because they hadn't been home when she'd called to tell them she was on her way back? She'd left a message with the information on the answering machine, but it wasn't the same. She'd wanted to talk to them. She desperately wanted to hear Cal's voice.

Loving him and leaving him was going to be harder than she'd first imagined. Life without him would be empty and cold for a long time. Logically she knew she wasn't going to die of a broken heart, even if it felt like it right now. And the worst wasn't over. She didn't just have to tell Cal about the job offers, she had to go through the trauma of hiring someone else.

There would be interviews, then making a final choice. Worst of all, she would then lie awake at night and picture that other person living her life, taking care of Cal the way she had. She wasn't sure how she would get over that.

If only she'd never fallen in love with him. Sabrina clutched the arms of the seat. Loving him was something she did very well. She couldn't regret that. In the deepest, darkest part of her she knew she would rather have loved him and miss him when she left, than be with someone else. Which made her a lovesick fool.

She reached for the headsets and put them on. With a little luck someone had written a country music song about her sorry life and she could find out how it was all going to come out in the end.

Chapter 15

Sabrina collected her carry-on suitcase and headed for the door. She hadn't bothered to arrange a shuttle for her return trip, so she was going to have to call the company when she retrieved the rest of her luggage. Or maybe she could take a cab. She followed the other first-class passengers down the jetway. There was the usual crowd of people, family members and friends to greet those arriving. She didn't bother to check for any familiar faces.

She'd already started toward the baggage claim area when she heard someone calling her name.

"Sabrina! We're over here."

She turned and saw Cal with Anastasia. The girl was grinning and waving madly. Cal's expression was more difficult to read, but there was a light in his dark eyes that made her hope he was pleased to see her.

"We missed you," Anastasia said, rushing toward her and giving her a hug. "We've had lots of fun doing stuff, but we missed you."

Sabrina brushed the girl's hair off her forehead. "I missed you, too." She looked up at her boss and gave him a shy smile. "Thanks for picking me up, Cal. I appreciate it."

"I know it's not fun to come home alone." He had a hand tucked behind his back, and when he drew it around in front of him, she saw he held a single red rose. "For you," he said. "Anastasia's right. We missed you very much."

She took the flower, brought it to her nose and inhaled the scent. The actions kept her distracted enough to allow her to blink back the tears that formed. The last time they'd seen each other, they'd come as close to fighting as they ever had in all the years she'd known him. She was three weeks away from walking out of his life forever. So why was he being so nice to her?

"Let's go get your luggage," he said as he put one arm around his daughter and the other around her. "So tell me about your trip. Was it successful?"

"Define *success*."

"Did you get any job offers?"

"Two." She mentioned the names of the companies. As they went down the escalator to the baggage claim area, then waited for the luggage, she talked about her interviews.

"They're both good companies," he said. "I don't know how you're going to like winters in either New York or Chicago, but you'll survive."

"I know." His touch was sure and familiar. She wanted to burrow closer to him and ask him to promise to always be there. What a mistake. So Cal had missed her. It didn't mean anything significant. He was probably regretting the fact that he'd had to do all the cooking. No doubt he wasn't looking forward to breaking in a new assistant. After all, they'd been together six years. For him it was an inconvenience, but for her, it was going to be major heartbreak. Still, she knew it was the right thing to do.

Anastasia stepped close and lowered her voice. "I met a boy," she said shyly.

Cal winced. "You did not meet a boy. I won't allow that. She went in-line skating with some kids her age. Children of both sexes. There will be no boy-meeting until you're thirty. Maybe not even then!"

Anastasia giggled. "His name is Jason and he's really cute."

"Cute is not allowed," Cal informed her. "I told you that already. No cute, no boys, none of that."

Sabrina grinned. "What's he like?"

When Cal would have started in on her, too, she pointed to the moving carousel. "That's my suitcase," she said. "The navy one."

He grunted, then went to pick it up.

"He's nice," Anastasia said in a low voice. "He's a year older than me and he's really great on blades. When I went skating with everyone, he showed me a couple of turns and stuff. I'm getting a lot better. There's a group of us going skating again tomorrow. Can you talk to Dad so he'll let me go?"

"I don't want to get caught in the middle," Sabrina started to say. At Anastasia's look of disappointment, she sighed. "Okay, I'll see what I can do."

"Thanks."

Cal returned carrying the suitcase. "What is she thanking you for? What have you agreed to do?"

Sabrina took his arm and led him toward the short-term parking. "Nothing you have to worry yourself about. Everything is going to be fine."

"You think I don't know when you're lying to me?" He gave her a mock glare. "Is this another of those 'he's male so he must be stupid' things? I'm not stupid."

Sabrina glanced at his daughter. "Wow, when did he get so sensitive about stuff?"

"I don't know. I guess it's because he's only around women."

"You're right," Sabrina said. "He needs some testosterone. Maybe he can get a shot or take vitamins."

"Like I need this," Cal muttered.

He caught her eye and grinned. She smiled back. It felt so right to be with him, she thought. She didn't know how much he'd really missed her, but she was willing to bet she'd missed him about ten times as much.

After unlocking the trunk, Cal handed his daughter the keys. She opened the car and scrambled into the back seat. Cal put the suitcase into the trunk and closed it. He turned to Sabrina.

"You deliberately stayed away from oil and gas companies, didn't you?"

She nodded. "I didn't want to create any illusion of conflict of interest."

"I'm not going to make you sign anything. If you'd rather stay in the industry, I wouldn't mind."

She looked at him. When high-placed employees left a firm in any industry, it was standard practice to have them sign a clause stating they wouldn't steal customers, compete directly or go to work for a competitor for a specified period of time. She'd just assumed Cal would want her to sign one.

"Why not?" she asked.

"You'll get a better job if you stay where you already have expertise. I want you to do well."

It was all she could do not to fling herself at him. "You're a really nice guy," she said.

"I know, but keep it to yourself. I have a reputation I have to keep intact."

"I won't breathe a word."

He walked around to her side of the car and held the door open. His hand rested on top of the window. She placed hers on his. "Thanks, Cal. I won't do anything to hurt the company."

"I know. That's why I offered."

"I'm going to find you the best replacement. You won't even notice I'm gone."

He didn't say anything for a couple of seconds, then he smiled. But it didn't reach his eyes, and she had the feeling it was more for show than because he was happy. "Let's not talk about that," he said. "Right now I just want to enjoy having you here."

Later that night Sabrina stood at the front of the porch and leaned toward the ocean. "I had a view of Central Park from my hotel room," she said. "It was nice, but nothing like this."

She heard Cal move up behind her, then he wrapped his arms around her waist. She hadn't realized how much she'd missed being close to him until that minute. Her body fit perfectly against his. He was warm and strong, and Lord help her, she wanted him.

"People say that folks from Texas talk funny, but if you ask me, those New York Yankees can be mighty tough to understand," he said, broadening his accent.

"I agree. Life is different there." She placed her hands on top of his. "Life is different here, too. More relaxed. I like it." She took a deep breath. "I'm sorry about Hawaii, not being able to go, I mean."

"It's all right. I was trying to extend the fantasy." His voice rumbled against her back. "Reality isn't so bad. I haven't forgotten what it was like, Sabrina. What we were like when we were together."

He rested his chin on her shoulder. She instinctively tilted her head, exposing her neck. He turned toward her and brushed his lips against her skin. A shiver rippled down her spine.

"I don't know that I've ever really missed anyone before," he said quietly. "But I missed you. I thought about you constantly while you were gone."

His confession touched her, making her want to confess all to him. That she'd missed him, too. That she wanted him, that she loved him and had probably loved him from the first.

"Between you and Anastasia, I think you're making a difference in me," he said. "I'm still something of a jerk, but I'm getting better."

She closed her eyes. "I never thought you were a jerk, Cal. I've always admired you."

"I'm glad. Your good opinion matters to me. I would do almost anything to keep it, but there are some things I just can't resist."

His hold on her loosened, and as he released her, he turned her toward him. She knew he was going to kiss her and she met him halfway, her mouth already parted and ready for him.

This wasn't like before. There was no playfulness, no teasing, little conversation. Last time they'd been caught up in exploration, this time they were drowning in need. The fire erupted instantly, surrounding them with passionate flames.

He held her face in his hands as he kissed her. His mouth was open, his tongue sought hers. Over and over he stroked and circled, danced and caressed.

"I want you," he murmured. "I want you in my bed. Naked. On your back, hungry for me. Wet and ready. I want to be in you, filling you, making you mine."

His words stunned her. When he broke the kiss and took her hand to lead her up the stairs, she followed mindlessly. If he'd sought to paint a verbal picture of them making love, he'd succeeded. She couldn't imagine being anywhere else or *with* anyone else.

They reached his room. Lights from the street filtered in through the vertical blinds. He didn't bother turning on any of the lamps. In the semidarkness, they reached for each other, hands touching, clothing falling, until at last they were naked.

He drew her onto the bed. She went willingly, wanting him to do all the things he'd talked about, wanting to feel those things with him. Only with him.

He kissed her passionately. As the world began to spin, he was her only constant and she had to cling to him to maintain her place in the universe. His muscles were warm and rippling beneath her hands. She moved up and down his back, rediscovering the familiar country that was his body. He, too, familiarized himself with her. He started at her collarbone and moved lower. When he reached her breasts, he cupped one yielding curve, learning its shape and weight. Her nipple tightened. He toyed with the taut tip, rubbing it with the pad of his thumb, circling around, sending waves of wanting through her.

He deepened the kiss. She closed her lips over his tongue and sucked gently. He groaned low in his throat. His arousal bumped against her thigh. She moved a hand down between them and encircled the length of him. His skin there was so soft, like shorn velvet, but inside he was hard as steel. She liked the shape of him, the definition, the vein running down the back, the way he flexed when she stroked him.

A single drop of moisture lay on the very tip. She used her forefinger to smooth it over him. The dampness made him slick and reminded her of what it would be like when he was inside her.

As if he read her mind, he moved his hand lower, over her belly, past the protective curls to that secret place between her thighs. She parted for him, wanting him there. His fingers were sure as they moved down into the moist heat. He caressed either side of the most sensitive part of her before dipping inside and mimicking the act of love.

Fingers moved in and out, preparing her until she felt she couldn't possibly be more swollen or wet. She moved her hand faster, urging him onward. He broke the kiss long enough to kneel between her legs and put on protection, then he slid home.

Within two thrusts she was on the edge of discovery. By the third, the familiar pressure began and she found herself spiraling out of control. But this was different from before. The release brought its own tension, and she knew she had entered a new dimension of pleasure.

He braced himself above her, eyes open, studying her. She clutched at him and urged him deeper. Love filled her, along with the desire. It was a heady combination.

A few more thrusts and another climax. She felt him nearing his release and her tension grew again. She tried to hold back, to contain herself.

"Don't," he ground out. "Don't resist. Give in. Come for me, Sabrina. Now!"

His words freed her. She exploded, deeply and completely, giving herself over to the spasms. He plunged into her one last time and groaned his own contentment. She felt herself milking him dry.

When they had caught their breath, they clung to each other. There was much to talk about, Sabrina thought, but she didn't have the words. Whatever happened, she would always be able to remember this night. She suspected no man would ever come close to touching her as completely as Cal. There might be other lovers, other good times, but he had possession of her heart. Perhaps she should try to reclaim it, if such a thing were possible. But in an odd way, she wanted him to keep it with him always.

She loved him, and right now, in his arms, with the scent of their lovemaking clinging to them both, it was enough.

The tinkle of glass followed by a muttered swearword woke her the next morning. Sabrina raised her head and saw Cal standing in the doorway to his bedroom, tray in hand.

"Sorry," he said when he saw she was awake. "I wanted to surprise you with breakfast. I know it's early, but I'd hoped we could have some time together before Anastasia woke up."

The combination of the thoughtful gesture, not to mention the little-boy smile, made him impossible to resist. She pulled the sheet up so it covered her breasts, then sat against the headboard.

"You're very sweet. Is there coffee, too?"

"What's breakfast without coffee?"

She glanced with interest at the tray. "And I wasn't sure you even knew how to work a toaster. I'll reserve judgment until I taste everything."

He set the tray next to her. "I'm crushed you don't trust me."

He'd dressed in shorts and a T-shirt, but he hadn't showered or shaved yet. Stubble darkened his jaw and his hair was mussed. She'd seen him in a perfectly tailored suit, even a tuxedo, but to her, he'd never looked more handsome…or appealing.

"Thank you," she said, and reached for the mug. "You are a prince without equal."

"No, but I am one of the world's most eligible bachelors."

She chuckled. "I'd forgotten about that. Getting any fan mail yet?"

But if he answered, she didn't hear. Sabrina wasn't sure of anything at that moment. Her gaze fell on the small white velvet box sitting in the center of the tray. The coffee mug had shadowed it, which was why she hadn't noticed it before.

She put the mug on the nightstand so she wouldn't drop it. Her stomach knotted until the pain was nearly unbearable. She knew her heart still had to be beating, but she couldn't feel it. She couldn't feel anything but the agony of knowing that it was over before it had begun.

He'd come to her last night knowing he was going to do

this today. The betrayal nearly made her gag. It was too early for him to have gone out to get the parting gift this morning. He'd planned ahead. Damn him. And damn her for believing in him. She *knew* better.

"Sabrina?" Cal sat down next to her. "What's wrong?"

He was going to tell her goodbye while she was naked. She wasn't sure why that particular thought stuck in her head, but it did. Naked and vulnerable and there wasn't anything she could do about it.

"Sabrina?"

She cleared her throat. "It's too small for a watch. Too bad, because we both know I can tell time the old-fashioned way."

Her voice sounded almost normal. If someone didn't know her really well, he wouldn't have been able to guess. Unfortunately, Cal did know her.

"A watch? What are you talking about? Tell me what's wrong."

She pointed to the jeweler's box, not daring to touch it. "That. The 'it's over' gift. How thoughtful of you to choose it yourself. Or did Anastasia help?"

"No!" He took her hands in his. "I'm sorry. I'm doing this all wrong, aren't I? I wanted to surprise you. I thought this would be romantic. I forgot about those stupid gifts I sent women when it was over." He stared at her intently. "You have to believe me. This isn't like that."

He released her long enough to pick up the small velvet box and open it. She forced herself to be strong and look inside.

Instead of a pin or a pair of earrings, a beautiful emerald-cut diamond solitaire winked back at her. She blinked. "I don't understand. You never give rings."

One corner of his mouth turned up. "I'm not telling you it's over. I'm trying to propose. Sabrina, I want you to marry me."

There was a rushing in her ears. She glanced from him to the ring and back. His smile broadened. "You're proposing?"

"Yes. Marry me. Please."

With the possible exception of telling her he'd had regression therapy and had remembered a past life as a dog, she couldn't think of anything he could have said that would have shocked her more. Marry him? Calhoun Jefferson Langtry was proposing to *her?*

The rushing in her ears turned to a ringing, and her stomach stopped hurting, but now it was flopping around. She felt light-headed and confused. Why did he want to marry her?

She searched his face, hoping to find a clue. She knew him well enough to know that he wouldn't have asked lightly. Nor would he change his mind and retract the proposal. Did he care about her the way she cared about him? He hadn't said anything about love, but obviously...

Then she knew. The ringing stopped, her stomach settled down to normal. She closed the velvet box.

"You don't want to lose me," she said flatly.

"Of course not." He touched her cheek. "You're a part of my life."

"You're right. We're good friends, we work well together. We get along. We're well matched, personality-wise and in bed. I keep your life running smoothly and I've already established a relationship with your daughter."

He frowned. "I want to agree with everything you've said, but I sense a trap."

"No trap, Cal. Just the truth." It hurt to breathe. She felt as if her heart had collapsed on itself. She'd come so close to realizing her dream. She hadn't known how much she'd allowed herself to hope until it was all snatched away from her.

"If I wanted to keep my job, would that be a problem?" she asked.

"No. Do you want to?"

She ignored his question. "Stock options? Are they available?"

The frown deepened. "You're making this sound like a business transaction. It's not like that. I want to marry you, Sabrina. I want a relationship. I will try to be a good husband."

She nodded. "I know you, and you *will* try. You'll be faithful and caring." He would drive her to the limits of pleasure in bed, too, if she let him.

It was so tempting. They could have children together. She would never have to worry about money. Of course she was already fairly well off now. But there would be security, and respect. Many marriages had survived on less.

But he didn't love her. He didn't love anyone, except maybe his daughter. She knew herself well enough to know that a loveless marriage would destroy her. After a while she would dry up and blow away. What was the saying? Ashes to ashes, dust to dust.

She loved him, therefore she couldn't marry him.

She climbed out of bed and slipped on her clothes, then crossed to the door. "I'm sorry, Cal," she said. "I…I can't."

Chapter 16

Cal wasn't sure how long he sat alone in the kitchen. It could have been ten minutes or two hours. He couldn't think, he couldn't do anything but wait for the pain to ease a little. He'd tried. That's what he told himself. He'd done his best and he'd failed. At the time it had seemed so simple. That he would propose and she would say yes, and she would stay with him always. That's what he'd wanted, but it hadn't happened.

He supposed he couldn't blame her for refusing him. He didn't have anything to offer her. After all, she knew the worst about him. She'd been there all the times he'd gotten involved with silly, inappropriate women. Women he'd chosen because they were pretty and easy and they didn't challenge him in any way. Women he could walk away from without giving them a second's thought. He'd been so afraid of someone real. Someone he could love, someone like her.

He'd thought being alone was the worst thing in the world,

but now he knew better. The worst thing in the world was being without her.

He heard a noise in the hallway and glanced up. His daughter stepped into the room. She walked over and hugged him. "'Morning, Daddy."

He held her close. "Good morning."

She stepped back and looked at him. "What's wrong?"

Apparently he was so transparent even his twelve-year-old kid knew something was troubling him. "Nothing."

"Da-ad."

"Don't 'Da-ad' me," he told her. "What do you want for breakfast?"

"Nothing. Did something happen with Sabrina?"

He couldn't tell her the truth. Not yet. She'd already been hurt by so much. He swore to himself. Not only was he going to have to figure out how to survive without the one woman he loved, but his daughter was also going to have to get used to living without her. It wasn't fair.

"Cereal or pancakes?" he asked, deliberately keeping his voice light.

Anastasia pushed her glasses higher onto her nose and sighed. "Cereal is fine. It's Sabrina, isn't it? Did you talk to her about staying?"

He got down a bowl. "Eat first, talk later."

Sabrina moved closer to the ocean. It was still early enough that she had most of the beach to herself. Which was good. She wasn't in the mood to smile at strangers, and she had a bad feeling that if someone asked even a simple question, like "How are you?" she would burst into tears.

What had gone wrong? Why had he proposed to her?

She shook her head. She knew the answer to that one. The problem was, she wanted it to be for a different reason. She wanted Cal to have asked her to marry him because he loved her and couldn't imagine living without her, not because she was a convenience. That made her feel like a dishwasher.

She shoved her hands into her jeans pockets and sighed. The worse part was, she was tempted. The weakness invaded her, making her want to go to him and tell him that she would agree to marry him under any conditions. After all, he would be a good husband. He would be faithful to her. She knew he cared about her and respected her. Maybe, in time, he could fall in love with her. Wasn't that a possibility? Wasn't that enough? A good man, Anastasia, children of her own. Was she wishing for the moon to want more?

She bit her lower lip. She couldn't settle. Not on this issue. It wasn't right. And if she did, she would never be able to respect herself. Some of Cal wasn't better than none. She would make a clean break of it. Sure it would be difficult, but she would recover and go on. There were lots of men out there who would find her interesting. She might fall in love with one of them. If not, she could like one a lot and try to make a go of it.

Which was settling in a different way, she thought sadly. So what was the answer?

She walked for several more minutes before turning around and heading back to the house. One thing she knew for sure—she was going to tell Cal the truth. Before she actually left, she was going to gather her courage together and admit that she'd fallen in love with him and that was the reason she couldn't accept his proposal. She had enough to regret already; she wasn't going to spend her life wishing she'd told him how she felt. She smiled thinking of his confusion when she carefully explained that the reason she wouldn't marry him was because she loved him too much.

As she neared their rented place, her mind filled with memories. There had been so many good times over the past six years. So much laughter and teasing, so many wonderful moments. The party he'd thrown for her when she turned twenty-five. How he'd come with her when her youngest sister had graduated from college. The extra-long weekend in Hong Kong after she'd won their stock bet last year. The specialist he'd had flown in when they were afraid that Gram had suffered a heart attack. So many wonderful gestures, so much affection. Cal might not have loved her, but he'd been a good friend. Along with her confession of love, she was going to tell him that, too. He was a wonderful man. Now that he'd let his daughter into his heart, he needed to make room for someone else. Someone who would treasure him and take care of him.

Thinking about him with another woman hurt too much, so she pushed the thought away. She crossed the sand to the boardwalk, then stepped into their patio. The sliding glass door was open. Cal and Anastasia were in the kitchen. They didn't see her as she stepped into the living room.

The preteen put a bowl into the sink and turned to face her father. "Okay, I ate my breakfast. Now tell me what happened."

Sabrina stopped in her tracks. Anastasia knew about the proposal?

Cal shrugged. "There's nothing to tell." He held up his hand. "I'm not kidding. I asked her to marry me and she said no. That's it."

"That's not it. Start at the beginning and tell me everything. She couldn't have said no. She loves you, Daddy, I know she does."

Even if Sabrina had wanted to leave, the girl's words rooted her in place. She shifted until she was concealed by the bookcase against the dividing wall and sucked in her breath. How had Anastasia figured out the truth?

"I wish that were true," Cal said. "But it's not. Sweetie, I know you wanted this to work out, and I did, too. Sometimes grown-ups make life complicated."

"What does that have to do with anything?"

"Sabrina and I have known each other for a long time."

"I know. You get along great. She wants to marry you. You must have said something to make her mad."

If she hadn't been so frozen with shock, she might have smiled at the preteen's assumption.

"I did not." Cal sounded indignant. "I took her breakfast in bed. There was an engagement ring in a velvet box on the tray. I asked her to marry me and she said no. End of story."

Sabrina heard a rustling sound, then Anastasia spoke, but her voice was muffled. "I'm sorry, Daddy. I really thought she loved you. I don't understand."

She risked a glance and saw Cal hugging his daughter.

"I've seen how she looks at you," the girl continued. "It's exactly how my mom looked at my other dad. You look at her the same way. I hate this. I don't ever want to grow up."

"Sorry, kid, you don't get a choice." He drew in a deep breath. "Don't blame Sabrina, okay? It's not her fault."

"Yes, it is!"

"No. I'm the one who…"

When he paused, Sabrina risked another glance. Cal stood with his back to her. He rested his chin on his daughter's head.

"I'm the one who messed up. See, Sabrina knows me too well. We all have bad parts, and usually we keep them hidden from the world. The problem is, Sabrina has seen those parts of me. They're pretty awful and she can't forget that. She's so wonderful. Bright. Funny. Pretty. She can do a lot better than me."

"No way," his daughter said loyally.

"Thanks, but on this one, you're wrong. Any guy would be lucky to have her."

Sabrina pressed her fingers to her mouth to keep from crying out. She knew the man, recognized his appearance and the sound of his voice, but she couldn't believe what he was saying. She'd never heard him talk like this before. What did it mean?

A gladness filled her heart. She didn't want to risk hoping and having those hopes dashed, but she couldn't control the feeling that grew and grew until it burned hot and bright like the sun.

"Daddy, if you love someone, you love all the parts inside. Sometimes I can be, you know, sorta bratty, but you love me."

"It's more than just sorta bratty, and yes, I do love you, but that's different."

"Why? You love Sabrina."

"Yes, but she doesn't love me."

Her legs nearly gave way. Yes. He'd said yes. As in yes, he loved her!

"What did she say when you told her you loved her?"

Silence.

"Daddy, you didn't tell her!"

"I couldn't. She wouldn't believe me."

"Yes, she would. I believed you."

"I know. It's just—"

Sabrina was near tears, but for the first time in months, they were from happiness, not pain. He loved her. *Her.* Was it true? Could she believe?

"Go," Anastasia was saying. "Go right now and tell her the truth. She has to know. You brought her a flower at the airport."

"Ah, yes, the universal love symbol."

"Daddy! I'm serious."

"Very well. I'll tell her, if only because I should have when I proposed. I was afraid to say it, but she deserves to hear it. Even if it doesn't matter to her."

Sabrina headed for the stairs. She barely made it into her room when she heard Cal climbing up behind her. She quickly brushed her cheeks and hoped that he couldn't tell she'd been crying, then reminded herself that even if he could, he would think that it was because she was sad.

There was a knock on her door. She braced herself against the window and tried to smile.

"C-come in." Her voice cracked. Had he noticed? Did it matter?

He entered the room. He was, she thought, the most perfect man ever created. So handsome and strong, so amazing.

He gave her a half smile that faded as quickly as it began. "Sabrina, I have something to tell you. I should have said it before. It's just, I was afraid." He shoved his hands into his shorts pockets. "I was just telling Anastasia that I didn't have much to recommend myself to you and I guess this proves it. I'm just some good ol' boy from Texas. My family has all the trappings of success, but they're not good people. You know that better than anyone. I'm a hard worker and I play hard. I can be stubborn. But you know that, too." He gave a short laugh. "Here I am, trying to sell myself. Pretty sad, huh?"

She shook her head. "I think it's charming. I also think you're wonderful."

He'd been staring at the ground, but now his head snapped up. "You do?"

"Yes. I have a confession to make. I, um, had a crush on you when I first came to work for you. But I knew you weren't interested in me that way, so I made myself get over it." She took a step toward him. "At least, that was the plan. I did get over my crush, but not the way I wanted. Those shallow, silly feelings deepened, and I fell in love with you. Only I didn't recognize that fact until very recently."

His breath caught audibly. "Sabrina?"

"I love you, Cal. I think you're an amazing man. I didn't agree to marry you because I thought it would only be half a marriage, and that would have destroyed me. I need to be with someone who loves me back."

"I do," he said, hurrying toward her and grabbing her shoulders. "I love you, I think I always have. I respect you and admire you, and, dammit, I want to spend the rest of my life with you. It's not about work or Anastasia. I'll hire a new assistant and a housekeeper and a nanny if that's what it takes to convince you."

She stared at the love burning bright in his dark eyes. "I believe you. To think we spent all this time not knowing."

He kissed her hard, then drew back. "I nearly lost you. I didn't know I had you and then I could have lost you. I wouldn't have survived."

"Oh, Cal."

She wrapped her arms around his neck and pressed her lips to his. The kiss went on for a long time. When at last they surfaced, he said, "What about the job offers?"

"Is that by way of another proposal?"

"If you want it to be." He touched her cheek. "I love you, Sabrina. Would you do me the honor of becoming my wife?"

"Yes."

"You still want to work for me, too? It's only summer. We do have a half year left on our stock bet."

She laughed. "I'm going to kick your butt on that one…again."

"Cheap talk, woman."

"You lost last year, and yes, I do want to keep working for you. I might have to cut back on my hours because of your daughter, but that's okay with me, if it's okay with you."

"It's more than okay. It's wonderful."

He held her close. She sighed with contentment. Who would have thought it would come to this?

"I was thinking," she said. "How about a honeymoon in Hawaii? We could take Ada and her nieces. That way Anastasia would have someone to play with, and she would have a good time, too."

"Because it's too soon to leave her alone."

She nodded.

He tucked her hair behind her ears. "This is why I love you, Sabrina. You are the best part of me."

"And you're the best part of me." She had a thought and giggled. "*Prominence Magazine* is going to be upset. Talk about a short-lived career as an eligible bachelor. You'll be married before the issue hits the stands."

"They'll have to get over it. I'm committed to you. For life."

"For life," she echoed. "Let's go tell Anastasia. She'll be thrilled."

"Are you kidding? She already knows. She's probably arranged the entire wedding by now."

"The alternative is her going on that skating date with a boy."

"She's not dating until she's thirty. Do you hear me? Neither are all the other daughters we have together."

She laughed as they walked down the stairs. It was barely eight o'clock in the morning, and it already promised to be the most wonderful day of her life.

* * * * *

To Susan Mallery—
together again after all these years. Thanks for
everything, but especially for the friendship.

IT TAKES THREE

Teresa Southwick

TERESA SOUTHWICK

lives with her husband in Las Vegas, the city
that reinvents itself every day. An avid fan of
romance novels, she is delighted to be living
out her dream of writing for Harlequin and
Silhouette Books.

Chapter 1

"Someone's been cooking in my kitchen."

Staring at the beautiful stranger in front of his stove, Scott Matthews figured he'd hit a low point even for him. His life was reduced to a culinary caper of *Goldilocks and the Three Bears.* Except the woman wasn't a blonde. She had hair like brown silk, eyes warm as hot cocoa and was *not* sleeping in his bed.

"Who are you and what are you doing here?" he asked, annoyed that the sleeping-in-his-bed thought sent a shaft of heat through him.

She wielded a spatula like a conductor's baton. "Who are *you?*" she demanded.

"I live here."

"You're Kendra's father?"

"Scott Matthews," he introduced himself.

"But you don't look old enough to have an eighteen-year-old daughter," she said, obviously surprised.

"Trust me, I am."

It's what happened when a guy thought with the brain south of his belt and had the first of two daughters when he was barely out of his teens.

"So you started your family when you were what? Ten?"

"Not quite." The compliment about his youthful appearance almost made him miss the fact that she hadn't yet told him who she was. This was his kitchen and he'd be the one asking the questions.

"Who are you?"

"Thea Bell."

"Why are you here?"

"Kendra didn't tell you?" Her confidence slipped and she looked uncomfortable.

What did his daughter have to do with anything? Was this woman using his child as an excuse to meet him? That wasn't ego talking. His wife had walked out on him thirteen years ago and after his divorce, he'd become fair game—fresh meat on the dating market.

At back-to-school night, there was always a divorced mom trying to get his attention. Or kids on his girls' sports teams had single mothers who invariably honed in on him. But they were barking up the wrong tree, because he had no interest in a relationship except the one he had with his daughters. After putting in a day's work at his family-owned construction company and then being both father and mother to the girls, dating didn't make the to-do list. And with Kendra just about to graduate and go on to college, he could see the light at the end of the parenting tunnel. Please, God, let it not be attached to a speeding locomotive.

He had news for Thea Bell. If her pickup approach was based on the way to a man's heart being through his stomach, she was dealing with the wrong man. He didn't care whether a woman could boil water or whip up a meal. He wasn't desperate for companionship. After his train wreck of a marriage, the single life was simple.

"What was Kendra supposed to tell me?" he asked suspiciously.

"She and I have an appointment to discuss her party."

The woman in front of him reached into the pocket of her tailored jeans and pulled out a card. He walked over to her and took it. Leaning his back against the refrigerator, he tried to ignore the sweet scent of her perfume as he read the name of her company printed in a no-nonsense font.

"For Whom the Bell Toils?" he said.

"Thea Bell toils for thee." One corner of her full mouth turned up as she shrugged. "I'm a caterer."

"Catchy." He set her card on the island in front of him and folded his arms over his chest as he studied her.

"I met Kendra at a birthday party I did for one of her friends."

"And?"

She frowned, her expression puzzled. "Did you not tell your daughter she could have a graduation party?"

"I did."

"Then why are you acting as if I'm a cat burglar who's just broken into your home to steal the fine jewelry?"

"I have no fine jewelry."

"You also didn't answer my question," she pointed out.

"I told her if she wanted a party she could be responsible for the details."

"She is being responsible for them. She's talking to a catering professional."

"When I said details, I meant buying burgers and buns at the grocery store. Not *hiring* someone to take care of the burgers and buns."

He hadn't seen her from the back, but he suspected Thea Bell had some fine buns of her own, because what he could see of her front was pretty fine. The silky white blouse tucked

into her tailored jeans accentuated her breasts and a slender
waist that flared into the delicate curves of her hips. He might
not date much, but he still knew she was the kind of woman
who would make any man instantly aware of her.

He drew in a deep breath to control the spike of his pulse.
"Didn't you wonder about dealing with a teenager? Or where
her parents were?"

"It's not unusual. Many parents work. They're busy and
give their teenagers a lot of responsibility, especially when
the teen is hosting the party. Not unlike what you said to
Kendra about handling everything."

She was sharp. Using his own words against him. "How
do I know you're a reputable caterer?"

"I have a list of references. You can check with the Better
Business Bureau and the Santa Clarita Chamber of
Commerce. If a complaint has been registered with either
agency, I'll eat my spatula." She glanced at it, then back at
him. "Your spatula."

It took several moments before he realized he was staring
at her mouth. Her lips were plump and pink and… And giving
them enough notice to attach adjectives really whipped up his
irritation.

"Where is my daughter?"

"You say that as if you think I've done something with her."

"Have you?"

"Of course not," she denied. "She went up to her room to
find a picture to show me, something for the party's theme."

"Graduation isn't enough?"

"She had something in mind. For the table decorations."

"She needs decorations?"

"Technically? No." She sighed. "But it's a touch that adds
an air of festivity to any gathering. It isn't just about food, it's
about ambience. When guests walk in, you want them in a
party mood. Decorations do that."

"And have you discussed with my daughter how much this is going to cost? And who's paying for it?"

"Not yet. I can't estimate until firm decisions are made about food, decorations and the number of guests."

"I see, so—"

Scott heard the unmistakable sound of his daughter galumphing down the stairs. A five-point-eight on the Richter scale, he estimated.

When Kendra entered the kitchen, she stopped so fast her sneakers squeaked on the tile floor. "Dad. What are you doing here?"

"I live here."

His dark-haired, blue-eyed daughter glanced from him to Thea and then back again. She had guilt written all over her.

Kendra moved closer to Thea. His daughter took after him in the height department. She was tall, nearly five feet ten, and made the other woman look even smaller by comparison. "I just meant, you're home early. How come?"

"I'm meeting a real-estate agent here to get a market evaluation of the house."

The teen speared him with a narrow-eyed gaze. "Define 'market evaluation,' Dad."

He should have channeled Kendra's question back to how she planned to get away with hiring a caterer when she hadn't cleared it with him. His lapse was directly due to the distraction of Thea Bell. When a man came home and found a beautiful woman in his kitchen, it tended to throw him off. Especially a man like himself, who was more comfortable with the tool belt and nail gun set. But he'd opened his mouth and now had to figure out what to do with the foot he'd inserted.

"The agent is coming to see the place and figure out how much it's worth on today's market. You know her. It's Joyce Rivers, Bernie's wife."

"I know Joyce," Thea chimed in. "We met at a Santa Clarita professional women's group. She's great."

"Why do you need Joyce to tell you how much the house is worth?" Kendra asked, refusing to be distracted.

His youngest child had been a handful since she'd turned twelve. Why should now be any different? Her older sister was an easygoing rule-follower who hadn't prepared him for Kendra's episodes of rebellion. But Kendra was going off to college soon and he wouldn't need this big house. That's why he'd arranged for Joyce to do the market evaluation and the best time for both of them happened to be when Kendra was in school. Speaking of which…

"Why aren't you in school?" he demanded.

"I told you last night," she said, sighing in exasperation as she rolled her eyes. "Today is a half-day schedule because the teachers had an end-of-quarter grading day."

"Oh. Yeah." He didn't remember her saying a word about it.

"As usual, you weren't listening." She put her hands on her hips. "You're going to sell the house, aren't you?"

Scott didn't want to have this conversation at all, let alone in front of a total stranger. "Can we talk about this later?"

"Maybe I should go," Thea said.

"Please don't," Kendra pleaded. Then she turned her patented drop-dead stare on him and huffed out a hostile breath. "Evasive tactics mean I'm right. I don't believe this. I'm not even finished with high school and you're selling my home out from under me. What if I go to the local junior college? Do you remember me telling you about that?"

"I'm not selling anything," he said, avoiding her question.

"Then why do you need to know how much the house is worth?"

"Maybe I want to refinance my loan," he countered.

"Do you?"

It was times like this when he wished he could lie. But

he'd made it a point to be as honest with his daughters as he knew how. "No."

"I knew it," Kendra said. "You can't wait to get rid of me. That's why you're pushing me to go away to college."

"You're wrong, Ken. I'm not pushing you to do anything."

"You didn't want to hear about the local community college."

"I want you to have the total college experience. Like your sister—"

"Perfect Gail." The aside was directed to Thea.

"I'm sure that's not what your father meant," she said, glancing at him.

"I'm sure he did. My sister does everything right and I'm the screwup."

"Coincidentally, Joyce did a market evaluation on my condo," Thea said, changing the subject.

"Are you selling it?" Kendra asked, toning down her hostility for the caterer.

Scott almost felt sorry for Thea, getting caught in the crossfire. But his empathy was mitigated by the fact that the woman had chosen to conduct business with a teenager instead of her parent. He decided not to analyze why it seemed better to focus on Thea's error in judgment rather than her noble attempt to defuse the situation. Or his daughter's rebellious streak that had created this multi-level farce in the first place.

"Actually, I am selling," she admitted. "I'm looking for a single-family home in a nice neighborhood."

Kendra cranked the animosity back up when she looked at him. "My dad just happens to have one for sale. Maybe he'll give you a good deal. He can't wait to unload this place, along with me."

"Ken, you're being overly dramatic…"

The ringing doorbell interrupted him. If only he felt saved by the bell. "That must be Joyce now."

"I'm going to Zoe's." Kendra grabbed her purse off of the built-in desk beside the pantry and stomped out of the room.

"Kendra, wait. You know how I feel about Zoe—" When the inside door to the garage slammed, Scott sighed. Then the doorbell rang again and he went to answer it.

Thea looked around the empty kitchen feeling about as useful as one chopstick. Could this be any more awkward? She'd had dealings with teens before, but always after first contact was made by the parent and the dynamics of the working relationship were spelled out. But there was something about Kendra. When they'd met at her friend's party, she'd felt the girl reaching out. Thea had seen something in Kendra's eyes that was an awful lot like sadness. Thea figured she recognized the emotion because she'd lived with it every day for the last two years.

When Kendra had called to inquire about hiring her for a graduation party, Thea had made an exception. Today she'd brought samples of food for the teen and showed her an album of pictures displaying her work. Thea had planned to get into the business details of a signed contract and a deposit check when Scott walked in.

Kendra had only said her father was a busy building contractor who couldn't be bothered with her party. The teen hadn't mentioned how very attractive the father in question was. His dark hair, blue eyes and good looks definitely made Thea's female hormones sit up and take notice. However, her hormones had been on high alert for a while now. So her noticing him could simply be chemically induced.

But clearly his irritation about finding her in his kitchen had been all too real. Maybe if he knew how very important the party was to his daughter, he'd cut her a little slack on leaving him out of the loop.

As she stood there trying to decide what to do, Scott led Joyce Rivers into the kitchen. The tall brunette looked around.

When she noticed Thea, she smiled. "Hello, there. I didn't know you and Scott knew each other."

"We just met," Thea said.

"Just," he agreed, his tone cool.

When he said nothing further, she figured he didn't want Kendra's role in their meeting made public. But the look glittering in his very blue eyes told her his daughter would get an earful when she came home.

Joyce tapped her lip. "You know, Thea, when we talked about what you were looking for in a home, I thought about this house."

"Really?" Scott said. "Even though I hadn't decided to sell?"

"You indicated to Bernie and me that when Kendra was finished with high school, you were going to downsize. Isn't she graduating in a couple of months?"

Thea stared at him. "So Kendra's right? Her teddy bears and Barbies aren't even cold yet and you're kicking them out?"

"She's blowing things out of proportion," he said.

"Clearly she thinks you're trying to get rid of her." Thea couldn't resist making him squirm a little. Scott Matthews had walked in and treated her like a breaking-and-entering suspect. Maybe his daughter's issues with him weren't just the rumblings of teenage independence.

"She's wrong. It's not getting rid of her when she's going to college. What do I need with this big place?" he defended.

With one eyebrow raised, Joyce looked from Thea to Scott and back again. "Am I interrupting something?"

"No." Scott blew out a breath as he ran his fingers through his hair.

Thea folded her arms over her chest. "She was only reacting to the information that you're going to sell her childhood home out from under her."

"I'm not selling anything yet," he said. "I'm simply gathering information."

"And let's do that," Joyce said brightly. Obviously she was grateful for the excuse to change the subject. "Thea, since you're here, why don't you tag along on the tour."

"If Scott doesn't mind." She looked at him and his expression said he minded very much.

"Why not?" His enthusiasm was underwhelming.

"Great." Thea didn't care what he thought. She'd been dying to see the floor plan. Already she'd fallen in love with the kitchen. The downstairs was charming, and she was curious about the rest of the house.

She turned off the stove, then followed Joyce who was just behind Scott as he led them upstairs. Peeking around the other woman, Thea got a glimpse of his broad back narrowing to a trim waist and one fine backside. She hadn't noticed men in general, or any man in particular since she'd fallen in love with David. He'd been the love of her life and she'd lost him. Odd that the first man to make her female antenna quiver was a man who was annoyed with her.

"This is the master bedroom," he said, leading them into the room at the top of the stairs. "It goes across the back half of the house. There are his and hers walk-in closets. Double sinks and a Jacuzzi tub."

Thea fixated on the large bed because it didn't dwarf the floor space. *Not* because its owner was a big man who needed a big bed. The completely innocent thought warmed her cheeks and she forced herself to focus on his words.

"Over there, two steps down, is an area for a parent's retreat." He looked questioningly at Thea.

Was he asking if she needed a parent's retreat? Whether he was or not, she wasn't in the habit of sharing personal information, let alone her house needs, with total strangers, even above-average-looking total strangers. So the silence stretched between them.

"I haven't seen this floor plan for a long time. It's a nice room, Scott," Joyce said, filling the void. "Very large and comfortable."

Beside the master bedroom was an open loft area with a huge corner group and a big-screen TV across from it. Built-in desks were under the windows and one of them was cluttered with books and papers next to a computer. Obviously this was Kendra's work space. Her perfect older sister didn't live here anymore.

Joyce looked around and took notes. "Teen rooms are popular, a good selling point."

"There's more this way," Scott said.

They peeked into the two bedrooms—one with the double bed neatly made, the other in a state of complete chaos. Obviously Kendra's. Thea didn't know why, but her heart went out to the teen who seemed to feel she didn't measure up.

Scott looked sheepish. "I had no idea her room was this bad."

"Teenagers." Joyce shrugged. "It goes with the territory."

Thea met his gaze and wondered. Shouldn't a parent have some idea about his child's environment? They lived in the same house, for goodness' sake.

"Brace yourself." He opened the bathroom door and stepped back. "I'm afraid to look."

Thea followed Joyce past him and breathed in the pleasant scent of cologne and man. Her stomach fluttered, but she chalked it up to the fact that it had been a long time since she'd experienced that particular scent. Ignoring him took some effort, but she managed to focus on the separate shower and tub area.

The vanity had two sinks and was littered with bottles of hair products and combs and brushes of various sizes and shapes. A curling iron, blow-dryer and makeup were scattered over every square inch of counter space. It seemed a million years since her biggest concern had been her hair. But she was grateful for those carefree days before she knew that life—and death—could bring her to her knees.

Sighing, she let her gaze wander. She saw flannel pajama bottoms and a coordinating top in a pile beside the overflowing wastebasket.

Scott was watching her and noticed the direction of her gaze. He hastily grabbed the handles of the trash bag, pulling it out of the container. "Sorry. I had no idea this bathroom was located in tornado alley."

Joyce arched an eyebrow. "I've seen much worse, believe me. This is nothing."

"Easy for you to say," he said, shutting the door. "I think it qualifies for federal disaster assistance."

Thea brought up the rear as they went downstairs. Was there a Mrs. Matthews? The interaction between him and his daughter gave her the impression there wasn't. The niggling sense of excitement in that thought brought her up short because it was so very unexpected.

In the kitchen, he set the bag of trash beside the tall circular metal container. "So there you have it," he said to Joyce.

She nodded. "This house will go fast on today's market."

"In spite of the biohazard bathroom?"

Thea laughed. Until his comments about Kendra's disaster of a bathroom, she'd thought the man had no sense of humor. She liked it.

"Forget it, Scott," Joyce said. "If you decide to list the place, you'll have time to clean it up."

"That will be Kendra's job," he said.

"Good luck getting her cooperation," Thea mumbled.

Joyce glanced at the two of them. "I gather she's resistant to moving?"

"She'll come around," he claimed.

"Of course she will." Joyce looked at her watch. "I've got to run to another appointment."

"So what do you think the place is worth?" he asked.

"Scott, you know as well as I do it's a gold mine. This

neighborhood is one of the most desirable in Santa Clarita. Houses sell as soon as they go on the market. There's a waiting list. You can easily get top dollar."

"What kind of top dollar are we talking?"

"Let me do some comparables and I'll let you know," she said. She looked at Thea. "I'll call you about listing your condo."

Thea nodded. After Joyce was gone, she was alone with Scott Matthews. For some reason he made her nervous, and not because he was annoyed with her. It had started after her assumption that he wasn't married.

"I guess I should be going, too," she said.

"Yeah."

She looked at the food she'd brought from a luncheon and reheated here for Kendra. It didn't seem right to walk away from the dirty dishes, so she moved several pots and pans to the sink and squirted soap from the container there into them.

"Just leave that," he said.

"Can't. Part of my job. A professional doesn't leave a mess in the kitchen."

"Even though you don't have a contract?"

"Even so. It's a service-oriented, word-of-mouth business. Someone you know might need a caterer and you'll remember the one who didn't leave a mess."

While she worked, Thea glanced at Scott who brooded beside her. "Kendra told me she's never had a party. Is that true?"

He met her gaze and his own narrowed. "It doesn't mean she's underprivileged."

"I can see that she's got everything she needs. Materially," she added.

"What are you saying?"

"Just that I got the feeling it was very important to her to have a party."

"What was your first clue, Dr. Phil?"

She ignored his sarcasm. "The fact that she didn't tell you I was coming. I'd have to guess she felt you would veto the catering idea."

"She didn't give me a chance to veto it."

"And if she had? What would you have said?" Thea asked, watching him carefully.

He sighed. "Probably I'd have said no."

"Look…" She rested her wrists inside the sink, letting the water drip from her hands. "Probably I should have asked if she had permission to hire me. And when it came to a signed contract and deposit check, the cat would have been out of the bag. But there's something about Kendra."

"Why didn't she come to me? That's a rhetorical question by the way." He shook his head, then met her gaze. "And I don't understand why she's so upset about selling the house. It's just a house." His tone oozed frustration.

"Men." Thea stared at him, not bothering to conceal her exasperation.

"What?"

His clueless expression was so darn cute, she couldn't help a small sigh. "How long have you lived here?"

He thought for a moment and said, "I guess ten or eleven years."

"So Kendra was about seven or eight when you moved in. She hardly remembers living anywhere else. She's facing big changes, like leaving high school and going away to college. Then she finds out you're getting rid of her anchor. Of course she freaked. Change is hard."

"I haven't gotten rid of anything yet."

"Just the thought of change is uncomfortable. It's human nature to fight against that."

Scott shifted his feet and brushed against the bag of trash on the floor. It tilted sideways, spilling the contents. "Damn it."

He bent to pick up the bag, giving her an unobstructed view of his backside. She was the first to admit she was out of practice in the fine art of observing men. And truthfully, she'd never understood the fascination for that particular part of the male anatomy. But Scott Matthews's fanny gave her a completely different perspective.

He straightened, pressed the latch on the kitchen can and dumped the smaller bag inside. Then he stooped again to gather up the stray trash on the tile. He picked up a slender plastic stick.

Frowning, he rolled it between his fingers. "Is this what I think it is?"

She saw the plus and minus symbols. "It is if you think it's a pregnancy test."

She should know. She'd used one not that long ago and hers had come up a plus.

Chapter 2

"Just shoot me now." A muscle jumped in Scott's lean cheek and tension made his already square jaw seem harder somehow. "Does this mean it's negative?"

Thea stared at the minus sign. "Not necessarily. The results are only accurate for a short time. There's no way to know if it's positive or negative unless you know how long it's been lying around."

His expression was dark when he looked up. "I feel as if I've been walking down the stairs and just missed the last three steps."

She wiped her hands on a dish towel. "Don't jump to conclusions."

Impossibly blue eyes narrowed on her. "What are you? Twenty-seven? Twenty-eight?"

"Thirty-four." But what did that have to do with anything?

"Married? Divorced?"

"Neither," she answered. "I'm a widow."

Something flickered in his eyes, but she was grateful when he didn't comment. The automatic "I'm sorry" was awkward and meaningless. She wasn't even sure why she'd clarified her marital status to him. Normally she didn't volunteer anything like that. But nothing about today was normal.

"Do you have any children?" he asked, exasperation lacing his tone.

Not yet, although she would soon. God willing. But this man was grilling her like raw hamburger. She'd innocently gotten caught up in his personal problems; that didn't mean she had to reciprocate with her own problems. When her husband had received his cancer diagnosis, she'd learned the very hard lesson that personal information should be dispensed on a need-to-know basis. Scott was a prospective client. Maybe not, she thought, noting his intense expression. But whatever happened, he wasn't entitled to her life story.

And she certainly wasn't going to tell this man, this virtual stranger, that she was now pregnant through in vitro fertilization with her dead husband's baby. She couldn't ignore the question, but there was no need to put a finer point on it.

"No," she finally said. "I don't have any children."

He slid her an I-thought-so look. "Then don't tell me not to jump to conclusions."

"I was simply trying to help."

"There's nothing you can do. This," he said, holding up the stick, "means she's having sex. Probably unprotected."

"I'm not an idiot, Scott. I know this is a serious issue."

"Really?" He put the test stick on the counter beside him, then met her gaze. "You know it intellectually? Or because you've watched Oprah and Dr. Phil? Or you've seen the teenage pregnancy statistics in *Newsweek?*"

"Of course, but—"

"But you don't have children. You have no idea what it's like to be nineteen and find out you're going to be a father.

You don't have a clue what it's like to be a kid yourself and find out you're going to have a baby."

"No, but—"

"I do," he interrupted. "It's damned scary. And everyone has an opinion about what should happen. My parents. Her parents. On top of that, she and I couldn't agree on what to do."

"What *did* you do?" Thea couldn't stop herself from asking. Just because she had a hang-up about sharing nonessential personal information didn't mean she wasn't curious about him. If he had a problem with it, he could tell her to mind her own business.

"I married her," he answered.

"Most people would call that doing the right thing."

"The right thing?" His handsome features turned harsh.

"No one could call your daughter ugly names or tease her about being born outside of marriage."

"Yeah, at least I prevented that." He smiled, but there was no humor in the look.

"And it can't have been all bad. You had a second child together."

He folded his arms over his chest. "Kendra wasn't planned. We were still too young and, I thought, perfectly happy with one child. Then we were careless. I was all of twenty-two when she came along."

Thea thought about her own struggle to become a mother. Ever since she was a little girl, she'd wanted to have a baby. When she'd married, she'd ached to know what it was like to feel a life growing inside her. She felt it now, mostly because she was tired and nauseous. The point was, she felt *different,* important. After the heartbreak of two miscarriages, she yearned to bring a healthy baby into the world and would do everything possible to make that happen. Now Scott was telling her his second child wasn't welcome.

She didn't try to hide the irritation and disapproval she suspected were visible on her face. "Some people would say having two children makes you lucky."

"I am. And very grateful they're normal, healthy kids. I love them more than anything. But the fact is I missed out on a lot. I hardly got to be a kid before I had two in two and a half years."

"But isn't it the tough times that forge the bonds in a relationship?"

"Not ours. That second pregnancy was the straw that broke the camel's back."

"What do you mean?"

"When Gail was seven and Kendra five, she decided the girls and I were cramping her style. She didn't want to be a mother and she left."

"She abandoned her children?"

"Define abandoned. Every once in a while she turns up. It was worse when they were little and all their emotions were stirred up. Now the girls have her pegged. They're polite but cool if she drops in."

"It must have hurt them a lot."

"They're better off without her." He shrugged. "They got over it."

Did they? And were they really better off without her? Thea wondered. Through no fault of their own or Scott's, Kendra and her sister hadn't been raised by Ward and June Cleaver. And Thea sensed ripples beneath the surface in the Matthews household. Sensed, heck. She'd seen for herself the tension between Scott and his daughter. Kendra was still hurting.

"Were you better off when your wife left?" she asked him. Again she wondered if he would answer. In his shoes, she wouldn't. But everything she'd just learned had her curiosity sparring with her better judgment.

He sighed. "That's not an easy question to answer. It was tough doing it alone. I still had to work to put food on the table and a roof over our heads. But I had two little girls depending on me when they got sick. Child care was a constant worry. And it's expensive. There was no one to share the responsibility."

That gave Thea a pang. Her plan of having a baby had always included sharing the experience with her baby's father. And the plan had always involved sex with said father. She'd never envisioned that the love of her life would get sick. That he would simply donate sperm and medical science would take care of the rest. She was having a baby. And she would be doing it alone. But in her case, she would never know what having help and support felt like, so she wouldn't feel the absence of it. But Scott *had* known.

"Did you miss her? Or was it just parenting alone that was a problem? I'm sorry," she said, before he could answer. She held up her hand. "That's really none of my business."

What was it about Scott Matthews that made inappropriate questions pop out of her mouth?

"Actually, the fact that I don't mind you asked is an answer in itself. Yes, I missed her. And not just because raising those two girls alone was the hardest thing I've ever done in my life."

He'd cared and then he was alone. She related all too well. "I'm sorry," she said again.

"I don't need sympathy. Raising kids is also the most wonderful, rewarding thing I've ever done." He blew out a long breath. "I'm not exactly sure why I told you all that."

"Maybe because I happened to be here when you found the stick?"

He frowned. "That damn pregnancy test."

"Sometimes it's easier to confide in strangers. Someone who doesn't have an emotional stake in any of this."

"Yeah," he said, running his fingers through his hair. "I don't usually spill my guts. But then, it's not every day I find out my daughter is sexually active."

"Shock will loosen your tongue."

He glanced at the evidence beside him. "I can't believe this. I don't want my daughter to be a mother while she's still a child herself. I don't want her to repeat my mistakes."

"I hate to think of children as mistakes," she said, a tad sharply. "They're a consequence of an action. A fact of life." Or in her case, combining her egg with her husband's sperm in a petri dish. In vitro fertilization was the miracle that had produced her fact of life.

"You're splitting hairs. I don't want them to do the same things I did. And now I find this."

"You were right when you said I've had no experience in this area. But you're obviously upset and I feel compelled to offer something. If Kendra is pregnant, it would be an experience that will take her down a different path. It doesn't have to mean failure for either of you."

"Hold on—"

"Think about it," she interrupted. "Can you honestly tell me you can imagine your life without your children in it?"

Hostility crackled in the air between them. Then the corners of his mouth curved up. "Actually, yes. I've been imagining Kendra going off to college."

"She'll still be in your life," Thea pointed out.

"I was kidding. She thinks I'm against junior college. Truthfully, I have mixed feelings about her going away. You're right. I can't imagine never having my girls. They're my reason for getting out of bed every day and putting one foot in front of the other."

Boy, in her current condition, she could really relate to that. It was on the tip of her tongue to tell him about her pregnancy, to share it with him. To bond. But she swallowed the temptation.

"Look, Scott, has it occurred to you that the test might not even belong to her?"

His face brightened. "Actually, no."

"You're obviously a glass-is-half-empty kind of guy," she said wryly. "It's always possible that it belongs to a friend who didn't want to take the test at her house. And Kendra was just being supportive."

"Way to put a positive spin on this."

His sudden smile had a very weird effect on her. She felt the force of it through her whole body. Her stomach dropped as if she were riding an elevator that suddenly plunged toward the basement. And her heart fluttered as if powered by a horde of hummingbirds' wings.

"I'm a pro at spinning," she finally managed to say.

"Spinning the facts?"

"No, actually. Salad spinning is more my style."

"Thanks for the benefit of an alternate perspective." He laughed. "But seriously, I'm sorry I dumped on you."

"Like I could have stopped you." She smiled.

"You could have left."

"No, I really couldn't. I've never met anyone who looked like they needed to talk more than you did today. And it is helpful, especially if somebody listens."

"I don't normally get carried away like that."

"No problem. Don't give it another thought."

Thea sincerely meant that. She had a feeling Scott's daughter was searching for an emotional *something*. And the pregnancy test was troubling. She was aware that the girl had reached out to her, even if it was behind her father's back. Obviously her graduation party was a big deal to Kendra and for some reason she couldn't tell her father.

"But do me a favor, Scott."

"Sure. What?"

"Just keep in mind that some girls confuse—"

The garage door slammed just before Kendra walked into the family room. She looked at the two of them. "Hi, Thea."

Scott felt the hostility radiating from his daughter. Even if he hadn't, he wasn't ready for the conversation he knew he had to have with her. "How is Zoe?"

"She wasn't home." She glared at him. "How come you're still here?"

Talking to Thea had begun to calm him down, but he could feel his blood pressure climbing again. He glanced at Thea and saw the sympathy on her face as she quietly watched Kendra.

"What does that mean?" he asked.

Kendra lifted one shoulder. The sullen gesture was one he saw from time to time and it never failed to fire up his frustration. "You're selling the house," she said. "Your work here is done. I figured you'd go back to the office."

He picked up the pregnancy test stick and held it up. "Not after I found this."

Kendra's eyes grew wide. Then surprise was replaced with angry resentment. "You were snooping in my stuff?"

"If you call dumping the trash in your bathroom snooping—yes."

Thea picked up her purse. "Scott. Kendra. You two need to talk. It would probably be best if I leave you alone."

"Don't go," Kendra said. "I want you to stay."

"But, this is private." Thea took a step back.

"Not anymore. Thanks to my Dad."

"Don't make this about me," he defended. "If you straightened up after yourself, I'd never have known. Your room—"

"You were in my room?" Her voice rose in pitch to just below what only a dog could hear.

"Yes. And you know why."

"To sell it." Kendra huffed out a breath.

"It's part of the house."

"I can't believe you let strangers in my room."

Thea cleared her throat and slid her purse on her shoulder. "I'll just get my things together."

"Please don't go," Kendra begged. "I didn't mean you're a stranger."

But she was. Practically. Scott looked between the two of them. "Why is it so important for her to stay?"

"Neutral third party," his daughter said, tossing a strand of hair over her shoulder. "I need a witness."

Scott looked at his daughter, the dark hair and blue eyes that were so like his. Maybe that's what scared him the most—that she was so much like him. A little rebellious. A little daring. Hostile and angry. The thought of her making the same mistakes and living with the consequences tied him in knots. He wanted her to have more choices, fewer problems. Hell, he wanted her life to be perfect, however unrealistic that was. How did he get through to her?

He looked at Thea, who was studying him. If it would help Kendra, he had no objection to Thea sticking around. After spilling his guts, there wasn't a whole lot she didn't know. He nodded slightly and she took her purse off her shoulder.

"Now, forget about the house," he said, glancing at the pregnancy test. "There's something more important we have to focus on."

"That's none of your business."

"I disagree," he shot back. "I'm your father. If you're having sex—"

"I don't want to talk to you about this."

"I don't care. Are you pregnant?" he demanded.

"That's none of your business," she said angrily.

"The hell it's not. You're my daughter."

"An accident of birth doesn't give you the right to tell me what to do."

"Actually it does. And another reason I can is that I pay all the bills around here."

"There won't be an 'around here' much longer, thanks to you," she said.

He glanced at Thea, who was diplomatically silent. Then he met his daughter's angry gaze. "It's not going to work."

"What?" she asked defiantly.

"You're trying to take the heat off by changing the subject."

"And you don't give a damn about my feelings."

"If you're talking about the house again, I'm not going there." He took a step forward. "Focus, Kendra. That pregnancy test tells me you're having sex. I need to know if you're going to have a baby and who the father is."

Like heat rising from blacktop, animosity rolled off the teen in waves. "I can't believe you. For the last eighteen years, you've practically ignored me. I'm eighteen. I'm an adult, too old for you to interfere in my life."

"You'll never be too old. And I'll always be your father. It's my job to interfere."

"Why can't you just leave this alone? Leave me alone?"

Scott felt frustration and anger coiling inside him, but struggled to control the feelings. Before he could, she turned and ran from the room. "Kendra? Come back here," he shouted.

The stomping on the stairs was a good indication that she planned to ignore him. He started to go after her.

"Scott?"

He felt a hand on his arm and looked at Thea. "What?"

"It might be best to let her go."

"But I have to know."

Thea's brown eyes were warm with sympathy. "And she'll just continue to stonewall you if you charge after her."

"So? I'll wear her down."

Thea shook her head. "Not in her present state of mind, you won't. You can talk, but you can't force her to reveal anything."

When she removed her hand from his arm, he missed the warmth of her fingers. "Do you have a suggestion?"

"Yes."

"Care to share?"

She nodded. "Give her some space. Let her calm down. You might want to do the same."

"I am calm."

"Oh?" Thea blinked up at him and then she smiled.

"What's so funny?" he asked.

"You're stretched so tight, if you were a rubber band and let go, you'd put someone's eye out."

He released a long breath. "Okay. Maybe you're right." He stared at the doorway where his daughter had stood moments before. "But I don't get it. What was all that about ignoring her for eighteen years?"

"I don't know," Thea said.

"Maybe this is payback."

"For what? Being a good father?"

He looked at her. "For how I felt when I first found out my wife was pregnant again. But when I saw Kendra for the first time…" He searched for words to express the power of his emotions and couldn't find any. "It was love at first sight," he finally said.

"Have you ever told *her* that?"

"I don't know." He rubbed the back of his neck.

"Under the circumstances, she might have some un-resolved feelings," Thea suggested. "Some girls confuse sex and love."

"Are you saying she's looking for love in all the wrong places because she thinks I don't care about her?"

"I have no idea." She sighed. "I'm just the caterer. They say the way to a man's heart is through his stomach. I'm not sure there's a parallel, but she contacted me to do her graduation party. And she didn't tell you she was doing the party on that scale. I'm no shrink, but it's obvious to me that she's sending you some kind of message."

"Can you decode it?"

"With my magic garlic press? Or maybe the decoder in my secret slotted spoon?" she asked, one corner of her full mouth tilting up.

"Okay. Stupid question. But you're a woman. Do you have any thoughts about what she's trying to say?"

"Yes."

When she didn't say anything further he added, "Any you'd care to share?"

"Do you really want me to? After all, I've never had any children," she said pointedly.

"Okay. I deserve that for patronizing you. But I'm desperate. Lady, I need all the help I can get. If you've got any ideas, I'm listening."

"Okay." She nodded. "I suggest you give her some time. When she's ready to talk, you listen to her."

"That's it?"

She nodded, then said, "And one more thing."

"Yes?"

"Think about having the party, and not just an average backyard barbecue. Give some thought to doing it the way she wants it," she added.

"Because you need the gig?"

She shook her head. "I don't need the job badly enough to take advantage of your situation. If one job was that important, I wouldn't be looking to take on a bigger house and mortgage."

"Okay. Then why should I think about doing the shindig her way?"

"Because my impression is that she's basically a good kid. And this was important enough to her to go behind your back."

"So you're saying I should reward her bad behavior?"

She thought for a moment and then said, "Think of it as hearing her cry for help. If she knows you're listening instead of lecturing, she's more likely to tell you what you want to know."

"How can I just listen when I need to make her understand that if she's not careful, she could ruin her life?"

"If I could answer that question, I'd be a financially independent woman." Thea shrugged and smiled a little sadly. "Goodbye, Scott. Good luck," she added.

It was odd, but when he'd found her in his kitchen, he'd been irritated. Watching her leave irritated him even more. And the implications of that didn't sweeten his temper.

Chapter 3

The following morning Thea parked her car in front of her office, then went to let herself in. She found the door was unlocked, which meant her workaholic partner was already there.

"Connie?" she called out, setting her purse and briefcase on her desk.

"Back here," came the reply.

She'd been best friends with Connie Howard since the seventh grade. They'd gone through everything together—their weddings, the birth of her friend's two children and the death of Thea's husband. She would have gotten through it without Connie, but probably not with her sanity intact.

Thea walked through the doorway separating the front office from the kitchen/work area in the back. She'd leased this space when her business outgrew her condo. Sometimes she cooked for a job at home, but mostly she and Connie prepared food here.

They'd furnished this office with a top-of-the-line double oven, a microwave/convection oven, a large side-by-side refrigerator and the best set of pots and pans their budget allowed. The drawers and cupboards were stuffed with the latest gizmos to make a cook's heart go pitter-patter.

Connie was industriously wiping down the countertops. As Thea approached, her tall, redheaded friend glanced over her shoulder. "Hi, T."

"Hi, yourself. It's only eight-thirty. What are you doing here so early?"

"It's not *that* early. Besides, I had a day off." She faced Thea and put her hands on her boyishly slim hips. "So how did your appointments go yesterday?"

The image of Scott Matthews instantly popped into her head. Not surprising, since thoughts of him hadn't been far from her mind since leaving his place yesterday. She'd wondered whether his daughter was going to have a baby. Some appointment.

"I took deposits for several parties," she said vaguely.

Connie's green-eyed gaze narrowed on her. "And?"

"And nothing."

"Don't blow me off, T. You've got a funny look on your face."

Thea sat on one of the tall stools outside the U-shaped work space and looked at her friend. "One of my appointments got a little weird. The initial contact was made by a teenager who didn't have parental permission for a catered graduation party."

"Bummer."

"Yeah," Thea said, sighing with what felt like regret. And she wasn't sure why. Like she'd told Scott—it wasn't as if they needed the catering job to survive. This business was thriving and word of mouth was their best free advertising.

Connie leaned forward and rested her elbows on the counter. "It's just as well you found out she was pulling a fast one before putting time, effort and money into the event. How did the underhanded little stinker get caught?"

"Kendra's father came home unexpectedly while she and I were discussing the party."

"What about the kid's mother?"

"Out of the picture," Thea answered. "And I get the feeling Kendra is having some feelings about it. She accused her father of ignoring her."

"I was going to high-five you on your perception, but most teenagers are giddy with happiness when their parents ignore them. I'd say that's a big clue she's got issues."

Thea laughed. "There's more."

"How can there be more? Is this kid in training for *America's Most Wanted?* How old is she?"

"She's eighteen, getting ready to graduate and go to college. Scott wants—"

"Scott?"

"Her father. He wants her to go away to school and she was talking up the local junior college. Reading between the lines, I think maybe she's getting cold feet."

"So she's acting out? Masterminding a covert event to get even with a pushy dad?"

Thea shook her head. "Your flair for the dramatic comes in handy for planning themed events. But in everyday life, not so much."

"I'm not the one trying to pull a fast one," Connie protested.

"Maybe she has reason. She was upset about her father getting ready to sell the house when she goes to college. He hadn't said anything to her about it yet. Selling, I mean."

"Still, he's the grown-up. I don't think a failure to communicate is cause to take him out back and beat the crap out of him. So to speak," she added.

Thea shrugged. "I think he's guilty of premeditated failure

to communicate. He didn't want to deal with his daughter's emotional fallout until it was absolutely necessary."

"Chicken," Connie said.

"I can't say I blame him."

"Now you're defending him?" her friend questioned.

"I guess it's my tragic flaw that I can see both sides of an issue. He was somewhat hostile in the beginning. But then I began to feel sorry for him."

"Why?"

Thea rested her chin on her knuckles. "I guess it was the pregnancy test he found."

"Whoa." Connie shook her head as if to clear it. "You're going to need to back up and explain that one."

"It's not that complicated. Joyce took a tour of the house for the market evaluation and I tagged along. It's a great place, by the way. Just what I've been looking for."

"Yeah, yeah. Get back to the test."

"Kendra's bathroom looked like a beauty supply store threw up all over it. He was shocked and appalled in equal parts and instinctively grabbed the bag of trash. When he was dumping it, the little stick fell out."

"Is she pregnant?"

Thea lifted one shoulder in a shrug. "Inconclusive because it's only accurate for a certain length of time. He didn't know how long ago she'd done the test before tossing it in the trash."

"Did you tell him you knew this because you'd recently used one yourself?"

Thea shook her head. "He was in a state of shock and didn't ask how I could read it."

"And if he had?"

"I'd have told him it's none of his business. My pregnancy has barely gotten off the ground. In my experience, it's bad luck bordering on a jinx to talk about it until I've successfully completed the first trimester."

"Okay."

The tone of that one word said she was crazy and superstitious.

"Connie, don't you go judgmental on me. You know better than anyone why I feel this way. In vitro fertilization is personal and private. I've done it twice and twice I thought I was pregnant. The first time, I told everyone. Strangers on the street, people on the phone, it didn't matter. And then I lost the baby. I had to go back to everyone I'd told and relive the pain of losing a child over and over. But once wasn't enough. I did it again because apparently I'm incapable of learning from my mistake. Third time's the charm. I won't do it again. Especially because I've got all my eggs in one basket. So to speak. I have no more eggs, at least none that are fertilized."

"I'm aware of that. And, by the way, that was quite a speech."

"It's from the heart, Con. If I lose this baby, too, it will be like losing my husband all over again." She took a deep breath to relieve the sudden pressure in her chest. "I promised David I would make sure part of him went on."

"And you've done that," Connie said, sympathy lacing the words.

"Not yet. Not until this child is born. To do that, I will not breathe a word to anyone—"

"What am I? Chopped liver?"

"You're my best friend. I had to tell you. Besides, you'd have known. Sort of a best friend ESP." She shrugged. "But I will not discuss this baby with anyone else until the first trimester is under my belt."

"So to speak."

"Yes." Thea reluctantly gave in to a smile.

"Not even your family?"

"Especially not them. Mom and Dad can't be emotionally involved until the risky first three months are done. They were crushed the other two times and I don't want them hurt again. Or my brother and sister, either."

"You don't need to protect everyone, Thea."

"Not everyone. Just my family, including this life inside me. Con, I can't remember a time when I didn't want children. Even when I was a little girl, I was drawn to babies. When I see a pregnant woman, or someone with kids in a stroller, the yearning to have one is so powerful, it's almost a pain inside me. Does that sound crazy?"

"Yes." Connie tucked a strand of red hair behind her ear. "But I understand. If I'd never had a couple of little misery-makers, I know I'd feel as if something was missing from my life."

Connie's choice of words belied the fact that she was a devoted wife and mother. She'd been Thea's rock through everything: when Thea and David were trying unsuccessfully to conceive; the subsequent exams that indirectly led to discovering his cancer; freezing sperm so they could have children following his chemotherapy; remission; the two IVF attempts that were unsuccessful and so incredibly heartbreaking; David's relapse and death. Now this one last try.

"I will do anything," Thea said, "to ensure the success of this pregnancy."

"And I'll help in any way I can." Connie made a gesture, as if she were zipping her lips.

"Thanks."

Connie grinned. "So tell me about Scott Matthews."

"He's got baggage, big-time."

"Who doesn't?"

"You, for one." Thea toyed with the diamond-studded heart on a delicate chain around her neck. "He's raised his two girls on his own—a father for the first time at twenty. It was an enormous responsibility and he was understandably upset to learn his daughter used a pregnancy test. And concerned she'll repeat his history."

"Wow, that's a lot of information."

"I guess he felt comfortable talking to me. That happens sometimes with a complete stranger."

"And how would you know that? Sharing information isn't something you do," Connie pointed out.

"And you know why. When David was sick, I found out the hard way that sharing details can be a huge mistake." One she didn't plan to repeat. Burn me once, shame on you. Burn me twice, shame on me.

"Still," Connie said, "there's something different about you since I last saw you."

"Probably the pregnancy glow," she said wryly. "Although I think that's an old wives' tale. I haven't got the energy to glow."

"Don't be so sure. There's a sparkle in your eyes. Could it be because of Scott Matthews?"

"I think someone's been whacked with the whimsical stick," Thea said. "I'm the same as usual. Besides, Scott joked about wanting to be alone when his daughter goes to college. But I think many a truth is spoken in jest."

Thea could tell him, alone wasn't all it's cracked up to be. She wouldn't share that with her friend and give her any ideas. But the truth was, as a caterer, she cooked for many people, but no one special. There was no one waiting for her at home, no one to take care of, no one to talk about her day with.

"No one's whacked me with anything," Connie said. "I just know you. What does Scott Matthews look like?"

"Oh, come on—"

"Humor me."

Thea let out a big sigh. "He's tall. Dark hair. Blue eyes."

"Not bad. What does he do for a living?"

"Kendra told me he's a building contractor," Thea answered. "And if his house is any indication, he does all right financially."

"So you had this communication thing going on, yet you're blowing him off?"

"He was annoyed that I met with his daughter behind his back. For Whom the Bell Toils didn't get the job. I have no reason to see him again. That doesn't constitute blowing him off. There's nothing to blow off."

She heard the ding-dong from the reception area indicating someone had come in the front door. "Anyone here?" The voice was decidedly masculine.

"I'll get it," Connie said, untying her apron.

"No. I'll go. Saved by the bell." Thea stood and grinned at her friend. "Now I know how Kendra felt when her father started in on her."

Thea walked through the door and was surprised to see the father in question standing there. Her stomach did a funny little shimmy. She knew it was too early for that movement to be about the baby. So it had to be all about Scott Matthews. She hadn't expected to be attracted to a man again. She'd thought that part of her had died with her husband.

She smiled at Scott. "Hello again."

"Thea." One corner of his wonderful mouth quirked up. "Or should I call you Obi-Wan?"

"Excuse me?"

"You did see *Star Wars?*"

"Of course. But I don't get the reference."

"The teacher and the student. Are you sure you don't have children?"

None that she'd cop to just yet. "No. I mean yes, I'm sure. Why? What are you talking about?"

"Wise you are, as well as beautiful," he said, imitating one of the movie characters.

"I think that's Yoda-speak. But if it was a bona fide compliment, thank you."

"It was. And you're welcome."

"Why am I wise?" she asked, refusing to acknowledge the beautiful part of that compliment.

"I managed to talk to Kendra without anyone leaving the room in hysterics, including me."

She laughed. "What happened?"

"I took your advice and simply listened and asked questions. I tried not to lecture or offer advice."

"And that didn't make you hysterical?" she couldn't resist asking.

"Of course it did. I'm a guy. And I build things. So the need to fix it *now* is especially strong. But I was a brave little soldier and didn't let it show."

"Wow. Congressional Medal of Honor material."

He leaned a jean-clad hip against her desk and half sat. "It almost killed me not to bring up the pregnancy test, but I tried it your way."

"And?"

"She admitted she feels bad when there's an event and her mother isn't there. Which proves your theory—listen you must, then talk to you she will."

Thea laughed. "I didn't say it like that."

"No. But the message was the same. I hope by not lecturing this time, she'll be more open to talking about it when I bring up the subject of the pregnancy test. Which I plan to in the very near future." He frowned and worry lines bracketed his nose and mouth.

"Good instincts. Pick and choose your battles. Figure out which hill you want to die on."

"Actually, I'd prefer not to die on any of them. But I suppose a single battle isn't critical as long as I win the war."

"Well said, General Solo." She saluted. His responding grin hit her in the midsection like a fireball. She backed away and rested her backside against Connie's desk.

"I—I'm glad you think I helped," she said, hoping he

hadn't noticed her stammer. And especially hoping he didn't get that her reaction to him caused it. "But, really, I didn't do anything. There should be some kind of a medal for raising a terrific young woman like Kendra. I'm sure your older daughter is just as wonderful."

"Gail," he said.

She nodded. "She's in college and on her way, thanks to you."

"I don't know how much is thanks to me. She's just a good kid. So is Kendra." He ran his fingers through his hair. "I always thought I was doing a good job as both mother and father. That they wouldn't miss their mother too much. After listening to my daughter, I realize I was wrong. She missed a lot."

"It's not your fault, Scott. You shouldn't feel guilty."

"No? I picked the woman who walked out so who else is there to blame?"

"You couldn't make her stay. Any more than—"

"What?" he prompted.

She'd been about to say any more than she could prevent her husband from dying. But this conversation wasn't about her. It was about a breakthrough with his daughter. Thea knew saying something about her own loss would completely shift the topic to her. Talking about herself could get awkward.

"I was going to say you couldn't make her stay any more than you could keep your girls from growing up."

"Isn't that the truth?" A tender look stole into his eyes. "But I wanted to give my kids everything, every advantage. And I couldn't give them a mom, which is what they needed most."

The words were like a stone pressing on Thea's chest. She'd made a choice to do everything humanly possible to ensure that a part of her husband went on. Now she was well on her way to keeping her promise. But she'd never stopped to consider the child's feelings. Scott's ex-wife was alive and well somewhere and, if she had a change of heart, could be involved with her girls. But there was no way her child would ever know its father.

How profoundly sad was that? When she and David had first started trying to have a baby, she'd had dreams about parenting together. She so very much wanted to share the experience with him. But fate had other plans. Now she was in this alone. And Scott was alone, too. For a long time now. Why was that? A good-looking guy like him. Was he commitment-phobic? If so, she certainly couldn't blame him.

"Thea?"

"Hmm?" She looked up and noticed Scott was frowning.

"You drifted off there. Anything wrong?"

"No." She took a deep breath. "I was just wondering—"

"What?"

"Feel free to tell me to jump in the lake. But I was wondering how a mother could simply walk out on her children."

"There's the million-dollar question." He lifted one broad shoulder drawing her attention there.

His light blue collared golf shirt molded to his upper body in a most intriguing way. He was alternately lean and muscular in all the right places. Her gaze slid to the sturdy work boots he wore and she tried to remember if she'd always thought the look was sexy. Or if it was more a matter of the man *in* the boots.

He sighed. "I was focused on how hard her leaving was on me and the difficulties of raising the girls alone. They seemed to be doing fine, so I took that at face value. I believed it because it was easier. I buried my head in the sand and left my backside exposed."

And a very nice backside it was, Thea thought. Unfortunately, she'd noticed a lot more than his backside and had the spiking pulse and sweaty palms to prove it.

"You've obviously done a fine job with the girls, Scott.

And that's the last time I'm going to pump up your ego. It's entirely possible that Kendra hasn't missed her mother all that much. Until now. Graduation from high school is a big step. I still remember the emotional trauma."

"Really?" He folded his arms over his chest. The movement showcased his superior biceps.

"Spoken like a man," she said, shaking her head. "She's grieving the loss of a comfortable way of life as well as the familiar faces she sees every day."

"But she'll make new friends in college."

"She doesn't know that yet. All she can see is what will be gone. What's changing. Maybe this has triggered some emotional upheaval she hasn't felt until now."

He rubbed the back of his neck. "Interesting theory. She's had bouts of rebelliousness here and there. But until yesterday, she's never done anything without running it by me first."

"Reading between the lines, I'd say that behavior is an indication of something pretty important to her."

"Yeah. When I listened to her, I got that impression."

Thea knew men were action-oriented, and Scott more than most. She wondered how many fathers would have taken her advice and actually listened to their daughters. She met his gaze across the space separating the desks and realized he was certainly more than just another pretty face. In addition to his good looks, he was thoughtful, introspective and boyishly charming. The triple threat.

She had a vague sense of relief that she hadn't gotten the catering job. He was the first man she'd noticed in a long time and the sensation wasn't the least bit comfortable. She didn't want to notice a man. It was act one in a play she wouldn't audition for.

Obviously Scott had dropped by to thank her for the advice. And the courtesy was very nice. But she was grateful she wouldn't have to see him again after this.

"I appreciate the 4-1-1 about Kendra."

"Hmm?" he said, obviously puzzled.

"Information. That she's communicating," Thea clarified.

"Yeah." He blew out a long breath.

She straightened away from the desk. "I'm glad things went well with the two of you. Now I have to get to an appointment."

He stood up. "And I have to get to work."

"Kendra said you're a building contractor?"

"Matthews and Sons Construction. My father is retired now, but my brother and I run the company."

"Aren't you doing that big housing project over in Northbridge?"

He nodded. "And I have a crew there waiting for me."

"You shouldn't keep them waiting any longer. Thanks for stopping by, Scott."

"Actually, I didn't come by just to give you an update. I want to hire Thea Bell to toil for me. Will you cater my daughter's graduation party?"

Talk about burying your head in the sand. Thea hadn't seen that one coming. Or maybe she just hadn't wanted to see it. Now what was she going to do?

Chapter 4

"You want to hire me?"

"That's what I said. You sound surprised."

"That's because I am." There was an understatement, she thought.

"Why?"

"I guess because you acted as if I committed a mortal sin when I treated your daughter like a grown-up."

"I may have overreacted," he admitted. "I might have come off a tad abrasive."

She couldn't resist needling him *a tad.* "Might have? You acted as if I was working black-ops catering with your teenager behind your back. I got the impression that my integrity was questionable in your opinion."

"Now that you mention it…" His expression turned sheepish. "I made some phone calls. You'll be glad to know your integrity checks out fine."

"What a relief. I was worried."

When he turned all the amps in his grin on her, Thea couldn't breathe. She began to straighten the already neat stack of receipts on Connie's desk, but the distraction didn't do much to take the edge off her reaction to him. He was offering her a job. The fact that she was even hesitating to take it spoke volumes. When she was dealing with Kendra, there had been no question about her doing the party. Now that she would be dealing with Kendra's father, everything was different. And it shouldn't be.

Thea had catered events for both women and men. She'd done functions for corporate CEOs—*male* executives. This man was no different.

And that was when she recognized the lie.

She liked Scott and that made him different. It made her as nervous as a dieter in a doughnut shop, which was why she wanted to turn him down flat.

Then she looked head-on into the intensity of his gaze and her stomach did that whole stop, drop and roll thing. From another lifetime she vaguely remembered this feeling. It was another good reason to refuse the job. But what did that intensity in his expression mean? Did he find her attractive? It had been too long since she'd wondered or cared about such things and she couldn't tell. Her feminine instincts, too long turned off, were now unreliable. He probably didn't care about her one way or the other and she was being a ninny.

"Earth to Thea. It didn't take this long to build the Suez Canal. So what do you say? Will you take the gig?"

"Do you have a date in mind?" she hedged. "I need to check my schedule."

"She's graduating the middle of June, assuming there are no unexpected surprises with her grades. But she's always been an honors student, so I don't expect that." He thought for a moment. "I think a Saturday night would work best." Moving closer to her, he glanced down at the large, desk-blotter calendar. "How about June nineteenth?" he said, pointing to the date.

She noticed the strength in his wide wrist and tanned forearm. She watched the muscles there bunch and ripple, making it difficult for her to take a deep breath.

"I'll check my day planner." She unzipped her briefcase and pulled out the leather-bound calendar. After opening it, she found the date and tried not to let him see her relief when she spotted a conflict. Loophole. She met his gaze. "I'm holding that date open for someone."

"Holding it?" He frowned. "I'm going to take a shot in the dark here. Do you have a signed contract? A deposit?"

"Not yet, but I promised to try and keep that date free and I feel an obligation to the client."

He pulled a checkbook from the back pocket of his jeans. "I'm willing to sign on the dotted line right now and put my money where my mouth is."

Of course as soon as he mentioned it, her gaze went straight to his mouth. Some subconscious part of her wondered how his lips would feel against her own and the thought made her shiver. What was that about? Fear? Awareness? Weather-related? Darned if she knew. But the reaction told her she should refuse his deposit and tell him if the date opened up, she would let him know.

He met her gaze and assumed a puppy-dog expression to ratchet up his persuasion. "Kendra would be very disappointed."

Drat. That was the only thing he could have said to win her over. Thea couldn't let down a teenage girl whom she suspected had been let down one too many times already.

"All right, Scott. You win. I'll do the party."

He grinned again, showing his straight white teeth and very attractive smile. She thought of Little Red Riding Hood and the Big Bad Wolf and couldn't help feeling she'd just stepped alone into the woods on her way to Grandma's house.

* * *

Scott looked at his daughter biting into her enchilada. "Thanks for throwing dinner together, sweetie. I planned to get home early, but there was a problem at one of the sites."

"That's okay. Do you like it?" she asked, about the meal.

"It's great." And that was no lie. "When did you get to be such a good cook?"

"Thea gave me the recipe when she catered my friend's birthday party. She said it wasn't hard to make and almost impossible to mess up. I guess she was right."

Thea Bell. He'd had trouble getting her off his mind since leaving her office that morning. And that wasn't at all like him. He'd dated here and there, but nothing serious. And it had been a long time, so he wasn't used to thinking about a woman. Normally work was the only thing that took his mind off the ups and downs of his kids. But he'd found Thea was one smart cookie and pretty intuitive. She'd been right about the fact that he should listen to his daughter instead of lecturing.

But there was still the matter of that pregnancy test and it was too important to ignore. He so badly wanted to tell Kendra to do as he said, not as he'd done. He didn't want her to learn the same lessons he had learned in the school of hard knocks. But how could he get through to her? How would Thea approach this potential minefield?

He started to say there was something he wanted to talk to her about, then checked himself. That would be his daughter's signal to shut down.

He looked across the dinner table and decided to try a different tack. "This is nice. Having dinner together."

"Yeah. Nice." Warily, she met his gaze.

"I don't stop to appreciate it enough. And I should," he added.

"Why?"

"Lots of reasons. Because I enjoy spending time with you.

And because when your sister was a baby, I hardly ever got to share a meal with the family."

"It's not that big a deal, Dad," she said. Her expression and tone told him she was ready to shut him down in a nanosecond if necessary.

"Yeah, it is. In those days, I was going to college at night and working during the day."

"But it's Grandad's company."

"That didn't mean I could slack off," he explained. "If anything, he was harder on me because we were related."

"I know the feeling," she muttered.

He refused to be sidetracked by even a mumbled verbal projectile. "The point is that between work and school, I put in a lot of hours away from home. It cost me time with you guys."

She pushed her plate away. "What are you really trying to say, Dad?"

So much for his different tack. He put his fork down. "Okay. Here's the deal. I made some choices that sent me on a path in life," he said, recalling what Thea had said. "I love you and your sister very much and wouldn't trade either of you for anything. But it was a path that took away my carefree youth. I don't want to see that happen to you."

She rolled her eyes. "Here we go."

"About the pregnancy test," he said. There was no subtle way to do this.

"I don't want to talk about it." She started to get up.

"Sit, Ken. I need to know. Was the test positive?"

"You saw the stick," she said, her hostility simmering. "Don't you know?"

"Thea said the results are inaccurate if it's been sitting for a while."

She'd known right off the top of her head what the stick was and how to interpret it. Along with the rules that would affect the damn plus or minus sign. He'd had no idea. It must be a female thing.

"Look, Dad, I really don't want to talk to you about this."

"Believe me, I don't like this any better than you. But I need to know if you're pregnant or not."

Her cheeks turned pink, and she stared down at her plate. "Not."

The weight he'd felt on his shoulders lifted and inside he was pumping his arm and hollering hallelujah with an exclamation point. Outside, he struggled not to react at all.

"Okay. That's good." Now part two of the conversation that was every father's worst nightmare. This was even worse than the birds and the bees talk that had led to an explanation of menstruation. At times like this, he was still angry as hell at his ex-wife for walking out. The hurt had disappeared long ago. But the resentment...he would carry that scar forever.

"The thing is, Ken, I'd have to be an idiot not to know you've had sex."

She looked at the table, refusing to meet his gaze. "I so don't want to talk to you about this. If you're going to force me to stay, can you just give me the Cliff's Notes on this lecture?"

"I'm not going to lecture," he said. "This is a dialogue."

"Meaning I have to talk?"

"That would make it less like a lecture," he pointed out. "Let me start by asking how you felt when you did the test."

She looked as if she wouldn't answer, then let out a sigh as she glanced up. "Scared," she admitted.

"I bet. Believe me, I understand. But you dodged a bullet. You get another chance to get it right. By 'it,' I mean birth control."

"I don't need another chance."

"If you think you're immune from the consequences of unprotected sex, I've got news for you—"

"I know, Dad. I got the message when my period was late."

"Then are we talking abstinence here?" he asked, his inner parent doing the dance of joy.

"Yes. I don't ever want to do 'it' again." Her eyes filled with tears.

He reached out and covered her hand with his own. It pleased him when she didn't pull away because he couldn't stand seeing her cry. Everything in him wanted to fix it—like he'd always done when she was a little girl. "What is it, Ken?"

"He was a creep. I can't believe I was so stupid."

"What?"

"In health class, the book said to use a condom because it's not only about not getting pregnant. I asked him to, but he said it doesn't feel as good. He said if I loved him I'd—" She met his gaze and said, "You know."

Yeah, he knew. Damn it all to hell, he knew. He tamped down the urge to put his fist through the wall. "So you did?"

She nodded, rubbing at a spot on the wood table with her thumb when she couldn't meet his gaze. "Then he dumped me. He went back to his girlfriend."

"Son of a bitch—" Anger swelled like a mushroom cloud inside him. "Who is he? Josh Hammond?"

"No. We broke up a long time ago. You don't know the guy."

"How can I not know him? I always screen your dates."

"Not always," she said.

He didn't have the reserves to deal with what he didn't know about his daughter. "I'll tear him apart. What's his name?"

"No way. I'm not telling you," she said, horrified. "I'd die. I'd have to go into the Witness Protection Program or something."

He blew out a long breath. "Okay. No names. For now. But you can't blame me for wanting to beat the crap out of him."

"I don't. But here's the thing, Dad. After I knew I wasn't

pregnant, what bothered me most was how stupid I'd been. How I'd misjudged him."

"Don't feel like The Lone Ranger. I think that happens to everyone when a relationship goes south."

"Like you and Mom?"

He'd felt betrayed for putting everything he had into making it work when she couldn't have cared less. After that, relationship abstinence looked pretty good. And still did.

"Yeah, like me and your mom."

Kendra shook her head as if she still didn't understand. "But I've known this guy since kindergarten. How could I have been so wrong? Worse, how can I trust my judgment ever again? How can I go to UCLA, which is like a small city, and tell the good guys from the bad ones?"

Scott felt the Aha! light come on. On top of what Thea had said about leaving the familiar behind, this was part of his daughter's problem with going away to school.

"You don't have to know," he said. "Don't trust any guy. And above all, don't sleep with any of them."

One corner of her mouth quirked up. "That doesn't help."

"It's good advice. Haven't you ever heard the only man a girl can trust is her dad?" He grinned. "Seriously, Ken, I've said this before. You shouldn't be—"

"Intimate until I'm in love or think I am," she quoted in a singsong voice. Who knew she'd been paying attention? "The problem is, I thought we were in love. I didn't know he wasn't." He opened his mouth to say something and she held up her hand. "Don't worry. The false alarm scared me. I'm never sleeping with a guy again."

He could tell her that in time she'd meet a nice guy who would appreciate the truly remarkable person she was. He could say that when she grew up, it would be easier to tell nice guys from the ones who were only after one thing. He could advise her not to judge all men by the one idiot. But he was a father, so he didn't.

He patted her hand and said, "My work here is done."

"Yeah, Dad," she said, and rolled her eyes. But she was smiling.

"I guess it's time to change the subject."

"Oh, yeah," she agreed.

"I have some news. I talked to Thea Bell this morning about catering your graduation party."

"And?" Her blue eyes brightened.

To see that sparkle back where it should be had been worth eating a little crow. And Thea had only poked a little fun at him. If her cooking went down as easily as that crow, it would be a great party. "She took the job. I gave her a check and signed a contract."

Kendra jumped up and threw her arms around his neck. "Thank you, Daddy. You won't regret it."

How could he regret anything that made her call him Daddy?

"I'm sure I won't."

She sat down and pulled her plate toward her. "Don't you just love Thea?"

Scott thought about the question and realized it was true. Not love; never again love. But he liked Thea. She was sweet, smart and sexy. Besides being all that and beautiful, too, she had an appealing sense of humor. And she was a widow. He realized that was all the 4-1-1 he had on the woman who knew so much about him.

He decided it would be a good idea to change that.

Several days later, Thea picked up the phone at her office desk to make a call when some movement on the sidewalk outside caught her attention. Her brain registered the fact that the strikingly good-looking man responsible was Scott Matthews. When her body got the message, her pulse and heart rate joined hands and started to boogie.

Boy, was she glad that Connie was in the back room. And

that was silly because she would bet everything she owned that Scott wasn't any kind of physical threat. Which could only mean some part of her believed he was an emotional hazard and her partner's presence could prevent a meltdown.

He pushed open the door and walked inside. "Hi."

"Hi, yourself." She replaced the phone and noticed her hand was unsteady. Linking her fingers on top of her desk, she said, "To what do I owe this visit?"

Before he could respond, Connie walked into the front office. "T, I think we need to order—" She saw Scott and stopped. "Sorry. Is the dinger down? I didn't hear anyone come in."

Thea hadn't heard the dinger, either, because she couldn't hear a smart bomb go off over the blood pounding in her ears. So she ignored her partner's question.

She held her hand out indicating the man in front of them. "Meet Scott Matthews. He's the recently contracted client I told you about. Scott, this is my partner, Connie Howard."

Scott held out his hand. "Nice to meet you."

"You, too," Connie said, blatantly checking him out as she shook his hand. "Thea didn't tell me you were so—"

"How's Kendra?" Thea shot her friend a warning look. "That's his daughter. She's graduating from high school and the reason he's having the party we're doing."

"Right. The teenager." Connie leaned against the desk without taking her eyes off him.

He looked from Thea to Connie and shuffled his feet. "Kendra's fine."

"Connie, don't you have a cake to decorate back there?" Thea stared daggers.

The other woman stared back, then blinked and straightened. "Oh. Right. The Swanson shower. Bridal. Heart-shaped devil's food with raspberry filling. Seafoam-green icing."

When she was gone, Scott said, "Seafoam green?"

"The color of the bridesmaid's dresses."

"Ah." He nodded. "How dense of me."

"Yeah, I was going to say—" She shook her head as one corner of her mouth quirked up. Then she met his gaze. "How is Kendra *really?*"

"Not pregnant."

"I'm so glad," she said.

"Me, too."

"Was the conversation that produced this good news more listening or lecturing?" she asked.

"Half and half, I'd say. Actually when I shifted into lecture gear, she admitted she'd thought she was in love with the underhanded little twerp. He told her if she loved him she'd have sex without a condom."

"Oh, no!" Shocked, Thea put her hand over her mouth.

"Oh, yes. But after sleeping with her, he dumped my daughter and went back to his girlfriend. I'd like to clock the little weasel."

"Can I watch?"

His mouth curved up. "Unfortunately, Kendra swore me to nonviolence."

"Too bad."

"No kidding." He folded his arms over his chest. "What's worse, I think this is part of why she's dragging her feet about college. She got burned by a guy she's known practically all her life—"

"How can she trust herself with strangers?" Thea finished.

"Exactly."

"Poor kid."

"The silver lining is that she's never going to have sex again."

"You don't really believe that, do you?"

He sighed. "No. But if you're the charitable sort, don't give me a reality check for a while. This is my fantasy and I'd like to enjoy it for as long as possible."

"Okay." Thea laughed. "But I hope you told her that a

man who really loves her wouldn't be as concerned with his own pleasure as much as protecting her."

"Actually, no. I was putting my testosterone to better use as I visualized the three hundred ways I planned to annihilate the little creep with my bare hands." He rubbed the back of his neck as he slid her a wry look. "Besides, I'm a little rusty in that department."

"Oh?" Did he mean sex? It was a lie. Had to be. A man as good-looking as Scott Matthews would have to beat women off with a stick. Surely he succumbed to physical temptation.

"Yeah. Between work and raising the girls, I haven't had the time or energy to be in the loop on this whole dating thing."

He looked charmingly sincere and her heart gave a funny little lurch at his admission. Women would fall at his feet, yet he'd channeled his energy into his children. How cool was that?

"So you're socially backward?"

"I guess you could say that." He chuckled and the sound was self-deprecating. "File me trying to advise my daughter under the blind leading the blind."

"Not entirely. You can clue her in on the male point of view."

"I guess that's something. And the next time we have a heart-to-heart, I'll be sure to mention that the guy who really cares about her won't push her to do anything she's not comfortable with."

"You might also bring to her attention that it's one way to know her knight in shining armor as opposed to the knave who's simply using her." Thea shrugged. "It's also a way to know if that someone cares about her."

"Excellent point," he said. "Not only does Thea Bell toil for me. She's the guru of good sense, and I will pass that on to my offspring."

Thea smiled at him. His compliment produced a glow that

had nothing to do with being pregnant. But it was familiar. She remembered falling in love with her husband. The ache inside when they were apart. The sheer giddiness when she saw him. The heart-pounding excitement. The anticipation of being together.

As she smiled up at Scott Matthews, her heart stuttered and her stomach fluttered. It occurred to her that this was very much like what she'd felt long ago.

But that was impossible.

Love like she'd had only happened once in a lifetime and she'd had hers.

"So what brings you here today?" she asked.

"The party. By the way, Kendra was very excited when I told her you'd be the caterer."

"I'm glad," she said. And she was. Until he moved closer.

Just like the last time he'd been here, he invaded her space and half sat on the corner of her desk. The pose pulled the denim tight across his leg, showcasing his muscular thigh. He folded his arms over his chest, in that oh-so-masculine way that drew attention to his above-average biceps. He was large and male and filled her personal area more than she was accustomed to it being filled. Or was it simply that he made her notice things she hadn't in a very long time?

She swallowed. "What about the party?"

"Have you had a chance to work up those figures for me on the cost yet?"

"I can't do it with any degree of accuracy because there are too many variables."

"Like what?"

"Number of guests. Choice of menu affects the cost of food. Theme impacts the price of decorations. You don't have to have a theme, of course. Although Kendra seemed excited about that. The two of you need to discuss it."

He nodded thoughtfully. "You mentioned that before. That day at the house."

"Right. I did."

If he remembered, why was he here? Until this moment the thought hadn't crossed her mind. She'd been too preoccupied with her reaction to him. He didn't have to drop by; he could have phoned to discuss this. Had he been looking for an excuse to see her face-to-face? She hoped not.

Why would he? By his own admission, he didn't have the time or energy for anything besides his work and his kids. And frankly, that was just fine with her. She was paddling the same canoe. Her work and her child-on-the-way were the focus of her world.

This was strictly business.

"Can you give me a ballpark figure?"

She thought about it. "I've done parties for a hundred dollars and some for over a thousand."

He whistled. "Whoa."

"It just depends. The cost of renting tables, chairs and linens is fixed, but without a number of people, it's meaningless information."

"I see."

"You should know that the cost of my labor is a good portion of the expense. Good caterers don't come cheap."

"I would never infer you were cheap," he said, raising an eyebrow.

"Good thing. Them's fightin' words."

"After all, you did say if you needed the gig that badly you wouldn't be considering a bigger house and a mortgage."

"True. And I have to tell you, your house fits my bill nicely."

"Have you listed your condo yet?"

"Yes. I'm hoping it will sell quickly, but Joyce said it's difficult to predict. Townhomes require a buyer with different criteria than single-family homes." Criteria like sending the last child off to college and downsizing. "Have you listed your house yet?"

"No. Kendra's reaction sort of put the brakes on that."

"I'm glad you're waiting. Maybe my place will sell and I can make an offer on yours."

"You liked it that much?"

"It's perfect, exactly what I was looking for. But we digress. Back to the party." And maybe there was another reason he was concerned about the cost. "Look, Scott, if money is a problem—"

He held up his hand. "I can afford you. But there's no harm in negotiating."

"Depends on the terms."

"If the cost of labor is the only variable, I say we start there."

"But I already know how much your daughter wants me to do the party."

"And I know how much you like my house." He grinned.

The smile was so devastating, it made her glad she was already sitting. "Did I tip my hand?" she managed to ask.

"Big-time."

"I didn't peg you for the wheeler-dealer type."

"I'm a wolf in sheep's clothing."

Her thoughts exactly.

He stared at her for several moments, and she could almost see the mental wheels turning. "How about this? I'll hold off on listing the house until there's an offer on your condo if you agree to discount your labor costs for the party?"

She thought about his suggestion. Basically, she would be trading her time for an insurance policy to have first crack at his house. Considering how much she liked the place, how perfect it would be for her needs and the fact that she knew it might get snapped up before she could sell her place, she figured it was a cheap insurance policy.

"I think you've got yourself a deal, Mr. Matthews." She held out her hand.

He took it in his big, warm palm and gave her a firm squeeze. "Glad to hear it, Ms. Bell."

When he released her hand, the palm tingled where he'd held it. And her cheeks felt warm. If there was a God in heaven, she wasn't blushing like a schoolgirl. For Pete's sake, his teenage daughter probably wouldn't redden like this simply because a man touched her.

She hated feeling out of her depth and less than in control. Too many things in life were uncontrollable, she'd learned. She should be able to deal with a man. But Scott Matthews wasn't like any man she'd ever met. And they'd just struck a bargain. She couldn't help thinking she'd just made a deal with the big, bad wolf. Except he'd said he wasn't and she believed him. Somehow that was so much worse.

He looked down at her. "So you're a widow."

The big, bad wolf had just stepped out of his sheep's clothing.

Chapter 5

Smooth move, Matthews, he thought.

He hadn't planned to blurt that out, but starting a conversation required personal information. The fact that she was a widow was all he had. On top of that, lack of dating experience put him at a distinct disadvantage. "What's your sign?" wasn't something he said to start up a meaningful dialogue with a woman. And he found he very much wanted to do that with Thea. But he didn't want it to be about catering, kids or real-estate contracts.

He kicked himself when his thoughtless remark turned her cocoa-colored eyes dark. And sad. She'd never said how long she'd been a widow, and he felt like the world's biggest jerk.

"I'm sorry," he said. "I didn't mean to bring up bad memories."

"That's all right. I've had time to deal with it."

"How long ago did you lose your husband?"

"David died two years ago."

At least it hadn't been two weeks ago. That made him feel marginally better. "What happened? If you don't mind my asking."

"Actually, I don't really like to talk about it." She stood up. "I try to keep my personal and professional life separate, Scott. You're in business. I'm sure you understand."

"Yeah." But he didn't really. She'd shut him down faster than a roofing crew in an electrical storm.

He also didn't understand what it was like to lose a spouse. His was alive and well somewhere—just not with him and the girls. Thea's husband was gone for good. The shadows lingering in her eyes told him she'd cared about the guy a lot. Or did she look like that because she thought Scott was trying to hit on her?

He'd told her he was out of practice. Hell, he'd never really been *in* practice. He'd been a family man when his high school buddies were perfecting their pick-up lines. He'd never had a chance to use his—"Hi, I'm Scott. How do you like me so far?" He took one look at her face and decided this wasn't the best time to take it out for a test drive. Besides, she barely knew him. She had no reason to trust him. But he wanted her to.

"Look, Thea, through a weird twist of fate, you were there for me at a very difficult time. As I recall, you said you'd never met a person who looked more like they needed to talk."

"Yes, but—"

"I could say the same about you. You told me—and I quote—'Talking is helpful.' I'd like to return the favor."

She smiled, but it didn't push the clouds from her eyes. "I appreciate that, Scott. But there's really nothing to say. It's in the past. I've dealt with it. But thanks for the offer."

"Anytime. I owe you one."

"No. Really." She looked at her desk calendar. "But we do

need to talk about details for your daughter's party. When is good for you?"

"Evenings are best."

"I figured. What about tomorrow?" She looked up and met his gaze.

"That would be Friday," he said, trying to remember if he had anything going on with the girls.

"Of course. The beginning of the weekend. You've got plans."

He shook his head. "I don't think so. My social calendar isn't exactly filled. But sometimes Gail comes home from college for the weekend. To do laundry."

"Not to see you?" She grinned.

The unexpected smile hit him between the eyes and jump-started his pulse. She should do that more often. It was like seeing the sun peek out from behind thick cloud cover. Not only did it chase away the lingering shadows, but it made her look so beautiful she took his breath away.

He couldn't help smiling back. "I used to think so, but I got real when I figured out she spent more time with the washer and dryer than she did telling me about her classes and friends."

Thea laughed. "I'm sure she misses you."

"You don't have to say that. I'm a father. I no longer have an ego. Tomorrow night is fine. Do you want me to meet you here?"

She thought for a moment. "How about if I meet you at the house? That way if your daughter is there, you don't have to leave."

"Great."

"I'll be there at seven, if that's okay?"

"Should be."

Scott said his goodbyes and walked outside. He was looking forward to Friday night in a way he hadn't since he'd been a teenager with a brand-new driver's license.

Thea stood to the side of the window where she couldn't be seen and watched Scott's truck pull out of the parking lot.

When he merged into the traffic on Valencia Boulevard, she breathed a sigh of relief.

"He's quite a hunk."

At the sound of Connie's voice, Thea whirled and splayed her hand over her chest. "You scared me."

"You should be scared. But not because of me. Thea," she said, tsking as she shook her head. "Tall. Dark. Blue eyes? Your description of him is as bland as unseasoned sirloin. And I repeat—be afraid, very afraid."

"Why?"

"The man practically issued an engraved invitation and you shut him down like a lid on a grease fire."

"Were you eavesdropping?" Thea asked, putting her hands on her hips.

"Of course." Connie didn't look the least bit repentant. "And spying."

"So we were listening to the same conversation?"

"Yes. And drooling over the same hunk."

"I wasn't drooling."

Connie met her gaze. "Okay. But this time, I'm absolutely sure there's a sparkle in your eyes. And after meeting Scott, I know the reason for it."

"Let's get back to the engraved invitation. What exactly would you be referring to? An invitation to what?" Thea asked.

"A personal relationship." Connie sighed. "That man is the hottest thing since habanero peppers."

"He's nice-looking," Thea hedged.

Connie stared at her for several moments. "Nice-looking? Tom Hanks is nice-looking. Colin Farrell is darkly intense and smoldering. He's your Colin Farrell."

"He's not my anything and I don't know who Colin Farrell is."

"You have to get out more."

"I get out plenty," Thea defended.

"No. You get out for work. There's a difference."

"How would you know? You're the married mother of two. Does your husband know about this?"

"My husband is the love of my life and the reason I'm living happily ever after. But he also knows I'm not dead. I know a good-looking guy when I see one."

"You're so lucky, Con," Thea said with a sigh.

Her friend sat down behind the other desk. "T, you've got to get back up on the horse. David wouldn't want you to be alone. To stop living."

"I haven't."

"I beg to differ. If you didn't get that Scott Matthews was hitting on you, then you're merely going through the motions."

"If he was hitting on me, I'll eat my hat."

"Better put lots of tenderizer on it. Maybe some marinade would help."

"Oh, for Pete's sake, Connie—"

"I didn't say he was hitting on you *well*. Based on his history, there's a good reason for that. He doesn't have to be a smooth operator, my friend. All he has to do is stand there. He's female fantasy material of the very best kind."

"I'm not blind. I can see that he's an exceptional-looking man. So, apparently, is this Colin Farrell person. But that doesn't mean I'm ever going to get it on with either of them."

"Yes, but Colin Farrell wasn't in our catering office telling you if you wanted to talk he'd be happy to listen."

"Scott was just being nice. Nosy, too. And you know how I feel about that."

"Look, T, you said his wife is out of the picture and has been for a while. What would be the harm in giving him a little encouragement?"

"I'll tell you what would be the harm. He's been hurt and

betrayed. That made his already difficult life even harder. He's not likely to want to risk that again."

"Is it him you're worried about? Or are you the one afraid to take a risk?" Connie asked, but her tone had gentled significantly.

"I'm not afraid. I simply don't wish to," she answered. "Look, Con, Scott and I couldn't be more *not* on the same page. I'm pregnant and starting a family. He's looking at shooing his last little chick out of the nest. In fact, he's going to be selling his house soon because it will be too big for one person."

"Funny," her friend said, tapping her lip. "You're in the market for a bigger place because you're welcoming a new little chick."

"Finally," Thea said, throwing up her hands. "You grasp the finer points of the situation."

"What I grasp is that you should sell him your condo so you can buy his house." Connie grinned. "I'm so brilliant, sometimes I scare myself."

"That's actually not a bad idea," Thea admitted. "My town house is a great place."

"See. So why won't you listen to me about the interpersonal relationship stuff?"

"Because nothing about it works."

"Except for the chemistry."

Thea wrinkled her nose. "I hated chemistry in high school. I barely passed."

"Don't underestimate it."

"I was wrong," Thea said.

"About what?"

"The other day when I asked who whacked you with the whimsical stick. There's nothing droll or capricious about this conversation. Or subtle, either, in case you were wondering."

"I wasn't."

"I have to ask who smacked you with the matchmaking stick."

"No one. I just know a winner when I see one."

"How do you figure?"

"You haven't dated because you're still living in the past and mourning your husband. He hasn't dated because his wife left him with two little girls to raise and he had to earn a living. You're both social geeks." She shrugged. "A match made in heaven, if you ask me."

"I didn't."

Connie glanced out the window where Scott's truck had been parked minutes before. "He did. He was trying to open the door and get to know you. He doesn't know anything about you, does he?"

"Only that I'm a widow. And I'm not sure why I let that slip."

"Because subconsciously you really like him."

Her friend knew her too well. But this was a pointless conversation. "Like I said, we're in completely different places in our lives."

"Don't you think you should give him the opportunity to decide that?"

"No. I'm not interested." She ignored her friend's snort of disbelief. "Statistics favor full-term pregnancies after completing the first trimester. I'm not talking about it until I'm over the hump. By that time, Scott Matthews will be out of the picture."

"Shame," Connie said. "Definite sparkle," she mumbled.

"You're impossible."

"And you love me."

"I do. The question is why."

"Because I have wonderful ideas. Like Scott should buy your condo so you can buy his house."

Thea thought about that. It made good sense.

"You're right. *Some* of your ideas are excellent. I'll mention it to him."

* * *

Thea stopped her car in front of Scott's house. It was her second visit and this time she'd driven around the charming neighborhood. Parents pushed babies in strollers. Kids played outdoors on the greenbelt areas. Neighborhood Watch signs warned the bad guys to stay away or face the wrath of the 'burbs. It looked like the ideal environment to bring up her baby.

She walked up the driveway and passed Scott's truck with the Matthews and Sons sign on the side. Casually she rested her hand on the hood and noticed it was still warm.

After knocking on the front door, her heart fluttered until Scott opened it. Standing there with a tool belt in his hands, he looked tired and dirty, as if he'd just arrived home. Instead of dialing down her awareness, the look seemed to take it up a notch. There was something about a man and his tool belt that set a woman's hormones bubbling and boiling.

"H-hi." Her voice sounded breathless and she hoped he would think it was the trek up the driveway.

"Hi. Come in." He closed the door. "I'm sorry. I just got home. There was a shortage of manpower at one of the construction sites and I filled in."

"A boss who's not afraid to get his hands dirty," she observed.

"And the rest of him, too," he said ruefully. "Look, I'm going to take a quick shower. I'll just be a few minutes. Make yourself comfortable. The girls are in the other room. Kendra will introduce you to Gail," he finished, just before he disappeared upstairs.

On her way through the living room and dining room, Thea heard female voices and giggling. Kendra and another girl were lounging on the corner group in the family room.

"Hi," she said, looking at both girls.

"Thea." Kendra stood. "I didn't know you were coming over."

"Your dad didn't tell you?"

"I've sort of been avoiding him." She looked at the other girl. "This is my sister, Gail."

"Nice to meet you, Thea," she said standing.

The older sister was the same height as Kendra, but her hair was lighter and shot with gold streaks. Her big green eyes sparkled with intelligence and were frankly assessing.

"My pleasure, Gail. I've heard a lot about you. All good." Thea winked at Kendra. "Your dad said you were happy about me doing the party."

She grinned. "I am."

"Good. I'm here to help you make some decisions so I can give him an estimate of expenses."

"Great. Gail's home for the weekend." She glanced at her sister. "She's good at the creative part."

"Not the food," she clarified. "But other stuff. I was on the decorating committee for my sorority. I've done a party or two."

Thea nodded. "Good. That's not my strongest area. I like the food part."

She studied the two sisters, side by side, and remembered when she'd first met Kendra at her friend's catered birthday party. While Thea had set up, the teen had asked a lot of questions. Was it hard to cook? How had she learned? Who taught her? Did she like it?

Thea had enjoyed spending time with her that day. She wondered if the child she carried was a girl and thought how lovely it would be to share her interest in cooking, clothes and other girlie things. She'd sensed something needy in Kendra when she'd first met her. Now that she knew her history, it didn't take a Ph.D. in psychology to get that it was about missing her mother. Anger curled through her toward the woman who'd deserted her daughters. It was reprehensible. There was no way to come out of that without feeling the effects.

Her baby would never know its father and nothing could

change that. It made her sad, but there was nothing to be done except give her child all the love and attention she had in her. Plus the best environment to bring up her baby. She looked around and knew without a doubt that she liked this house even more the second time.

She heard the water go on upstairs. An instant visual of a shirtless Scott Matthews jumped into her mind. Her stomach lurched and she wished it was about the pregnancy. Why had she volunteered to come here? She looked at Kendra and remembered.

"So," she said, "why are you avoiding your dad?"

The teen glanced at her sister, but before she could say anything Gail spoke up. "There's an overnight freshman orientation coming up that he wants Ken to go to."

"And you don't want to?" Thea asked.

"He's just trying to get rid of me."

"Oh, for Pete's sake, Ken," her sister said. "Dad's not doing that. You're just a big chicken."

"You're afraid?" Thea asked.

"No." Her mouth took on a stubborn slant, remarkably like her father's.

"You should give it a try," Thea advised.

"What if it's lame?" Kendra looked up and for just a moment there was apprehension in the blue-eyed gaze she'd also inherited from Scott.

"What if it's not?" Thea sat on the arm of the wing chair in the family room. "You've got nothing to lose by checking it out. That's what orientation is all about."

"You've been talking to my dad, haven't you?"

"Yes," Thea admitted. "But not about this. I'm not taking his side if that's what you're implying. It simply makes good sense."

"Why?"

"You get a taste of what college life will be like. You do want to go, right?"

"Of course."

"You have an opportunity to go to one of the most prestigious colleges in the country. UCLA is an excellent school and it's practically in your backyard. You're far enough away to get a taste of being on your own, but close enough if you need—" she glanced at Gail "—laundry facilities."

"Is that what my dad told you?" she asked, grinning.

"He actually said that when you come home, you spend more time with the washer and dryer than you do with him."

Just then a buzzer sounded from down the hall. Gail rubbed her nose sheepishly. "Right on cue. That would mean my darks are done." She left the room to tend to her clothes.

Thea laughed. "He wasn't complaining. Just stating a fact. You're growing up," she said, looking at Kendra. "And he wants you to have the best possible education. What if you like it?"

"What if I don't?" the teen asked.

"Then you can enroll at the local junior college. There's more than one way to get from point A to point B. But don't limit yourself because you're afraid."

"I'm not afraid," she said. "Just a little nervous. It's a big place."

Thea remembered what Scott had said about doubting her ability to judge people after her unfortunate experience. She knew it would embarrass the teen to know that she knew. Instead of bringing it up, she said, "It *is* a big place. That can work in your favor. Makes it easy to blend in. To not be noticed. Has it occurred to you that you're not the only freshman who feels this way? There will be a whole crop of newbies feeling just as insecure as you do."

"Yeah," she said a little doubtfully.

Thea put her hand on the girl's arm. "Just don't let fear stop you. Take the steps. Your dad will be there to catch you if you fall."

Kendra shrugged. "I've always hated the first day of

school. Especially in elementary school. Not knowing which teacher I'd get—would she be nice or the Wicked Witch of the West."

Elementary school. It would come in handy for her child. She would check out the school system. But this was an opportunity to get information from someone who'd walked the hallowed halls.

"What did you think of your elementary school?" Thea asked her.

She thought for a moment. "It was good. I liked it."

Thea couldn't resist. "A few years from now you could be saying that about UCLA."

"Maybe." Kendra grinned. "When I was in grade school, I remember a lot of the parents would ask for their kids to be with certain teachers, but my dad never did."

"Why's that?"

"He said in life you don't get to pick people. You have to learn how to get along with anyone and everyone, no matter what."

Very practical, Thea thought. "So overall you'd say your experience in elementary school was positive?"

Scott walked into the room. "What's this about school?"

"I was just asking your daughter about her experience. When one is interested in the educational system, one should go to the person who's walked the walk."

"Why are you interested?" He folded his arms over his chest.

This wasn't the time to share that she was concerned about the future education of the child she was carrying. But she also couldn't ignore him or blow off the question. So she seized the only thing she could think of. "Have you forgotten our deal?"

"No."

"Okay, then. It's something any prospective buyer should be aware of. One should always be concerned about resale. And the school system is important in that regard."

"It was one of my concerns," he agreed.

"What deal?" Kendra looked at her. "Are you going to buy the house?"

Uh-oh. She'd stepped right on that land mine. She didn't want to make things more difficult for Scott, but she also wouldn't lie to the girl.

"I'm looking for a bigger place and I love this house. But I have to sell my condo first and that could take a while. So your dad agreed to hold off on listing the house until my condo sells and give me first crack at making an offer on this house."

Kendra nodded. "Cool."

Thea looked at Scott, who was staring at his daughter as if she was an alien from another planet. "Cool?" he said.

"Yeah." She cocked her thumb toward the laundry. "I'm going to help Gail."

"Okay." Scott stared after her, scratching his head with a puzzled expression on his face.

The scent of soap and some spicy cologne tickled Thea's nose and she looked at him. His damp hair was darker and showed marks where he'd run his comb through the wet strands. He'd put on fresh jeans and a black T-shirt that clung to his flat abdomen and the impressive contours of his chest. The muscles in his upper arms flexed and rippled as he rubbed the back of his neck. She'd forgotten how good a man looked and smelled fresh out of the shower. A feeling of longing sliced through her, making the empty place inside her echo with the pain of what would never be.

"Just the other day she had a meltdown about selling the house. Now it's 'cool'? I will never understand the complexity of the female mind," he said, the corners of his mouth curving up.

The bemused look was so darn cute. Thea felt a tug in the region of her heart, and it chased away the yearning she'd felt just a moment ago. How could this happen? She was the one who'd planted both feet solidly on her soapbox while delivering the lecture about keeping her personal and professional lives separate. She didn't need a visit from the common-sense fairy to know it was time to do what she came here to do and then beat a hasty retreat.

"So what kind of food did you have in mind for the party?" she asked Scott. "What does Kendra like?"

"Chicken," called out a voice from the other room that belonged to Gail. Good-natured chatter followed the remark.

When Thea laughed, Scott looked puzzled. "Apparently I missed something."

"Not important." She picked up her briefcase and walked to the kitchen dinette to open it. She took out an album of pictures from parties she'd done. After opening it, she stopped at a page. "This is a party I did with Greek food. But it was for a wedding shower and the couple was going to Greece for their honeymoon. And the bride was a vegetarian."

He nodded as he studied the pictures. "I'm trying to remember if I was ever that young."

"I know what you mean," she said. "But it was not my intention that you get philosophical on me. My purpose in showing these is to demonstrate how theme can complement the menu—and any dietary idiosyncrasies."

"As long as there's meat." He arched an eyebrow at her.

The girls walked into the room, Gail carrying a basket filled with folded clothes. "Dad, Ken and I are thinking about going to a movie."

You're leaving us alone? What's wrong with you? Thea wanted to shout at them. But she managed to hold back.

"Kendra, don't you want to be in on the menu discussion?" she asked instead.

"You're the one who wanted this party in the first place," Scott said. "I thought you'd want to help plan it."

"You didn't tell me Thea was coming over," she defended.

"Okay. But I thought this party was important to you. Now that she's here, the least you can do is hang around and tell her what you want."

"But Gail and I don't get to spend a lot of time hanging out together."

"Tell me about it," he said.

Gail set down the overflowing laundry basket. "What about a balloon theme? Something like, 'The sky's the limit.'"

Scott glanced at Thea. "Are balloons expensive?"

"Depends on how many you have and if they're the Mylar ones filled with helium. But you can do a few of those and some you blow up yourself."

He nodded. "Then I think it's a brilliant idea."

"Dad, you squeeze a penny till it shrieks," Gail needled.

"Someone around here has to be frugal," he defended. "You guys think money grows on trees."

"It doesn't?" Kendra said, eyes wide as she glanced from him to her sister.

Scott reached over and tweaked her nose. "Very funny."

"I think it's a brilliant idea, too," Thea agreed. "So we have a theme. What about food? Anything ethnic you're particularly fond of?"

"Mexican," Gail said.

"Chinese," Kendra chimed in.

Scott looked at them. "Steak and baked potatoes."

"Anyone can do that," Kendra pointed out. "Thea's food is special."

"So what do you want?" he asked.

"To go to the movies with my sister."

"But Thea gave up her evening to come over here."

She hadn't given up much, she thought. Just her empty condo and a frozen dinner. "Don't worry about it, Scott."

"It's not about worrying. It's about inconveniencing people," he said, giving the girls a stern look.

"But they didn't know I was coming. Besides, you guys can't even agree on what kind of food you want." She tapped her lip. "I think I have a suggestion that might help."

"What?" he asked, sounding doubtful.

"Why don't I come back at a mutually convenient time for everyone and we'll do a tasting to see what you like." She watched the three of them nod. "I'll pick some dishes that have received the most positive feedback—"

"No pun intended," Scott said.

"Right." She grinned. "I'll cook and maybe we can pin down the food. What do you say?"

"Are you sure you don't mind coming back?" he asked.

Of course she did, but not for the reasons he thought. But now she was in for a penny, in for a pound. And she wouldn't let Kendra down.

"It's fine. That way the girls can go to the movies and hang out."

Scott let out a long breath. "I suppose it's all right since we're just in the discussion stage."

The girls stood on either side of him and kissed him on each cheek. "Thanks, Dad," they said in unison.

Gail put her laundry basket by the stairway, while Kendra picked up her keys and purse. Then they were gone and the energy level dropped. But when Thea looked at Scott, the level of something else went up.

"So when are you coming back to cook for me?" he asked. "How about next Thursday? You just got a crash course in how complicated weekends are around here."

She nodded and checked her date book. "That works for me."

And the words were barely out of her mouth before her anticipation to see him again set in. That did not work for her.

Chapter 6

He'd seen women more beautiful, but Scott couldn't remember who or when.

Thea was standing in front of his stove, about where he'd seen her for the very first time. Now she was wearing jeans, a soft fuzzy green sweater that brought out hints of hazel in her big brown eyes and an apron with her catering logo—For Whom The Bell Toils. The "O" in *Toils* was in the shape of a bell and the dinger looked like a wooden spoon. It was catchy. And, like her, it was cute, clever and captivating.

She glanced at him over her shoulder as she sprinkled grated mozzarella cheese over lasagna noodles. "Scott, I can call you when everything is ready for you to taste."

Right. The party menu. The reason she was here. Pretty soon he'd get his head into making a decision on that, but right now all he could think about was tasting the comely caterer.

"Scott?" Her hand hovered above the baking dish as she studied him with a puzzled expression. "Is something wrong?"

"Nope. Everything is peachy." He took a drink from the beer in his hand. "Are you sure you wouldn't like a glass of wine? I've got a nice bottle of cabernet. Been saving it for a special occasion."

She turned back to the stove. "I've learned never to mix work and wine unless it's called for in a recipe."

"Probably wise," he said.

"This will take at least a half hour to heat through. I would have put it together at the office, but the luncheon I did today ran a little late."

"No problem," he said. "It's exciting to stand around and watch the cheese melt."

"Ah. Sarcasm." One corner of her full mouth tilted up. "So don't stand around. Go watch the grass grow or the car rust. The cheese will melt whether you're here or not. You must have something better to do than hang around with me."

"Not really. For a change it's kind of nice to not be the one cooking." At the moment, he couldn't think of anything he'd rather do than watch her. "So what have you brought to taste? Besides the lasagna?"

"I have a Greek salad," she said, indicating a bowl of greens on the counter. "Some egg rolls I made from scratch. They're left over from the luncheon today and they're really good if I do say so myself. I assembled quesadillas—they're simple—tortillas and cheese—but if you like them and want more pizzazz, I can use salsa, guacamole and beans. Jalapeño peppers can spice them up and make them hotter."

He could think of ways to spice things up, he thought, staring at her mouth. And that definitely made him hotter.

"Sounds like you've put together a veritable United Nations for the palate."

"I like that," she said with a grin. "And once we have an ethnic direction, I can narrow down your choices and fine-tune the recipes, taking into consideration your personal preferences. Also, you don't have to stick with just Italian or Mexican food. You can mix and match if you want."

"That wouldn't be breaking any catering code?"

Her eyes sparkled. "None I'm aware of. Some clients like to stick with one direction, but it's not carved in stone. It all depends on what you want. The customer is always right." She stuck her hands in the pockets of her apron. "Seriously, if you have something you need to do, I'll just let you know when everything is ready."

That was the third time she'd hinted he should hit the road and get out from underfoot. Did he make her nervous? Or was she a temperamental chef who didn't like anyone peeking over her shoulder? He sort of liked that he might make her nervous—if it wasn't nervous in the "temperamental cook" kind of way. If it was the sort of nerves that meant she was as aware of him as he was of her, he could go for that.

"Don't worry about me," he said. "I can take care of myself."

"I'm not worried. You're a big boy," she said, not quite meeting his gaze. "Where's Kendra? I haven't seen her."

It was a natural question, considering the fact that his daughter had initiated this whole thing in the first place. But it was the way Thea had asked, as if she were hoping. As if *she* were worried—about being alone with him.

"She's at a friend's house."

"But she was supposed to be here."

Scott shrugged. "I know. Something came up for school. I was going to call and cancel but she talked me out of it." And that had taken precious little effort.

"I see." She tapped her lip. "When will she be home?"

"Ten at the latest. That's her curfew on school nights."

"Hmm." Thea met his gaze. "It would be nice to get her input. Since this party is for her. And that's why I came back."

"She said everything you make is to die for—that's a direct quote—and I should pick what I like." His gaze zeroed in on the slender column of Thea's neck, which he liked very much. He noticed her pulse fluttering and his own kicked up to keep pace.

"Okay." She nodded. "She can reheat the leftovers and let me know what she thinks. Often they're better because the flavors have time to blend. But I have to warn you, if there's anything you love and she hates it, her opinion as guest of honor carries the most weight."

"Even though I'm paying the bill?" He couldn't resist teasing her. Maybe he could shake her out of this stiff, professional pose. If he'd never seen her sympathetic-listener side, he wouldn't miss it now. But he had and he did.

"You're paying the bill because you love your daughter and want her to be happy."

"You're sure about that?"

"Absolutely," she said, nodding emphatically.

"I'm that transparent?"

"Like plastic wrap."

"You've learned all my secrets," he confirmed.

"Then my work here is done." But her gaze skittered away. She pointed at the clutter on the refrigerator beside him. "Does it always look like that?"

He studied the mass of magnets, some of them with clips holding coupons, school memos and pictures. "Yeah, pretty much."

She tapped her lip. "I can't decide if it's a fire hazard or a work of art."

"Probably both," he said with a grin.

She plucked off a magnetic frame with a photo in it. "Which one of the girls is this?"

He moved in close to look, even though he knew exactly which one of his daughters it was. "That's Kendra. She was three months old."

Gently, she traced the picture with her finger, as if it were a real, live baby. "She's so sweet."

As sweet as you smell, he thought, breathing in her floral scent. A soft, tender look crept into Thea's face as she studied the small photo. He hadn't thought she could look more beautiful, but she did. It took all his willpower to keep from reaching out to trace the curve of her cheek and the line of her jaw. The skin there looked incredibly soft and smooth and perfect. Her small nose turned up slightly with a dusting of freckles splashed over it.

Strands of hair shimmered around her face like brown silk. It was all he could do to keep from tangling his fingers in it and pulling her to him to taste her mouth, see if it was made for kissing as he suspected. The sight of her made his chest tight and for the first time in a long time, he felt the emptiness inside.

"She's completely adorable." Thea looked at him. "I can't believe you know exactly how old she is in this picture."

"Besides the fact that it's written on the back," he said, "I remember everything. I've been involved in all my girls' activities—fairy princesses, sports, school."

"Did work get in the way of being a father?" she asked wryly.

"Sometimes. But since my dad owns the company, it was a little easier to juggle my time. Any pressure about work came from me trying not to take advantage."

"So much for trying to make me believe you're a tough guy where your daughter is concerned." She looked around the kitchen and into the family room. "Your girls practically grew up in this house. For a man who remembers everything, doesn't that make you think twice about selling it?"

He shrugged as he followed her gaze. "It's just a house. The memories are up here," he said, tapping his temple. "I've got a ton of pictures, ninety-nine-point-nine percent of which are *not* in albums. I wish digital cameras had been around when my girls were growing up."

"Do you have a good one now?" she asked, a spark in her eyes.

"Yeah. Today's technology makes storing the memories easier and that appeals to me. Are you interested?" He looked into her eyes and wished they were talking about something more personal than the latest photo technology. Then he realized how his question might sound and added, "In cameras?"

"Yes. I'm going to need a good one for—" She stopped, looking uncomfortable. "F-for business. I like to take photos of my parties," she said quickly.

"I remember. We looked at them the other night when you were here."

"Right," she said, nodding emphatically. "But I'm not into technology much. Connie keeps trying to get me to join the twenty-first century, but my heels are dug in and I'm hanging on to the past with both hands."

He laughed. "In certain things I can understand that."

"Meaning?"

"I've tried my damnedest to keep my girls from growing up. But apparently they didn't get the memo that they're supposed to stay small."

"So you do have mixed feelings about your daughter leaving home and selling the place."

"Yes. But soon I'll rattle around this big house. It's time for something smaller."

Looking unconvinced, she leaned back and studied him. "Fibber. I think you're a big softie."

Shaking his head, he said, "No way. I'm hard as nails and practical. It's going to be quiet and peaceful around here. When Kendra goes to college, the phone won't be ringing off the hook and the energy level will drop to normal proportions."

"*If* she goes away."

"Even if she decides on the local junior college for now, I'm looking at two years tops until she transfers to a four-year school. The handwriting is on the wall. She's going to leave whether or not I want her to and I'll need a smaller place."

"And when you're alone, you're going to miss her—teen problems and all."

He scoffed. "I'll miss her. But after recent events, I will never miss teenage problems."

Thea looked down at the picture in her hands and smiled, softly—sadly. Why sad? What was she thinking to make her look like that?

He wanted to know. And it hit him like a two-by-four to the head—he wanted to fix whatever was bothering her. But he couldn't do that without knowing what was wrong. Only the last time he'd tried to draw her out, she'd refused to co-operate. Should he try again? The answer was yes, although not tonight. He didn't want to give her a reason to hide behind her professional demeanor. Or worse, head for the hills. He was enjoying her company too much.

He felt a click with her and suspected she felt it, too. He'd admit to being out of practice with women. His experiences were few and far between, but he didn't remember feeling an attraction like this before. Even if he wanted to, a man couldn't forget a woman like her.

Thea put the magnetic frame back on the refrigerator. "So you're absolutely and completely committed to getting a smaller place?"

"Yup. Like I said—hard as nails and practical. What do I need with this big house just for me?"

"What if the girls want to come home for a visit?"

"I'm not going to live in a cardboard box under the freeway. Wherever I move will just be smaller, but I'll want a couple of extra bedrooms."

One of her delicate eyebrows arched. "I happen to know of a place like that."

"Oh?"

"Yeah. My condo." Before he could say anything, she rushed on. "Actually it was Connie's idea. I told her you were downsizing and, being Connie, she said in her flippant way that maybe we should trade spaces."

Scott rested his forearm on the refrigerator, leaning in close to look down at her. "Intriguing idea."

"Isn't it?" She blinked as she gazed up at him and swallowed. "She actually called it brilliant, but humility has never been her most attractive quality."

"I hadn't gotten as far as thinking where I'd move to, but a condo makes a lot of sense."

"It's practical," she said, lifting that eyebrow again.

"Have I mentioned I'm a practical guy?"

"No way," she said in mock surprise.

"Yeah." He grinned.

"Then you should check out my place and see if you're interested."

He was interested, all right. Checking out her mouth, he felt the blood flow in his body shift to points south of his belt. Some rusty instinct warned him that this wouldn't be the best time to check out if her lips were as soft and sexy as they looked. Not if he wanted to know her better. And since she'd just given him a gold-plated invitation to do just that, he could wait.

"I'd like very much to see your place."

"Great. Let's look at our calendars and we'll set up a time." He could hardly wait.

A week after her visit to Scott's house, Thea looked at the clock on her microwave. He was due any minute. Instantly, the threads of nerves in her stomach tied into one gigantic knot.

At this moment, and every one since the words had come out of her mouth, she wished for the invitation back. She was as tense as a chef watching a soufflé. Which was silly because this was business. Sort of. He had a big place and needed a smaller one. She had a smaller one and needed a bigger one. Simply business.

But it felt very personal and complicated, which made her uneasy.

The doorbell sounded and she pressed a palm against her abdomen as the knot grew. She glanced in the peephole to check to make sure it was Scott. It was. And even distorted by the peephole, just as Connie had said, he was female-fantasy material. Not for her, of course. But the average woman would be putty in his hands.

Bracing herself, she turned the dead bolt. With her practiced, professional smile firmly in place, she opened the door. "Scott. I'm glad you could make it."

"Me, too." He walked in and smiled.

"You're right on time."

She shut the door after him, then turned to find him looking around. He'd walked the length of her entry and waited to step down into her great room. As always, her gaze was drawn to his impressive physique, and it occurred to her that this was the first time she'd seen him in something other than jeans and work boots. In his khaki slacks and the navy knit shirt molded to his broad shoulders, muscular back and trim waist, he cleaned up pretty good. She marveled at her instantaneous female response to that realization. It was nice to know that part of her still worked. Nice, but nerve-racking. In order to avoid more of the same, she resolved to suck it up and get this over with.

She looked up at him. "I'll show you around."

"Okay."

With her arm out, she indicated the long kitchen with a nook at the end where her dinette sat. "This is where For Whom the Bell Toils was born."

"I can see why you lease an office. It doesn't have a lot of counter space."

"Is that a problem for you?"

"On the contrary," he said. "Less is more as far as I'm concerned."

"This is my living room. There's my office where I do paperwork," she said, indicating the room set off with French doors. "It could be a downstairs bedroom if you wanted. Although, obviously a solid door would need to be there."

He grinned. "I'm a builder. Doors are my domain."

"Oh. Right. Of course. That would be a piece of cake for you." She indicated the stairway. "I'll show you the upstairs."

"The last time we did this, there were surprises." He held out his arm for her to precede him. "You go first."

"I guarantee there's nothing to be afraid of," she teased.

"I'm not taking any chances."

She led him up, past where the stairs turned, opening to a loft on the left. Through double doors, she took him into her bedroom. "It's spacious. Big, walk-in closet, double sinks, separate stall shower."

"Nice," he said, looking around.

She'd chosen roses and ruffles for her bedroom. The walls were painted a neutral rosy beige color and there were vases of dried flowers and a dish of potpourri on her nightstand. It couldn't be more feminine. And he couldn't possibly look more masculine and out of place in her froufrou space. The thought was like a speed bump to her racing heart and just as surely it shook her up.

"There are two more bedrooms." As he looked in, she swallowed the breathlessness she'd heard in her voice. When she felt in control, she said, "These would make perfect guest rooms for Gail and Kendra when they come to visit."

He met her gaze and the corners of his mouth turned up. "I can see why you're such a busy caterer. Never miss an opportunity to market your product."

She shrugged. "I'm not doing a sales presentation. It's the truth."

When they were back downstairs, she wasn't sure what to do. Should she ask him to sit down? Offer him a drink? At his place it had thrown her when he'd offered her a glass of wine. If she hadn't been pregnant, she'd have been tempted to take it. That reaction had unnerved her. She was the businesswoman; he was the client. But with Scott, the line between business and pleasure blurred. Something sizzled between them that fried the professional parameters and turned the politically correct into soot.

But she'd been taught that you could never go wrong being polite. Her mother's voice in her head wouldn't let her be anything less. Maybe he had to get home and would turn her down. "I'm sorry I don't have any beer. Would you like a glass of iced tea? Or a soda?"

"Iced tea would be great."

She should have known. But since she'd opened her big mouth again and made the offer, she couldn't very well take it back. If only she didn't feel the power of his appeal every time they were in the same room.

She walked into her kitchen and reached into the cupboard beside the refrigerator for a glass. After putting in some ice, she pulled out the tea pitcher and poured. "Would you like lemon and sugar?"

He shook his head and took the drink. After sipping, he looked at the glass, then at her. "What flavor is that?"

"Passion fruit."

As soon as the words were out of her mouth, she blushed like a teenager. She hadn't blushed this much around a guy even when she *was* a teenager.

To his credit, he didn't say anything except, "It's really good."

She leaned her back against the counter. "Town house living is ideal for a busy professional like yourself."

"How so?"

"Outside maintenance is taken care of by an association. I

have a small yard in back—patio large enough for a barbecue and a bit of grass and flowers. But essentially there's no upkeep."

"Good to know."

"It's important information to have when one is phasing out responsibility."

"That's something impossible for a father to escape. With two kids in college I'm looking at mega-obligations for a long time to come. And if either of the girls wants to go for a master's degree, I'll be doing dad duty even longer." He lifted one broad shoulder. "I'm just looking to simplify my living arrangements."

Thea understood that. This town house was where she'd moved to escape the painful memories after her husband died. It became her haven, allowed her to uncomplicate her life. Now she was ready to take on the responsibility of being a mother. She ached with the need to hold her baby in her arms.

She looked at Scott and said sincerely, "This is the perfect place to simplify your lifestyle. It's a little over twenty-three hundred square feet, by the way. Big, but not too big. Just the right amount of space without being overwhelming."

He set his empty glass on the counter. "You're preaching to the choir. I like your place. A lot. It's exactly what I need."

When he said the last words, his gaze darkened with intensity as he looked at her mouth. The realization made her skin grow warm and put a hitch in her breathing. She felt as if she needed to suck in air, yet she couldn't manage to because of the tightness in her chest.

She cleared her throat. "Maybe it's something we should pursue. The real-estate deal, I mean."

He nodded. "I agree."

"I'll call Joyce. If you're serious about swapping spaces, maybe she can cut us a break on her commission. This deal would be half the work."

"Maybe." The soles of his shoes scraped on her tile floor as he shifted his weight. "We can look into that. But—"

"Yes?" she asked eagerly, excited at the prospect of buying his house. It was everything she wanted. A kitchen large enough to do a lot of her work in, as well as being in the school district where she wanted her son or daughter educated. The perfect place to raise her child. And, she thought, the house had a positive parental vibe. She would be living in the same place as the man who'd successfully raised two fine young women.

He jammed his hands into his pockets as he shifted his feet. "There's something I'd like to ask you."

"Okay." He looked nervous. What was that about?

"Would you have dinner with me sometime?"

Dinner? To talk things over? Just the two of them? Not a good idea. "That's very nice of you, Scott. But it's not necessary for you to take me out to dinner to discuss real-estate details."

He shook his head. "Actually, talking business was the furthest thing from my mind. I meant, I'd like to take you out for a meal and discuss anything *but* business."

"You mean, a date?"

"Yeah." His expression went from tense to sheepish. "But if you have to ask, I guess I'm way rustier at this whole thing than I realized."

He wasn't the only one. If she was more with it, she'd have seen this coming, but she hadn't.

"No." She shook her head. "Dinner's out of the question."

He stared at her with a puzzled expression. "The last time I checked, dinner was a meal that most people take for granted they're going to eat."

Drat. He wasn't going to let it drop. But a date simply wasn't going to happen. And she couldn't violate her prime directive to explain why. She refused to talk about her baby yet. Call her superstitious, but it felt like asking for trouble— a challenge to the fates.

"I'm just too busy right now. We're on the cusp of summer.

That means weddings. Where there are weddings, there are bridal showers. And all of that is in addition to graduation parties. On top of which people still celebrate birthdays."

"You don't even need to check your schedule?" he asked.

This was awkward. Actually, she amended, she was awkward. She didn't know how to do this. She didn't want to do this. And, for Pete's sake, what part of *no* didn't he understand?

"Look, you said yourself that you're trying to simplify your life. You're going to be an empty-nester soon. I think this dating thing is a knee-jerk reaction to that."

"You're wrong. It's a knee-jerk reaction to wanting to see you socially."

Now what? Straightforward refusal, that's what. "I just can't. I'm sorry, Scott."

"I'm sorry, too." After an awkward moment, he turned and walked to the door, putting his hand on the knob. "Thanks for letting me barge in. I hope it wasn't too much trouble."

"Not at all. It was my idea."

"Yeah. I remember. Good night." Then he was gone.

Feeling like the slime that formed on rotten vegetables in the refrigerator, she stared at the spot where he'd been standing a second before. She was relieved that he'd finally accepted her no. But she couldn't help the tiniest bit of disappointment, too. Which was stupid, since she didn't want to go out with him. She didn't have room in her life.

Shaking her head, she realized it had been a long time since she'd thought in terms of having a life. After losing David, it had really and truly felt as if a part of her had died, too. Coming back had been long and painful but she was getting there. The problem with having a life was the potential for complications.

There was no question she found Scott attractive. Everything about him appealed to her. He was a good man and a good father. It was impossible not to like him. But that was useless information. She was going to have a baby. Thanks to modern science, she didn't need a man and that was just fine with her.

Having her husband's baby wasn't the only vow Thea had made on David's deathbed. She'd also promised herself that she would never want or need a man again. And she'd just made sure there was no chance of that happening.

Chapter 7

Scott walked into his younger brother's office at Matthews and Sons and slapped a folder down on the desk.

Mike Matthews glanced up from the spreadsheet on his computer screen. "Something wrong?"

Scott looked at his brother, working at the computer as if he didn't have a care in the world. And he probably didn't, because he'd never married and had kids. Not that Scott regretted his kids. He did, however, regret the woman he'd chosen to be their mother.

People had always said the two of them looked like twins. But that was where the resemblance stopped. Mike wore wire-rimmed glasses, compliments of being a computer geek. And his position as a desk jockey, instead of out in the field doing construction, meant that to stay fit he spent lots of time in the gym. Other than the fact that he envied his brother's simple lifestyle—no commitment, no way, no how—they were good friends. But he didn't really want to answer the question—was anything wrong?

"No," he finally said. "Why?"

Mike swiveled his desk chair and faced front. "Scuttlebutt has it that mortgage rates are expected to creep up. That could slow new home sales."

Scott shrugged. "Not in this area. Santa Clarita is booming and shows no signs of slowing down."

"I heard Josh McCardle is quitting. Isn't he your best crew foreman?"

"Yeah. Richmond West is really busy and offered him a better deal than we could. I told him to take it."

"He's been with the company for ten years. You taught him everything. Doesn't it tick you off that he went with a busy company—and our biggest competitor?"

Busy. That's what Thea had said. She was too busy to go out to dinner with him. She might just as well have said he was ugly and his mother dressed him funny. Too busy meant the same thing. Everyone had to eat. How could you be too busy to go out to dinner? It wasn't like he was asking her to sleep with him. He just wanted to take her out to a damn dinner.

Hell, who was he kidding? He wanted Thea any way he could get her. And if a romantic rendezvous afterwards at her place was in the cards, he wouldn't wimp out and throw in his hand.

"Scott?"

"Hmm?"

"You look like someone left your favorite drill out in the rain to rust. What's up with you?"

"Nothing."

"Something wrong with the girls? Did Kendra get turned down at UCLA?"

"No. The girls are fine."

His brother leaned back in his chair and linked his fingers

over his abdomen. "Look, bro, you've been in a crap mood for a week now. I'm trying to be supportive, but I gotta tell you, playing twenty questions is getting real old. Either you tell me what's wrong or get out of my office. I don't much care which."

Scott released a long breath and stared out the window for several moments. "Okay. You win. Besides, I'm going to explode if I don't talk to someone about this."

"I'm here for you, Scott, you know that."

"I know you've had a lot of experience with women."

Mike's eyebrows shot up in surprise. "This is about a woman?"

The skeptical look on his brother's face didn't do anything to sweeten Scott's mood. "Don't look so shocked."

"Sorry. I can't help it. It's been a long time between women for you." He shrugged. "I just didn't think—"

"That I could have a problem with one?"

"Well, yeah." He grinned. "You made it clear that your personal life ran a distant third behind the girls and your job. It never occurred to me that you've been walking around in a black funk for a week and it was all about a woman."

"So it's breaking news?"

"I'm proud of you, bro."

"Don't be." Scott snorted. "She turned me down flat."

"Who is she?"

"Her name is Thea Bell and she owns a catering business here in town. I've hired her to take care of Ken's graduation party."

"And she's hot?"

"She's a very nice, very attractive woman," he answered. His tone must have held a warning because Mike lifted a hand as if to say she's all yours.

"She must be all that and more to get your attention."

"What does that mean?" Scott asked.

"Just that since your divorce, you haven't shown enough

interest in any woman to walk around in a funk for a day, let alone a week."

Scott sat on the corner of the desk and blew out a long breath. "Here's the thing, Mike. She's different. She's not the type who talks much about her personal life."

"So ask her out and get to know her."

"I did. Like I said. She rejected me."

"What did she say?"

"That she was too busy."

Mike winced. "Ooh. That's bad."

"Even I know that. But it gets worse."

"How?"

"She knows Kendra is graduating from high school and going to college. She said that my asking her for a date was a knee-jerk reaction to the fact that I'll be an empty-nester."

"Ouch." Mike shook his head. "But you defended yourself, right? Set her straight?"

"I didn't think my ego could handle it. I got the feeling she was trying to let me down easy. It seemed to me if I pushed her, and she let me down any easier, I'd be a rust-colored stain on the carpet."

"Yeah. I can see how you'd get that impression."

Scott rubbed the back of his neck. "But here's the other thing, Mike. I really like her. And I know I'm not the sharpest tool in the shed where women are concerned, but I would bet my favorite hammer that she likes me, too."

"So?"

"So, I guess I could accept a *No* more gracefully if she just flat out said she's not interested."

"You want it up front and right between the eyes?" Mike asked.

"Yeah, I guess I do."

That was preferable to having children and spending years with a woman only to find out he didn't know her at all. After

Kendra was born, he'd thought things were better than ever between him and his wife. So when she gave him her sweeping pronouncement that she wasn't happy being a wife and mother, it had come out of nowhere. And her timing couldn't have been worse. He'd been patting himself on the back for making it over the speed bumps in their marriage. Hell, he'd taken pride in the fact that they'd nipped their problems in the bud and were going to make it as a family. Then, to find out he'd been so wrong, he'd felt like the world's biggest chump.

"Maybe Thea's married," Mike suggested.

Scott shook his head. "She's a widow."

"Could be she's already got a boyfriend." Mike leaned forward and rested his forearms on his desk. "But if she does, wouldn't she just say so?"

Scott would be the first to admit he wasn't the best judge of character. But his gut was telling him that Thea was outspoken and direct. If she was personally involved with another guy she wouldn't hesitate to say so.

"Yeah. She would have been up front about dating someone else."

"So what's her deal?" Mike asked.

"Damned if I know."

And that was the hell of it. He didn't know. Not even what tragedy had taken her husband from her too soon. If he knew what was good for him, he would just drop the subject. Get through his daughter's party and walk away in one piece. Forget about Thea Bell. Why should he stick his neck out? Why put himself on the line again? He didn't much enjoy feeling like he'd been flattened by a speeding locomotive.

The thing was, he had a feeling Thea had been flattened even worse than he had. And he'd been telling the God's honest truth when he said he liked her. How long had it been since he'd met a woman he could say that about? He wasn't willing to blow it off without at least giving it another try.

He met his brother's gaze. "Mikey, I'm going to find out what her deal is if it's the last thing I do."

"That's the spirit. But, Scotty—"

"Yeah?"

"Don't ever call me Mikey again. If you do, I'm gonna have to hurt you."

Scott grinned. "You and what army?"

But he felt better than he had in a week. Because now he had a plan. Come hell or high water, he intended to find out personal information about Ms. Thea Bell.

"I'm grounded."

"But why?" Thea asked, settling herself on the sofa.

She'd arrived for her appointment with Scott at the agreed-upon time but he wasn't home from work yet. Kendra had let her in and invited her to sit in the family room. The first words out of her mouth were about her punishment.

"He's so unreasonable. I came in just a little after my curfew."

Thea remembered what Scott had told her about the rule. "I guess he figures if he gives an inch, you'll take a mile."

"But it's not fair."

"He said you were working on something for school. Did you need more time?"

Kendra shrugged. "It took a little longer than we thought."

"I don't get the impression your dad is completely unreasonable. Did you call and explain the situation?"

"With my dad that's a waste of time and cell phone minutes."

"So you didn't even try?"

The teen flopped back on the couch. "My battery was dead. I tried to explain, but he said being grounded will give me time to think about remembering to plug it in."

Scott *was* tough as nails, Thea thought. In the same situation, she'd have been tempted to relax the rules, as long as schoolwork was involved. But she could certainly see the wisdom of running a tight ship the way he did.

"But what about your friend's house? Is it a cave without phone service?" Thea's mouth curved up. "No, let me guess. Both of your hands were broken and you couldn't dial the phone. And all your friends had the same problem."

The girl grinned reluctantly. "No. Zoe's house has a working phone. But I forgot because…"

"What?" she asked, when the girl got a funny look on her face.

She didn't quite meet Thea's gaze. "Because we left."

"And? What aren't you telling me?"

"Zoe wanted to go to Java 'n Jazz where her boyfriend works. He was going to ask her to prom and we all got excited. I didn't think. And—"

"There's more?" Thea asked, surprised.

"Dad says Zoe doesn't have enough parental supervision and he's not happy about me hanging out with her."

The way things turned out, he was right to be concerned, Thea thought. But all she said was, "A rule is a rule."

"You sound just like him. He said the same thing. Followed by—and I quote—next time you won't forget." She heaved a big sigh.

Thea reached over and patted her arm. "I'd love to bash your father with you," she lied. "Except I agree with him."

"Traitor." But there was no heat or hostility in the word.

"Tell me honestly that if he relaxed the rule on this, you wouldn't push the envelope again under the same circumstances. Or next time you're out on a school night working on a project with your friends, tell me you won't remember this consequence and be home by curfew."

Kendra tucked a strand of long dark hair, the same shade

as her father's, behind her ear. "Okay. You might have a point."

"I knew you were a reasonable young woman the first time I met you."

"Not so much," the girl said. "I plan to stay mad at my dad for a long time."

"You might consider one thing."

"What?"

"He's letting you have a catered graduation party *and* picking up the tab. And I'm not just saying that because I got the job."

Kendra's shoulders slumped as she shook her head. "I hate it when people are rational, logical and sensible."

"I can be annoying that way," Thea agreed.

The teen met her gaze. "So you think I should be nice to him?"

"I think you should accept your punishment gracefully and move on." She tapped her lip thoughtfully. "If you really want to freak him out, tell him you completely understand why he punished you, then thank him for caring so much."

Kendra grinned. "You're diabolical."

"It drove my parents crazy," she agreed. She opened the notebook on her lap. "Did you taste the dishes I left?"

The teen nodded. "I loved them all. Especially the lasagna and quesadilla. The Greek salad not so much. Egg rolls," she closed her eyes and heaved a huge sigh. "To die for."

"So do you want to do an international sort of menu?"

"Dad said you didn't mind if that's what I wanted."

Thea nodded. "It makes no difference to me. Like I told him, the client is always right."

"Then how come I got grounded?"

"Because you were wrong not to follow your father's rules." Thea looked at her. "You might want to consider law school after college. Way to twist the daylights out of an innocent remark."

"Thanks." Kendra grinned proudly. Then she asked, "Isn't it more expensive to mix up different foods?"

Thea shook her head. "It's all about the ingredients. If you wanted a recipe with shrimp, lobster or crab or something with expensive fixings, I'd have to pass on the cost to your father."

"What are the most expensive things you make?" the girl asked, a gleam in her eyes.

"Oh, no you don't. I'm not getting caught in the middle of World War III."

Thea heard the front door open and close and her heart skipped a beat. Scott was home. She'd been half relieved and half disappointed he wasn't there when she'd arrived. Although mostly she dreaded seeing him again after their awkward last meeting. If only he hadn't tried to make things personal. Under different circumstances, she would have been like a teenage girl at her first boy/girl party. But letting things between them become more than a simple business association was a recipe for disaster. And she'd had enough of that to last her a lifetime.

The teen grinned at her just before her father walked into the room. "Hi, Dad."

"Hey, sweetie." He looked surprised, as if he'd expected hostility. "Sorry I'm late, Thea."

"No problem. It gave Kendra and me a chance to talk things over."

"What things?"

The teen stood and walked over to him. She kissed his cheek. "I just wanted to say thanks for grounding me. I deserved it, and I'm sorry I broke the rules."

He stared at his daughter as if she'd beamed down from the Starship Enterprise before his very eyes. "You are?"

"I'm going upstairs to do my homework."

"Okay," he said.

"See you later, Thea. Thanks for talking with me."

"Anytime," she said.

Although she'd rather the teen stick around and not leave her alone with Scott. But after advising her to shake him up, she couldn't very well ruin this Kodak moment.

After his daughter disappeared upstairs, Scott slid her a shell-shocked look. "Do you want to explain that?"

"No."

"So there is an explanation?"

"I didn't say that."

"It was implied," he said.

"She's your daughter."

"Maybe." He glanced up at the ceiling, where his child had disappeared. "Or maybe my daughter was kidnapped by aliens who left a very cooperative, very scary clone in her place."

Thea laughed. "She's a good kid. Leave it at that."

"Okay." He set his briefcase on the floor by a wing chair. "I hope I didn't keep you waiting too long. I got hung up in a meeting with my brother Mike."

"No problem. It gave Kendra and me a chance to discuss what she wants for food. She decided to do an international smorgasbord. Lasagna, quesadillas, egg rolls. I recommend a big green salad and fresh fruit salad with that."

"So are we talking a second mortgage on my house to cover it?" he teased.

"Actually, I explained to her that the ingredients of a recipe determine the cost. She wanted to know what my most expensive main dishes are."

"And?" he said cringing.

"You walked in and she became a teen angel." Thea shrugged. "Actually she approved all of your choices. Apparently you have similar taste."

When he smiled, she felt instant heat roll through her followed by a melting sensation that made her thighs quiver. Why did this have to happen to her now? Everything in her life was going perfectly. Her business was better than ever. Financially she was secure. She had a baby on the way that would fulfill a deeply personal promise as well as a powerful maternal yearning. And now she was attracted to *this* man.

Since she couldn't deny it any longer, she would simply have to deal with it. She stood. "Now all you have to do is give me the number of people and I can work up the figures for you."

"Ken and I will talk that over. Now that we're talking, period. I have a feeling that change in our communication is thanks to you," he added.

"Sooner or later it would have blown over. Talking just made the process go faster." It was nothing more than the truth because he'd done a wonderful job with his children. He was a terrific father. And that thought shook her, convincing her it was time to get back on task before she had to examine her feelings too closely. "When you have a guest list, I'll know how many tables to reserve."

He folded his arms over his chest, and the impossibly masculine pose snagged her feminine attention in spite of her best intentions. She noticed that whole heat thing again with the fireball effect in the pit of her belly. Every nerve ending in her body zapped a hormone, which she had in spades at the moment. The chain reaction let her know how aware she was of this man.

"What about setting up outside?" he asked.

She glanced out the slider into the backyard. "Good idea. The pool will make a wonderful focal point. And you have lots of room, so table arrangements shouldn't be a problem."

"Unless Kendra wants to invite the equivalent of a third world country."

"Yes." She inched toward the exit. "But that's for the two of you to work out."

His gaze narrowed. "What's your rush? Do you have another appointment?"

"No, I—"

Whenever she was around Scott Matthews, she felt like a pacemaker too close to microwaves. All her brain functions went haywire. He'd just given her an out. All she'd needed to say was that she had to be somewhere. It wasn't even a lie. She did have to be somewhere—anywhere but spitting distance from this man would do.

"I have to get going," she said, hoping to salvage the situation. "I need to—"

The doorbell rang and he held up a hand. "That's our pizza. Hold that thought."

She didn't want to hold anything. She just wanted to go and distract herself from thoughts of Scott Matthews. After she'd refused to go out with him, she'd feared a cool and distant working relationship. He was anything but. *Charming* was the word that came to mind. Talk about diabolical. But his lack of a grudge wasn't something she could let herself get excited about.

It had been a long time since she'd felt anything but emptiness. But her baby and meeting Scott had changed that. She couldn't stop the feeling. It was exciting to be attracted to a good-looking man. But fate had a twisted sense of humor because he was the wrong man.

He walked back into the kitchen with a large flat box and a bag on top of it. "Dinner is served." His expression turned wry. "I'm sure it's not as good as what you could make."

"I love pizza."

"Stay and have some with us."

She'd done it again. If this kept up, she'd have to find a good recipe for foot-in-mouth. "I don't want to intrude."

"It's not intruding if I invite you. Besides, anyone who can get my daughter to thank me for punishing her is someone I want to know better."

"It's only because I'm not an authority figure."

Scott studied her. "How did you get to know so much about teenagers? Did you study teen psychology in school?"

"I was a business major, actually." Wow, did that pizza smell good.

"Did you go to college in California?"

"UC Santa Barbara."

"Did you grow up here?" He flipped back the square top of the box and the mouth-watering smell permeated the room. "Do you have family in the area? Brothers and sisters?" He handed her a paper plate with a triangle of pizza on it.

She took it and after taking a bite and chewing, she said, "My parents live in Northridge. I have a brother in San Diego and a sister in Marina Del Rey."

"A boyfriend?" He took a bite of his own pizza and met her gaze.

She put her plate down. "If I did have one, I would have said so the last time we were together." When he'd asked her out, but she didn't want to say that. Wasn't he the nosy one. It was time to put the brakes on that. "Thanks for the pizza, Scott. But I really have to go."

"Why? You don't have an appointment."

"That doesn't mean I don't have things to do."

"What is it with you and questions?"

"An exchange of personal information is a technique for bonding. Since we have nothing more than a short-term business contract that would be a waste of time."

"We can't be friends?"

"This can be a friendly *working* relationship," she said, emphasizing the key word.

Scott put down his paper plate and frowned. "I don't get you."

It's really not that complicated, she thought. One tidbit of info would lead to another and another. It could take them to a place she would rather not go.

"I'm sorry. But you know better than anyone that there are rules. Your daughter can't stay out past ten on a school night. I make it a point not to get too close to my clients." She shrugged. "I've found it's better that way."

"For who?"

"Everyone." She picked up her things. "Call me when you and Kendra have the guest list together."

Thea walked out the front door before he could say anything more. When she was inside her car, she had the most absurd desire to burst into tears. It was really stupid since she was the one who had done the walking out. She felt so bad curbing her normally friendly nature, but Scott seemed determined not to let it go. She was a couple weeks shy of completing her first trimester and discussing the baby until then was out of the question.

But how she wanted to. The temptation to laugh and talk with him about it was almost too much to resist. He'd been a father twice over and knew what to expect. Just being in the same room with him made her feel—

What? More than simple attraction, that was a given. He was strong and conscientious, the kind of man who took care of his own. She'd missed sharing the load with someone. And she was tired of being alone.

She wouldn't be for very much longer. Soon she'd have her baby. And she'd be raising it alone. It wasn't as if she hadn't known before the IVF, so she had no right to whine. But she was acutely aware of coming back to life because Scott made her ache for what she couldn't have.

If she *were* a whiner, that was prime complaint criteria.

Chapter 8

Thea closed the book she'd just finished and set it on the end table beside her. She wondered if she'd have time to read after the baby was born. Pressing her palms against her abdomen, she longed for the six and a half months to pass quickly. If it weren't for the weariness and nausea that were tangible signs of her pregnancy, she would have her doubts about a baby growing inside her.

It seemed like forever until she would be able hold it in her arms. She prayed the child she carried would be healthy and perfect.

A knock on her door startled her and she looked at her watch. "Eight-thirty? I'm not expecting anyone."

At the door, she stood on tiptoe to see through the peephole as she called out, "Who is it?"

"Kendra Matthews."

Several things went through her mind at once when she recognized the teen. It was too late for a strictly social visit.

Scott must have shared with his daughter the location of the condo he intended to buy. But why would she come here? Something was wrong and Thea wasn't sure she wanted to get involved. Shaking her head, she realized there was no choice. She hadn't been able to ignore this girl from the first time she'd met her.

Thea sighed as she turned the dead bolt and opened the door. "Hi, kiddo. Come in."

"Hi, Thea." The girl walked inside and stood in the entryway twisting her fingers together. "I'm sorry to bother you."

"You didn't. In fact your timing is perfect. I just finished my book." She frowned as she recognized the intensely tragic expression on the girl's face. "What's wrong?"

"I had a fight with my dad."

"I'm sorry." Thea was no expert on teenage behavior, but it seemed weird for Kendra to show up here instead of going to someone her own age.

"Can I talk to you?"

"Of course. But I'm surprised you didn't go to one of your friends."

"They're gone. Zoe invited all of us to go to the Colorado River with her and her mom and stepdad."

"Your dad wouldn't let you go," Thea guessed.

She nodded miserably. "He says she's not a good influence after what happened to get me grounded. She's a new friend, and he's never met her parents. So he just put his foot down and said no. He wouldn't even listen to me or give her another chance. I got so frustrated, I just left."

"He doesn't know where you are?"

She shook her head. "I turned off my cell phone."

Thea wanted to insist the girl call her father. If she were in Scott's shoes and her child had stormed out of the house, she would be frantic. But she had a feeling if she insisted, the teen might take off again. Then she would be behind the wheel of a car with her emotions all over the map. Not a safe situation.

"Come in and sit down," she invited. "Can I get you a soda? Something to eat? Have you had dinner?"

"I'm not hungry." She sat on the sofa and set her keys on the coffee table.

Thea understood Scott's protectiveness. Her baby wasn't even born yet and she was bending over backward to make sure this child would have a full-term pregnancy and safe delivery into this world. She could only imagine how her instincts to safeguard this child would escalate when she held him for the first time and watched him grow.

Scott had nurtured his daughter for eighteen years. Even when his decisions were met with hostility and rebellion, he kept his head and tried the best he knew how to do the right thing. She couldn't fault him.

"You know, your dad doesn't take pleasure in telling you no."

"He's so unreasonable."

"Translation—he wouldn't let you do what you wanted."

The teen met her gaze and her eyes widened in surprise. "You're taking his side?"

Thea refused to be put on the defensive. "Why did you come here, Kendra?"

She lifted one shoulder. "To talk, I guess."

"And I'm happy to do that," Thea said, sitting beside her. "But part of talking is listening. And I'm not the kind of person who will say what you want to hear. I'll tell you what I think."

"You think my dad is right? That Zoe is a bad person?"

"I have no opinion on your friend. I've never met her. And I'm not convinced your dad thinks that, either."

"He doesn't trust my judgment."

"Think about it from his point of view. All he knows is that you went to her house to study and then you broke the rules."

"His rules are lame." She slouched against the back of the sofa.

"Maybe. But as long as you live under his roof and he's paying the bills, he's entitled to set any parameters he thinks best."

"So you think I should go away to college, too."

Thea stared at this woman/child who'd just leaped from the specific to the general. "It doesn't matter what I think and that's not what we were talking about. Here's the thing—even if you go away to college, your dad will still be paying the bills. He's still going to have some input in your life. Not as much input, and not on a day-to-day basis. The only way to have things your own way is to be independent. And the only way I can see for you to do that is to suck it up and get the best possible education so you can support yourself and not rely on your father."

The girl's eyes grew wide. Obviously she hadn't expected to hear she needed to snap out of it. Finally, one corner of her mouth turned up. "It will take forever to get through college."

"'The journey of a thousand miles starts with a single step,'" Thea quoted. "Besides, I bet when you were a freshman in high school you thought you'd never graduate. Yet here you are."

"Yeah. It seems like a long time ago. How did you know?"

"Because I remember. It felt like I'd be in high school forever. Suddenly I was a senior and saying goodbye to my friends. It was a scary, exciting, traumatic time."

"I know what you mean," she said, sitting up straight. "I get so weird sometimes—"

A knock on the door interrupted her. "I wonder who that could be," Thea said. She stood and walked over, too tired to strain and see who was there. "Who is it?"

"Scott Matthews."

At the sound of his voice, Thea felt the shivery sensation

he always generated flutter through her. The good news was it chased her weariness away. The bad news: as much as she knew it wasn't smart to be in the same room with him, she just couldn't turn him away.

"I'm going to let him in." She glanced over her shoulder. When the girl nodded, Thea put her hand on the knob and opened the door.

"I saw Kendra's car," he said, before she could greet him.

The expression on his face was grim, ragged, intense. When he looked past her and saw his daughter, relief was stark on his features even before he released a long breath. He walked inside. "Hi," he said to her.

She stood up. "How did you know I was here?"

"When you didn't answer your cell, I decided to drive around and see if I could spot your car. I knew all your friends were gone, so I came by here on a hunch. Process of elimination." He shrugged. "I was worried about you, Ken."

"I'm sorry, Dad. I just needed some space. I get so frustrated." She twisted her fingers together.

He nodded. "Me, too. Welcome to my world."

"Thea made me look at things from your point of view."

"Good. But I think we've imposed on Thea long enough."

When he glanced at her, Thea couldn't tell what he was thinking. But she was thinking how good it was to see him.

Kendra picked up her keys from the coffee table, then met Thea's gaze. "Thanks for making me listen."

"Anytime."

The teen looked at her father. "I'll see you at home."

"Okay," he said. When she was gone, he finally looked at Thea. "I'm sorry she bothered you. But I have to ask what you said to her."

"I simply tried to give her a different perspective on the situation."

"So you didn't take her side?"

She put her hand on her hip. "What is it with you people? You're so hung up on taking sides. She accused me of taking yours. And you thought I'd take hers."

He grinned. "So you didn't hang me out to dry. I like that in a friend."

"Are we? Friends, I mean?" What had made her ask that? She was the one bending over backward to keep it professional. A *friendly* working relationship, she'd said.

"You tell me." He ran his fingers through his hair. "I've always made it a point to get friendly with the people surrounding my children. Kendra trusts you. You obviously have some influence over her. A positive one," he said, glancing at the door where his daughter had just left. "That is not the same girl who screamed that I was ruining her life just before she slammed out of the house a little while ago. And whatever you said to her is responsible for the attitude adjustment."

"I'm glad I could help."

"Me, too." He folded his arms over his chest. "But to answer your question. Are we friends? I don't know. But I'd like to be. Except I was taught that it's a two-way street. With you, I feel like a jaywalker every time I try."

"It's not you, Scott. It's me."

Suddenly he walked over to the end table and picked up an eight-by-ten picture frame sitting there and looked at it. "Is this your husband?"

"David," she said, as the familiar feeling of sadness washed through her.

"What happened to him?" When she hesitated, he said, "I wasn't aware that your life was subject to government security clearance. Besides the fact that in my world friends share things, I figure it's my job to know the people who influence my daughter. But that's just me. I'll try to make sure she doesn't bother you anymore." He turned to leave.

"Wait!"

She didn't want him to leave like that. Somehow he'd become more than just a client. And she hadn't meant to hurt him.

"It's not just you," she said with a sigh. "I don't blurt out my personal information to just anyone. And I have my reasons." When one of his eyebrows lifted, she shook her head. "I don't expect you to understand. But I've learned to be cautious about sharing details."

"What about sharing the burden? When you mentioned David, you looked sad. What happened to him, Thea?" he asked, setting the picture back on the end table.

Looking at the familiar and beloved face, she realized that without a photo she had trouble remembering her husband's features. She couldn't figure out when that had happened.

"He died of cancer."

"I'm sorry," he automatically said.

"Me, too. He was way too young and it stinks."

"I'm sorry," he said again.

"It's all right. I'm over it."

"Yeah. I could tell by the 'it stinks' part. And the fact that you look like you're going to cry."

"Just hormones." Which was the truth.

During the in vitro process, she'd been pumped full of them to get her body ready to accept and nurture the implanted embryos. Now that she was pregnant, the hormones were still creating havoc in her body. But that didn't always explain why her eyes filled with tears. It was simply the reason she couldn't stop crying once she'd started.

Gently, Scott nudged her chin up with his knuckle and forced her to meet his gaze. "Thea, you don't have to do it alone. I'm here to listen."

When he curved his fingers around her upper arms, she allowed him to pull her against him. She rested her cheek on his chest, savoring the strong and steady beat of his heart. It had been so long since she'd leaned on anyone. God help her, it felt so good to be held. The circle of Scott's arms was a place she wished she could stay forever. Which was exactly why she pulled back.

When she did, she saw the hungry expression in his eyes. Part of her brain registered the fact that she recognized it. With the other part, she acknowledged her own corresponding sensual awareness that had been dormant for a long time.

It was the only explanation for her sigh of satisfaction when Scott eased her closer, then lowered his head to touch his mouth to hers. Instantly, liquid warmth trickled through her. He tunneled his fingers into her hair and lightly applied pressure to make the meeting of their mouths firmer.

Tenderly he moved his lips over hers, touching the corner of her mouth, the curve of her cheek, her nose and eyelids. The sweetness of it created an ache inside her. Moist heat settled between her quivering thighs and almost of their own will, her arms found their way around his neck. Then he slanted his mouth across hers again as his arm came around her waist, settling her against the solid, muscled length of him.

Her breath caught at the incredibly wonderful sensation of a man's hard body pressed to her feminine curves. The thought was like tossing a lighted match to bone-dry twigs. The resulting inferno threatened to consume her and she couldn't find the will to care.

Scott held her tightly to him and heaved a ragged sigh. She heard it at the same time his breath fanned her face and cranked up her need. When he pulled back a little, everything inside her cried out against ending the embrace.

"I didn't mean to do that," he said, resting his forehead to hers. "I'm a little out of practice."

"You couldn't prove it by me," she whispered.

As soon as the words left her mouth, she wanted them back in the worst way. She'd barely acknowledged her feelings of friendship for this man and now she was revealing how much she'd enjoyed his kiss—so much, she'd have willingly followed him anywhere.

That thought scared Thea to the core of her being.

Carved on the wall of the church where she'd had her husband's funeral were the words "Grief is the price we pay for loving." In the weeks and months following, she'd decided the price was too high.

Only her promise to have this child had brought her through and given her the will to go on. But she wanted no part of loving a man ever again.

She stepped away from Scott. "Kendra will be waiting for you." She let out a long breath and stuffed her shaking hands into her pockets.

"Yeah." He ran a hand through his hair and she noticed he was shaking, too. The realization gave her no satisfaction. "I'll call you."

"Okay. There are still party details to work out."

She knew she was ducking behind her professional facade, but she had nowhere else to hide. Fortunately, he didn't comment. He simply nodded, then left her alone.

She locked the dead bolt and leaned back against the door, completely appalled at her behavior. She wished she could blame him. Heck, she wished she could dislike him.

But she couldn't do either. She could only put the brakes on her emotions to keep from liking him any more than she already did.

Thea hummed a popular tune as she walked into the office and set down her purse and briefcase. "Isn't it a beautiful day?"

"Good news?" Connie asked. She was sitting at her desk in the front office.

"The best."

Thea didn't need a mirror to see that she was beaming. She could feel it. Along with the pregnancy glow she'd heard so much about. It had to be evident to everyone who saw her. Flush, blush, shine, whatever. She could practically feel it radiating from her and bouncing off stationary objects.

"So what did the doctor say?" her friend prompted impatiently.

"She said everything is progressing normally."

Connie sniffed. "I could have told you that."

"Yes, but she had the ultrasound results to prove it." She put a hand on her abdomen. "Seriously, Con, I'm so relieved. She said there's no reason to expect anything out of the ordinary, even though this baby was conceived through in vitro fertilization."

"So you're just like every other hormone-riddled woman who's going to give birth in six months?"

Thea nodded enthusiastically. "The method of conception doesn't make me any more vulnerable to miscarriage or any other pregnancy trauma than a woman who gets pregnant the old-fashioned way."

Speaking of sex, Thea flashed back to the memory of Scott kissing her. She couldn't help wondering if her baby was the only thing responsible for her glow.

"Speaking of sex," Connie began.

They'd been friends too long. It was as if they could read each other's mind.

Thea knew what was coming and didn't want to go there. "We weren't talking about sex. I was referring to the miracle of modern science that made this baby possible."

"No, you were referring to the time-honored tradition of the horizontal hokey-pokey that sometimes results in pregnancy if the sperm is not deflected from its intended target."

"No. I was referring to the fact that simply because my baby was helped along in its existence, that doesn't mean I can't enjoy a routine, worry-free pregnancy. Using common sense, there's no reason I have to limit my normal activities."

"So you're cleared for sex," Connie clarified wryly.

"Sex might be listed under normal for most pregnant women, but not for me. And it hasn't been for over two years."

"Even more reason to be open to the possibilities."

Thea narrowed her gaze. "What does that mean?"

Connie stood and crossed her arms over her chest as she leaned back against her own desk. The expression on her face said what she had on her mind wasn't the usual attitude-laced, bracing, rah-rah pep talk. She had something serious to say.

"David died, Thea, not you."

"I'm aware of that."

"He was your husband and you loved him. He was my friend and I loved him. I introduced the two of you in college. I wish I could say I did it because I thought he was perfect for you, but that would be a lie. I simply got tired of you whining that you never met any nice guys."

"I didn't whine."

Connie's grin was fleeting. "So not the point. Here's the thing, Thea. David loved you very much and would want you to get every last drop of fun and fulfillment out of life."

"And that's what I'm doing," she defended. "I'm going to have a child."

"David's child."

"Yes. I promised him."

"Are you sure it's not just another barrier to keep anyone from getting close to you again?"

A knot formed inside her and Thea fought down the annoyance. "How can you say that? You knew David almost as well as I did. You know how much he wanted children. We wanted to create a child who would inherit the best of our combined DNA. His brains, my—"

"Stubbornness?"

"That's not what I was going to say."

Connie sighed. "You met a terrific guy—"

"I meet lots of guys."

"Okay, you want to split hairs, I can get specific. Scott Matthews."

Thea's heart pounded merely at the mention of his name. "What about him?"

"He's better looking than the average bear. He's pretty well-off financially. He seems like a great guy and his daughter likes you."

"And what's your point?" As if she didn't know.

"He's interested in you."

"Get real," Thea scoffed, hoping to pull off disinterest so her friend would drop the subject.

"I will if you will." Connie braced her hands on the desk, then slid her fanny on top and let her legs dangle. "He's interested. And I think you are, too."

"Oh, for Pete's sake."

"No, for your sake. And your baby's. That child is important. No one understands that better than me. But you're poising yourself to make it the center of your universe and that's just not normal."

"I'm not doing that," she protested.

"You are. You're shutting down feelings with real potential."

"How do you know this?"

"Because I'm your best friend." When she started to protest, Connie held up her hand. "Can you honestly tell me that Scott Matthews hasn't made your inner woman sit up and do the happy dance?"

Thea shifted uncomfortably as she sighed and looked away.

"What?" Connie demanded. "I know you. What happened? Tell me everything. I can't believe you've been withholding details."

Thea finally met her gaze. "I could have told you my inner woman was comatose. And it would have been true before—"

"What?"

"Before Scott kissed me."

"Hot damn and hallelujah," Connie cheered.

"I don't know what you're so excited about. It didn't mean anything."

"Uh-oh." Her friend's gaze narrowed. "Please tell me you're not going to pooh-pooh it."

"Why not?"

"It's just wrong to spit in fate's eye like that."

"What are you talking about?" Thea asked. But the question was simply a stall, because she knew what was coming.

"There must be some kind of cosmic rule against turning your back on possibilities. For throwing away the opportunity for happiness."

"It's not happiness I object to," Thea said. "But the emptiness and pain that happen when it's taken away."

"So you *are* turning your back," Connie said in her aha-I-knew-it tone of voice.

"I'm being realistic. Scott Matthews is everything you said. And in case there's any doubt, I did, in fact, notice he's not hard on the eyes."

"I hear a but."

"But he's nearly finished raising his children."

"Look at it this way. He brings experience to the table."

"That's just it. He doesn't want to sit at the table. He wants footloose and fancy-free. But I'll be tied down for the next eighteen years."

Longer, really. She could see that because of what Scott was dealing with. The hands-on responsibility would change, but it would always be there. Because the love would always be there.

"You're having a child. It's not one of those prisoner ankle surveillance things," the other woman said. "You can still have a personal life with all the lows, highs and in betweens. You're entitled to the joys of living. Including sex."

Thea was living. She knew that because of the way her body had come alive and burned at the feel of Scott's mouth on her own. What scared her the most was that she would have slept with him. She wasn't sure how or why she'd gotten to that point, but she had.

And it would have been wrong. For both of them. For so many reasons.

She looked at her friend. "I know I have a life to live. Now I have this life inside me. This baby is the most important thing to me. I don't need the distraction of interpersonal relationships."

"Translation, you're running away."

"No. I'm running to. I'm looking forward to being a mother."

"What about a father?"

"That's out of my hands."

"No—"

"Stop, Con. I can't go there."

Connie emitted a huge sigh that meant defeat and Thea was grateful. She didn't want to argue. Her life was moving forward according to plan. And Scott Matthews was not now nor could he ever be a part of that plan.

After two miscarriages, this baby—her baby—had finally made it safely through the first trimester. With the baby growing inside her she'd kept her promise. She couldn't hope for more happiness than that.

She was afraid to.

Chapter 9

Thea sat down at Scott's kitchen table and tried to forget that the last time she'd seen him he'd kissed the daylights out of her. It was time to pull herself together. Only a difficult, persnickety client got as much attention as she'd given him. And he was neither difficult nor persnickety. Which meant she'd subconsciously wanted to be with him. That had to stop. Firm decisions needed to be made so she could keep her distance.

"Okay. It's crunch time," she told him. And she didn't mean crunched up against that hard, strong body. So much for getting a grip.

"Are we really short on time?" he asked.

She shrugged sheepishly. "We're doing okay. I just like saying that."

"Ah, the dramatic type," he said with a quick grin. "I'll remember that. Before we get started, would you like a drink?"

"No, thanks."

"I've got coffee made."

She shook her head. "I'm off caffeine."

"Doctor's orders?" He glanced at her over his shoulder as he pulled a mug from the cupboard above the coffeemaker.

"Why would you think that?"

"No reason. You just seem nervous."

Not because of caffeine, she thought. Because of him. Because of that kiss.

"It's just a busy time of year for the business. I'm being pulled in a lot of different directions right now."

One of them was her attraction to Scott, a direction she refused to go. She'd been there, done that, and didn't want to participate ever again. It was exciting at first, but the potential for pain was too great. Best to just do this job and that would be that.

He set his mug on the kitchen table and sat down at a right angle to her. "Okay. Then we'll nail down this menu for Kendra's party so you can relax."

Like that was going to happen with him sitting a foot away from her. "Okay," she said, glancing at her notes. "We've got international delight here. And Kendra liked everything but the Greek salad. I had an idea how we could pull it off and still do justice to the food."

"I'm all ears."

If only that were true, she thought wishing he had Dumbo ears. If only he had a flaw to detract from his overwhelming appeal. Then her heart would idle in neutral instead of racing like a runaway locomotive.

She cleared her throat. "I was thinking we could serve the quesadillas and egg rolls as appetizers, then bring out the lasagna and garlic bread. I'll do an antipasto salad with a light Italian dressing. And the previously agreed-on fresh fruit salad."

Sipping his coffee, he nodded slightly. "Sounds good."

She lifted one eyebrow. Right. Neither difficult nor persnickety. "You're awfully accommodating. Why is that?"

"You'd rather I was a pain in the caboose?" He smiled. "I
hired a catering professional. It wouldn't be especially bright
to ignore her advice."

"I suppose not. What about dessert?"

"I'm always in favor of it," he agreed.

"I was thinking about a cake iced and decorated with her
school colors. What are they, by the way?"

"Red and black."

"Yikes."

"Problem?"

"Challenge." She tapped her lip thoughtfully. "I have a
recipe for a red velvet cake garnished with coconut. I'll put
Connie to work on a creative angle to work in the black."

"Something that won't be too gross?"

"Guaranteed. Trust me."

He winced. "People always say that when it's the last thing
you should do."

"I wouldn't steer you wrong." She made some notes, then
met his gaze. Her heart stuttered at the intensity there as he
studied her. "Shouldn't we run this by Kendra?"

"She's not here."

"I thought she was grounded. Did she have a get-out-of-
jail-free card?"

"She had freshman orientation at UCLA. College always
trumps consequences. It's a two-day overnighter."

"Wow. That's a major breakthrough for her. You must be
happy."

At least one of them was. Now that she knew they were
alone, she was anything but thrilled. It was her cue to finish
up and get the heck out of Dodge. She wasn't far off the mark
when she'd said it was crunch time. Because she wanted so
badly to kiss him again. She'd replayed the last one over and

over in her mind and each time she was left with a yearning to feel his lips against hers one more time. With hormones spiking the way they were, she couldn't be held responsible for her actions.

"I have mixed emotions about her college weekend," he admitted. "And I understand I have you to thank for this."

"Should I be afraid?" she asked, leaning away from him.

He laughed. "No. She said she talked to you and you challenged her—pointed out that she had nothing to lose by gathering information."

"I did," she said nodding. "But I don't understand your reaction."

"That's because you don't have kids." He sighed. "As graduation gets closer, the local junior college looks more appealing because she could live at home. Considering recent bad choices on her part, that wouldn't be a bad thing. On the other hand, I'm glad she's at least exploring her options. Thinking about spreading her wings. But that's a scary thought, too."

Thea empathized with him, and, at the same time, she admired his parenting skills. He stepped in when necessary and stood back with bated breath the rest of the time. She thought about the baby she was carrying and what she would have to deal with when her child was a teenager. She'd be alone like Scott and hoped she handled it even half as well.

But that was personal and she was here on business. "So she gave you full discretionary powers," she said to get them back on track.

"Yup. I get to pick whatever I want."

Thea met his gaze and her pulse skipped at the dark intensity there. He looked as if he'd like to pick *her*.

She stood suddenly. "Okay. I think we're finished with this part."

"We are?" He stood, too.

"You said, and I quote, 'Sounds good.' That's good enough for me. Now all I need from you is a maximum number of guests attending the party and I can firm up a price."

Scott put a hand on her arm. "Don't go, Thea."

"But I have stuff—"

"To do," he finished. "So do I, but that's not what this is about."

"No?" she said in a small voice.

He shook his head. "Caffeine isn't making you nervous. It was that kiss." She opened her mouth and he silenced her with a finger on her lips. "I think you liked it just as much as I did."

He'd liked it, too? Warmth spread through her until she threw cold water on it. One of them had to be realistic.

"It's not that simple, Scott."

"It can be." His expression sobered as he studied her. "Is this about your husband?"

"That's part of it."

"It's been two years, Thea. You're allowed to have a life." He took her hands in his and squeezed reassuringly. "You shouldn't feel guilty that you didn't die, too. There's not a doubt in my mind that if you could do anything to bring him back, you'd do it in a heartbeat."

She simply nodded when words stuck in her throat.

"Thea, I can't imagine you loving any man who wouldn't want you to move forward and be happy."

"It's not just that, Scott. There's more. I have to tell you—"

"Me first," he interrupted, then took her face in his hands and lowered his mouth to hers.

The tender touch set off a firestorm inside her and instantaneously passion ignited. Thea felt a hunger that had nothing to do with food and everything to do with her craving for a man's touch, the feel of his lips on hers, the taste of him, the longing to be in his arms.

She pressed as close to him as she could get, reveling in the feel of her softness against his rock-solid body. He groaned and tightened his hold on her. When he traced the seam of her lips, she opened to him. Heat billowed through her as his tongue invaded her mouth, the motivation imitating the act of lovemaking.

She heard a moan and it took her several moments to realize that wanton sound had come from her. Was it reckless? Maybe. Probably. But she couldn't find the will to care. The pleasure was vaguely familiar from another lifetime. Familiar, but so very different and new. Hot. Intense. Frantic.

Yet, she knew where she was going, what she was doing. And she could no more stop herself from experiencing the sensations of happiness in Scott's arms than she could flap her arms and fly to the moon.

This was sex. The affirmation of life. And the physical expression of her femininity. It was reassurance that she was a woman. She was alive and this man was attracted to her. That realization was more intoxicating than any alcohol.

A frightening excitement exploded through her body, unlike anything she'd ever experienced before. It went beyond pleasure and became simply a demanding need. One she couldn't deny.

Scott lifted his mouth from hers. "Thea," he said, his breath ragged. "I want you. If that's not okay, you need to tell me now."

She studied the sincerity on his face and realized she didn't have the words to express the depth of what she was feeling. "I want you, too," she simply said.

He shut his eyes for a moment and let out a long breath. "Thank God." Then he looked at her, his expression wary. "But I think it only fair to warn you I haven't done this in a pretty long time."

His admission only endeared him to her more. If he'd been arrogant and condescending, resisting him would be a piece of cake. But he was sweet, sexy and so very masculine. She was a goner.

"Me, either," she said. "We can muddle our way through together."

"I like the sound of that." His grin made her weak in the knees.

As if he'd read her mind, he scooped her into his arms. She squealed with surprise as she encircled his neck with her arms. "Scott, put me down. You'll hurt yourself."

"Way to make me feel manly," he teased. "You hardly weigh anything."

He headed for the stairs and easily carried her up to his bedroom. If she wasn't already a sure thing, she would be after this. The sheer romance of the gesture melted her insides like a Fudgsicle left in the sun.

Beside his bed, he removed his arm from behind her knees and let her body slide down the front of his. She felt the bulge in the front of his pants and reveled in the knowledge that he wanted her as much as she wanted him.

He took her face in his hands and kissed her thoroughly, nibbling his way across her cheek and over her jaw to the indentation beneath her ear. When he touched his tongue to the oh-my-God spot, her breath caught.

He slid his fingers up under her sweater and settled his palms on the bare flesh at her waist. The warmth of his palms felt too good and she realized how much she'd missed a man's touch. Did he miss being touched by a woman?

She slid his T-shirt from the waistband of his jeans and imitated his actions. When she settled her hands on his chest, he sucked in a breath. The sound of his approval was sustenance to her soul.

He looked at her, his expression tight and strained from passion and need. "Don't you think we have too many clothes on?"

"Yes," she said breathlessly.

In a frenzy of activity they pulled off shirts and pants and everything in between and stood there naked, simply looking their fill of each other. And suddenly the perfection of his body was too much for her. Thea knew if she didn't explore the muscular perfection with her hands, she would shrivel up and blow away.

She settled her palms on his chest again, loving the tingle from the dusting of hair. Sliding over the contours of his muscles, she felt his ribs and the firmness of his abdomen. Again he sucked in his breath and she knew where to touch to get his attention.

He lowered his head and kissed her. The assault of sensations made her dizzy: the firmness of his mouth; the taste of coffee; the startling, stimulating intimacy of his tongue stroking hers. She'd shut out memories of the warm smoothness of a man's skin, the spicy scent of his aftershave, the safety of his arms around her.

Suddenly her tender breasts were pressed against the unyielding wall of his chest. Her nipples tightened and throbbed in a way that made her revel in her femininity.

When he pulled back slightly, the intensity of his gaze burned her like twin blue flames. He half turned and yanked the bedcovers back. Then he scooped her up again, settled her in the center of his big bed and came down beside her.

His passion-filled gaze locked with hers. "I'm safe."

Desire made her brain misfire, but she got his drift. The only response she could manage was, "Me, too."

He nodded and settled his lips on hers. As he took her breast in his palm, she was swept away on a tide of emotion, excitement, anticipation. Need built within her as he rubbed her nipple between his fingers. He swallowed her moan of pleasure, then slid his hand down her abdomen and cupped her most feminine place in his palm.

Her already ragged breathing stuttered at the intimate, exquisite contact and liquid heat pooled there, getting her body ready for him. Then he slipped a finger inside her and she welcomed the intimacy. He explored the folds of her femininity and found the small nub encompassing all the nerve endings of her pleasure.

He stroked and rubbed until she was mindless with want. Tension built inside her and begged for release. Without warning, the pressure stretched and tore and exploded. She shattered into a million brilliant points of light, and her breath caught in her throat. Cares and worries and stress drained away and she felt boneless, like a rag doll.

Until he touched his tongue to that sensational spot by her ear. Just like that, her senses came to life. When he settled himself between her legs and nudged her knees apart, she gloried in the closeness. Then he slowly eased his way into her feminine passage. Her body was unaccustomed to this sort of intrusion and the care he took showed that he was aware. His tender sensitivity brought tears to her eyes.

He moved slowly at first, giving her time to become accustomed to him. When she arched her hips and accommodated his rhythm, he increased the pace, stroking in and out. His movements grew faster and more intense until he thrust one last time. His body went still as he groaned out his release and satisfaction.

Thea held him in her arms until his shudders stopped and he finally rolled away. She turned her head on the pillow and opened one eye. She saw that Scott was smiling.

"What's so funny?" she asked.

"Not a doggone thing. That was pretty sensational."

"It was amazing," she agreed, returning his smile.

He rolled to his side, then reached over and brushed her hair from her cheek. "I'm glad," he said sincerely.

"Me, too. I'd say we muddled through pretty well. You, sir, were way too modest about your muddling skills."

"As were you." He slid his arm around her and nestled her to his side. "If you're game, we can muddle again in a little while."

"I'll be a muddler if you will."

"Lady, I'll muddle with you anytime, anywhere. Just say the word."

"Muddle," she said with a sigh.

For just this one night, she thought. Surely no one could begrudge her a single night of sweetness and light after so much darkness.

Scott felt something soft and warm move beside him. Then he got a jab in the chest and opened one eye. He smiled when he saw Thea with her shiny, silky brown hair spread across the pillow beside his. He opened his other eye to see her better.

He felt the need to touch her, make sure she was real. Gently, he smoothed a strand of hair from the corner of her mouth. Heat shafted through him when he remembered how those full lips had aroused him the previous night. He'd seen her outer beauty the first time he'd laid eyes on her. Smooth, flawless skin, small turned-up nose, big brown eyes—the combination was a package that could turn a man into a quivering mass of locked-and-loaded testosterone.

But he'd learned she was beautiful on the inside, too. She'd taken his daughter under her wing at a time when Kendra was insecure, confused and scared about the future. How many women would do that?

As he studied her face, he noticed the shadows beneath her eyes, highlighted by her high, sculpted cheekbones. She'd told him several times that this was a very busy time for her. Was she working too hard?

A sensation of protectiveness expanded inside him. It wasn't unfamiliar; he felt it for his girls. But it was different. A man for his woman? Wow, that thought got his adrenaline pumping.

He pulled the covers more securely around her naked body and a wry thought occurred to him. At least he wasn't a do-as-I-say-not-as-I-do kind of father. He had feelings for the woman he'd slept with. He just wasn't sure what they were.

The insistent throbbing in his groin was proof that he wanted to make love to her again. But his gaze was drawn to the circles under her eyes and he didn't want to disturb her sleep.

Carefully, he slipped out of bed and slid into a pair of sweats and a T-shirt. He went downstairs and put on a pot of coffee. While he waited for it to be ready, he leaned his elbows on the island, stared into the family room and listened. There were no sounds. No thumping overhead to signal Kendra's footsteps. No galumphing down the stairs because she was late for school. No phone ringing off the hook. No loud music vibrating the second story of the house.

Nothing but damn peace and quiet.

And this is how it would be if she went away to college.

He remembered Thea teasing him about not being ready for his daughter to leave home and he'd assured her he could picture it clearly. There was a part of him looking forward to the break in 24/7 responsibility. But he had to admit he hadn't really known what an empty nest would feel like. He did now. And it felt weird.

"Good morning."

"Hey, sleepyhead." He smiled as Thea walked into the kitchen.

She'd put on his navy-colored terry-cloth robe and the abundance of thick material only made her look smaller and more fragile. His protective urge jabbed him again as surely as her elbow had just a little while ago.

He went to her and put his hands at her waist. Lowering his head, he kissed her and felt a sublime satisfaction when she shivered and sighed. "How did you sleep?"

"Good." She thought for a moment and added, "Better than I have in a long time."

"I'm glad." He traced the shadows beneath her left eye. "You need to work on getting rid of these."

"No. I just need to spread on the concealer with a palette knife."

"I think you look beautiful without makeup."

She grinned. "Silver-tongued devil."

"Busted."

He noticed the coffee had stopped dripping and went to get a mug. "Want some?"

She shook her head. "No caffeine. Remember?"

"Yeah. Right." He poured the strong, black brew into his mug and took a sip. "You don't know what you're missing. Guaranteed to put hair on your chest."

Her gaze dropped to his chest. "And a fine job it's done on you." Her grin faded and she said, "You were looking awfully pensive about something when I came in."

He set his coffee on the island and folded his arms over his chest as he leaned back against the cooktop. Thea stood with the island between them and he wondered if she was distancing herself on purpose. He knew last night's passion had caught her off guard. It had him, too. He hadn't meant for things to get out of control like that. But he couldn't regret what happened and didn't want her to, either.

"Earth to Scott."

"Hmm?" He met her gaze. "Oh. Why was I looking thoughtful? I was thinking how quiet the house is with Kendra gone."

"Surely this isn't the first time. Hasn't she spent the night with friends?"

He nodded. "But this is different. Her going away to college is looming over me."

"Let me see if I've got this straight. She's facing the leap from high school to college, but this is all about you?"

"Of course."

She leaned her elbows on the island and rested her chin in her hands. "Might I point out that you wanted her to go away to school? To have the total college experience by living on campus the way her older sister is?"

"If I'd known you were the kind of woman who actually listened to me and then throws my words back in my face—"

"Yes?"

"I'd have been more careful about what I said."

She laughed. "I'm just playing devil's advocate."

There was nothing devilish about her. She looked like an angel, even though her hair was sexily tousled and traces of a seriously satisfied woman lingered in her brown eyes.

"I guess I thought the feelings would be the same as when I sent Gail off to school. But they're not. Because I still had Ken. Now I'm actually looking at an empty nest."

"I thought you wanted to downsize."

"I think it's being forced on me because my rebellious children insist on growing up."

She moved around the island until she was no more than a foot away. There was a soft, tentative, tender sort of expression on her face that made her even more beautiful.

"Scott? You obviously care very much about your girls. And you're a terrific parent. You've done a wonderful job with them under circumstances that were less than ideal. Single parents everywhere could take lessons from you."

His eyebrows shot up at her praise. "Wow. I thought you weren't going to feed my ego anymore. You make me sound like a candidate for canonization."

She lifted one delicate shoulder swathed in the robe that was too big for her. "Can't help it. You're a good man doing a good job. And I have a feeling you don't get enough pats on the back."

"You can say that again."

She moved beside him and patted his back with her small hand. His skin burned even through the material of his shirt. "There."

"Thanks." He noticed when her expression turned thoughtful. "Speaking of pensive—"

"Hmm?"

"What's on your mind? I can see the wheels turning and if you don't spit it out, there's going to be a power drain in Santa Clarita."

She laughed. "I don't know. I just had a silly thought."

"Want to share?"

"I was just wondering. You're obviously going to miss Kendra when she leaves home. It occurred to me—have you ever thought about having more children?"

He shook his head. "To start again with two o'clock feedings, diapers. Teething. Nursing them through colds and the flu. Worrying about juggling child care and work. Worrying about everything…. I don't think so."

"You've had basic training. This time you'd bring seasoning and skill, knowledge and maturity to the experience."

"I've learned that life is always a trade-off. As much as I'd like to keep my girls small and run interference for them, protect them from all the bad stuff in life, they grew up and are eager to see what the world is all about. The trade-off is that now it's my turn to do what I missed out on when I took on responsibility too young."

"But you wouldn't have an empty nest," she said in a small voice. "Another child would—"

"No way."

His reaction was instinctive, straight from the gut. And the words must have come out sharper than he'd intended because Thea looked shocked and backed away. The startled expression on her face compelled him to explain.

"Sorry. Didn't mean to sound harsh. Apparently you struck

a nerve. I just don't want more children, Thea. I'm very sure about that."

Thea's eyes grew wide and she looked shell-shocked. "I s-see."

Why did he feel as if he were the slimeball who just shot Bambi's mother? Irritation laced through him. He couldn't shake the sensation that he'd somehow let her down. That he'd disappointed her. Which meant she was judging him. And that wasn't fair. He'd gone through hell and tried to do the right thing. And she'd said herself that he'd done a good job. He'd had his two-point-whatever children and anyone who'd traveled the same path he had would probably feel the same way.

The truth hit him between the eyes. She hadn't traveled the same path. Her husband had died and she had no children. Did she want them? She was still a very young woman. How did she feel about kids? His gut clenched.

"Look, Thea, I—"

"Wow, it's getting late," she said, glancing at the clock on the microwave. "I have a bridal shower to get ready for. I better get dressed. Excuse me."

Scott ran his fingers through his hair as he watched her hurry from the room. So much for the postcoital glow. It was nice while it lasted. He was so out of the loop on this man/woman thing. Maybe it would have been better if he'd lied to her.

He shook his head. If telling lies was a prerequisite for a relationship, then he was destined to be alone. That just wasn't his style.

Thea was back a few minutes later dressed in the clothes she'd worn yesterday. She briefly met his gaze before hers skittered away. "I'll work up those figures for you on the party."

"Okay." He moved toward her. "I'll call you—"

"I'm going to be out all day."

He followed her to the front door. When she opened it and

started to leave, he curved his fingers around her upper arm to stop her. She glanced up, her eyes shadowed and questioning.

He leaned down and brushed his lips over hers. "Have a good day. Drive careful. You look tired. Don't work too hard."

"You don't have to worry about me."

"I know," he said.

As he watched her get in her car and drive away, it struck him that not worrying about her was easier said than done.

Chapter 10

After the bridal shower, Thea ladled the remaining iced tea—passion fruit flavor—into a container. As if she needed a reminder that she'd engaged in the fruits of passion. That she'd spent the night with Scott, tangled in his sheets and in his arms. It was so nice while it lasted. As she continued to empty the contents of the decorative jar, she remembered in painful detail Scott's adamant declaration about children.

Connie appeared beside her with the leftover shrimp dish and fruit salad. "Are you okay?"

"Yeah. Just moving slow. Sorry."

"No problem. Everyone is gone, including the party hostess. I told her we'd lock up when we were finished putting the house back together."

"Good." Thea was glad it was just the two of them, although she'd have preferred to be alone.

"I'm going to strip the linens off the dining room table and put the chairs back."

"Okay. I'll take care of these leftovers and leave them in the fridge."

Thea took some of the disposable containers she always brought with her and scooped the shrimp into one, then labeled it. She did the same with the fruit and put the bowls away. It was part of the service she offered. Thea Bell toils for you and makes your life a little easier.

If only someone would do that for her. She'd felt as if life was finally starting to go her way when the IVF was successful. Then she met Scott. It had been downhill ever since, capped by sex with him. No, that was the high point. Even though all the signs had been apparent, she'd harbored some misguided notion that he might be open to the possibility of another child—her child. Until he'd told her in no uncertain terms how he felt, she hadn't even realized the hope was there. Because she didn't dare to hope anymore.

"Thea, are you all right?" There was sincere concern in her friend's voice.

She turned away from the open refrigerator. "Yes. Why?"

"Because you've been standing there with the fridge door open staring off into space. That's not like you. In fact, you haven't been yourself all day. So talk to me. You know I won't let up until you do."

Thea shut the door and released a long breath. "Okay. I'm not okay."

Connie was beside her in a flash. "What's wrong? Is it the baby?"

"The baby's fine. I slept with Scott Matthews last night," she said in a rush. Then she looked at her friend whose expression went from worried to shocked to smug in three seconds flat.

She held up her hand. "High-five, girlfriend."

"No. I should bend over and let you kick me in the fanny. It was probably the dumbest thing I've ever done. It was a mistake."

"Why? Was he bad in bed? Did he not know what he was doing?"

Thea shivered at the memory of what Scott had done to her, how he'd made her come alive with his hands, his mouth, his body. "No. He knew what he was doing, all right."

"Then I don't get it. What part of it was a mistake?"

"The whole thing. It never should have happened. We were friends. And now…"

"You're friends who had sex."

"It's not that simple. Don't you see?" Thea held out her hand in a frustrated, helpless gesture. "We were intimate."

"Yeah. That's kind of the point of sex. A man and a woman getting intimate."

"You are the most exasperating woman. If I didn't like you so much—" She shook her head, but couldn't suppress a small smile.

"I'm not exasperating. I'm clueless. The man is a hunk and a half. He's gainfully employed."

"And then some," Thea agreed.

"He's interested in you. You're obviously attracted to him. More important, you like him. What is the problem?"

"He doesn't want any more children," Thea said miserably. "That's a deal breaker."

"It would be if he really meant it."

"Oh, he did."

"Lots of people say it. Including me. But if the situation arises, you roll with it," Connie said.

"Not him."

"How can you be so sure?"

"He told me so." Shaking her head, she blew out a long breath. "He took on heavy responsibilities at a very young age. Now it's his turn to do his own thing. And that doesn't include another baby."

"But, T—"

Thea held up her hand. "You should have seen his face when he talked about all the negatives—two o'clock feedings, flu and fevers, teething. He loves his children but he doesn't want the responsibility that comes with a baby."

"Did you tell him you're pregnant?"

Thea shook her head. "I got out of there as fast as I could."

"You should tell him."

"There's no need to. Now that I know how he feels, there's no chance of taking anything between us to the next level."

"I think you're wrong, Thea. There's always a chance."

"Speaking of fevers," she said, reaching over to touch the back of her hand to her friend's forehead.

Connie ducked away. "I'm serious. And completely in my right mind. He obviously likes you a lot. Maybe more than like. If I'm right, and he finds out you and a baby are a package deal, he might accept it."

"I don't want 'acceptance' for this baby," Thea said sharply. She meant that with all her heart. "David would have loved being a father, but that wasn't meant to be. Now it's my responsibility to raise our child the way he would have wanted. That doesn't include letting a man into my life who would simply tolerate the child I'm carrying."

"But if you tell him—"

"No. It's my personal business," Thea said. "And there's no reason now to share it with Scott."

"Even though you're friends?"

"We're not that close."

"I don't know," Connie said, tucking a strand of copper-colored hair behind her ear. "Sex, by definition, means you get pretty close."

"You know what I mean," Thea said, just this side of ex-asperated. "Besides, we won't be having sex again. I intend to let him know it was a mistake. Hopefully that won't impact his feelings when I make an offer on his house. And he indicated he's interested in my place. He's condo and I'm single-family home. We're wrong for each other and at completely different places in our lives. It was a terrible mistake to let things get out of hand like they did."

"Maybe. But once you've crossed over, it's hard to go back," her friend pointed out.

Especially when one didn't want to, Thea thought. But the bigger mistake would be in letting things go on knowing how he felt.

"I'll just have to find a way to make sure he gets the message. After our real-estate deals are finished, any association with Scott Matthews will be finished, too."

"Don't be too sure," Connie warned.

Thea ignored her. There couldn't be a game if only one person participated. Scott was a bright guy. Smart, handsome, tender, loving, strong, reliable—

She put the brakes on that train of thought before she derailed her own best intentions. He was a really terrific guy who deserved to find an equally terrific woman to care about. Someone who met his criteria. And she wasn't the one.

It didn't matter that the thought of him with anyone else made her heart hurt.

Scott dialed Thea's number without looking it up. How quickly he'd memorized it, he thought. That happened when you phoned a woman over and over because she hadn't returned your calls even after you'd left numerous messages.

"Hello?"

Finally, he thought, muting the TV as he sat up straighter on the sofa. "Hi. Thea? It's Scott."

"Oh. Hello," she said, breathlessly. It sounded as if she'd just come in and raced to the phone.

Or just finished making love.

That thought generated a shaft of heat that shot straight to his groin. At the same time, just hearing her voice produced a yearning so deep inside him it was almost painful. That had happened almost as fast as memorizing her phone number. And wasn't that the pits. The last time he'd needed a woman, his whole life had turned upside down when she'd walked out. He'd promised himself never to need anyone again.

"I guess you've been busy," he said casually.

"Yes." The sound of crackling came over the phone, as if she were setting bags down. "Why?"

"Because you didn't return any of my messages."

"Oh. Yeah."

"Or have you been avoiding me?"

He winced when the words came out. He'd just finished warning himself not to get sucked in. Now he was quizzing her about why she hadn't called him back. Stupid move, Matthews, he thought.

"Why would I do that?"

Classic avoidance technique. Answer a question with another question. "I'm not sure. Maybe because things are moving kind of fast between us."

"You mean because we—you know."

He heard the embarrassment in her voice and could almost see the blush he knew would be coloring the flawless skin of her cheeks.

"Yeah. That."

"No—I mean, yes, things did move fast."

"I refuse to say I'm sorry it happened, Thea. And I hope you're not sorry, either."

"You have nothing to be sorry for. It takes two to tango, as they say. No one forced me."

He noticed she hadn't said she wasn't sorry. "So that's not why you haven't returned my calls?"

There was a telling silence before she said, "Of course not."

"Good, then—"

"Did you get the estimated cost of food per person for Kendra's party that I faxed to your office?"

"Yes. Why?"

"I thought maybe you had a question about it," she said.

"No. It's fine."

"Good. All right, then, if there's nothing else—"

"Whoa. Wait a minute."

"Yes?"

"What's with you?"

"I don't know what you mean," she hedged.

"The heck you don't. First you don't return my calls. Then you change the subject to business. Now you're trying to get me off the phone. You are avoiding me."

"Why would I do that?"

For the same reason he'd been avoiding emotional entanglements since his wife had left him and their two little girls. "Because you're afraid of being hurt again after losing your husband," he said.

There was a loud sigh on the other end of the line. "There could be some truth to that," she admitted.

"You can't run forever, Thea."

"Wanna bet?"

"Seriously, sooner or later you have to take a chance and get back on that horse."

"And you know this because you've had so much experience taking chances?" she asked sarcastically. "Do I file that advice under, 'Takes one to know one'?"

"Touché. I've been reluctant to dip my toe in the cold water of relationships," he said. "But after meeting you I find that I'm inclined to want to dive in."

"It's all about sex, isn't it?"

"No." And he truly meant that. Mostly. "Although I can't tell a lie. I'm all in favor of sex. With you."

She sighed again. "Look, Scott—"

"I'm not going to like this, am I?"

"I couldn't say. But I can't tell a lie, either."

"Sure you can."

"No," she said with a small laugh. "Since we met—"

"And made love," he interjected.

"That, too, I've realized I'm not ready to take a chance and get back on the horse. Or dive into the waters of a relationship. Or whatever else you want to call it. And to be honest, I'm not sure I ever will be."

"There's that honesty thing again," he grumbled.

He didn't especially like the way this was going and wished he'd let her continue avoiding him.

"I don't know any other way to be."

That was refreshing, anyway. He'd lived with a woman who told him what he wanted to hear until the day she said she couldn't stand her life and was leaving him. But Thea's truth was only marginally better.

"Look, Scott, I just want to be fair to you," she said, filling the silence.

"I don't know what's fair. All I know is that there's something going on between us. Or am I the only one who feels it?"

"I feel strongly that the wisest course of action is to nip this thing in the bud. Before either of us realizes we want more than the other can give."

Scott wasn't sure what he wanted except he knew he didn't want to simply end it. Thea Bell was a pretty amazing woman and it didn't feel right to walk away from her just like that. Wasn't it just his luck that the first woman he'd met who made him want to take the risk was afraid to go there with him.

"Look, Thea, let me take you out to dinner and we can talk about this."

"I don't think so, Scott."

He would bet if he brought up Kendra's party she'd change her tune. Since the day he'd caught her cooking in his kitchen, she'd backed away from the personal and taken cover behind the professional.

"What about my house? Didn't you want to make an offer?"

"Yes, but I still have to sell my condo."

"What if I want to buy it?"

The silence on the other end of the line told him her eyes widened and she was blinking in surprise.

"Do you?" she asked.

"It's exactly what I pictured myself in after the girls were gone."

"Then we should get Joyce to write up offers on each other's property."

But that would mean I can't see you, he thought. He also suspected if he pushed any harder, he'd push her away. That was the last thing he wanted. "Okay," he agreed.

He didn't think he could persuade her to go out with him just yet, but he didn't want to hang up without knowing when he would see her again. "What's the next step for the party?"

"When you know the number of guests who will be attending, I'll reserve tables and chairs. Then I'll need to take a look at the backyard and figure out where to set everything up."

"Okay. I'll sit down with Ken when she comes home from UCLA and we'll finalize the guest list."

"Good. If that's all, Scott, I have to run. I'll talk to you when you've got all that information."

"Okay, good—"

He heard the click and stared at the receiver. When it sank in that she'd hung up on him, anger churned in his gut. He should be relieved that she didn't seem to want anything serious between them. But he wasn't. She'd basically told him that if not for Kendra's party, she would have nothing to do with him.

And he didn't like it one little bit.

Chapter 11

Scott slammed the phone down and ran his fingers through his hair. "Son of a—"

"Dad?"

He looked up. Kendra and Gail were standing in the family room staring at him. He hadn't even heard them come in. Thea was some distraction. No wonder they named every other hurricane after a woman.

"Hi," he said, then released a long breath.

"Something wrong?" Kendra asked.

He glanced at the phone. "It's no big deal."

So much for not being able to tell a lie. He didn't need a shrink to tell him his over-the-top reaction meant it was a very big deal.

"So," he said, looking from one daughter to the other, "how was your weekend?"

"Awesome," Kendra said. She was beaming.

He hadn't seen her this happy since she'd scored the

winning goal for her soccer team and sent them to the playoffs.

But he had to be cool and let her open up on her own. "Oh?" he asked, looking at Gail.

"It was great, Dad. I showed her the campus and where my classes are. Then there was a—"

"Whoa. Time out." Kendra dropped her backpack in the family room and walked into the kitchen, straight to the refrigerator. "It's my orientation," she said sliding a good-natured glare in her sister's direction. "I'll tell him."

"I'm listening," he said.

"Dad, it was so cool. There was a meeting of all incoming freshmen. I thought it would be lame, but Gail made me go. She said she did it and met some cool people. There was an exhibition basketball game at Pauley Pavilion."

"And?" he prompted.

Kendra popped the top on her soda can and took a sip. "I had the best time. I met a ton of kids who are starting classes in the fall."

"Are any of these people guys?"

"Da-ad." She rolled her eyes.

"It's my job to ask," he explained.

"Okay. Yes, some of them were guys. And they seemed really nice."

"Don't worry, Dad." Gail sat down beside him. "I already gave her the 4-1-1 on not trusting every college guy she meets. It's cool."

"Okay." He met Kendra's gaze and she nodded slightly, letting him know she'd explained her unfortunate experience to her sister. Her eyes narrowed slightly and he figured she was warning him to let it drop. He got the message.

"So where did you stay?" he asked.

"In Gail's dorm. It's pretty small," Kendra explained.

"Like living in a cardboard box," Gail grumbled.

His youngest nodded eagerly. "But if you're organized, there's lots of storage in the closet. And space under the bed."

"When's the last time you saw any space under your bed? Or anywhere else in your room for that matter?" Scott teased her.

"Don't start, Dad. Let the euphoria wear off naturally," Kendra advised.

"Okay." He looked at the glow on her face. "I guess this means you're going away to college?"

"Yeah."

"I'm not sure I want you to," he admitted.

He'd realized how much he would miss Kendra the morning after making love to Thea. Just thinking Thea's name tied his gut in knots. He didn't get her at all. But while she was there, he'd gotten how much he was going to miss the energy his youngest daughter brought into this house. Then he remembered—this was the house that Thea was going to buy. Somehow, the woman had woven herself into the fabric of his life.

"Now you *don't* want me to go?"

He shrugged. "I missed the heck out of you."

Kendra looked surprised. "You missed me?"

He nodded. "Like crazy."

Gail took a sip of her water. "See, I told you, sis."

"Told her what?" Scott asked.

"That you loved her and she was nuts."

"That, I get. But why do you think so?" he asked, grinning when Ken huffed loudly.

"She thinks you didn't want her. That you wished she'd never been born," Gail explained.

He stared at his youngest daughter. "Why would you think such a thing, Kendra?"

She looked down at her sneakers and rubbed the top of one against the calf of her leg. "I heard you tell Uncle Mike. You said you wished I'd never been born. That it would be easier. It was right after Mom left."

Scott couldn't have been more shocked if she'd slugged him in the stomach. He couldn't have said that. She must have misunderstood. "I don't know what you overheard, but the truth is that after you were born, I couldn't imagine my life without you in it. I fell in love with you the moment I laid eyes on you."

She nodded. "Thea told me the same thing."

Thea. She'd somehow become important in their lives. But he tucked thoughts of her away for later, when he could sort them out. "Ken, your mom and I had a complicated relationship. After you were born I thought things were fine, then found out I was wrong. It was a rough time. But whatever you heard me say to Uncle Mike, I'm sure it wasn't that I never wanted you."

Kendra nodded. "It's okay, Dad. I understand better now."

"So we're clear. You don't think I wish you'd never been born?"

"Nope." She reached over and gave him a hug, then pulled back.

"Good."

It was possible that with her own pregnancy scare, she had put herself in his shoes as much as she could and was able to imagine a little of what he'd gone through. When Scott met her gaze, there was no hostility in it, thank goodness. Maybe this was the silver lining of that whole fiasco with the weasel who'd used her. Although he'd still like to rip the jerk's head off for hurting his little girl.

"I love you guys," he said. He hated the fact that life was changing and the three of them weren't together all the time. These two were his family and he loved them with everything he had. He'd die for them.

"I love you, too, Dad," the girls said together.

Smiling, he glanced from one daughter to the other. Kendra was dark-haired; Gail's hair was streaked with blond. One was blue-eyed; the other's eyes were green like her mother's. His gut clenched at the thought. He'd tried to give his girls a solid foundation and understanding of right and wrong so they'd never turn out like their mother. That time had nearly brought him to his knees and he'd sworn never to trust a woman again. Somehow Thea had sneaked past that promise. So maybe she'd done him a favor by shutting down things between them.

"Earth to Dad." Gail was moving her hand in front of his face to get his attention.

"Hmm?" he said blinking.

"You look like you did when you wanted to beat up Doug Satterfield." Kendra looked horrified and instantly clamped her hand over her mouth.

"Is that the toad's name?" he asked.

"Dad, if you really love me, you'll forget I said that."

"I can't promise to forget. But I won't do anything about it unless you give me the green light."

"Not in this lifetime," she said, looking relieved. "But what's wrong? You look like someone dumped you."

"Dating happens before dumping," Gail pointed out. "And you don't date. Do you?"

If you didn't count the deposit he'd given Thea for the graduation party, he hadn't spent money on her. He wasn't sure if making love to a woman could be classified as dating and tried to decide how to answer the question.

"It's Thea," Kendra guessed. "Are you dating her?"

"No," he said. Technically that was the truth. She'd essentially told him to take a flying leap.

"But you want to?" Kendra guessed again.

Did he? He'd gotten a glimpse of life post-child-rearing and it loomed lonely. On the other hand, his spectator seat had included a view with and without Thea. The outlook with her had been far more pleasant and exciting.

But he didn't want to open that door and have it slammed in his face again. So the answer to his youngest daughter's question was, "I don't know."

"If you like Thea, don't give up," Gail advised. "Remember, it's better to have loved and lost than never to have loved at all."

Kendra snorted in disgust. "Spoken by someone who's never been through a major heartbreak."

"Yes, I have," her sister shot back. "Remember Greg Smith?"

"No."

"Well, it's not important that you do. *I* remember the pain of rejection." She glanced at the clock on the microwave. "More important, I have to get back to school. I have an early class in the morning." She smiled at her sister. "In a few short months, we'll be there together."

"I can't wait," Kendra agreed.

Scott watched the girls hug, grateful their relationship was so close. Gail would watch out for her little sister. She gave him a hug and whispered in his ear, "Perseverance. Wear her down."

She left and Kendra went upstairs to her room. And he was alone.

"Better get used to it," he said to himself.

He thought about what Gail had said—better to have loved and lost. That was the biggest load of crap he'd ever heard. He and Kendra—and Thea—were all casualties of love. Pain was not better.

He'd give anything for his daughter to have never been hurt and disillusioned the way she'd been. The experience had almost impacted her college plans.

And Thea. The man she'd loved had died and she was still dealing with it. He'd bet she didn't buy into the saying any more than he did. He'd wager she wished she hadn't lost the man she'd loved.

And Scott figured it was a no-brainer that he'd rather not have his relationship scars. If he'd never cared about his ex-wife, there wouldn't *be* any scars. He and Thea were damaged goods.

Tonight she'd told him she didn't want to pursue anything of a personal nature.

He didn't, either. He didn't want to take another chance.

There was only one problem with that.

All he could think about was Thea Bell. What was he going to do if he couldn't get her out of his mind?

Thea filed the folder with her accepted offer on Scott's house. Then she started another one for the deal on her condo with his offer inside. They were in escrow—actually switching spaces. There would be no living with Connie's ego when she found out. To put her ego and meddling tendencies in line, Thea would have to share that she'd put the lid on anything personal between herself and Scott.

Even though it had been a week since they'd last spoken on the phone, thoughts of him made her sad. Shouldn't she be over that by now? Shouldn't she be over missing him? The fact that she wasn't and she did, miss him that is, proved she'd been right to end it. Things between them had escalated at the speed of light. If she hadn't put a stop to it, they'd have gone beyond the point of no return. That would have been a disaster.

Her focus now had to be the baby growing inside her. She put her palms over her still flat belly. "You're not growing fast enough, little one."

She went into her living room and took a throw pillow from the couch. Stuffing it beneath her T-shirt, she tried to imagine how it would be when the baby was that big and she could feel movement. She stood in front of the entry mirror to see herself.

Grinning at her image, she said, "I never thought I'd say this, but I can't wait to be as big as a house."

Suddenly her doorbell rang, making her jump. "I'm not expecting anyone," she said to herself. "Maybe it's Connie."

She looked through the peephole and was startled again. Scott Matthews stood there. Instantly her pulse cranked up in direct proportion to the joy she experienced at the sight of him. How pathetic was she? The bell rang again, more insistently this time. If she knew what was good for her, she would ignore it. But the fact was she couldn't resist the temptation to see him up close. When her awkward belly brushed the door, she removed the pillow from beneath her shirt and set it on the table in the entryway. Then she slid the dead bolt off.

After opening the door, she said, "Hi, Scott."

"Thea." He met her gaze and his own was sizzling with emotion. "I need to talk to you."

"If it's about our real-estate deal, I'd prefer you direct any problems to Joyce." It was so hard to turn the conversation to business when her nerve endings were snapping with excitement and energy was humming through her.

"It's not about that."

"Then what?"

She thought she'd successfully sidestepped an emotional confrontation, but the expression on his face told her differently. It was common knowledge that the average single man looked for an excuse to avoid entanglements. It was completely unfair that she'd met one who wouldn't take the out she'd given him.

"It's about needing to see you," he said.

Her insides melted like sugar glaze over warm cake. All of a sudden, she couldn't be sorry he hadn't listened to her.

He moved in closer and stopped so that their bodies were

an inch apart, but not touching. She loved the way he smelled. When she breathed in the wonderful masculine scent of him, it burrowed inside her and set off a chain reaction, a heat-activated response.

"It's about not being able to stop thinking about you," he said, his voice hoarse and rough with feeling.

"Oh?"

"And I tried," he said, anger lacing the words. "I tried my damnedest to put you out of my mind." His voice was low and rough and exciting.

"I see."

"The hell you do. Do you think I'd be here if I had a choice? Do you think I like running into a brick wall?" He shook his head and a muscle jumped in his cheek. "I can't think about anything but you. You're in my thoughts when I'm dreaming and when I'm wide awake."

The anger and frustration in his gaze startled her with their intensity. His words were like salve to her shattered soul. She caught her breath at the power of the passion emanating from him. Was she really and truly responsible for his profound feelings? It had been so long since she'd felt wanted and, most especially, *needed*.

"Scott, I don't know what to say—"

He cupped her left cheek in his palm. "Me, either."

She looked into his eyes, saw the tension in the line of his mouth and felt the weight of everything separating them. She'd been such a fool to think this moment would never come. This was the point of no return. He had to know about the baby.

"Scott, there's something I have to tell you—"

He touched a finger to her lips to silence her. "Didn't you just say you don't know *what* to say? In my opinion, talking is highly overrated."

He removed his finger, then lowered his head and with exquisite tenderness, touched his lips to hers. Thea couldn't agree with him more about talking. Her heart stopped momentarily, then thumped painfully against the wall of her chest. His lips were soft and warm, and he nibbled hers for several seconds before nipping a spot just beside the corner of her mouth. Her fully charged nerve endings combusted on contact, sending all coherent thought down the tubes.

All she could think about was the way her skin was sensitized to his touch. Shivers and tingles danced over her body. It felt as if a boulder were sitting squarely on her chest, as if she couldn't draw enough air into her lungs.

And she didn't want to. She wanted only to concentrate on the feelings he generated inside her. She needed to touch and be touched. Like the last time she'd been with Scott, everything spiraled out of control as soon as he brushed his lips over hers.

He pulled her into his strong arms and trailed nibbling kisses over her cheek and jaw to that place he'd discovered just beneath her ear. When he touched the tip of his tongue there, it was like a lovely electric shock. Sensation arced through her and all she could think was that she wanted more. His tender touch filled the emptiness inside her and torched the banked fire of her need. Woulds, shoulds and coulds were burned away by the heat his mouth generated and the pleasure evoked by his warm hands as they moved tenderly up and down her spine.

He pulled back, his breathing ragged. "I didn't mean for that to happen. But I saw you and—" He shrugged as his mouth curved up on one side. "I just couldn't help myself. I'm sorry."

"I'm not."

And she meant that with every fiber of her being. Even if it damned her to hell for eternity, she could no more deny herself the sweetness of being with this man than she could refuse air to breathe.

"No?"

Instead of wasting her breath with words, she smiled and

took his hand, leading him upstairs to her bedroom. The walls were pale pink, the bed skirt and quilt were covered with roses in variegated shades of crimson. An arch of dried flowers was the focal point of a grouping of needlepoint blossoms on the wall above the bed. Everything about the room spoke of femininity, yet she'd never felt like a complete woman in it.

Until now. With this man.

Scott took the hem of her T-shirt and she raised her arms, encouraging him to lift it over her head. Then he undid the button at the waist of her jeans and slid down the zipper. She pushed the material over her legs and stepped out of them. Too late she realized her bra and panties were plain white cotton, not the stuff of seduction. What she wouldn't give for a matched set of red satin. Then it ceased to matter as he looked at her and his gaze grew hot.

"You're so beautiful," he said, the words hardly more than a breath of air.

"You don't have to tell me that."

"Would you rather I lie and say you're so homely you'd have to sneak up on a glass of water?"

She laughed. For some reason that reassured her more completely than flowery words and practiced phrases. He was telling her the simple truth the way he saw it. Which meant when he looked at her, he saw beauty.

Her heart filled to overflowing with emotions she couldn't name. Then he reached behind her, unhooked her bra, and she didn't want to think at all. As the material slid away and the cool air touched her breasts, so did his gaze.

"Beautiful," he said again.

He reached around her to the bed and yanked down the quilt, blanket and sheet. When he pulled his shirt over his head without bothering to unbutton it, her heart beat so furiously she thought it would fly from her chest. He slid his feet from his shoes and then went to work on his pants. Fascinated, she watched the ripple of muscles across his chest and arms as he unbuckled his belt, then pushed his jeans and briefs down over muscular thighs and calves. His erection sprang free and her breath caught in her throat. Fearing her trembling legs wouldn't hold her, she sat on the bed and then moved to the center, making room for him.

The mattress dipped from his weight as he put one knee on it then slid closer and settled beside her—the first man ever in this bed. In this room. It felt so right that Scott was the one.

When she shivered, he pulled her close and brought the sheet up over them. "Better?"

"Yes," she whispered. "But only because you're here."

He grinned as he pressed her even closer, nestling her naked breasts to the wall of his chest. "Shared body heat is an amazing thing."

"I couldn't agree more." She liked the rough texture of his chest hair on the tender skin of her breasts. Was there anything that could make a woman feel more feminine than that?

He reached down and slid her panties off. Then he rubbed his large palm over the dip of her waist and down the length of her thigh. In the wake of his touch, heat exploded. Liquid warmth spread through her, settling in her center, readying her body to accept him. And that answered her question. A man's possession could definitely bring out the woman in her.

He took her lips with his own and kissed her thoroughly, with exquisite tenderness. She opened, admitting him inside, savoring the invasion. She traced the roof of his mouth, taking profound female satisfaction when he groaned deep in his throat. His chest rose and fell rapidly.

"Wow," he said, struggling to catch his breath. "Lady, you pack a wallop."

"You're no slouch yourself," she breathed. Then she touched the tip of her tongue to his earlobe.

"Oh, God—" he said.

She felt his erection pressing into her belly and again felt the power of her femininity. It seemed the most important thing in the world to touch him, to know the texture of him, to feel the essence of his maleness in the palm of her hand.

"Thea—" His voice was raspy and strained.

For so long she'd existed in a haze, but Scott had brought her out of the clouds and into the light. She'd felt the weight of too many things out of her control. Now, with him, she felt as if she could take command. When he rolled to his back, it was as if he could read her mind. She knelt beside him, then settled herself over him.

Groaning with satisfaction, he put his big hands on her hips and guided her, showing her the rhythm, urging her faster. Her breathing kept pace and her heart hammered as if she were running the hundred-yard dash. Pressure built inside her until she felt like a volcano about to erupt.

He reached out a hand searching for and finding the nub of her femininity pressed to the shaft of his masculinity. Her engorged bundle of nerve endings was exquisitely sensitive to his touch. He stroked her gently until the pressure released into a thousand points of light and she collapsed against his chest.

When she recovered enough, he urged her hips into motion again and seconds later, he stilled her as he groaned his own release.

It seemed an eternity until she could move, but when she stirred, he nestled her against his side with her cheek on his chest. The musky, life-affirming scent of sex drifted in the air. They were skin to skin and the warmth of him wrapped around her. With the taste of him still on her lips, she savored the rise and fall of his chest, the sound of his breathing. The power of the moment hit her. All her senses told her she wasn't alone. The thought brought tears to her eyes.

Because it felt so good.

And because it was way past time for her to tell him about her baby.

He kissed her forehead. "Thea, I hope you know I didn't come here just for...you know."

"I know," she said, her stomach knotting. "You came here to talk. And I agree we need to. Can you stay?"

"The girls are due home soon. I wish I could. But I need to be there when they get back."

"I understand."

"I don't want to be a do-as-I-say-not-as-I-do kind of dad."

"I know. But you've got a few minutes?"

It was time to tell him everything and see where they were going with this crazy whatever-it-was between them. She knew now he had feelings for her. Maybe, just maybe, they were strong enough to bear what she had to say.

He glanced at the clock on the nightstand. "Not really. I have to go." He threw back the sheet and sat up. "I'm taking the girls to brunch tomorrow morning before Gail goes back to school. Would you like to join us?"

What she wanted was to run her hands over his back and memorize every hard angle and muscular contour. But she didn't. "I think it would be best if I didn't go along," she said.

"The girls wouldn't mind. They like you."

"I'm glad."

"In fact, they're the reason I came over tonight. Last weekend they encouraged me not to give up on you."

"And it took you all week to decide they were right?" she teased.

"I may be slow," he admitted. "But once I make up my mind, look out." His expression turned sheepish. "That didn't sound right. I really did come here just to talk."

"I believe you." If she hadn't needed him so badly, that's probably all they would have done. "But you won't have many opportunities from now on to have them all to yourself. I'd love a rain check, though."

"You got it."

He slipped out of bed and dressed quickly as she lay on the bed watching him and loving every minute. When he was finished, he leaned over and ran his hand over her breast and to her abdomen, over the life growing there. She sucked in a breath as her chest tightened.

"I'll call you," he said.

"Okay."

Then he was gone. She wasn't a coward. Not completely. She should have told him. But he was looking forward to tomorrow with his girls. She wasn't certain if her news would cast a cloud over his day, but why take a chance.

A chance. She clung to the word with all her might. God wouldn't be so cruel. There was always a chance Scott cared enough that he wouldn't give up on her when she told him about her baby.

Chapter 12

Thea set a plate with soda crackers on the coffee table, then put her feet up on her couch and rested against the throw pillows. Morning sickness strikes again, she thought. Except it wasn't morning and it was after the first trimester, so shouldn't it be over? Her stomach rolled right over on that damn pregnancy glow.

She sighed as she patted her belly. "From everything I've read, little one, the hallmark of being a mother is to expect the unexpected. Thanks for the reminder." She closed her eyes against the nausea and said, "I think."

Connie had sent her home with specific orders to put her feet up. In fact, they were finished for the day, so Junior's timing was actually pretty good.

When her doorbell rang, she decided someone else's timing wasn't so good. Unless it was Scott. The last time she'd had an unexpected visitor, it was him. And he'd made such tender love to her, the memory of it made her heart ache to think about it.

With very little effort, she could fall for that man.

When the doorbell rang again, she sat up and swung her legs to the side. The thought of seeing him was about the only thing that could get her off this couch.

She peeked through the peephole and recognized Kendra. The last time the teen had dropped in, there was a crisis in the Matthews household. This was becoming a habit, a thought that pleased her very much. Not the crisis part, but the fact that the girl felt she could come to her.

She threw the dead bolt and opened the door. "Hi, there. Is everything all right?"

"Yeah. The best." Kendra smiled. "Didn't my dad tell you when he was here the other night?"

The other night when her father had been here, they hadn't talked about much. Their mouths had been otherwise occupied. Thea felt the heat rushing to her face and hoped the teen didn't notice.

"He said he was taking you and Gail to brunch. But that was about it. How was orientation?"

"Awesome," the teen said, grinning from ear to ear. "I met some cool kids. The campus is the best. I can't wait to go."

"So you're not afraid anymore?"

She shook her head. "And I have you to thank for talking me into giving it a try."

"No. You're the one who took the steps." She held out her arm. "Come in."

"I can't stay long." Kendra slung her backpack over one shoulder. "I stopped by your office, but Connie said you'd already left for the day. Are you okay?" she asked, looking closer.

"Fine. A little tired. I've been busy the last few weeks."

The girl looked uneasy. "Then I don't want to bother you."

Thea sat on the couch and patted the space beside her. "Sit. Tell me what's up. It's no bother."

"You might change your mind about that when I tell you."

"Let me be the judge. What can I do for you?"

Kendra took a big breath. "Mother's Day is coming up in a couple weeks."

"Yeah."

Thea was well aware. It would be her very first. But given Kendra's history with her mother, she couldn't imagine where she was going with this. Was she going to reach out to the woman who'd abandoned her?

"I want to surprise my dad with a party and I was hoping you'd help me pull it off."

"On Mother's Day?" she asked, surprised.

The teen twisted her fingers in her lap as an earnest expression crept into the blue eyes so like her father's. "The fact is, he's been both mother and father to me for as long as I can remember. I—I've been a pain in the neck to him lately and it's a way to say I'm sorry."

Thea reached over and squeezed her hand. "He loves you. No matter what."

"I know. In spite of everything. And he's always been there for me." She shrugged. "I guess there's something about going away to college. It feels final even though I know I'll see him a lot."

"It's a change," Thea agreed. "Everything will be different."

"That's for sure. But it feels like the right time to try and thank him for everything. I've been a big job and I want to do this in a big way."

"On Mother's Day."

"Yeah," she agreed. "Because he won't be expecting it. And I really, really need you to help me."

Thea smiled. Something about this girl always tugged at her heart. Was it because she was so much like her dad? Or that she seemed to be reaching out for something missing from her life? Either way, she was a sweetie. And the bottom line was Thea couldn't say no.

"Count me in," she said.

Kendra leaned over and hugged her. "Thank you."

"What can I do?"

"Help me plan the food. And we need a theme. I was hoping to have it at my grandparents' house so Dad won't know. And combine it with a Mother's Day celebration for my grandmother."

"So you're going to let her in on the surprise?"

"No, I want her to be surprised, too. I have a key to the house so you can set up. And I'll figure out a way to get everyone out of there."

"What about a movie?" Thea suggested. If the teenager couldn't pull that off, it would be déjà vu all over again when they walked in and found her cooking.

"Good idea," Kendra agreed.

"That would make it an evening event," she said, tapping her lip. Thea usually spent the morning with her own mother on that day, so there wasn't a conflict. "What kind of food do you want?"

"I'm not sure."

"Your dad likes Italian—"

"Yeah. Good idea."

"We could do stuffed shells or manicotti. Antipasto salad, garlic bread. And dessert. For how many people?"

"Just the family. Gail, me, Dad of course. My grandparents and Uncle Mike."

"A small celebration," Thea said.

"I can't afford more than that."

Thea hadn't even thought about charging her. When something didn't feel like business, it made her nervous. But that wasn't Kendra's problem. "Don't worry about the money."

"But I can't ask you to do this for free."

"We can work something out." Thea shrugged. "Actually, you can help me with everything. As I explained to your father, labor is the major expense."

Kendra raised one hand and put the other over her heart. "I swear I'll be your willing slave and promise to do whatever you tell me without complaint, whining, or eye-rolling."

Thea laughed as she pointed at her. "I'll hold you to that."

They talked for several more minutes, exchanging pertinent information. As they did, Thea noticed the sparkle in Kendra's eyes. She was different from the girl Thea had met a few months ago. She seemed happier and more confident. The result of a young girl whose father had given her space here and advice there. It was all about balance and Scott had pulled it off. Twice, when you counted Kendra's older sister. Thea put the date in her book and Kendra wrote down her grandparents' address.

The teen nodded eagerly. "You'll love Grammy and Poppy."

"I have no doubt." Children were a reflection of their parents, Thea realized. And Scott's mom and dad had raised a fine man.

After seeing Kendra out, she leaned against her door and sighed. He was a fine father, too. The kind any kid would be lucky to have.

She looked down and wondered about her own baby. He'd never know his father. Before undertaking the IVF, she'd rationalized that you couldn't miss what you'd never had. After meeting Scott and his girls, she wasn't so sure the rationale held up. Kendra missed her mother. Would her child miss his father? Would he turn out all right without one?

Scott had so much to offer—in every way. And he seemed to care. Chance, she reminded herself. There was always a chance for them.

If he could accept her baby.

Maybe Connie was right. Maybe if he fell in love and a child was part of the package, he would be happy about it, in spite of his past.

Thea checked over the Mother's Day fare she'd set up in Scott's parent's home one last time to reassure herself it was perfect. So far, their covert operation had come off without a hitch. The night before, Kendra had helped her assemble the food and decorations, deciding a big banner and balloons were inexpensive and easy. When Thea had arrived, the house was empty so she assumed the movie idea had worked like a charm. Thea had decorated and set out the food, plates and utensils.

Now that everything was ready, she had a few moments to catch her breath and look around. The elder Matthews lived in a sprawling ranch-style house not far from Scott's in a gated community. The living and dining rooms were situated on either side of the entryway that led to the huge kitchen with an island in the center. Thea browsed through the adjacent family room with its used brick fireplace and matching raised hearth that took up almost a whole wall.

Family pictures were everywhere, including some of Scott and his brother. She studied a photo collage on the wall and recognized Scott's formative years. There was one of him as a little boy playing T-ball, a grade school play, junior high, high school football, then him with an infant in his arms. It hit her that the pace of his formative years had suddenly increased at the speed of light. There was no picture parade of girlfriends like his brother had. He'd gone straight from high school football to fatherhood.

Before the knot in her stomach had a chance to tighten, she heard a car in the drive. Peeking out of the living room window, she saw doors on two vehicles open and the Matthews clan spilled out. Her gaze was drawn to Scott like a magnet to true north and her heart skipped in a way that was becoming familiar at the first sight of him.

His brother, Mike, bore a striking family resemblance. He was as tall as Scott, with the same dark hair and hunk quotient. But the family photos hadn't revealed a Mrs. Mike and she wondered about that. Kendra and Gail were both there with an older couple who must be their grandparents. Laughing and talking, the whole Matthews family walked up the brick sidewalk. Thea hurried into the kitchen. When everyone walked in, they stopped and stared—first at her, then at the banner.

Thea looked at Kendra and grinned. Together they said, "Surprise!"

Scott read the words on the hand-lettered sign—Happy Mother's Day, Grandma. Happy Mother's Day, Dad. With a pleased, yet puzzled expression on his face, he looked at his daughter. "What's all this?"

Kendra stood by the kitchen island and twisted her fingers together. "You've been both mother and father to Gail and me, and Father's Day didn't seem like enough. I just wanted to do something special to say thanks."

The older woman hugged her granddaughter, then sniffled and wiped away a tear. "Now I know why you were so insistent about getting us out of the house to that dreadful movie. That business about starting new family traditions. And this is why you threw that fit about not wanting to go out to dinner afterward. All that drama about starving to death while waiting to get a table." She shook her head as she smiled fondly at the teen.

Kendra shrugged. "I didn't know what else to do when you suggested that new restaurant by the theaters. I worked my fingers to the bone on this."

"You certainly were a big help," Thea agreed wryly.

"Thanks." Kendra grinned at her. "Are you surprised?" she asked, looking from her father to her grandmother.

"Absolutely," they both said.

"So was I," said the older man, who was obviously Scott's father. Tall, silver-haired, distinguished, he was the image of what his son would look like as he aged.

And Thea realized how very much she would like to know Scott for a long time and watch him grow distinguished. But the thought scared her because she didn't trust the future.

Before she could process that information further, Scott met her gaze and smiled. "Kendra, this is obviously your gig. Maybe you should introduce everyone to Thea."

The teen nodded and cleared her throat. "Family, this is Thea Bell, from For Whom the Bell Toils catering. Thea, this is my family."

"Smart aleck," Scott said, shaking his head. He put his arms around his mother and father. "These are my parents—Betty and Tom."

The older woman was a short, slim brunette. Her brown eyes still sparkled with a suspicious brightness. "It's nice to meet you, dear."

"The pleasure is mine, Mrs. Matthews, Mr. Matthews."

"It's Betty and Tom," the older man said. He indicated the man beside him. "This is our youngest son, Mike."

Scott's brother studied her openly. "I've heard a lot about you. It's nice to finally meet the woman giving my brother fits," he said, smiling.

She was dealing with the fact that he was every bit as good-looking as his older brother and it took several moments before his words sank in. "Fits?"

Scott looked uncomfortable. "Mike has a big mouth."

Betty glanced from one son to the other, her gaze finally settling on the youngest. "Michael, what are you talking about?"

"Nothing, Mom. Call it payback for years of sibling oppression."

"I never picked on you," Scott said with over-the-top, self-righteous indignation.

"Okay." Mike's grin was full of the devil. "And because you're lying, I will revert to junior high mentality for just a moment. Scott likes Thea."

"I can see why," Tom said, studying her. "And we all know the way to a man's heart is through his stomach. Why do you think I married your mother?"

But the levity did nothing to disarm the glare Scott turned on his brother. "You just violated some serious sibling code. And, for the record, I never picked on you."

"You still pick on him, Dad," Gail said. "Hi, Thea."

She was glad to have the focus off her and Scott. But it was clear he'd talked to his brother about her. Was that good or bad?

"Hi, kiddo," Thea said. "How's UCLA?"

She beamed. "Way cool. Although finals are coming up fast."

Thea nodded and glanced at the Matthews clan. "It's nice to meet you all. Now it's time to get this celebration on the road. I've set all the food up in here." She indicated the hot trays on the kitchen island containing lasagna and stuffed shells. "Your backyard and patio are so beautiful, I decided to set up the picnic table out there."

Scott went to the window and looked out. "Wow." He glanced back at her. "It looks great. You did a terrific job."

His compliment pleased her more than a compliment usually did, proving that she was in a lot of trouble. "I'm glad you approve. Now everyone, the plates are here. Fill them up and I'll get drinks when you're all settled at the table."

"Of course you'll join us," Betty said.

"Thank you, no. I'm working," she explained.

"I don't know how Kendra roped you into this," the older woman said, "but I'm going to make an educated, instinctive guess that she's supposed to be helping."

"Yes, but she's part of the family and this is a family party. You all don't want a stranger intruding."

"You're not a stranger." Scott's mouth turned up at the corners.

The twinkle in his eyes told her he was thinking about seeing her naked, which supported his statement. Thea's cheeks couldn't have been hotter if she'd been cooking over an open fire.

"I'm the caterer," she explained. "It's my job to be unobtrusive—to not be seen or heard."

"I thought that was kids," Mike Matthews said.

"No, Uncle Mike." Gail huffed out a breath. "Kids should be *seen* and not heard."

"Then how come you didn't get the memo?" Mike playfully grabbed her and rubbed his knuckles over the top of her head until she shrieked for mercy.

Betty Matthews stepped forward and handed Thea a plate. "You may be the caterer, but this is my house and no one goes hungry. Besides, you're too skinny."

Scott shrugged. "I think you just had your first example of what Mike and I learned many years ago."

"What's that?" Thea asked.

"Don't mess with Mom."

Thea smiled at the woman who'd taken back control of her kitchen, removing plastic from the salad, uncovering steaming dishes of food and directing traffic through her domain.

"Well, I tried," she said to Scott. The two of them were at the end of a line of Matthews family members filling their plates as they filed past the food. "Your mom is obviously happier running the show."

"She is now that food she didn't have to prepare is here and assembled," he said. He sniffed the fragrance of basil and garlic wafting through the air. He sighed dramatically. "You're amazing. I think I've died and gone to heaven."

"Not yet." Mike turned and looked at him. "But I can arrange it."

Thea laughed. "You remind me of my brother."

Mike looked offended. "Not exactly what a guy wants a pretty girl to say."

"Not so fast, little brother. I saw her first."

The tone got Thea's attention and when she looked at Scott, she wondered if he was angry. Did he think his brother was hitting on her? The idea that he might be jealous filled her with a sense of awe. She wasn't the sort of woman men fought over. And it certainly wasn't her intention to manipulate the two of them, but the fantasy of two such attractive men vying for her attention was so incredibly lovely. The rush of exuberance filled her with sheer happiness to be alive.

And for the first time since losing her husband, that thought wasn't followed by a flood of guilt.

"That was a test." Mike grinned. "And I found out what I wanted to know."

"I should have taken you out when I could have," Scott mumbled, flexing his wide shoulders as if they were tense.

When all the plates were full and everyone else was seated at the table beneath the patio cover, Scott pulled a chair up beside his own for Thea before the two of them sat down. Her heart stumbled at the masculine gesture that was just shy of possessive.

She dug into the food on her plate, realizing she was very hungry. Fortunately, the Matthews clan went into action, laughing, talking, teasing. This gave her a chance to observe them.

The mutual love, respect and acceptance was evident in the good-natured banter and joking. They reminded her of her own family. She'd been raised in a similar environment and had always yearned to have that same kind of life. But fate had stepped in and robbed her of the chance.

"So, Thea, I understand you'll be catering Kendra's graduation party." Betty took a bite of garlic bread and closed her eyes for a moment as she chewed, an expression of sublime enjoyment suffusing her expression.

"That's right." She looked at the teenager. "In just a few weeks, she'll be the proud owner of a high school diploma."

"And it's about darn time," Scott said. "What took you so long, kidlet?"

The words, teasing though they were, twisted in Thea's chest. He was obviously happy to be almost finished with child-rearing and she'd barely begun. He was such a good father, with so much to offer. And that was when she pushed the thought away and ate as if this were her last meal.

When everyone declared that they couldn't eat another bite, Thea stood to clear the dishes and Kendra helped.

Gail joined them in the kitchen, resting her elbows on the island. "The food was great, Thea."

"I'm glad you liked it."

"The most important thing is that Grammy did. And Dad. Way to go, sis," Gail said. "Wish I'd thought of it."

"Thanks." Kendra flashed a grin over her shoulder as she loaded the dishwasher. Then she looked at Thea. "What about your mom? I'm sorry. I didn't even think. Was she okay with you doing this on Mother's Day?"

"My brother and sister and I took her and Dad out for brunch," she explained. "That's been our tradition for several years, which left me free this evening."

"We're glad you're free, too. If you were a mom, you wouldn't be," Gail said. A thoughtful expression settled on her pretty face. "How come you're not? Do you want children?"

"Yes."

"How do you know? How do you decide when it's right to have kids?" Kendra asked.

Thea knew the question was generated by her family

history. Her father had never had the opportunity to choose when he wanted to *be* a father.

"I don't know about timing," she admitted. "But I do know that ever since I was a little girl, I've wanted to have a baby."

"So how come you don't?" Kendra asked.

Thea couldn't say anything to them about her dream nearly come true—not until she told Scott about the baby. When he walked through the sliding glass door connecting the kitchen to the patio, she knew she had to tell him soon.

"Hey, you guys," he said to his daughters. "I can't hold your grandmother back any longer. She's opening your gifts whether you're there or not."

"No," Kendra said. "I want to see her face."

"Me, too," her sister said as the two of them hurried back outside.

Scott came up behind her and slipped his arms around her waist. "I thought I'd never get you alone."

"So you lied?"

"How did you know?" he asked, chuckling into her ear.

"I thought you never lied."

"It's not a lie as much as a man's gotta do what a man's gotta do."

His breath stirred the hair around her face and raised tingles all over her body. How she wanted to lose herself in his arms.

But Scott must have felt her body tense because he turned her toward him. "Is something wrong?"

"No," she lied. Correction: a woman had to do what a woman had to do. And right now she didn't want to spoil his night.

His gaze skimmed her own and he shook his head. "I can see it in your eyes. What's going on?" He pointed a finger at her. "And don't tell me it's nothing."

"It can wait," she hedged. "This isn't the time."

"If you're upset about something, I'll make time. Spill it,

lady. It's not good to keep things bottled up." She started to put him off again, but he silenced her with that same pointed finger over her lips. "Just so we're clear, I don't intend to let this drop until you've come clean."

Interesting choice of words. But now she really had no choice. As if she ever did. Twice she'd tried to tell him and both times he'd interrupted her with a kiss that scrambled her brain function. This was lousy timing, but there simply wasn't going to be a perfect time and place for this announcement. And one thing she'd learned about Scott—when he made up his mind, he wouldn't back off. Now that he'd insisted, she needed to just say it.

"I just have something to tell you."

"What?" He frowned as he studied her face. "Interest rates went sky-high? You're moving to Micronesia? Global warming ruined the world's garlic and herb crop?"

She shook her head and took a deep breath. "Mother's Day seems as appropriate a time as any to tell you I've always wanted to be a mother."

His hands stilled on her arms. "You have?"

"Yes. In fact, I'm going to have a baby in about six months."

Chapter 13

Scott couldn't have been more shocked if she'd stripped naked and slugged him in the gut. He would have bet everything he owned that she hadn't been intimate with another man since her husband died. How could he have been so wrong? The bitterness of her betrayal slammed through him.

"So that's what you meant when you said you were okay. If you're already pregnant, I suppose that qualifies as birth control," he said, his throat tight. "Were you going to try to pass it off as mine?"

She took a step back, looking genuinely shocked. "Whatever you're thinking, you couldn't be more wrong."

"I'm thinking who's the father?"

"My husband."

"That would take a miracle."

"Exactly." She nodded. "A miracle of modern science. The magic of IVF."

"What?"

"In vitro fertilization."

"But your husband's been gone two years."

Thea leaned back against the sink and folded her arms over her chest. The smooth skin of her forehead puckered. From outside, sounds of laughter drifted in through the open window. At least his family was having a good time.

"When David was diagnosed with cancer," she finally said, "we were trying to have a baby. The oncologist told us that chemotherapy was the only chance to save his life, but it would make him sterile. It would be impossible for him to father the child we so desperately wanted. We were advised to freeze sperm."

"I see."

"When the treatment put him in remission, we didn't want to waste any time. We consulted a fertility specialist who guided us through IVF. He injected me daily with ovulation stimulants before my eggs were harvested and combined with his sperm in a petri dish."

"Then what?"

"The cells multiplied and divided. After that, three fertilized embryos were implanted and the rest were frozen. We thought we'd hit a home run the first time at the plate. I was pregnant." Anguished sadness crept into her face. "Three months later, I had a miscarriage. We were crushed. Then we tried again, but the same thing happened. We were devastated. But there was more bad news. David's cancer came back."

Scott tried to wrap his mind around what she was telling him. She was pregnant. Her dead husband was the father. The words banged around inside him and he felt as if he were slipping into a black hole. At the same time he was angry that she looked so sad for another man. A man who'd lost his fight to live. What kind of bastard was he to be resentful because she'd loved the guy with everything she had?

"Scott, I promised my husband that I would do everything in my power to make sure a part of him went on."

"But it's been two years. Why now?"

"Lots of factors. I had no reason to believe the results would be any different this time, but time was the operative word. I'm thirty-four years old. Twenty-five percent of women under thirty-five achieve live births. After that, the rate drops with each year over thirty-five. Also, I had to make a decision about what to do with the frozen embryos. I couldn't give them to strangers or pull the plug and let them go. I had enough left for one more try and figured I had nothing to lose."

Maybe *she* had nothing to lose. But he felt as if he was losing everything. If only she'd said something…

Anger churned through him and settled in his gut like acid. "What I don't get is why you didn't tell me right away."

"I should have, I guess."

"You guess?" His voice rose as waves of what ifs washed over him. If only he'd known. If only he could have insulated himself. If he'd simply shut down his instantaneous attraction to her from day one. If he'd done any of the above, he wouldn't be fighting off the pain that threatened to pull him under now.

"After everything I'd been through, I didn't know if I could survive another miscarriage. Emotionally, I mean."

"What does that have to do with telling me the truth?"

"You make it sound like a deliberate lie."

"Isn't it?"

She shook her head as something—anger, irritation, fear—flashed through her dark eyes. "I'm not in the habit of blurting out my personal information to complete strangers."

"I'm not a stranger."

"You were at first. When you got to *not* be a stranger, the situation became awkward. How do you slide something like that into a conversation with a client? I make a mean egg roll. Oh, and by the way I'm pregnant? It wasn't any of your business. Besides, I'd made a promise to myself not to say anything to anyone until after I made it safely through the first trimester of my pregnancy."

"And are you? Through the first three months?"

His gaze dropped to her still flat stomach. He'd seen her naked, the feminine beauty of her soft curves, her full breasts. Not a single sign had alerted him to the fact that she was carrying a baby. But he hadn't been looking for signs. He'd been too busy savoring the feel of her and wondering how he'd gotten so lucky the day he'd come home and found Thea in his kitchen. He figured his bad karma was over. No one told him karma had a sick sense of humor.

"I completed the first trimester not long ago."

"Before we had sex the first time?" She flinched, then met his gaze and nodded. "At that point, I'd say it was definitely my business."

"I'd been trying to find the words to tell you, then you kissed me," she said, twisting her fingers together.

"You're blaming me for the fact that you didn't clue me in about something I had every right to know?"

"Of course not." Her eyes flashed again, and her lips pressed together for a moment. "I distinctly remember saying I had something to tell you. Your response was 'me first' and then you kissed me and I couldn't think about anything else."

"Oh, please. You think flattery is going to make this better?"

"It's not flattery. The truth is it felt good. I'd forgotten how good it felt to be in a man's arms. Your arms," she said, putting a finer point on the statement. "And making love. I simply couldn't think about anything else. It was wonderful to reaffirm that I'm still a woman. Not just a vessel for my child or a glorified science experiment. But a flesh and blood woman with wants, needs, passions. And to know that you wanted me. Do you have any idea how much that meant to me?"

He had a clue. What she said touched a nerve with him. "That still doesn't justify what you did. Or should I say didn't do."

"It's still something that's my personal information. I was trying to find a way to tell you, then you shared how adamantly opposed you are to having children. After that I knew there could never be anything between us and figured there was no reason to tell you."

"That's where you're wrong. There was a damn good reason. I don't sleep with someone I don't care about. So where does that leave me?" He saw the shadows in her eyes and couldn't find the will to care that he was being harsh. "All you had to do was be upfront and everything would have been fine."

Scott realized there was more than one way to be trapped. He'd felt that as a young father, his choices taken away when he did the "right" thing. Then his wife had walked out leaving him alone and solely responsible for their two small children. Now he was torn between his powerful feelings for Thea and his desire not to be tied down again.

"I'm sorry, Scott. If there was something else I could say or do, I would. But there isn't. So take me out back and throttle me."

"I'm not in the habit of throttling women." He ran his fingers through his hair. "But for God's sake, Thea. I've been in the parenting trenches for twenty years. My kids are almost independent. To start all over—"

"I've heard that children keep you young," she said.

He stared at her and hated the hope he saw in her eyes. "Twice I was robbed of choices. After that, I did something to make sure I was completely in control." That was a laugh. Control was a pipe dream. "I had a vasectomy."

"Oh. That's what you meant when *you* said you were safe."

Her eyes widened and her mouth trembled before she caught her top lip between her teeth. That told him she understood how much he didn't want to be responsible for another child. But he couldn't help feeling he'd drop-kicked a kitten and the thought ticked him off. He hadn't done anything wrong.

"I can't believe this." He slammed his fist on the counter, ignoring the pain that vibrated up his arm and settled in his shoulder. "I finally connect with someone—with you—and now this."

"Don't feel like The Lone Ranger. I didn't expect to ever have strong feelings for another man. Yet here I am."

In spite of everything, pleasure shot through him at her admission, but he tried to ignore it. This was an impossible situation.

"Yeah, here we are. With a baby standing between us."

She tipped her head to the side as she studied him. Anger flashed through her eyes and mixed with the pain. "You know, Scott, I never expected to feel alive again and didn't care to. You were right. I've just been going through the motions. It never occurred to me that I would care for someone again. And it especially didn't cross my mind that someone I liked and respected would view a new life as a negative."

"Don't you dare make this my fault," he ground out.

"Nothing could be further from the truth. I'm just explaining that this child is the most important thing in the world to me. I lost two babies. The crushing pain of that taught me it's not just about having a child. I learned how desperately I wanted to be a mother."

"So what are we going to do?" he asked, frustration roiling through him.

"Under the circumstances, it might be easier if you found

another caterer to do Kendra's party. I can recommend some good, reputable ones."

He shook his head and didn't want to think about why everything in him cried out against that suggestion. "Time is getting short. And besides, Kendra wanted you. The party is about her, not us."

"I agree. And there's no way I would do anything to hurt her, but I had to offer." She sighed. "And I understand if you want to back out of the house deal—"

"Why would I? To hurt you?" The thought never crossed his mind.

She lifted one shoulder. "I wouldn't blame you."

"No. That, at least, still feels right." In fact, it felt more right than it did before, reaffirming that he was going to control his life if it was the last thing he did.

"Okay." She nodded. "Then we'll get through everything the best we can. After that, we don't have to see each other again."

As Thea turned away to pack up her things, Scott felt as if she'd already left. He hated the thought of not seeing her, of not having her in his life. The emptiness hit him low and deep. He hadn't known he could feel so much so fast. Possibilities had dangled in front of him and now they were snatched just out of reach.

Maybe he was a selfish bastard, but he wanted time to think only about himself. Hadn't he earned it? His head said yes. The tightness in his chest told him something else.

Thea checked the heat beneath the chafing dish to make sure the flame wasn't high enough to dry out the lasagna. She'd set up the food for Kendra's party on the kitchen island and dinette. All the guests had moved through, filled their plates and then filed out the slider to the tables set up around the pool in the backyard. Now she was checking everything to make sure the remaining food would hold up to second helpings. Sometimes they were better than the first time around. Other times, not so much.

Kind of like her and Scott. Both of them were each other's seconds and they'd been a disaster. He'd been conspicuously absent today when she'd set up for the party. And tonight she'd managed to look extremely busy when he'd gotten his food. How could she have been so stupid as to think he might care enough about her that a package deal would be okay with him?

She thought about his vasectomy and wondered why she'd been so shocked that he'd taken the ultimate step to make absolutely certain he would have no more children. From the first moment she'd met him, he'd made no secret of the fact that his youngest child was almost on her own. He had mixed feelings about it but he couldn't keep her from growing up. He was moving on and making the best of it.

For the record, she was never listening to Connie again about hoping for something she knew in her heart wasn't going to happen.

From her vantage point in the kitchen, she surveyed the Matthews backyard. She'd messed up with Scott, but at least she'd done a good job for his daughter's party. The decorations looked great. They'd strung white lights in the trees and set up tables on the brick deck surrounding the pool. Centerpieces were mortarboards and balloons—the sky's the limit. Napkins for each place setting were rolled up and tied with a ribbon to look like a diploma.

Everyone seemed to be having a good time, she thought, glancing around at the group of relatives and friends. Thea recognized the Matthews clan. They'd all been very friendly tonight so she guessed Scott hadn't clued them in on anything. She thought about the first and last time she'd seen them. Pain rolled through her and she knew it would be hard from now on to celebrate Mother's Day without remembering how she'd had her heart broken for the second time.

As much as she tried not to, her gaze continually strayed to Scott. She'd caught him looking at her more than once. Every time, his mouth tightened and he looked angry as he immediately glanced away. She didn't blame him for any of this. It was all her fault. He was right. She should have said something. But she'd thought she was doing the right thing. After losing her babies, it had been beyond painful when people had asked how she was feeling. She'd had to put on a brave face and say over and over what had happened. This time, keeping her condition to herself had been every bit as painful—in a very different way.

Kendra walked inside with her empty plate. "Wow, that was really good. Is there anything left?"

"Everything. What can I get you?"

"Actually, nothing. I'm stuffed," the teen admitted. "I was just making an excuse to talk to you."

"You don't need an excuse. Why would you think that?"

"I don't know."

"Well, I'm glad you did. I wanted to thank you for the graduation invitation. I wish I could have gone, but…" She shrugged, unable to find the words.

"That's okay. Thanks for the gift."

"You're welcome." Thea had sent a very feminine, cloth-covered photo album that tied with a ribbon so that Kendra could keep memories of this time. But as she studied the girl, she realized something was bothering her. "What's wrong, sweetie?"

She lifted one shoulder. "It's just that everything feels different."

"With your dad?" Thea asked. "Did something happen?"

Kendra shook her head. "No. At least not between Dad and me. But he's been weird."

"Weird how?" It was nothing more than a stall tactic.

"Grumpy. Testy. Crabby."

"Sounds like three of the Seven Dwarfs from the dark side," Thea commented.

Kendra laughed. "He's like he used to be. Only worse."

"Like he used to be?"

"Yeah. Before he met you."

"He changed?" Thea asked, hating that she couldn't stop the tiny little glow inside her.

"Yeah. For a while there he was happy. And cool. And he listened. Now he's not happy. Ever since that Mother's Day party."

"Oh."

"I was just wondering. Maybe that idea wasn't so hot. Did I do something?" she asked, clearly confused and upset.

"No, of course not." Thea touched the girl's arm, feeling the need to connect and make her understand.

"How can you be so sure?"

"Because it's me he's angry at."

The girl's eyes grew wide. "That's why he got so irritated when I wanted to give you an invitation to my graduation."

It warmed her heart that this young woman she'd grown fond of had wanted her to be a part of her commencement day, enough to send the invitation against her father's wishes. She also understood Scott's negative reaction, but his daughter didn't.

Kendra nodded. "Dad went ballistic and said I couldn't invite the whole universe."

Thea wasn't that big with child yet. "Who else did you want there?"

"My mom." Shadows lurked in her eyes. "He was mad, but I sent it anyway. It came back stamped Not At This Address."

"I'm sorry," she said, squeezing the girl's forearm reassuringly. She was even sorrier she hadn't attended the ceremony, even though Scott would have been annoyed. She'd let this girl down and that bothered her a lot.

One shoulder lifted in a careless shrug. "It's okay."

"No, it's not. And I think it's unconscionable the way that woman treats her children." Then rational thought returned. "I'm sorry. I should keep my opinion of your mother to myself."

Surprisingly, Kendra didn't look upset. "No. I think she's pretty lame, too. But I'm sorry Dad wouldn't let you come to the ceremony. What happened between you two? I thought he kind of liked you. And you liked him, too."

Thea wasn't going to tell this young woman that her father was giving up on a promising relationship because of the baby Thea carried. It would be too easy for Kendra to go to the bad place where she blamed herself for his not wanting more children. The issue was complicated and Scott should be the one to explain his feelings.

"I think that's something you should ask your father," she gently suggested.

"But he won't tell me. He'll just pat me on the head and tell me not to worry about it."

"That's his prerogative."

"But it's not fair. He butts into my life and it's okay because he's my dad. But it's not okay to know what's bothering him?"

"He doesn't want you to be concerned." His single-minded determination to protect his children was one of the things Thea liked best about him. That and his outstanding butt, she thought a little sadly.

"He wants me to be responsible. He wants me to be a grown-up. It would help if he started treating me that way." Kendra looked confused and angry—and so much like her father that Thea's heart ached.

"He has mixed feelings about you growing up," Thea said, willing her to understand.

"No kidding. That's why I asked you. You've never sugar-coated anything for me. You've always been straight even when it wasn't something I wanted to hear."

Except this was different. It concerned hang-ups of Scott's that Thea wasn't at liberty to be straight about. But she felt she couldn't hang the teen out to dry completely.

"I can't speak for your father—"

Kendra cocked her hip and jammed her fist on it. "Please don't shut me down, Thea."

"You didn't let me finish," she pointed out. "I can't speak for him, but I can tell you how I feel. He's a wonderful man. He's kind, considerate, conscientious—"

"And hot?"

"Hard-working," she went on, ignoring the interruption. "He's a fabulous father."

"And you think he's really hot, right?"

"He's reliable and caring."

"Okay," Kendra said rolling her eyes. "I've had about all the grown-up treatment I can stand. Do you or do you not think my dad is the hottest thing since green Tabasco sauce?"

Thea laughed. "Okay. You win. I think your dad is a very nice-looking man."

Kendra shook her head. "Better, but no cigar. So you like him?"

"Yes."

"Then what's the problem?" she said, throwing up her hands.

"You're going to have to ask him that question."

The girl tapped her lip. "Then I have to assume you wouldn't kick him out of bed."

"What?" Thea's cheeks turned hot and it wasn't because the chafing dish flame was too high. Did this teenager know she'd slept with her father?

"Translation: you admitted you like my dad so that means he dumped you."

"No one dumped anyone." One had to be in a relationship for that to happen. She and Scott had sort of eased into something neither of them wanted to label and then they'd had mind-blowing sex. She didn't know what to call it.

"Then you guys still have a chance?"

"You're relentless," Thea said, shaking her head.

"Dad says determination is a good quality in a grown-up."

Like father, like daughter, she thought. He was the one who had refused to take no for an answer. If he had, neither of them would be in this mess now.

"Not being nosy is another admirable quality in an adult."

Kendra assumed a pathetic expression—big, wide eyes and semi-pouting mouth. "C'mon, Thea. Tell me something. I think I have a right to know. I liked you and my dad together. It made me feel better that he wouldn't be alone when I go away to school."

Hah. Wasn't that ironic. And Thea couldn't tell her that alone is exactly what Scott wanted. She wouldn't even tell her about being pregnant. It was the clue Kendra needed to put two and two together, but she might add it up to five. Scott needed to be the one to tell her and explain his feelings. He already blamed Thea for this lousy situation; and she'd accept a good portion of the responsibility. But she didn't want his daughter to jump to wrong conclusions because of anything she said. Still, she felt compelled to give Kendra something.

She sighed. "All I can tell you is that your father and I have something standing between us. And before you ask, there's no way for us to compromise on it."

"But if someone bends—"

Thea shook her head. "Ask him to explain."

"Why are all men dorks?" the girl asked, then heaved a big gusty sigh.

"Not all of them are. And when you meet a man who rings your chimes, I guarantee you won't think he's a dork."

"I'm never falling in love."

"Like I believe that." Thea laughed. "Now go back to your party. It's almost time for cake. And Connie worked long and hard on it."

"Okay." But the teen hesitated. "Can I call you? I mean, if there's anything I need to talk over, when I get to UCLA?"

Impulsively, Thea hugged her. "You can call me anytime, sweetie. I sincerely mean that."

"Thanks." Then she walked outside and joined a group of teenage girls at a table under the trees.

Tears filled Thea's eyes as her gaze automatically went to Scott. A profound, aching sadness filled her as she stared at his handsome profile, smiling at something his brother said. Soon the party would be over and their only connection would be their respective escrows. When they closed, any link to him would be history.

If, as the saying went, timing was everything, then she had nothing. She'd been lucky enough to meet another wonderful man and she found it unbelievably tragic that there was no way to resolve their differences.

She'd worked so hard to keep from falling in love with Scott because deep down she'd known her heart would get broken.

And this was one time she hated being right.

Chapter 14

The day after Kendra's party, Scott opened his door to the last person in the world he expected to see. The sight of Thea sent a jolt of joy arcing through him, followed almost instantly by a shaft of pain.

"Scott." She backed up a step, obviously surprised to see him. "I'm sorry. I—I…Kendra said you weren't home," she finished lamely. Nervously, she tucked a strand of hair behind her ear.

So that was why his daughter had looked so funny after answering the phone and out of the blue said she was going to the mall. She was playing matchmaker. "Sorry. I still live here until escrow closes."

He hadn't meant to sound so abrasive. But it was hard to concentrate when his brain was busy memorizing the way the sun picked out the red in her brown hair and made it flash and sparkle with even the slightest movement.

She was staring at him, too. "I don't mean to bother you.

But last night I left some serving dishes and a few other things after the party. I stopped by to pick them up." She met his gaze, then half turned away. "But it's all right. I can do it another time."

He shook his head. "Now's fine."

Even though it hurt to look at her. Deep inside, where no woman had ever touched him before, he ached. Watching her throughout the party last night had been a mixture of pleasure and pain. Pleasure because just looking at her did that to him. And pain because he couldn't have her, not under the circumstances.

When she'd left last night, it was as if some light inside him sputtered and went out. He figured that was the last time he would see her. And he was resigned to that. The lie was bitter inside him, although he would make it the truth if it was the last thing he ever did. But at this very moment, he couldn't make himself send her away.

"Come in."

"Thanks. Kendra said she stacked the things on the island in the kitchen. I'll just get them and be out of your hair."

Just because she walked out of his house didn't mean she would be out of his hair. Not as long as he couldn't stop thinking about her.

He sighed as he followed her to the back of the house. It took every ounce of his self-control to keep from pulling her against him and kissing her until they were both breathless and wanting.

In the kitchen, he spotted her stuff on the island, just as she'd said. He cleared his throat and, if there was a God in heaven, his voice would be normal, or at the very least, neutral.

"Yeah. Here it is," he said.

She inspected the sizable stack of serving dishes, warming trays and assorted spoons and linens. "It looks like everything is here."

When she started to grab the collection, he put his hand

on her bare arm to stop her. Warmth from her skin zinged through him, leaving sparks that threatened to reignite that light inside him.

He took his hand away and forced himself to ignore the tingle that wouldn't stop. "I'll take that out for you."

"Thanks, but that's not necessary. It's bulky but not heavy. I can handle it."

"You're pregnant," he said simply. But there was nothing simple about those two words. They changed everything and turned his world upside down.

"Having a baby, true. But I'm not handicapped. I carry things all the time."

"Maybe you shouldn't. Why didn't you send Connie to pick this up?"

"Because I can handle it."

"For someone who was so cautious she wouldn't even talk about her condition, this attitude seems a tad cavalier."

The angry words told him he hadn't achieved neutrality toward her yet.

A muscle moved in her jaw as her eyes flashed. "Okay. If you're going to keep up the martyr routine and be snarky, there's no reason I should soft-pedal anything. I didn't send Connie to pick up these things because she's pretty angry with you and I couldn't guarantee your safety."

He was the one who'd been kept in the dark from day one, he thought. Although her "martyr routine" crack cut deep.

"What the heck did I do?" he asked.

"You hurt me."

"*I* hurt *you?*" he said. "Excuse me, but weren't you the one withholding pertinent information?"

"Think back, Scott. And be honest with yourself. I tried to keep distance between us. I tried to get you to back off. But you and your pesky determination wore me down."

"You knew from day one how I felt about being finished

with raising children. All you had to say was, 'I'm pregnant.'"

"I hardly knew you from a rock," she snapped. "I'm not in the habit of revealing intimate details of my life to any Tom, Dick or Harry on the street."

"You were in my house."

"Don't split hairs. You were a client. That didn't entitle you to my personal, private information."

He put his hands on his hips as he stared at her. "Has your life always been this top secret?"

"As a matter of fact, no. I used to be much more open. But that changed when I opened my big mouth to people I thought were my friends. I found out you can't trust anyone."

He had a bad feeling about what had put the wary, wounded look in her eyes. Maybe she wouldn't answer, but he decided to ask anyway. "What happened?"

Her eyes glowed with anger. "It was right after David was diagnosed with cancer. He had a lot of paid time off that he could take for treatment and wanted to keep his condition just between the two of us."

"What happened?"

"I decided that for him to successfully fight the disease, he needed the support of everyone around him, including his coworkers."

"And?" This was like pulling teeth.

"And I found out the hard way that my husband's instincts were right. He was one of two candidates in line for a promotion with more benefits. The other guy went to his boss and revealed David's condition. He was advanced. David was put on administrative leave—sick leave, they said. And claimed it was in his best interests so he could concentrate on getting well. But we had to pick up the cost to keep our medical insurance in force. Administration wanted to unload deadweight." She laughed harshly. "No pun intended."

"That doesn't seem right. Surely you had some recourse?"

Her mouth tightened for a moment before she said, "I wanted to fight it, but David didn't have the stamina to battle on two fronts. And his health was the most important fight. That was when I started catering on the side to earn extra money. I was an office manager by day. But we'd opted to take our medical benefits through David's job and after his diagnosis, he had a pre-existing condition and no insurance company would touch him. So they got away with it."

He ran his fingers through his hair. "That's rough."

"It was a nightmare. A painful lesson. But it taught me to play my cards close to the vest."

"Yeah. But, you and I—this was an entirely different situation."

"Oh? I was here for a catering job. How was I to know you wouldn't say pregnant caterers need not apply?"

"Now *you're* splitting hairs. Besides, pretty soon you won't be able to hide your condition."

"I wasn't hiding anything. And like I said, I tried to get you to back off, but you wouldn't. I didn't set out to make you fall for me. And I certainly didn't intend to—" She brushed the back of her hand across her cheek. "Oh, never mind. This is pointless."

"No. You didn't intend to what?"

Her eyes blazed when she met his gaze. But mixed in with the sparks were tears. "I didn't intend to fall for anyone. My goal is to bring a healthy baby into this world and raise him or her by myself to be the best human being possible. This child is a part of David. After the way I betrayed him, the least I can do is make sure his DNA will go on."

"Are you still in love with him?"

Scott wasn't sure what made him ask. But suddenly it was damned important for him to know.

Her chin lifted just a fraction and the sparks in her eyes burned out, leaving only the tears. "I'll always love David."

She looked at the stack of things beside her as she rubbed a knuckle beneath her nose. "You know, suddenly warming trays and serving dishes aren't so important. Since we're closing escrow soon, just leave them for me when you move out."

She slid him a weak smile, then walked past him and out the front door.

Scott felt as if he'd been flattened by a three-hundred-pound linebacker. She still loved her husband?

"This bites," he snapped.

He wanted to hit something. The pain might take the edge off what he felt inside.

And he had to admit Thea was right. He'd noticed her putting distance between them. And he'd planned to play it her way until his brother talked him into giving it one more try.

"Remind me to thank Mike," he said to the empty room.

He was angry at Thea. Angry at his brother. But mostly, he was furious with himself because he still wanted her.

And he didn't know how to make it stop.

Thea walked up the plant- and shrub-lined sidewalk to the escrow company. When the loan officer had called to set the time for signing papers, Thea had made sure Scott was already scheduled in the morning before settling on her own last appointment of the day.

As much as she ached to see him, just to catch a glimpse of him, it was best that she didn't. He was angry and she couldn't really blame him. It was all her fault—wrong thing, right reason. Lousy result. She had to move on with her life. She'd done it before, after David's death. She could do it again.

After muscling open the heavy glass-and-chrome door, she walked into the lobby. Searching the building's directory there, she found the suite number and then took the elevator to the third floor. When the doors whispered open, she stepped out into the reception area. It should have been empty. It wasn't. Scott was there, dwarfing one of the standard waiting-room chairs.

Her body betrayed her good intentions to move on without him. Her traitorous heart hammered almost painfully, making it difficult to draw in air. On legs that felt about as sturdy as limp noodles, she moved farther into the room.

He looked up. For a split second, she'd swear he was glad to see her. Then his mask of cool indifference slipped into place. It was the expression he'd worn the day after the party, two weeks ago, when she'd told him why she didn't share her personal information. She hadn't seen or heard from him since.

"Hi," she said.

He stood. "Hi."

Then she got a bad feeling. "I thought you were signing papers this morning. Is there a problem?"

Translation: had he changed his mind about the real-estate deal? God knows she'd had second thoughts about living in the house that would forever hold his essence. In a weird way, that thought had actually brought her comfort. Probably because she was completely pathetic.

"No problem. Except I had to reschedule my appointment." He lifted one broad shoulder in a careless shrug. "A crisis at work."

At least he didn't think she'd scheduled her appointment in order to manipulate him somehow. "I hope it was nothing serious."

She meant that. Really she did. But it was difficult to be completely sincere. Not when the crisis had allowed her one more chance to memorize the laugh lines around his eyes, the mesmerizing blue there, and his strong, square jaw. The irony of the situation didn't escape her. They were buying each other's homes because they were at different places in their lives. And she had that to thank for this opportunity to see him one last time.

But the differences were also what stood between them.

"Nothing serious," he said absently, not looking away. "How are you?"

"Fine."

"And the baby?" His gaze dropped to her abdomen.

Her body was beginning to change and her clothes were getting a little snug. Her tummy was rounding nicely and all was as it should be, her doctor told her. Everything was fine except for her heart. It would bear the scars of knowing Scott forever. But if he made love to her now, he'd notice her belly and know about the baby. The thought put a catch in her breathing at the same time it made her profoundly sad. A time that should have been perfectly joyful was marred by things that couldn't be changed.

"The baby's fine." She slid her purse strap higher on her shoulder. "My last ultrasound was normal and showed everything looks good."

"Did you find out the sex of the baby?"

She shook her head. "I want to be surprised."

"Are you hoping for a boy? To carry on David's name?"

How like a man to think of that. "It never occurred to me. I guess because girls are raised knowing their last name will change when they marry. But this child will carry David's DNA whether it's a girl or a boy. And that's all I care about."

He frowned and a muscle in his jaw jerked. "You look tired. Are you sure you're all right?"

"Fine," she said, with a snap in her voice that she couldn't suppress.

His rejection of her and the baby had absolved him of the right to be concerned about her. His being sweet and caring and tender was frustrating and just made everything harder.

"How's Kendra?" she asked, to change the subject.

"I haven't seen much of her. She's been shopping and getting ready to move down to school. There's a program for incoming freshmen to help them acclimate and get the most out of the college experience. It was her idea to do that and I agree it's a smart move."

If she'd just met him, she might have thought he was trying to get rid of his daughter. But she knew him too well now. He only wanted what was best for his child, like any loving parent.

The last time Thea had seen Kendra was the night of the graduation party. She recalled the girl asking questions about their relationship and wondered if she'd quizzed him yet. If not, Thea should warn him so he could spin it whatever way he wanted.

"There's something you should know—"

"I hate when someone says that. The 'something' is never good."

She smiled and marveled that he could make her do that, what with all the pain bottled up inside her. "I didn't mean to be overly dramatic. It's just that I talked to Kendra the night of the party."

"And?"

"She asked about you and me." Thea couldn't quite meet his gaze. Her own settled on a spot just below his jaw, a place she'd very much enjoyed kissing.

"What did you tell her?" he asked sharply.

"Not much. I suggested she ask you."

"She hasn't said anything. What does 'not much' mean? She didn't even know there was a you and me."

"That's where you're wrong. She noticed. And she especially didn't miss the tension between us the night of the party."

"So what did you tell her?" Speaking of tension, his jaw tightened noticeably.

"I just said you were angry with me."

The last time she'd seen him, Thea had forgotten to warn him about this. Not surprising since she'd had a lot on her mind. Actually not a *lot*. Just Scott. But he felt like everything.

"Did you tell her you're pregnant?" he said, frowning.

"No. I thought it best that you explain."

He ran his fingers through his hair. "Swell."

It was on the tip of her tongue to say she was sorry, but Thea suppressed the words. Enough apologizing, already. She hadn't set out to hurt anyone. She'd tried to be true to herself and her child. If she had it to do over, she would do things differently. Hindsight was twenty-twenty. But she could have given Kendra an earful and didn't.

She put her hands on her hips. "Look, Scott, she asked and I had to tell her something. She's smart as a whip and noticed things changed between you and me after Mother's Day." How ironic was that? "She was afraid it was her fault somehow and I wouldn't let her think that. I told her there's something standing between us and there's no way to compromise."

"Hmm." His comment was just shy of a grunt.

Not especially helpful communication. "I didn't think it was fair to you that I explain your feelings to her. She's just gone through an insecure time and I didn't want to make it worse."

Thea stared at him, wondering how it was possible to be so angry with this man and so in love with him at the same time. The realization stunned her. She'd believed love would never again be in the cards for her. Yet it had happened. But no way would she admit as much to him. What was the point?

The door to the back offices opened and a plump blond woman stood in the doorway. "Ms. Bell?"

Thea looked at her. "Yes?"

"I can help you now."

No you can't, she thought. The woman had done the paperwork to make the rift between she and Scott official. He was condo; she was single-family home.

Single being the operative word. She glanced at Scott and the pain inside her expanded like a parachute after the rip cord had been pulled. It had been devastating to lose her husband to a disease she had no control over. And while he'd battled to survive, everyone had said where there was life, there was hope. She'd learned it was a lie. Scott was full of life, with so much to offer, and she had so much love to give. But it was never to be.

She met his gaze and hoped her own didn't betray what she was feeling. "I can wait to move into the house until after Kendra leaves for school."

He nodded. "Thanks. I appreciate that."

"I'm ready," she said to the escrow officer. She looked at Scott again feeling anything but ready—this was goodbye. And she couldn't bring herself to say it. "Good luck, Scott."

Then she turned away and followed the stranger past the point of no return. It was time to focus on her new home and getting it ready for her new baby. Forgetting the man who haunted every room wouldn't be easy, but she would do it.

She'd learned once that life is risky and love was the biggest risk of all. She'd just lost again.

Chapter 15

Shaking his head, Scott surveyed Kendra's room. This time, the chaos wasn't her fault. Moving boxes designated for his town house were stacked against the wall. She had suitcases, several backpacks and a duffel filled with the personal stuff and school supplies that she was taking to her dorm room. All in all, the place didn't look much different from its normal disastrous state. Except this time, *he* was different. He knew she was taking the clutter and confusion with her to college, and a sinkhole of loneliness opened up inside him.

Kendra walked in and stuffed a brush into the side of her backpack. "I'm starting to freak about forgetting something."

Gail stood in the doorway. "It's not Timbuktu. It's UCLA. If you forget anything, I guarantee you can find a store that carries it."

Scott settled his arm across her shoulders and forced himself not to grab her to him and squeeze her tight. He didn't because it's what he wanted to do to Kendra, to hang on and never let her leave home. But the reality was, they were all leaving this house.

Movers were scheduled to arrive tomorrow to take their belongings to Thea's town house. His now. They'd choreographed moving day carefully, both of them loading up at the same time, then the trucks passing like ships in the night. As always, thoughts of Thea sent a shaft of pain-wrapped regret slicing through him and he wondered if it would ever get better.

"What do you guys want to do about dinner?" he asked. "How about I take you to L'Italiano's. They have your favorite bread and that ravioli with the tomato cream sauce."

The girls looked at each other for a moment, then shook their heads. How did they do that silent communication thing? he wondered.

"I want to stay here," Kendra said, settling her duffel beside the suitcase at his feet. "It's my last night in this house."

"Mine, too," Gail echoed. "Although I don't think I feel it as much as Ken because I've been away for a couple years now."

"Then what about a pizza?" he said.

They looked at each other again and nodded. "That sounds good." Gail leaned her head against his shoulder.

His heart squeezed tight as he hugged her close for a moment, then dropped his arm. "I'll go call."

"Get it from Vincenzo's," Gail suggested. "It's my favorite."

"Mine, too," her sister echoed. "I think they deliver here so much, the driver could find his way blindfolded."

"Yeah," Gail said. "I've missed it."

"I'm going to miss it, too. And this house," Kendra said, a wistful expression on her face as she glanced around her room.

Gail sighed. "I keep telling myself change is part of being a grown-up. But myself answers back that I don't have to like it."

"Are you guys upset that I sold the house?" Scott asked.

He'd thought Kendra had come to terms with it after that first negative reaction. And the girls had seemed genuinely happy that Thea was buying the place. They approved of turning their house over to someone who would take good care of it. He'd tried to tell them it was business. But now that it was real, they were all feeling pretty darn personal about the change.

Kendra looked at him, her blue eyes shadowed. "We grew up here. All of my memories, good and bad, are here."

Gail met his gaze. "We moved here after Mom left. I've always wanted to ask you—" She caught her bottom lip between her teeth.

"What is it, honey? You can ask me anything."

"Well, I'm about the age now that you were when I was born. I guess I've been thinking about this since Ken went through that thing about you not wanting her. At school, I go to classes, hang out with my friends, do pretty much what I want. But you never got a chance to do that."

"So what's your question?"

"Do you have any regrets that I was born? Because of all you missed?"

"Never." He slung his arm around her again and this time, he did hug her close for several moments. "The two of you are the best thing that ever happened to me."

"But if Mom hadn't gotten pregnant with me, you'd have been able to go away to college. You didn't get to do a lot of things."

"I got to do other things, more important things. Like being a father to the two most terrific kids in the world." He rubbed his knuckles across the top of her head until she giggled and begged for mercy. Spinning away from him, she flopped on the bed beside her sister.

He crossed his arms over his chest as he leaned against the door frame. "But I will admit that I wonder sometimes what it would have been like to be ready for the experience of fatherhood."

Thea was responsible for that. She wanted it so much and had waited so long, he couldn't help thinking about what that would feel like. She had made him see a lot of things differently.

He looked at his girls. "I love you guys and I wouldn't trade the two of you for anything."

"Speaking of love," Kendra said, a glint in her eyes, "what happened between you and Thea?"

Uh-oh. Thea had warned him this question might come up. How did he explain his feelings to them? The last thing he wanted was for them to feel insecure about their place in his heart.

"It's complicated," he finally said.

"Is it anything we did?" Kendra asked, glancing at her sister.

"Why would you think that?"

She shrugged. "I don't know. Maybe because of Mom. If it hadn't been for us, she might still be around. Maybe we chase women out of your life."

Residual anger and resentment churned through him, aimed at the woman who'd made his children blame themselves for her actions. He walked over to the bed and sat down between them, taking each of their hands in his.

"Okay, you two. Here's the deal. Straight, no bull. The reason your mother walked away from us had nothing to do with you. It was all about her and her selfish needs. It's as simple as that."

Kendra still looked unsure. "And what about Thea?"

How did he answer that? Kendra had brought her into his life. In spite of how it turned out, he couldn't regret knowing her. She was probably the most unselfish person he'd ever known. "She's one of a kind."

Gail snorted. "And that tells us exactly nothing. Do you like her? Are you dating? And what about—"

The doorbell rang and Scott was grateful. His eldest had a habit of blurting out personal questions, and he had a bad feeling he knew what she'd been about to say. He'd been saved by the bell and he couldn't quite suppress the hope that it was Thea Bell.

"I'll get it," he volunteered.

He started out of the room and glanced back at his girls. The sparkle was back in their eyes, just as it should be, and he went downstairs with a lighter heart.

He opened the door and found his brother on the porch. "Mike. What are you doing here?"

"I thought you might need some help with the move."

Scott didn't buy it. "You know this is Kendra's last night home and you came over to see her off."

"I'm that transparent?"

"Like plastic wrap," he said automatically.

He winced when he remembered Thea saying that to him. How long before he stopped thinking about her? Repeating her words? Seeing her face? Dreaming about her? Hoping she'd come to see him one last time to change his mind?

"Can I come in?"

"Yeah." Scott stepped back and pulled the door wide.

"I'm going to help myself to a beer."

"Get one for me."

When they were in the family room, long necks in hand, Mike looked at him. "I didn't just come to see Ken off."

"No?"

"I wanted to talk to you."

"About what?"

"Something's wrong, bro." He held up his hand when Scott started to protest. "Can it. You haven't been yourself since Mother's Day. Before you deny it, you should know the folks have noticed, too. Mom thinks it has something to do with Thea."

Scott thought about telling his brother to take a flying leap. But the truth was, he needed to talk about this. Maybe if he did, he could get her out of his mind.

"She's going to have a baby, Mike."

Unfortunately when he said that, his brother happened to be taking a drink. He choked for several moments. Finally he said, "I know it's not yours."

Scott shook his head. "It's her husband's."

"I thought she was a widow."

"She had in vitro fertilization, a promise she made to him before he died."

Mike blew out a long breath. "That would make a man stop and think."

"And this is me we're talking about." Scott shook his head. "My youngest is on her way to independence practically as we speak. To start again with night feedings, walking the floor, worrying. That's the hardest. Worrying about every little thing that could go wrong with that tiny human being who's looking to you for everything."

His brother stared at him. "It occurs to me that not once did you say you don't care about her."

"It doesn't matter—"

"That's where you're wrong, big brother. Caring is everything."

"But the baby stuff. Been there, done that. I don't want to do it again."

"With Thea, you wouldn't be alone this time."

"I wasn't alone the first time."

"Yes, you were. And I don't mean just after she left you." Mike leaned forward and rested his elbows on his knees, his beer in his hands. "Even when you were married, she wasn't ever really there for you. And she didn't care. If she did, she'd still be here."

"And your point?" Scott asked angrily.

"Thea's different."

"You hardly know her. How the heck can you decide that?"

"Actions speak louder than words. Your wife declared her undying love right up until she walked out. Thea loves so much, she moved heaven and earth to have her dead husband's child."

"I think she's still in love with him," Scott admitted. It was the first time he'd voiced that out loud. He wasn't sure if he felt relieved or not.

A gleam stole into his brother's gaze. "So that's what your problem is."

"What are you talking about?"

"You're looking for an excuse to turn your back because you might not measure up. She might reject you."

Scott snorted even as he felt the words strike a chord. "Stick to numbers, Mike. It's what you're good at."

"It doesn't take a psych degree to see you got the shaft real bad, bro. Even a spreadsheet guy like me can see you don't want to put yourself on the line and risk a repeat. But I saw the way she looked at you."

"How was that?" Scott kicked himself for asking, but couldn't stop the words.

"Her face lit up whenever she laid eyes on you. She's different, Scott," he said again. "And if you let her get away, you're an idiot."

Scott had one of those moments of absolute crystal clarity. Thea was loyal and loving and beautiful and smart. She was everything he'd ever wanted. And he was an idiot for building barriers to keep it from working between them.

He was in love with Thea Bell.

Scott felt one corner of his mouth curve up. "How the heck did an emotional train wreck like you figure all this out?"

"I'm the sensitive sort."

"Mom told you, didn't she?"

Mike grinned. "She thought the information would be better received if delivered man-to-man by someone closer to your age. She also said I might learn something."

"If you were smart enough, you'd have already learned from the two of them long before this."

"Right back at you," Mike said.

"Mom and Dad are the best," Scott pointed out, ignoring his brother's jab.

Mike didn't pretend to misunderstand. "Yeah. The folks are pretty lucky. I'd give a lot to find what they've got. I envy you, bro."

"Why?"

"A woman like Thea to care about. The chance to raise a child with her. Face it, Scott. You're a family kind of guy."

Mike was right. Damn it. Scott should have figured it out himself. He would have if his emotional baggage hadn't been stacked so high he couldn't see over it. He hoped his brother wasn't premature in patting him on the back. Scott knew it was entirely possible he'd blown the best thing that had ever happened to him.

He'd used the baby to push Thea away because it hurt when someone you cared about walked out. He'd successfully avoided caring too much until Thea somehow managed to infiltrate his heart.

The truth was family meant everything to him. It was how he'd grown up; it was how he'd raised his girls. He liked being a family man. He was good at it, if he did say so himself. Thea had a family in need of a man. And he was the right man for the job.

All he had to do was convince her of that.

Thea put a box filled with kitchen paraphernalia on her new island, then brushed the sweat off her forehead with the back of her hand.

"As God is my witness," she said to the room that looked like it threw up, "I vow two things. I'm never moving again. And if I buy a new kitchen gadget, I will throw an old one away."

She had entirely too much stuff. Thank goodness for all the cupboards she had now. Maybe she would renegotiate with God about throwing things away—if she ever forgave Him. It wasn't entirely His fault, but somewhere between running the world and being all-powerful, He could have worked a little miracle on her behalf with the former owner of this house.

But when she felt a little bubble move across her abdomen, she was reminded that her baby was a living miracle. "And I guess there's only one to a customer. Anything more would be greedy."

Besides, self-pity was a waste of energy. She'd been blessed, even though Scott didn't want her and the baby. It was his loss. Along with her son or daughter, she was going to have a good life in this house.

She looked around. The movers had left several hours before. After delivering all of her furniture, she realized the family room was still empty. A trip to a home-furnishing store was in her near future. And whatever she bought would need Scotchgarding. Not unlike the way her heart needed Scott-guarding.

"And procrastinating will not get the rest of the stuff out of my car."

She walked through the living and dining rooms, which were marginally more organized, but only because there were fewer things than in the kitchen. After walking out the front door, she followed the L-shaped walkway to where she'd backed her SUV in the driveway. With the back seat down, she'd been able to fill the car with the remainder of her things. The last minute stuff, like cleaning supplies and vacuum. She'd cleaned as the movers worked so Scott wouldn't have to worry about it.

Although it would have served him right if she'd left the dust bunnies and let them party hearty in every corner of the place. She knew she couldn't keep up this high level of anger and irritation toward him indefinitely. But she planned to maintain it for as long as possible. Because she knew from past experience when that was gone, she would be inundated by the pain.

When she rounded the garage, she stopped so fast her sneakers would have squeaked if she'd been standing on anything but cement. Speak of the devil.

"Scott," she said.

"Hi, Thea." He peeked into the back of her car. "That's quite a load."

"Yeah. I've got a million things to do. But you know how that is, what with moving into my place."

"Yeah." He had a weird expression on his face as if he'd eaten bad seafood.

"Is something wrong?"

"You could say that."

"But the condo passed inspection with flying colors. Everything was okay when I left."

"It's still fine."

She walked closer. The nearer she got to his tall, attractive self, the harder her heart pounded. "Then I don't understand. Are you having buyer's remorse? Because escrow is closed. You've taken title. There's no going back—"

He held up his hand. "No second thoughts. Not about buying the condo."

"Then what are you doing here?"

"I'm having second thoughts about you."

She couldn't believe she'd heard him right. But her heart kicked into high gear anyway. "What kind of thoughts?"

He ran his fingers through his hair. "Mike says I'm an idiot."

"You'll get no argument from me." She covered her mouth with her hand. "Sorry. Just popped out," she mumbled.

His expression turned sheepish. "I suppose I deserve that."

"No. What you deserve is a good swift kick in the caboose."

"Okay. I deserve that, too. I just didn't know what I had until it was gone."

Her gaze narrowed on him. "If you're talking about me, you never had me. If you're talking about your daughter—"

"It's not about Kendra. Unless you count that she was the one who made me start thinking about you."

"She finally asked you what happened between us?"

He nodded. "And you were right. Discussing it with her could have poured salt on the wounds of her insecurity. Especially since it came up the night before she left for school."

"Could have?" Thea stared at him. "What did you tell her?"

"Fortunately, I didn't have to say anything. I was saved by the bell."

"I'm going to take a wild guess here and assume you're not talking about me."

"Mike came over to say goodbye to Kendra."

"Okay. But I still don't see—"

"Just stop interrupting and I'll get there faster. Mike said I was an idiot if I let you get away. I should have figured it out for myself, but—" He shrugged. "I didn't."

"Figured what out?"

"That I was looking for an excuse to walk away from you. I've been single for a long time because putting everything on the line, risking it all again, was something I didn't want to do. I didn't want to get burned again."

"And now?"

"You made me want to get burned," he said, heat sparking in his eyes. "I'm ready to take a chance again."

A few weeks ago, the words would have sent her over the moon with happiness. But now she'd managed to stanch her bleeding emotions. She couldn't afford to be a basket case. Not again. Not with the baby coming. She didn't trust this sudden about-face. She refused to have expectations or hope. Most of all, she wouldn't let herself need him. He might be there today and possibly even tomorrow. But what about the long haul? She couldn't let her guard down.

She could only count on herself. Strength was her middle name. Independence was her new best friend.

She looked up at him and a shaft of sunlight caught her in the eye. With a hand on her forehead to shade her gaze, she saw the hope in his expression and steeled herself against it.

"I'm sorry, Scott. I can't take the chance that this change of heart isn't just about Kendra leaving home. You made it clear you don't care enough about me and the baby."

"That's just it. Don't you see? I'm willing to accept the baby."

Her heart twisted at his words. "The problem is, you don't see. I can't be with a man who's 'willing' to 'accept' my child. It's not fair to me, or the baby, or you for that matter. Don't misunderstand, I want this baby to have a father. It breaks my heart that he or she won't have one. But that man needs to be with us because he wants to. We need a man who sees a baby as a blessing, not a burden. And you've made it clear from the first day I met you how you feel about it."

"Thea, listen to me—"

"No."

She stepped to the back of the SUV and started to slide a box toward her from the rear hatch. Scott moved beside her, close enough for her to feel the heat of his body. He reached out and moved her aside.

"You shouldn't be carrying stuff in your condition." His voice was rough yet warm, like sandpaper dipped in whiskey.

Through a blur of tears, she saw the muscles and tendons in his forearm flex with harnessed strength. Not now, she thought. She'd managed to get through everything without dissolving in a puddle of tears and she was awfully proud of herself for that. It hadn't been easy, what with her jam-packed, hormone-ridden body. Now he had to go and do something sweet like this.

"I won't hurt my baby. Now will you please go away? I don't want to see you anymore."

"Too bad." He glared at her. "I'm going to unload the back of this car. If you have a problem with that, don't watch. But if you pick up anything heavier than a throw pillow—"

Thea didn't wait to hear the rest. She couldn't stand this. He was showing her what it should have been like and it was too cruel. It was a glimpse into what might have been—like a peek into heaven when your soul was damned to hell.

She turned on her heel and went inside, upstairs where she could be alone. In her master bedroom, tears trickled down her cheeks while she ripped open boxes. Finally she found the one with the towels. She grabbed one and buried her face in it so he wouldn't hear her sob.

She didn't know how long she cried, but she stayed like that until she had no more tears left. Before going back downstairs, she peeked out the window and saw that his truck was gone.

"I guess I got through to him," she said.

But the thought held no satisfaction, just a mother lode of pain from a broken heart she knew would never heal.

Now who was the idiot who needed a good swift kick in the caboose?

Chapter 16

Scott walked into For Whom the Bell Toils and saw the flowers he'd sent to Thea on her desk, but she was nowhere in sight. And he hadn't seen her SUV outside. It had been a week since they'd made their respective moves. A week since he'd seen the tears in her eyes as she'd turned her back on him. Seven days since he'd watched her stiff back as she'd walked away from him. One hundred and sixty-eight hours during which he'd called and left messages she hadn't returned. He was going out of his mind.

"Hello?" he called out.

Connie appeared in the doorway to the back room. She frowned when she saw him and the look of hostility on her face clearly said what she thought of him. "We've got to get that dinger fixed."

"I don't give a damn about the damn dinger. Where's Thea. I need to talk to her."

Her expression went from hostile to stubborn as she folded her arms over her chest. "She doesn't want to talk to you."

"She's made that clear. But I've got some things to say to her."

"Don't you get it? She doesn't want to hear any more from you."

"I get it, I just refuse to accept it." He ran his fingers through his hair. "Look, Connie, I know I've made a few mistakes—"

"A few?" she said, one auburn eyebrow going up.

"Okay, a lot. And they're really big mistakes. Whoppers. But I need to explain to her. I've tried sending flowers, calling, leaving messages she doesn't return. I don't know what to do if she won't even talk to me. I need help."

She sighed and moved farther into the room, stopping by Thea's desk. Leaning forward, she breathed in the scent of the blooms. "She loves these lilies. How did you know?"

"I didn't. Just a shot in the dark. But I'm glad. Here's the thing. If I'm going to convince her I'm sincere, I need someone with the inside track. I need to know how to get through to her."

"What if I help you and she never speaks to me again?"

Something in his own chest pulled tight. "If you don't, you'll be responsible for two people missing out on an opportunity for happiness. Thea and I will be miserable for the rest of our lives. And it will be on your head." He watched her face, the emotions shifting there and decided to keep pressing. "You don't have to like me, but this is your chance to be her friend."

"As her friend, I will honor my promise to run interference."

"Is she happy?" When Connie didn't answer, he swore silently. He wished she wasn't fitting the profile of the stubborn redhead. "If you can honestly tell me that she's better off and completely content, I'll back off."

He mentally crossed his fingers and prayed she wouldn't call his bluff.

Connie's forehead creased with doubt. "What if I help you and you break her heart?"

He let out a long breath. "I already did that by being a jerk. She's the best thing that ever happened to me. I need to put her heart back together and spend the rest of my life making it up to her."

"I can't stand to see her so sad," Connie said, and he knew she was relenting. Then she glared and pointed at him. "But if you let her down again, I'm coming after you, buster. And it won't be pretty."

"I won't hurt her, I swear. Now help me. What should I do."

"Court her."

"Tried that," he said, pointing to the bouquet in the vase beside her. "I even sent some to her at the house and she still won't speak to me."

"Flowers, candy," she said, ticking off on her fingers typical courting gestures. "Candy's out. She's watching her weight with the pregnancy. Her motto is anything over twenty-five pounds isn't baby. So food would probably earn you demerits." She looked at him. "You've got your work cut out for you."

"Has she mentioned me at all?"

Connie shook her head. "Thea internalizes everything. I watched her go through David's death and the stages of grief. I've watched her do the same thing with you."

"I'm not dead."

"To her you are. And right now she's working on acceptance. If she gets there—" She shook her head and he didn't want to think about what that meant.

"How do I keep her from getting there?"

"Shake her up. Make promises—preferably ones you intend to keep."

"That's the only kind I make."

She studied him as if she was gauging his sincerity. Whatever she saw seemed to satisfy her because she nodded her head. "Somehow you need to get her off balance."

"How?"

"I haven't got a clue. But it needs to be big. Look, Scott, she got clobbered really bad. The lesson she learned was that if she doesn't let herself care, she won't be hurt again."

"I get that, but—"

She held up her hand. "Let me finish. Now she's got the baby to think about. All of her maternal instincts are on high alert. You turned your back on her because of her baby. She's not likely to give you another chance to hurt her child."

This wasn't making him feel better. "I made a mistake. I admit that, but—"

"I'm not saying you're a bad guy. Look, I've got kids. I know how hard a job it is. And consciously choosing it again is a tough decision."

"No, it's not."

He knew he'd given the correct answer when a small smile curved her mouth. "I'm not the one you have to convince."

"How do I do that? Especially when she won't talk to me."

"My best advice is show up and keep showing up. When you do, speak from the heart and do what you do best."

"That's not especially helpful since I'm just a dad who happens to be a building contractor." He shrugged.

"Then do dad stuff and build something. I don't know what else to tell you. If that doesn't help, you're on your own, pal."

"Can you at least tell me where to find her?"

She shook her head. "She just said she had time between appointments and she was going to check out baby furniture."

"Where?"

"She didn't say. But I know she's planning to furnish the nursery soon."

Scott nodded. "Okay. I appreciate the help, Connie."

"Good luck."

"I'm going to need a miracle," he said, then walked outside.

Glancing up at the sky, he thought about David. He would never see the baby Thea had fought so hard to bring into the world. Would he want another man to be there for her and his child? "If so, now would be a good time for a little divine inspiration."

Thea had been in Scott's house for several weeks when she realized she was still thinking of her new home that way. It was time to stop. Partly because every time she did, there was that annoying empty feeling followed swiftly by a sensation of pressure around her heart. This was *her* house, damn it, and she was going to be happy in it.

But she couldn't stifle her disappointment that he'd stopped calling and sending flowers. Apparently he'd given up trying to communicate with her, just when she'd been on the verge of giving in. How perverse was that?

But it was for the best, she told herself. Herself replied that it didn't feel best. Loneliness was funny that way.

The timer on the microwave signaled that her frozen dinner was ready at the same time the doorbell rang. She wasn't expecting anyone and was surprised to have company. It was probably Connie. She'd talked about a housewarming gift.

But when she opened the front door, the man standing there didn't look anything like her partner. The man standing there was Scott. Her heart did a happy little dance, proving that all her conditioning to accept their situation had been a waste of perfectly good mental energy.

"Hello, Thea."

He looked good—really, really good. Better than she'd ever seen him. Or was that because she'd missed him so deeply? Or because she hadn't expected to see him again?

"What are you doing here?"

"I have something for you."

She didn't want anything but him. The thought made her

work harder at steeling herself against loving him. "I can't accept anything from you."

"Will you at least look at it?"

She couldn't resist the pleading expression in his eyes. Not to mention the pleading in her heart. "Okay."

He nodded and said, "Hold that thought. I'll be right back."

Then he was gone. She heard the microwave timer beep, reminding her with its relentless, annoying chirp that she hadn't taken her food out. She walked into the kitchen to do that and shut the appliance up. After grabbing a pot holder, she removed the steaming cardboard-encased meal and set it on the island. Then she heard the front door close.

"Thea?"

She went into the living room. Scott stood there and at his feet was a wooden cradle, with the curved runners to make it rock. She'd expected flowers maybe. Or a plant as a house-warming. But this looked like handmade furniture, a fine sturdy piece of wood with two intertwined hearts carved into the headboard and footboard. Her own heart pounded when she realized the significance of a baby's first bed and the intricate carving. She was speechless.

"I made it for the baby," he explained.

She wanted to ask what it meant, absurdly hoping for the moon, the sun and the stars. "Why?" she finally said.

"Because I can." He shrugged.

"Scott, I'm not sure what this is about, but you and I are over—"

He shook his head. "Don't say that. As far as I'm concerned, things between us are just getting started."

Her whole body began to shake. "I don't understand."

"I do. I get that you're afraid to care again. I was, too. But something scared me more."

"What?" she whispered.

"Living without you." A muscle in his jaw moved. "When

you walked away from me that day, I got the worst feeling deep in my gut. It got bigger when you wouldn't speak to me or return my calls. Every day that went by, it got worse. Because I love you, Thea."

Her eyes grew moist as she looked at him, making his image waver. She'd longed for and dreaded hearing him say those words.

"It's too late for us, Scott. It can't work." She shook her head. "You've already raised two kids. 'Never again,' you said."

"How come it's a woman's prerogative to change her mind, but a man has to live and die by whatever stupid words come out of his mouth?"

"I don't know," she admitted. "I thought when you stopped calling and sending flowers that—"

"I'd given up?" He shook his head. "I just decided to invest my energy in the future." He stepped closer and took her hands in his. "Thea, this isn't simply a cradle."

"No?" She nudged it with her bare toe and watched it rock. "Looks like it to me."

"It's a symbol. Of my commitment to you and the baby."

"How can I believe you mean what you're saying?"

"Life doesn't come with a guarantee. Sooner or later you're just going to have to take a leap of faith. This is my way of prodding you over the edge. Take a chance, Thea. I'll make sure you don't regret it."

"If only I could be certain—"

Gently but firmly, he squeezed her hands. "I only do two things well. I'm a builder and a father. The cradle I built will keep the baby safe and secure until he outgrows it. The father in me wants to see him grow. I want to build this child with you. I want to make a difference for the better—with you."

The tears gathering in her eyes spilled over her lower lashes and rolled down her cheeks. But her voice was steady when she spoke. "I don't know what to say."

"You've said you want your child to have a father. Someone who sees him as a blessing. I'm your man—a family man."

Her heart swelled to bursting with happiness. Thea could no more turn him away than she could turn her back on the promise she'd made to the other man she'd loved. And somehow she had the absurd feeling that David heartily approved of Scott Matthews. Maybe because she'd found love again and it felt so very right to her.

Scott squeezed the hands he still held. "I mean this with all my heart, Thea. If you'll give me another chance, I'll spend the rest of my life multiplying your happiness and dividing your sorrow."

She smiled through her tears and whispered a single word past the lump in her throat. "Okay."

He pulled her into his arms and drew in a shuddering breath. "Thank God."

She savored the strength and heat of his body to reassure herself that he was real, that this wasn't a dream. "You called the baby 'he.' Do you know something I don't know?"

"Nope. I just couldn't call our baby 'it.'"

The words warmed her as surely as the Sterno flame on a chafing dish. "Well, it's official. I'm head over heels in love with you, Scott Matthews."

When he looked at her, his mouth curved up. "Good. That tips the scale in my favor for the question I'm about to ask."

"Ask away," she said, sniffling.

"Since you're officially in love with me, and I'm officially in love with you, what we need here is an official proposal of marriage." He got down on one knee and lifted a jeweler's box from the cradle. He took her left hand, then slipped the ring on the appropriate finger. "Will you marry me?"

She saw the hope and sincerity in his eyes and had no more doubts. There was only one right answer to his question. "Yes," she said without hesitation.

She borrowed hope from him and transplanted it in her own heart to grow again. For a while, hers had been lost. Not anymore, thanks to Scott.

Epilogue

Scott stared into the cradle he'd made and watched the month-old baby boy squirm and squeak. Glancing at the clock on Thea's side of the bed, he read 2:00 a.m.

"Right on time, T.D.," he whispered, stroking a finger over the infant's perfect head full of downy dark hair. "But your mom could use a little more sleep, so I'm on diaper duty. Maybe I can hold you off just a little bit before she feeds you."

Gently, he lifted the child and carried him into the other bedroom of the house he'd sold to Thea. He chuckled as he thought about the nightmare of paperwork they'd gone through to change the title on this house and the condo into both their names after getting married. Now they rented out the town house and set up a home in the bigger house where he'd raised T.D.'s two sisters.

"Kendra and Gail are coming home tomorrow. Your sisters wouldn't come home for your mom and me, but they can't wait to see you on the weekend," he said to the little guy.

When he was finished changing the baby, he put his hand on the boy's belly and stared in awe at this beautiful child, truly a miracle. Scott was more grateful than he could put into words that Thea had let him into her life. Not only that, she loved him. God knew why, but he was glad she did and wasn't going to question her judgment. He was a lucky man, he thought, remembering the man who would never see his son's face.

"David," he whispered into the night, "I love Thea and this child with all my heart. I'll be the best father I know how to be and guide him with all the wisdom Kendra and Gail gave me. Granted, they're girls, but—"

When he felt a small hand on his back, he looked into his wife's warm brown eyes. At that moment they were suspiciously bright.

"Hi, sweetheart," he said. "Didn't mean to wake you."

"You didn't. I guess it's a mom thing, but I sort of know when Thomas David needs something."

He pointed to her chest. "It couldn't have anything to do with the fact that you're ready to breast-feed T.D.?"

She laughed. "Maybe. And about those initials—"

"It means touchdown," he defended.

"So you've said. But we spent many hours picking an appropriate name for our son."

Scott remembered. They'd teased about Hildegard for a girl or Ichabod for a boy. "And your point?"

"We picked the middle name David for the man who gave him life. And Thomas for the man who gave you life and raised you to be the special man you are."

He leaned down and kissed her nose. "Thank you."

"You're welcome. But if T.D. sticks, all those hours spent agonizing over his name will be a waste of energy."

"And if you insist on calling him Thomas David, he'll get beat up every day after school."

"You're right," she said, sighing.

He blinked. "That easy?"

"It's not easy. It's all about balance. And thank goodness you're here to do that for us. T.D. is very lucky to have you."

"He's more lucky to have you for a mother."

Leaning her cheek against his arm, she put her hand beside his on the baby who was dozing on the changing table.

"You and I are so lucky," she said. "To have such special children. We met thanks to Kendra, who was reaching out for the mother she missed. And now we're raising this little guy who won't have to reach out for a father he doesn't have."

"I'm not perfect," he reminded her, not for the first time.

"Perfection is highly overrated." She gazed up at him. "Do you know why I fell in love with you?"

"No." He couldn't resist asking. "Why?"

"Because you were such a good father to the girls."

"But I made so many mistakes."

"To be sure. In spite of that, you kept trying, doing more right than wrong. I love and admire you more every day."

"Do you know why I fell in love with you?"

"No. Why?"

"Beats the heck out of me," he teased.

She slugged him playfully. "I take back everything nice I said."

"Okay. Seriously. I fell in love with you because you're hot." He braced himself for another assault.

But she stood on tiptoe and kissed his cheek. "That's the nicest thing you could have said to a woman who recently gave birth and has the postpartum body to prove it."

He shook his head. "Not once have you ever done what I expected," he said, shaking his head. "And I really think that's why I fell in love with you."

Gazing up at him, she smiled the sweet smile he loved so much. "It doesn't really matter why. The important thing is that we do."

"Yeah."

"I thought I loved you before, but sharing this child with you, watching the way you care for him, makes me realize the capacity for love is endless and forever."

"Amen," he said. "But I'm not ashamed to admit that I love you because you're hot, too."

The sound of her laughter warmed his heart. As he looked up, he thought of David. A feeling of peace settled over him and he knew all was right in the universe. And he knew his love for this woman was eternal. Just as he knew that Thea Bell Matthews would forever ring his chimes. Once upon a time, he'd thought she was all he needed to be happy. But her special brand of love showed him it takes three.

* * * * *